He's waited 100 years for her to arrive.

MIDNIGHT WITCH HOUSE

JULIE CATHERINE

MIDNIGHT WITCH HOUSE

MIDNIGHT WITCH HOUSE
BOOK ONE

JULIE CATHERINE

EDITED BY
ALLANA STUART

To all my ladies still waiting for the right vampire
to give you the chills.

1

PERSEPHONE

"I'll miss you the most, Persephone."

"You'll forget me before your butt hits the rocking chair," I said.

"Rocking chair? I'm not that old, dear." The old bookseller who smelled like leather and cinnamon laughed out loud. She *was* that old. The librarian with the curt sense of humor and the voice that bellowed was the best sort of woman. The only mother figure I'd ever known.

"But retirement looks good," she agreed. "*You'll* miss all the free books you could read," Marjorie Long was not foolish enough to believe she'd make my list of missable things. But she was wrong. I'd miss this store, these books and her company more than she'd know. Still, there was no point in romanticizing things. She was retired. And the job was finished. The store was closed. There were no real permanent ties between us now. We'd both move on.

"I'll miss the sort of people who chose to spend their time in your store." I shrugged. The concession split the difference. The woman nodded wistfully.

"Salt of the earth," she said.

Just like you, old bird, I thought, but I didn't give it voice.

The fact that I was here, saying goodbye, was enough. She must have known how I felt.

We stared at the hollowed out shell of the bookstore on Radler Avenue. Everything sold or packed. A disappeared world. Only remnants of memories and lore. For decades this retail space had been an adorable bespoke paper and specialty book shop. Since before the time of the internet and cell phones and ebooks. Marjorie Long had seen it all. You might have thought the rise of technology would have killed her dainty paper business, but instead, she evolved. One had to evolve. Or die.

The store became a niche. A specialty shop for a certain kind of people. Humans who loved the feel of fountain ink, pretty papers, books with sprayed edges, and limited printing runs.

At least, that's what it was.

It was dead now.

Marjorie was ready to move on and none of her grown children wanted to take over the shop. They didn't care about a small business that none of them visited, and the senior citizen had had enough of running things on her own. It was time to shut down.

It was the only job I'd ever known.

I'd studied for every college exam while perched on the register stool. I received my first peck on the lips in the back row of the stacks. I'd read every hardback that I could, but ensured that I never cracked a spine. If she had asked me to take over the store I might have said yes, but it never came to that.

I wasn't her kin.

Plus, it was pointless to dream of more, as I didn't have the kind of money needed to buy her out. I didn't have *any* money, if I was honest about my bank accounts. And she was my boss and a proud and solo entrepreneur with a savvy head on her shoulders, not my mum.

This wasn't my life.

So, now the final moment was here. A legacy finished. I heard the space would soon be a martial arts dojo studio. Where men could learn how to throw ninja stars and spin chain-whip weapons around their thick necks. Someone else's dream life.

I watched as she locked the door for the final time and spun the key in her hand. She interlocked the spiky pieces between her fingers, like she always did. One could never be too careful. I sighed.

"And they lived happily ever after," she whispered, mostly to herself.

It was the exact opposite sentiment of what I'd heard from my landlady when I explained that the bookstore was shuttered and I'd need to look for new work.

"Time to live in the real world," she had grunted.

Yeah. The real world.

That was something that hadn't been particularly kind since the day I was born.

We stepped back from the closed door and took in the front side. Years of sun damage showed the unpainted outline of the original sign, *Ever After Books,* bleached on the wall. The dojo would have to paint over that.

"You'll be alright?" The older woman wondered.

"I'll be fine," I forced a grin. She patted my shoulder.

"You always are."

There was nothing else to be said. The car was packed. The door was closed. Time to get on with our lives.

We parted with a stiff hug and an awkward wave. I thought about putting my feelings into words. Not just all she had meant to me, or what this store did for my work experience, not even the biweekly pay, but the bigger truth: Marjorie's little store had become a soft spot in a very hard life.

"I—thanks for a great ride."

"Take care of yourself, Seph."

"I will." I watched her adjust the final box in her trunk, but didn't wait until she drove off. This was the natural evolution of her life plan. Not mine. In truth, I had no idea what might come next. I'd made it through school. I had a stupid English degree that I couldn't use. A lot of student debt. Technically, I was the embodiment of an adult. But I didn't feel grown. I didn't feel much of anything these days.

Or the days before that.

There wasn't a lot of wisdom or guidance imparted in the group homes where I grew up. Not with eight to twelve random children's mouths to feed day in and day out. A revolving door of childhood trauma and complacent authority figures. Now I lived in a stop-gap roommate flat for ex-fosters, newly out of the system. I was legally a fully functional adult. With no future, no prospects, and no parents to fall back on. My saved up bookshop funds earned me room and board at the place through 'til the end of the month. I had that long to figure things out.

"Sephy, is that you?" My House Mum called from the front lounge as soon as I let myself into the house.

"Yes." I groaned. I closed both eyes, annoyed. I should have climbed up the old oak tree and snuck in through the bathroom window like I did after hours. Years of living under strangers' roofs taught me to use clandestine points of entry and egress. It helped you disappear from the eyes of the world. You could avoid a lot of conflict if no one knew when you came home or what time you left. Today I'd been too distracted and waltzed in the front door. I now stood in the foyer with one foot on the treads to go up to my bedroom, but ignoring my House Mum's shout-out would be rude. And she never spoke to any of her charges just for fun. "How are you doing, Mum?" I came forward in the house, hoping to make the briefest eye contact with my landlady then take off.

My House Mum spent all her time in the kitchen. She had six

charges like me living in six tiny rooms, two upstairs, four in her basement. That meant six tenants, plus two of her own kids. She always had something cooking on the stove. The meals were never particularly good, but they were warm. Her birth children were six and eight, and were currently screaming in the living room, fighting over the remote, simultaneously trying to watch cartoons and play video games on the same device, each starfished on the threadbare rug. I passed without intervening in their fuss. I found the woman in her usual spot.

"Oh, Sephy. Life is hard and then you die. What did I expect?" my House Mum grumped. A general complaint. Maybe she didn't have specific news after all. I caught one look at her staring at her cell phone and turned to go.

"Right. Well, I–"

"–a letter came," she interrupted my getaway. This perked me up.

"For me?"

"No, for Hansel and Gretel. Of course for you."

My House Mum held up the envelope but never looked away from her phone. She swiped and swiped. I took it from her, but couldn't escape her concern. Even if she didn't look up from the never-ending stream of crap on her device, I wasn't free to leave.

Not yet.

I ripped the notice open and read it in front of her.

"It's a lawyer informing me that my uncle died." I explained, though she hadn't actually asked. My House Mum finally looked up.

"Didn't know you had an uncle, I coulda charged you a proper room and board all this time."

I could've lived in a better place than this dump, I didn't reply.

My House Mum frowned. "Who is he?"

I read his name.

"Cornelius Child." It meant nothing. My full name was Persephone Dawn. Apparently, my last name had come from some other part of my family? Or maybe from nowhere at all.

"He sounds fancy." Her son piped up from the floor.

"Name's don't mean nothin'." My House Mum shut him down. "They're given, not earned."

"I'd call you Doo-doo-head," his sister giggled.

"I'd call you Fart!" They roared with laughter at their own terrible jokes. Over their fits and squabbles, I read the letter again. The professional jargon was a lot to take in, but the message was clear. "It says he left me something in his will. I have to go to a testament reading in Plumpkin."

"Where the hell is Plumpkin?" The little boy squawked.

"*Language,*" Mum snapped. "Where is it?" She also asked.

"Hell if I know," I confessed, winking at the boy. His eyes went saucer wide.

"Why does *she* get to say it?" He immediately complained.

"'Cuz Sephy is grown," his sister defended me. "Momma swears too. I heard her."

"Mind your business." Their mother snapped. The kids immediately lost interest in us.

"It's my turn!" The boy tried to take the tv remote from his sister by force. She screamed in reply. I looked through the envelope again.

"It also says they provided enough money for the train fare to town. Did you see any cash?" The envelope had been closed, but she could have easily opened it and sealed it back up.

"Does it look like I'm made of money?" My House Mum shot back, not actually answering the question. She cocked her head to the side with an aggressive frown.

No. I sighed. *It looks like you stole the only thing ever given to me by a relative. The first real relative I've ever known.* I held my tongue. No point in pissing her off. The money wouldn't magically reappear. I stared at the letter again.

"You gonna go?" My House Mum asked with a frown.

"*Nah.* I mean, I might. Depends how soon I get another job."

"Rent is due at the start of the month," she said. Her real point. My pittance and her other tenants' rent money funded this fabulous lifestyle. She went back to endlessly scrolling on her device.

"I'll keep it in mind."

Without any new information to divulge, I'd been dismissed. I climbed the stairs to my room, which was basically a single bed, a laptop computer, and three piles of books all crammed into a hole in the wall. It had once been a closet. It had no window and met no fire codes. All the novels and notebooks I'd been gifted and/or purchased on my delightful staff discount were totally flammable. Luckily I never lit candles, so it was fine. And it was my home.

For now.

After being relocated so many times as a kid, I didn't easily put down roots. And now that Ever After was gone, there was nothing holding me to this place. The letter was intriguing. I had relatives in some distant, small town.

Real family.

I just had to find them.

I lay on my stomach, pulled out my computer and opened a map. I searched up Plumpkin. The place was hours away from where I lived now. But I could get there by train with one ride.

I'd lied to my Mum.

I would go check it out.

I would listen to the last will and testament of this stranger, this uncle, I'd accept whatever I'd been given, then I'd meet every member of my family that I could find.

After all, Plumpkin looked like as good a place as any to start a new life.

2

PERSEPHONE

"Come on, Benny," I leaned on the counter in full groan.

This was the third pawn shop I'd been to, selling everything that I could sneak out of the house without my House Mum growing suspicious.

All my books were gone. I couldn't take them with me. The ones that had no monetary value, I distributed to local libraries across the city. I sold my computer. I was down to one final set of earrings. I really needed to cash them in. Today.

"*No way.* I'm losing out on the deal." Benny threw up his hands and fidgeted like he always did when he was bilking someone.

"I need to buy a train ticket. Seventy-five." I pushed back.

"You're leaving? That means this stuff is hot. Fifty, not a dollar more. I'm taking too much of a risk."

"It's not stolen." I lied. It sort of was. I'd swung by the local high school's lost and found. Any valuables the students misplaced were kept in an office drawer, but I learned a long time ago, the secretaries didn't care who picked the stuff up as long as you looked stricken and young. I put my hair in high ponytail buns and lied and said my sister was missing a priceless family valuable and had they seen it? The unsympathetic woman pointed me right to the stash then went on with her life. I'd taken the earring set because I'd guessed the stone setting was legit and left the other valuables in case their real owners came looking for their lost stuff. Now I realized, I should have grabbed more. "Fifty won't get me half way out of town."

"Not my problem, kid."

"I'm your best customer."

"And you're *leaving*. Sounds like you're not coming back." He had me there. *Crap.*

I closed my eyes. The earrings weren't much, but the sparkly stones were definitely worth more than fifty bucks. I had an eye for this stuff. I bet they were real diamonds and Benny was getting a steal, that's why he hadn't appraised them up close... only today I was too desperate to sell to try to find out their real worth. I needed the cash. Now.

"I don't know what else to do," I whimpered, trying to soften my eyes. If I couldn't get a ticket to Plumpkin, I couldn't see what my dead uncle had bequeathed me in his will. What if it was something of value? What if I had other family there? The testament reading was scheduled for tomorrow. I had to be present.

"I'll take your necklace too," Benny said, going in hard for the kill. "Three hundred large for both. Four hundred," he countered himself. I had always maintained my chain was not for sale. That one did have significant worth. Way more than four bills.

"No way." My hands went up to my neck.

"Fine, take the bus. Walk, all I care." Benny checked on another customer who was interested in knives. I looked down at the measly earring jewels. Maybe they weren't true diamonds after all.

Suddenly, I felt a terrible chill.

When I glanced up, in the absence of Benny, my reflection

mirrored back at me from the glass wall behind the counter, but I didn't stare at my own face. There was someone else there, deeper in the store, behind the technology and camera collections. A sleek man with dark, wavy hair. He was tall and filled out. Handsome as hell, with a cut jaw, sharp blue eyes, and an expensive looking coat. The dress shirt underneath lay flat against his stomach. His shoulders were back and proud. Not the sort of guy you saw in the shops around here. His beauty caught my eye, but his danger drew me in. And warned me off.

There was something wrong.

Or... more accurately, something too right to be trustworthy or real.

Little wrinkles crinkled around his eyes. He was standing all the way on the other side of camera lens display but it still felt too close. Like his very presence in the store tickled my skin. I rubbed the new goose bumps that appeared. He stared at the jewelry around my bare neck. He was fixed on my skin and the way the tendrils of my red hair touched the gold jewelry and swayed as I moved. His mouth tightened, his head slightly tilted. I put my fingers protectively up to the chain and glared at him in the mirror. His eyes came up to my aggressive frown, surprised. And through the mirror, he also locked me in his gaze.

Tit for tat.

I thought he'd be embarrassed to be caught looking at me, but he wasn't. Instead, he raised both eyebrows like some slick invitation. His jaw flexed in half a smile. All I'd have to do was turn around and we'd be face to face.

Was he lost?

Maybe that's why he didn't know it was rude to stare or listen to another patron's sale.

"Do you mind?" I asked his reflection, not bothering to turn around. His jaw lightly flexed again.

"I was just thinking you're selling yourself short." He smirked.

I spun around, ready to bite off his head and tell the busy-body no one to back the hell off, but the man had already stepped out of range. In fact, he strolled himself right out of the store. The bell jangled as he left. I glared after.

"You scaring customers away?" Benny groaned.

"He wasn't about to buy something," I sneered. "He was dressed too nicely. A rich boy slumming."

"A rich *man*," Benny countered. The stranger had been over six feet and filled out his dress shirt beautifully, I'd give him that. "Or a cop." We both laughed. They didn't make many officers who looked like *that*. Either way, I hadn't lost the pawn shop owner a sale. I was still trying to make mine.

"Sixty-two dollars for the pair." I pushed the earrings towards him. "Take it before I change my mind."

Benny's mouth kicked up in the corner.

A winner this time.

I'd offered a cheaper final price point than he'd been willing to pay.

"You have one month to change your mind, that's how this works." He lectured, as if we hadn't done business a hundred times. He wrote me up a pink slip for the stuff and popped open the register door. I pocketed the cash and the slip. There was no point in saying he could sell them today. Benny was right on all accounts. It was stolen property and I was permanently leaving town. But the pawn shop owner wouldn't care. We weren't friends.

I pushed out of the store with all my belongings now in the pack on my back. I didn't get enough for a hotel, a meal, and the train, but possibly a snack and the bus. If I found a free place to crash, I had enough money for a few meals after that. I started to walk towards the depot, according to the map on my phone. But as I rounded the first corner away from the pawn dealer, I felt the chill again.

I wasn't alone. He was there.

The expensive guy from the store.

Dressed in black and shades of expensive gray.

He perched his butt on a sleek burgundy sports car, chest slightly concave, shoulders relaxed, hands resting near his pockets, his black wool coat now strung over one arm. Benny was right, he was a *man* for sure, not a boy, but he was still young. Late twenties, slightly older than me, but worlds apart from where I was. Around here, this guy stuck out like a sore thumb. Clearly, he didn't belong in this part of town. But he also didn't care.

Out of the shop, he read as even more styled and expensive than before. He wore slacks, not pants–though I couldn't really verbalize the distinction, I knew it when I saw them. Maybe it was the fact that there was a pressed crease down the center of his legs. Maybe it was the way the trousers lay smooth and flat on his hips. He was fit. His posture was straight but not rigid or tight. The pants draped over his lower assets perfectly. One knee was casually bent to his bumper. The other foot held his weight. His rear leaned back on his car hood. A belt buckle shone at his waist. It drew all my attention to his hips and the fly of his crotch, which was definitely enticing too. I looked away, fighting the urge to grin or blush.

But his patience drew me back.

He merely waited for me to pass by.

Still as a stone.

Where his non-coat carrying hand rested on his hip, I observed an expensive watch peeking out. Selling that timepiece would fund me across the country and back. Both his elbows were bent. His too-casual arms were strong. He was high-born, from a privileged social class, and he worked out. Probably just for fun.

I had his number totally pegged, until I noted his shoes.

Heavy black boots.

Well worn.

They carried the weight of the world.

A working man's boots.

Those were out of place.

As was the stillness in his limbs. It was unnatural.

We both knew he was waiting for me, but as I approached, he didn't move. Didn't straighten or fidget his hands. Instead, as I observed him, he took in all of me too. Watched every inch. There was something about that gaze. An undefined intensity that he'd set on me from our very first glimpse. It drew me to him and repelled us apart.

While I often held my tongue in public, knowing it rarely served me to fight back, somehow I wanted to grind him to dust. Whether it was his obvious privilege or his perfect appearance, it was the strongest reaction to someone's existence I'd ever had in my life. But we were strangers and I intended to keep it that way. I did not open my mouth. We grew closer and closer together. My sidewalk path closed our gap to his spot on the road.

I braced for what was coming.

Something obviously was.

But, he didn't say a word. The perfect man let me get so close to him I'd soon just pass him by. So I was wrong, he wasn't waiting for me at all. Just a weird coincidence.

Then he spoke.

"I didn't mean to invade your space." He lied.

His hair almost fell over one eye.

Those damn eyes.

Two pools of blue shining light. With little crinkles and wrinkles around the edges on the outsides. More than his obvious money, his chisel-set jaw, or his stoic mouth, it was the smile lines around his blue eyes that set him apart. He had thick lashes, the kind women paid to glue on, and bold eyebrows. He was gorgeous and he knew it. Delicious and calm.

"You drive a car like that 'round these parts and you're gonna get robbed," I half-warned, half-mocked, not slowing at all.

"I can handle myself," he said. Then, he pushed off the car with liquid speed that proved his point. His concave chest straightened into a trim, straight core. He slid between me and the route I intended to go. His muscles were evident. My stranger knew his way around a weights gym or perhaps a boxing ring. Maybe both.

Beauty and danger pervaded who he was.

He was also now fully in my way. I had no choice but to stop.

"Did you sell your bracelet?" He asked.

"It was earrings."

I didn't say yes.

People were sometimes known to beat others up for their pawnshop sales. Lousy as the payout was. Was this beautiful man going to try to hold me up and take the cash from me now? A measly sixty bucks while he relaxed his butt atop a hundred-thousand-dollar car?

"Enough for your train ticket?"

"I'm in a hurry," I said. I could have pushed around him, but to do so would appear weak. I stood my ground.

"What if I were to help you out?" he offered. This made me pause. "I'll buy your necklace." His eyes flickered down to the skin above my breasts. His casual tone made me feel stripped, like he'd already taken it off of my body with his bare hands. My fingers fluttered there. "You want me to buy your necklace," he said in a new tone, leaning forward. His light eyes seemed to blaze into my soul.

I stared at him.

Those blue eyes were all I could see.

His smell, his intensity. It caused a weird tingle in my head. I shook it off.

"It's not for sale."

His jaw flexed in disappointment at my words.

"Two thousand," he countered.

I half-gaped. I managed to keep my mouth shut. But my pupils weren't in my control. I was sure they dilated twice as big as they were moments before.

Two thousand dollars was a life-changing amount.

"Four thousand… plus my watch." He upped his own price. *Twice.*

This was definitely a trap.

Or a trick.

Something was wrong.

"I'm trying to help you out. Take the deal."

"No. Throw your money at some other girl." I made the move to push by, half afraid he would grab my arm and spin me around.

But the stranger let me pass, unmoored.

I stalked down the street so fast, my hair bounced. I could feel him follow my efforts with his gaze for the whole block. Still standing there on the sidewalk. The man didn't budge. He openly stared. Tempting my return. I refused to look back.

At the depot, it turned out that the cross-country bus tickets were expensive too, so I bought a cheaper fare for a destination near the city and then snuck onto the Plumpkin-bound bus when the driver stepped away for a smoke.

My subterfuge complete, I sat low in the stiff upright chair. I let out a big sigh.

What a weird guy on the road.

My stalker. My stranger. With serious cash to burn.

I shook him out of my head. Four thousand bucks and an expensive watch for an old-timey pink metal chain that might not be real gold? That sale would have been dumb. And I was stupid for not taking it, maybe… but it was a family heirloom, and he was strange in ways I couldn't explain. All my red flags flapped in the sky.

Plus, the necklace was all that I had of my Mom... at least for now. Until I learned about my dead uncle, I supposed. Maybe there was plenty more where that came from. Maybe I should have accepted his price.

Forget about the weird deal, I shook it off.

What was done, was done.

I'd already moved on.

I was starting over in a new town, with a new life. I'd finally be a capable adult with a family of my own. And I could learn more about my past. And meet my relatives...

Was my uncle from my Mom's side or my Dad's?

The two parents were only vague concepts in my mind.

People had family. That was normal. But I'd always been on my own.

Since the day I was born.

And I managed just fine.

When the bus driver returned, he shut the door and turned the cab lights off, washing the whole vehicle in muted dimness to help his passengers relax as he drove. I settled in, like the others. The road trip would be long and slow. Overnight.

But as we turned out of the depot, I shot up in my chair.

On the road beside the exit, my stranger was there.

Him and his expensive car.

The man leaned against his burgundy car in the same damn pose, butt on his hood, watching the bus leave.

Not a care in the world.

The blue-eyed gaze goose pimpled my skin.

I wanted to look away, but I couldn't help but stare. He locked eyes with me from his perch on the road. He flexed his jaw into a half-grin. He raised both eyebrows my way. Then, he distinctly mouthed three words. I stared at his lips as they moved.

See you soon.

3
LARK

The girl was impossible.

Beautiful, sure, in that bee-stung sort of way full of tanned skin, and scraped knees, and messy wild red hair she never bothered to straighten or comb. The esthetic looked totally natural, but took forever to get just right, I knew. Just ask an immortal. I rolled my eyes.

I also knew, Child's niece was clearly trouble. She was used to protecting herself. I shouldn't have gotten so close. Shouldn't have pushed so fast or direct. That was my fault.

In retrospect, I should have just posed as the owner of the pawnshop and handed her wads of cash for her dumb jewels. But even that wouldn't have worked as she seemed to know her stuff, what it was worth, and she also knew all the sly pawn shop owners behind their registers.

The biggest trouble was that damn necklace.

With Electrum on, she couldn't be compelled.

She could still be... helped.

I could have forced the girl into my car, I thought, flexing my arms. She didn't weigh much. Her body could snap like a twig in my hands. I might have tossed her in the back and just driven off, but that would have become a headache of a ride back. My job was to guard and protect until the task was complete. Not babysit or cajole.

And Child's niece was on the right bus.

Headed to the right town.

So that was enough.

At least for now.

4
PERSEPHONE

I half-expected to see the stranger waiting for me, leaning against his damn car in Plumpkin, the same smirk on his face when the bus dropped me off. With the fancy engine under the hood he could have driven us both here in half the time and I wouldn't have achieved the unpleasant side effect of smelling like old feet when we got here. But when the bus stopped the next morning, he wasn't there.

There was no way I saw what I thought I'd seen.

He didn't say '*see you soon.*'

That was unreal.

It was a weird send off from my old life but good riddance, I decided, heading straight for the law office of Dunwoody and Barge. The bus had directed me into the heart of Plumpkin just in time. It was impossible to get lost in the one-main-street town. When I located the law office door, the receptionist led me into a small room with a red brick feature wall. I was slightly early, but not by much. I wasn't sure if there'd be a bevy of grieving mourners I'd have to contend with, but I was all by myself. There were four chairs and an empty table, but there was no one around.

Nervously, I put my bag on the floor. I'd never been in a law office conference room before. I felt underdressed in my jeans and t-shirt and sneakers and sloppy ponytail. I wanted to fix it, but I also didn't want to get caught fussing. Just when I started to get antsy, a woman in a smart white suit with a pin-stripe of navy blue at the seams walked in, her arms full of papers and files. She wore glasses two sizes too big for her nose. They gave her an owl-like appearance I liked.

"Persephone Dawn?" She dropped the paperwork on the table and extended a hand.

"Uh, hi." We shook. She pointed to the opposite chair, then sat herself. "Are you Dunwoody? Or Barge?" I asked.

"Neither." She pushed the glasses up the bridge of her nose. "I am, er, *I was*, your uncle's paper master. Bonnie Main. I'm so sorry for your loss." She seemed both scattered and kind. Those big sad eyes waited for a response. I shifted uncomfortably.

"I didn't know him, so–"

"Yes. Right. Well, this is him." She fished out a picture and handed it to me. "Let me walk you through–" She turned on a business switch and began to go over all the documents that she'd brought. The phony sympathy gone.

I stared at the picture.

There was a robust man in the photo. He looked old. Fifties? Late forties at least. Wrinkled with time, but stern and proud. A powerful man. The only thing we had in common was our fiery hair. He could have been any other stranger in town. When I finally looked up, I realized the paper master had been talking for a good twenty minutes and I didn't hear a word that she'd said. She'd noticed too. "He looks a bit like you," she finally conceded.

"I didn't know him."

"Well," she took off her glasses. "The boss of any organization is usually a tough man to know... your uncle was a polarizing-entity in this town. He lived in Child Manor. Up on the hill?" I shook my head. "You'll see it soon. It's now yours. Or it will be." She turned a heavy file folder towards me. I blankly stared. Barely understanding. "That's what I've been telling you, Persephone."

"What?"

My estranged dead uncle left me a house?

"He left you his home. Sign here and here." She pointed at marked spots. The paperwork was prepared with little red arrow stickers to help. There were twenty similar markings in most of the folders she held.

"What do you mean? The house is mine?" I signed everywhere that she pointed out. Not reading the words. Was this how houses were sold?

"Absolutely, yes. He bequeathed the home to you in his will. Plus his bank accounts. A substantial amount."

This time I let out a little peep. "How much?"

"Oh, I don't know. You'd have to tally it all up. Several hundred I'd guess." She put back on her glasses and poured over the paperwork.

"Right." I sat back in my chair. Hundreds. That was manageable.

"Uhhh, four hundred thousand." Bonnie came up with the number. "Give or take."

"What?" I blinked several times. "Holy crap."

"There are some requirements," the paper master quickly warned. She looked nervous now.

A catch. There was always a catch.

"Like what?"

"You didn't hear my earlier information?" She chose her words carefully. "There is a... lock... on the building to keep you out, and the home and the accounts won't be released to you until you complete Cornelius Child's final wishes."

"What did he want?"

"Ah, well... it says you have to go to school."

"I have an education. I'm grown."

"Yes, I know, I can see that." She gave me a forced smile. "This is, er, a different sort of education, taught by Lady Mauve."

I scrunched up my eyebrows. "Who's that?"

"She's an instructor at... a nearby institution... It's kind of a secret establishment in town, very hush hush, although right now the academy is changing its rules. Since your uncle's passing there's been some restructuring happening and... I'm not sure if I can explain it to you," the paper master squirmed.

"I don't understand."

"I'm being terribly vague, I know. It's just, it's not my place." She looked more and more uncomfortable. "At least, it isn't *yet*. Mauve will know what to do." Bonnie declared. "She'll..." she tried to start again and failed. "Well, I'll leave it to her. She couldn't make it today, but come back here tomorrow, same time, same place, and all will be revealed. I hope that's alright."

Out of the corner of my eye, I noted the address of the house for Child Manor.

My house.

For four hundred thousand dollars? Hell yeah, I could wait overnight in this small town.

"Can I ask you a question?"

"You can ask as many questions as you like," Bonnie collected the signatures in a pile.

"How did he die?"

The paper master went white. She looked even more nervous than before.

"Child?"

I nodded. Who else?

"It was several months ago. It took a while to locate his papers and then the will had to go through probate and I'm only taking care of the estate," she hedged.

"I know." I waited.

"He was killed," she said.

"How?"

"I believe he was stabbed in the back."

"By who?"

This time, the paper master made a small gurgling sound. "I'm sorry. This isn't my place. I'm so sorry Persephone, again, I'm sorry for your loss. We'll leave the details to Lady Mauve. Tomorrow will be here before you know it." The paper master managed to blow out of the office before I could even agree or say goodbye.

So much for asking whatever I want.

I had hours to kill before the meeting tomorrow so, after my strange visit to the law offices of Dunwoody and Barge, I looked up directions to my new house and went for a walk. Child Manor was on a rolling farm road. The houses were well spaced out. My uncle's old house was positioned back from the lane. There was nobody home, which made sense since apparently *I* was the new owner now.

I climbed over the gate and dropped to the grass. I sunk my feet onto his grounds and dropped my backpack there. I'd just take a quick look around.

Was it possible this would soon all be mine?

The manor literally had gardens and grounds.

They were a bit wild and grown over from the passage of time, but the house was beautiful and large. I walked up the driveway. The classic architecture was cool. Not that I knew what any of the woodwork details were called. They gave the home character. And authority. And it looked... old. Like the previous owner had been. Sort of a reflection of his life.

I went up to the front door and throttled the handle.

Ow.

It gave off a sort of a jolt. Locked. Like the paper master had warned. I went around and tried the other doors. All jolted too.

Some sort of alarm. I looked for an open window. I didn't want to smash my way in, but I might. After all, it wasn't breaking and entering if it was a house that you owned... or almost owned. Had I finished the paperwork yet? I wasn't sure. Just another question for Lady Mauve.

I peeked in the windows at the furniture. Classy antiques.

There were plenty of things in the home I could pawn, or maybe I'd sell the whole lot to an auction house. People loved old heirlooms. They'd pay well for the stuff.

I didn't feel a sense of belonging to anything in the house.

Strange things from a strange man. A stranger in my life.

I picked up a stone. I felt the weight in my hand, then chose a point of entry, a window on the right side of the property.

"This is gonna hurt you more than it hurts me," I admitted to the house. I reared back to throw, but just as I did, I heard someone call.

"I wouldn't do that if I was you."

I spun.

The guy from the pawn shop? My stranger?

But no.

A new guy with an orange crew cut watched me turn. I instinctively lowered the rock. Why'd I think it might be the guy from the pawn store? A man I'd literally met one time, yesterday, in a distant town.

That was odd.

I'd almost hoped it was him, even though his fierce intensity unsettled me.

This guy was chill. His green eyes smiled. He sauntered and strolled.

"What are you doing here?" I asked him. He had his hands in his pockets, a grin on his cheeks. Red hair like me, like my uncle. Were we related?

"I could ask you the same. Skulking around Child Manor. Picking up rocks. *Tsk, tsk.*"

"I wasn't skulking."

"What would you call it?"

"A homeowner checking out her new digs. I own this place now."

"The owner is dead."

"The *old* owner died. The new owner is right here," I said. At least, I would be the new owner soon. As soon as I explained my previous educational qualifications to Mauve. Shouldn't take more than a few minutes to clear up.

"You didn't come through the gate," he mused. "*New owner.*"

"Did you?" I shot back, but when I looked at the driveway, the gate was now open, so it was clear that he had.

"You knew Cornelius?" His interest had changed. Sizing me up.

"I'm his niece. Estranged niece. I actually didn't know he existed until I learned of his passing and I came here today for the will."

"I'm sorry for your loss." He examined me to find any sadness.

"Thank you," I shrugged. "Are you related too?"

"Why? 'Cuz of the hair?" He bowed a bit to show it off. I nodded. "Would you like me to be related to you?" It was so slimy I knew at once I shared no blood with this man.

"I'm good." I shrugged.

"You *are* good," he agreed. He'd gotten quite close. Too close. "But you shouldn't throw that rock."

"I don't have a key."

He still hadn't explained why *he* was here.

I'd let my guard down. That wasn't like me.

"This is my future home," I defended my actions. "What's a damaged window to the person with the deed?"

"Well you should know, your uncle put a spell on the house," the man warned.

"A spell." I frowned.

"Throw the rock," he shrugged towards the house. I narrowed my eyes at him, but since that was my plan all along, it couldn't hurt. I did as he said. I hurled the stone at the intended window.

It hit it hard.

Instead of cracking or smashing, the window shone bright with sudden glow. The house made a sudden zinging sound and the stone bounced back. It reversed so hard I had to dodge. The guy simply laughed.

"What the hell?" I could have been hurt.

"Told you." He came closer. I stared into his eyes, surprised, trying to figure him out. Then I saw them, the same crinkle eye lines as my stranger in the pawn store had.

"Your uncle was a wicked wizard," the redhead said. "The biggest spell jockey in town."

He'd gotten so close, he made me feel small. I suddenly wished we were having this discussion somewhere far more out in the open. I threaded my old house keys between my fingers, just being prepared. In case something bad was coming.

"There's no such thing as witches and wizards," I told him.

"Tell that to the house. It's magically sealed." The man picked up another rock, he whipped it at the window. Way harder than I had. It ricocheted off the glass with another blinding flash of light and a zinging sound. I flinched as it flew by. He laughed, a little too loud. But the act wasn't funny. Not at all.

Suddenly, I was very aware of how alone I was with this man.

I didn't know him.

We were standing on the far side of the lawn of the yard.

And he still hadn't told me why *he* was there?

"Are you a wizard too?" I asked. I couldn't believe the words coming out of my mouth.

"I have some tricks up my sleeves." He slyly grinned. A fresh chill washed over me.

"Like what?"

"Like this." Suddenly, he thrust his face into my personal space, staring me down, grinning hungrily. Way too close. His hands gripped my arms.

"*Whoa*, stop." I pulled back but he didn't release.

"You are going to give me this house," he said. Low and slow. With weird eye contact.

I felt a strange tingle in my brain.

"*No, I'm not.*"

"Child Manor is mine." He hissed, gripping my arms. Harder.

"Get off me, weirdo." I shoved him. I stumbled, managing two steps back. His eyes flashed wide in surprise, then his gaze went down to my neck. When he saw my mom's chain hanging there, he practically growled. Instinctively, I covered the spot. He lunged again, only this time, I was prepared for the worst. When he came for me, I clawed him with my keys interlocked between my fingers. The keychain didn't even open anything of purpose anymore, but it worked as a weapon just fine. Thank you, Marjorie Long. Then I kicked the redhead in the groin.

"*Leave me alone!*"

I crushed his dick. I didn't hold back.

Time to go.

Now.

I took off towards the street, running fast. But changed plans mid-stride. It would be better to lose him in the trees. Easier, maybe. If I went straight out to the street, there might be nobody out on a farm road. Then I'd still be alone.

I could hide from him better in the thicket, I hoped.

I made the quick calculation and swerved.

Rawrrrr!

As I turned, the redhead was on me lightning quick. Tackling me like I'd never kicked him at all. He smashed me down to the ground. I screamed, taking a mouthful of grass.

"*No.*" I squirmed under his body weight.

He was big.

Way too heavy for me.

"*Get off! Get off!*" I battered his hands and chest. He laughed at my struggle, fighting right back. He reached for the necklace from my mom. "Leave me alone!" I tried not to panic. It didn't help. I didn't want him to take it, but I was no match.

He looped his fingers around the chain and pulled. The clasp snapped open, throwing me to the dirt. I gasped. But he wasn't done. On top of me. He lunged for my bare neck.

Ahhh! I screamed and wrenched. I managed to swerve, and we both floundered on the grass. But he climbed back up. Him on top. Me down below.

"No, *no. Get off.*"

"*Leave her!*"

Suddenly, someone smacked my aggressor off my hip bones. The impact sprawled the redhead onto the ground a few feet away from me. Our new joiner pounced on the man with a thump. Two bodies, thick and hard on the ground. Swinging with punches.

Oh thank god. I scrambled to get up. Then I saw who it was.

That black wool coat, the dark wavy hair. The stranger from the pawn shop was on my uncle's lawn, grunting and fighting the other stranger on the ground.

What the hell?

My savior had just knocked the terrible guy from atop my chest. But the fight wasn't done. Each rose up to full height. My stranger wiped the fat lip he'd incurred with his opening shot. The redhead leered my way. He refused to go down without a fight.

"You? What are you doing here?" I stared in shock.

The monkey in the middle between two mysterious men with murderous intent.

And fists cocked full of rage.

"Come to me!" My stranger ordered.

"Are you insane?" I bolted into the forest instead. Fast as my legs would run. I thought they'd be on me any second, one or the other. Maybe both. I didn't think that they were working together. But I wasn't sure. Was this some kind of trick? I really didn't care. I only thought of running. Departing as fast as I could. The branches hit me in the face as my boots shredded the forest. Sticks slapped my cheeks. My hands couldn't protect me from them. I blindly reached out. My fingers didn't stop them. I just ran.

Behind me, on Child's lawn, I could hear the men throwing punches. Fists sacking raw meat. They went at it like some kind of battle to the death.

What was wrong with this place?!

No, no, no.

I burst through the trees and glimpsed an old barn up ahead. A neighbor's house. The battered wood looked safe and contained. It seemed familiar as I ran, like I'd been there before. I blinked twice. I pushed my unruly curls out of my face. It couldn't be. I'd never even heard of this ridiculous town before that letter arrived. Still, I didn't slow down my pace.

It was so familiar.

Had I been there before?

Impossible.

The fall must have done something to my brain.

I'd been concussed in the attack.

I ignored the weird deja vu and lunged at the sturdy barn door. I tugged wildly on the handle, desperate to put firm walls and distance between myself and the two men that I'd left behind.

Argh! I shook the handle. But it was no use.

"It's locked," a new voice offered. "There's a chain."

I spun to face this new foe or friend.

He was male, but younger and softer.

A gangly guy.

A few years younger than me.

His shoulders were hunched in worry and fear. He glanced back at the forest I'd just burst through, and the distant sounds.

"If you wanna be safe, come underground. There's a room down here." Instead of the barn, he disappeared through storm cellar doors in the nearby farmhouse.

I looked over my shoulder one more time, then agreed with my instincts.

I followed the boy down the stairs out of sight.

5
PERSEPHONE

"Go, go, go." I shoved the kid inside his own house.

With awareness, he turned back once we were both ensconced and systematically shut the double storm cellar doors by sliding a heavy beam across them as an old-fashioned lock. As a final measure, he applied a tiny padlock with a minuscule key on a small latch. My stomach heaved as I tried to catch my breath.

"All safe." He jangled the ineffectual protection.

"What was *that*?" I asked.

"If I were to guess, I'd say you came across some witchcraft at the old Witch House."

"The what?" When I could breathe again I noticed more of his face. Soft and smooth like a baby's skin, with little baby cheeks and a baby face, though he was closer to my age than I originally thought. He wore an oversized tan golf shirt that didn't quite fit. Part of the collar stuck awkwardly out and his hair was meticulously combed, thrust to the right-hand side, out of his face. It was extreme, but other than the poor cosmetic choices, he was cute.

Youthful.

And safe.

And the most important feature on him? His brown eyes were kind.

"Wait, don't you know?" His eyebrows shot up like inquisitive hummingbirds. "Why were you at Child Manor?" He was curious and not critical of my choice.

"Apparently, he's my uncle." I straightened my clothes, picking off grass.

"He died."

"Right."

"Months ago."

I nodded again. "I just found out."

"I'm sorry for your loss." It was everyone's automatic response.

"Thanks. This whole town is nuts." I sighed. "Sorry," I realized that lumped him into the lot. "Not you," I offered. "You just saved my life. Those guys were crazy out there." He shrugged.

"Maybe you shouldn't explore strange, magical places all alone." His matter-of-fact analysis made me chuckle.

"Magical? Huh?" I checked. The boy nodded. "Maybe you're nuts after all."

"So you're not a witch?"

"No, I'm not." I deadpanned. But this wasn't a joke. "I didn't even know who Cornelius Child was… but… you do…" I realized.

"I did."

"It must have been scary to know you had a powerful wizard living beside you." I tested my words, feeling crazy myself, but he wasn't fazed.

"It was… but at Halloween, he always gave out full-sized candy bars, so in the long run, it worked itself out."

I stared at him, *was this guy serious?* But then his baby face cracked open into a loopy grin. We both laughed. Relief flooded out of my pores.

"Right." I rolled my eyes. "Thank god for Halloween." And he chuckled some more.

"It's a lot to take in?" The boy asked.

"You could say that."

"I just did."

The lunacy of everything that had just happened to me felt normal with him. I finally relaxed enough to look around at the room that I'd fled to. It was the basement of a farmhouse. A stunted teenage boy's domain. His bedroom and home. It was clear he'd lived on his family's subterranean floor for quite a while. And that he loved bugs.

A lot.

They were everywhere. It was gross.

Bugs were housed in little glass structures. Pinned down with signage. Insect drawings hung up on walls. There were even spider cartoons on his bed comforter. And a grasshopper print on his bed sheets.

"What is that?" I noted a large glass enclosure near the storm cellar doors. It was large like an aquarium, but full of sand and soil and twigs instead of water. I squinted, trying to see what was inside. *Please don't be a snake.*

"It's a terrarium," he followed my gaze. "You build a home by layering the container with rocks and dirt. Provide food, moisture and the periodic cleaning. There's no one big in it today. Just worms. The insects come and go." He shrugged.

"A bug hotel?" I checked.

"*Uh huh.* I love bugs," he agreed. "They're a magnificent source of life and all that is under the moon and the stars. There's even a worm moon, it's coming soon."

"If you say so," I sighed, relieved. If there was no snake and no creepy crawlers in the terrarium tonight, a bug hotel was fine by me. Better than the alternative.

"People call me Bug." He chewed his bottom lip.

"Oh, I'm Seph, Persephone Dawn." I shook his hand. A limp shake. "Because of your hobby?"

"Not really, no. Bug's kinda short for Ugnacious Frankel, I mean they're not identical but it's close and it also fits in other ways. It's always been my nickname. Forever. Since I was a kid. I didn't like it in school, but as Mom says, if the shoe fits. Anyway, I wear it... you should know I'm a witch."

I tugged my hand back from our shake. "Are you serious?"

"Yes. My powers are not very impressive. I harness bugs. Girls don't like bugs."

"You're saying all this witch stuff is *real*?" I'd already brushed it off in my head.

"Yes, of course. Wait. Define *real*."

I looked at him like he had two heads, but he was looking for an actual definition.

"There are spells?" I asked. I pictured the flash-bang at the house.

"Oh, yeah. Sure. Those are made by chemists. I'm an empath. Like I told you, I harness bugs. Want me to show you?" He brightened at that.

"Absolutely not."

His face fell. He nodded. "Girls don't like bugs."

"It's not that. I've had a big day," I softened the blow. "What with finding out about my uncle, learning witches exist, almost dying–"

"You should talk to Josie! Josie Jiu?" He checked as if I might know her. I shook, no. "She could help. She knows everything about everything in this town." His eyes bulged at the idea. "*Uh huh, uh huh*. That would be good. I'll go with you!" His voice rose an octave or two. "We should go. Now. The store's gonna close."

"Whoa." I hadn't really thought beyond the present moment until now. Did I plan to stay in my new friend's basement the whole night? No. I didn't have anywhere else to go, but that would be super weird. Of course we should go out. "You think it's safe?"

"It'll be fine. They would have either killed each other or left by now."

I didn't love the casualness with which he gave the lethal options. But now that the idea had set upon him, Bug would not be deterred.

"You're gonna love her, Seph. She's super smart, and–" He tried to undo his tiny padlock, "super cool, and–" his fingers refused his brain's flustered commands, rushing to get out. "Oh, sorry." He dropped the key for the narrow lock twice.

"You have a thing for this girl?" I narrowed my gaze.

"No!" He practically yelped.

Busted.

On his third drop, I took up the key and used it to open the tiny lock. I handed it back. "I'm not risking my life for your crush."

"She's not my crush." He practically melted on the spot. "I just told you, she's super smart. She'll tell you everything you need to know about magic. She's like an open book."

"Is she hot?"

He gave up. "She's the most beautiful girl in the world," he confessed. I hid my smile. The sweet adoration he held for his girl... this boy was alright.

"Okay, fine. Take me to see Josie Jiu."

"Really?!"

"Why not?" I needed to learn as much about this new magic stuff as I could. Together, we shoved the heavy beam aside from his doors, and opened the storm cellar exit back up. But that was a mistake. The moment we stepped out of the stairs, I had a bad feeling about this plan. It was only around 7 p.m. but the sun had already set. It was dark. With today's heavy cover of clouds glooming up the skies, it felt like midnight. No one was out on the road. The air was too still.

It was quiet.

Too quiet.

Even for an old residential farmhouse in a very small town.

"We can take the bikes," Bug nodded at the front of his house. His footsteps crunched the gravel, moving too fast. Tension wound itself onto my bones.

"Bug, slow down." I said. "Maybe we should just call her?" I suggested, glancing around.

"Wait, why? What's wrong?" Bug immediately stopped, but he failed to hide his disappointment.

"I dunno. It's too quiet."

"Oh, I can fix that. How 'bout this?" Bug squeezed his hand closed and the buzz of nature filled the evening with calming sounds. Flying bees, groaning cicadas. A nearby hum. It was actually quite comforting. Like summer. And starry nights with campfires.

"How'd you–"

He held up a balled fist.

"Magic," Bug beamed.

"Right. You harness bugs."

The insect witch blushed.

What a weird skill, but Bug was being so nice. He was doing everything to help.

"That's quite a talent." I lied. He jutted out his chin, proud as punch.

"They're mostly hemiterra," he told me the insects' proper names. "I can make a huge swarm."

"Let's see it," I agreed.

Bug grinned. He placed his feet hip width apart, put his hands at his side, kept the palm closed, and shut his eyes. The buzzing sound grew. It came over the horizon, growing in sound. Then sight. Hundreds of bugs leapt in from all sides, humming, buzzing, jumping, flying. They kicked off of our skin, and landed everywhere that I turned.

"*Whoa*, stop. Okay, that's enough. Let's just stick to the ambient sounds," I shut it down. Bug immediately relaxed; things went back to the quiet hum of a summer night.

"Pretty cool, right?"

"It's... something." My mind whirred.

So it was real.

Magic potions.

Witches and wizards.

Harnessing bugs? Chemistry spells?

It was a lot.

Way too much.

And my uncle was the king of this kind of stuff? The leader of this—*what did they call a group of witches? A coven? Was my mother a part of this?*... The questions just kept piling up.

"Over this way," Bug took off again. This time, I jogged too. We rounded the corner to the front of the house and headed straight for the bikes, two mountain-style vehicles with chunky wheels, left haphazardly on their sides near the wooden front porch.

"You can use my sister Una's." Bug picked up his first then gestured to mine. It was smaller, and painted pink with purple streamers hanging out of the handlebars, but it would work fine.

Una and Ugnacious. Their parents hadn't been particularly kind naming their kids.

"Thanks, Bug."

He plopped his helmet on, pushing down his brown mop. It smushed his hair out around his ears and eyes. The provided helmet for my smaller bike was also sized small. For a much younger brain. There was no way all my wild hair would fit inside. We both stared at it.

"You want mine?" He asked.

"I'll be alright." I tossed it back on the grass beside the walk. We both straightened the wheels and straddled the bikes. To properly ride, Bug had to drop his harnessing palm. The warm hum of bugs stopped. The quiet rushed back.

"I'll start it again, when we get to Jo," he offered.

"That's alright. I feel better now." I lied. I glanced up at the house. In fact, I had the distinct feeling of being watched. Combined with a new strange sensation that I'd experienced all this stuff sometime before in my mind? But that made me sound nuts. The world looked just fine. There were lights on inside the Frankel house, illuminating Bug's family inside. There were no dark shadows peering out.

Just a dumb feeling, I shrugged.

A new place, a new time.

It had been a shaky start coming here, but now things were safe.

Bug started forward on his bike. I sat my butt back on the seat, kicked up my stand and was about to ride, when from the driveway two high beams flashed on in a waiting car, blinding us in their light. A fancy sports car. Bug hadn't noted it at all. I just assumed it was another family vehicle in their driveway.

But why'd it turn on? No one should have been sitting inside a car, waiting in the dark.

Ahead, Bug skidded to a halt, kicking up stones. His fingers flew high to block the sharp glare. So did mine. I watched as a figure leapt out.

"No. Bug! Watch out!" I recognized him immediately. The heavy wool coat flared around his legs like a cape. "It's a witch!"

The man rushed at Bug. Their shadows struggled and merged, intertwining.

Ahhhh!

A scream ripped from my throat as the boy who had been so sweet to me seized up, flopped, then collapsed. His bike crashed down to the ground. My stranger held Bug's limp body for a second more, then draped him down on the earth. His shadowed figure looked up at me and then stood.

"*Oh, hell no.*" I kicked my pedals. The bike skidded. I took off on the gravel, pumping my legs hard to escape.

The door to the old farmhouse banged open behind me. An older man in jeans and an untucked flannel shirt stomped out onto the porch.

"Bug!" He barked. His son didn't budge. "Ugnacious, answer me."

"He can't," I whimpered, looking over my shoulder as I tried to escape. Behind Bug's Dad, a woman in a floral dress and a tiny young girl, only seven or eight, in matching flower fabric, stepped out. When they saw their poor boy flopped on the earth, his Dad raised a shotgun at the blackened shadow still in the headlights.

"He's a witch!" I screamed, trying to help. My split attention caused the bike to skid. I fell to the ground. "He'll get you, run!" I tried to help.

"He's no goddamn witch," Bug's dad muttered. He fired at once.

I gasped. I'd never heard a gun go off so close.

Never seen someone decide to use one.

Never had to before.

The explosion of sound made tears leak from my eyes.

Smoke hazed on the porch.

I didn't know what to think in the dark. It seemed like a direct hit. The man was close enough to strike, I hoped. I expected my stranger to fall.

Like in the movies, the dark figure would clutch his chest then collapse. Blood would dribble down his chin. But it didn't happen like that. Instead, the monster moved lightning quick. The man in the wool coat whirled, seemingly avoiding the close-range shot, then he raced towards the family. His coat-cape flapping in his wake.

"Watch out!" I yelled from the grass. I checked the bike wheel, it was slightly bent but it didn't need to be straightened out before I could still ride. It'd be alright. At least, it would if I could still move my legs.

Terror froze me where I was.

I couldn't run.

I had to watch.

My stranger was on them before the old man could reload.

I stared in horror as the terrible man pounced on Bug's family one-by-one. Taking the father down first, then his wife, and little Una last. They succumbed onto the wooden slats of their porch. The door still wide open to their safe, internal world. Inside the house, a mocking television audience hummed and laughed.

No, no, no.

Suddenly, I was moving again. I found my legs. I pushed the pedals hard, pumping the little wheels of the bike as fast as they would go, careening down the farmhouse lane and out towards the road.

Behind me, the man in the wool coat wasn't done. The car door slammed. His engine roared. My stranger gunned towards the road. He could hit me.

He *would* hit me.

I pumped my legs more.

The car screeched by me, incredibly close.

I clenched my eyes as it blasted past.

Breathless and wild.

He spun the wheel and blocked the road, skidding his car directly in front of my route. With silky skills, he killed the engine and emerged.

I shredded the gravel to a stop. The bike groaned.

Where to go now?

Bug and I never should have left the safety of his house.

I launched my body off the bike. It was too dangerous to stick to the road and the terrain was too bumpy to veer off. I ran on foot. I refused to look back. Blood pounded in my chest and my head, clouding my brain. It filled me with shock.

He just took them.

They all caved in his hands. I was next.

Go, my body said. So I ran.

No plan, no destination. I just fled.

What did he want with me?

What had I done?

I heard him coming behind me. Twice as fast.

At an impossible speed.

I put my head down and sprinted. But he was on me before I got a further two lengths.

He snatched my arms, picked me up. My feet kicked the air.

I flailed the best that I could.

"No, stop! Get away. *Help*!"

But everyone in hearing distance was dead at this man's hands.

My stranger spun me around and stared right in my face, his blue eyes taking up my whole world, all I could see. He stared and stared, hard and firm.

"Orphan girl, can you please stop running and fighting? I've had a long day."

My brain flooded with tingles and fear.

I immediately gave in.

I couldn't fight anymore.

My body relaxed.

"Okay." I fell still in his hands, staring, helpless to the whims of the horrible man.

6

LARK

As soon as she stopped struggling, I released her.

"Good girl," I purred.

"You killed them!" She spit out the words.

My hands balled in fists. Is that what she thought? That I was just this horrible monster who'd followed her here and murdered that young witch's innocent group?

She wasn't far off.

Tears of anger crowded her lashes, but she blinked them away.

It wasn't sadness, it was rage.

She wanted to punch me in my face, scratch out my eyes and flee. I couldn't blame her. I didn't want to compel the girl, but after the vamp at the house yanked off her necklace, it was an available choice, and the quickest option, even if it did make me feel… gross.

Here she was, rooted to the earth.

She couldn't move.

She couldn't do anything unless I gave the word.

Totally under my control.

Other men used the skill to get women to do all sorts of things, but I wasn't like that.

"They're not dead. I compelled them," I explained to her. "Just like I compelled you right now."

"What are you talking about!?" She glared and glared.

I admired the fire in Child's niece, after everything she'd just seen and learned. If it had happened to me, I doubted I'd still be standing, let alone going toe-to-toe with my foe.

She was cute when she was angry.

"They're not dead." I repeated. She still didn't get it. "And you're still here, aren't you?" I smirked. "Still by my side? Haven't hit me yet?" She looked down at her helpless fists, confused. Like she wished that they'd strike. But neither moved.

"*So?*"

I raised a single dark eyebrow, surprised she couldn't make the connection herself. "So... I asked you to stop running and fighting. You obeyed. "

She tried to take a fresh swing at me but I was right. Her arms didn't work. It was like the neurons weren't listening or firing from her brain to her hand. Which, in fact, was true. I politely grinned.

"I asked them to sleep soundly and awaken in a half hour or so."

"Why?" She stared. Half my face was illuminated from the lights of the car, the other half was pitch black. Light and dark. In a gross way, the contrast suited me. After all, I was an angel and a devil all rolled into one.

"Go back and check on them if you like." I nodded towards the farmhouse.

"You're not gonna force me?" She frowned.

"I'm not compelling you now." I rolled my eyes. "That little tingle in your brain?" She nodded. "That's a compelled thought taking root." She seemed so blank I wondered if she'd fallen into shock, but just as suddenly, she spun to locate the boy witch in the dark. She kicked up small stones and ran to him. She collapsed to her knees by his helmeted head. She took off the useless protection and cradled his brain in her lap. He was snoring softly. The insect witch was sleeping. Quite sound.

"Bug," she shook him gently. The baby-face didn't stir.

She looked back, but I didn't follow her across the lot. I didn't have to. My headlights merely illuminated the scene. I leaned on the hood of my car, arms crossed. Watching. Waiting for her to return.

The illumination from the headlights made her crazy curls glow. A halo around her head.

"You're alright," she told Bug, putting him gently back on the drive. The girl checked the other family members on the porch. Bug's mom, dad and sister Una were all sleeping, just as I said. I wasn't the monster she'd thought.

Not tonight, anyway.

Slowly, she stood and walked back to me.

"Who are you?" She asked. But I declined.

"Mauve asked me to keep you safe."

Her ears perked up. I'd name-dropped the person she was supposed to meet with tomorrow. The teacher mentioned in her dead uncle's will.

"You know Lady Mauve?"

I waited for her to catch up a bit more. "I do."

"She's a dangerous witch, like my uncle, isn't she? The whole town is full of magical people and stuff. That's what the paper master didn't want to tell me."

"Yes." My jaw flexed, pleased she'd connected more than I thought.

"But you're not a witch?"

"I'm not."

"What are you?" The way the headlights brightened her

clothes and skin made her look radiant, and she didn't look scared, even after everything that I'd done.

"I'm a friend... be glad for that."

"Because that wasn't witchcraft? Magic?" She gestured to the family snoozing behind us. "You hypnotized them?"

"As I already said, we call it compelling."

Perhaps I was giving away far too much.

"We. You and Lady Mauve."

Again, a piece I hadn't meant to reveal.

"Can this inquisition be over? As I said, I've had a long night." I frowned. But she wasn't done.

"Did you compel the man back at my uncle's house?" She squinted as if she could look straight through the forest. No one was there. I paused.

"No," I said. "I dispensed of him." Dreven's underling was gone.

Neither of us explored what that meant.

"Please." I opened the passenger side door and gestured for her to get in.

It was ridiculous. Suddenly I was brimming with manners?

"You want me to go with you?" She bitterly scoffed. "In that?"

"You could take the bus again if you like," I sniped, then caught myself. "I will take you to Mauve." Persephone still didn't budge. "*Please.*" I gestured again.

She didn't move. But I didn't compel her.

I just waited for her to acquiesce.

After all, this was the option she truly wanted. I was offering it up.

"It's my choice?" She finally uncrossed her arms, though her feet remained planted on the earth.

"I wouldn't dream of telling you what to do," I agreed. She glared, so I broke. "Mauve wanted you to come of your own free will."

"I have a meeting with her at the law offices tomorrow," Persephone hesitated again.

"You want to wait until then?" I asked, crooking an eyebrow.

Was she finally scared?

I'd just stalked her from her previous town, I'd killed someone on her future front lawn, I'd collapsed a family of innocent observers with a twist of my tongue, I'd enforced my compulsion on her when I instructed her to stay, not to fight, and now I was asking her to ride along with no clue where we'd go... *this was her choice?*

"Lead the way."

7

PERSEPHONE

The man from the pawn shop stripped off his wool coat and tossed it into the backseat of his car. He slid into the seat beside me, filling the vehicle. He wore black on black on black, a black dress shirt rolled at the sleeves up to his elbows, black pants, a black belt and the earlier black boots. His forearms flexed as he punched through his gears. He drove way too fast. I clung to the seatbelt across my breasts and held on with each turn.

"You'll be fine," he grumped when I couldn't help but let out an excitable yelp.

Still, he didn't slow down.

I don't know where I expected some secret meeting with Lady Mauve to be held. I was acting faster tonight than my brain could process the choices. Maybe we'd drive into a secret castle? Or onto the grounds of a magnificent school? My stranger took me to a parking lot of a small roadside diner. He whipped his car into a parking spot at seemingly full speed, then killed the engine.

"We're here."

I looked up at the sign.

Spaghetti Joe's.

Through the restaurant window I could see the diner looked like any other worn-down roadside attraction. With 1950s booths and stools at an island, facing a long kitchen counter where the staff worked. The whole place looked old and rundown. But a hot coffee sounded great.

"Come on." Lark poured himself out of the car and strode around the vehicle. He opened my door. This wasn't good manners. I may not have gotten out of the car if it wasn't for him. But since this stalking brute was leading the way, I slowly rose. I ignored the jellied fear in my knees. He closed the car door shut behind me and we went in.

There was only one waitress in the place.

"Two coffees. Please. And a sandwich. Turkey on rye." He said to the woman behind the counter. She nodded at him. "Sit," he ordered me. I tucked into a booth and he sat across from me on the stiff rubber bench.

I stared everywhere but his face, as if I could glean more information about this secret rendezvous if I observed it well enough, but the old diner was just a location. Any place.

Like roadside restaurants all over the world.

Now my stranger watched my face. He tried to connect with my gaze. It was such an intimate space, across the table, just me and the man. I finally gave in.

"There she is." He wagged his eyebrows at me. I might have ripped his face off if the waitress hadn't arrived with two cups of coffee and a sandwich just then.

"Anything else?" The woman asked.

"Another coffee for our friend, when she arrives," my stalker smiled sweetly at the woman. The diner waitress merely nodded and strolled off to kill the rest of the night, one slow minute at a time. He pushed the sandwich my way. "You must be hungry."

"You don't know anything about me," I grumped. But I could

be full of a delicious sandwich or I could be proud, so my hunger won out. I dug into the brown bread and meat with a thick helping of mayo. I ate the whole thing while he watched, an amused smirk on his lips.

He wasn't as old as I first suspected, maybe within a few years of my age, but the distinct smile lines around his blue eyes crinkled his face. They were beautiful in their own way. And everything else about him was gorgeous in the diner's amber lights. His blue eyes caught every motion I made. When the waitress came back, he smoothly lifted the empty plate.

"We'll have another, if you don't mind." He flashed a smile at her long enough to make the cordial request. The waitress vaguely nodded. Then the man turned back to me. I almost blushed.

"Was I supposed to share?" I swallowed the last bite. Not really caring if crumbs littered my mouth.

"No. The next one's for you too. Wouldn't want you to starve." He almost smirked. "A hangry girl's a cranky girl."

"Where's Lady Mauve?"

The man shrugged. Infuriatingly calm. "We've got all night."

"Speak for yourself."

He leaned forward, his voice dropping low. "Where do you have to go? You've been hexed out of your new home."

I shuddered at this stranger knowing fresh details of my life. "Who are you?"

Just then, the diner door rattled and opened, ringing a little bell above the hinge, and a woman marched in.

"Coffee, black." Her order was decisive and loud. She stalked straight to our booth. My stalker slid out of the way, his gaze still locked on my face, his lips still in that infuriating half-smile. I glared right back as long as I could. I only broke off to look up at the new woman who'd arrived. She unceremoniously plopped herself into the booth.

"We'll take it to go," the man told the counter girl of his

second sandwich. The server nodded and poured a coffee for Lady Mauve. I watched as the new, older woman took my captor's place. Barely half the size of the man and twice his age, her presence still took up the whole booth.

A tiny powerhouse.

Plus, my stalker didn't go far. He spread out on a stool at the table's end, still watching me with a half-grin. The waitress dropped off the take-out sandwich for me, and a coffee for Mauve. Embarrassed, I tugged the food bag off the table and slid it onto the bench. Unlike my stalker, Mauve didn't thank the diner staff, look at her, or try to make nice. She only regarded me through narrowed eyes. Her hooded lashes had seen a lifetime of terrible stuff. It was etched into her hollowed cheeks and her frown. Lady Mauve wore spiky gray hair that suited her angular face. She had sharp, light-colored eyes. Every action she made was curt enough to freeze the people in her path. She easily assumed control of the room. And I could tell that her position was earned.

"You're Lady Mauve?" I checked.

"Who else would come here?" She snapped back.

"You set the location," I pushed. "I'm just along for the ride."

My captor sat a bit back, hiding his smile.

"Are you gonna be cheeky, Red, or shut up enough for me to tell you why you're here?"

I spread my hands. "By all means."

"Let us have the place for a while," my captor said to the waitress. I noted the way he said it, and the way he stared her way.

Like he could see straight through her.

His voice flexed, from kindness to command.

The waitress went a touch limp, then she recovered, nodded and ambled away. When we were the only ones visible in the place, Mauve started right in.

"Your mother's side were witches. Your father's side were morons. Far as I know," she began. The mere mention of the woman who birthed me caused me to touch to feel my chain, only, it was gone. My eyes went wide. I'd completely forgotten. When the creep on the lawn attacked me, he ripped it away. It slipped my mind in all the chaos.

"You dropped this." My stalker shifted on the stool to reach in his pocket and pulled out my mother's pink-gold chain. I stared in shock.

"She *lost* it?" Mauve stared at him. "Did you retrieve the lost object?"

"No, he *took* it." I snapped, grabbing it back. He shook his head at Mauve.

"In a fight she was having, it dropped to the grass." They exchanged a knowing glance.

"You probably stole it from me," I grumbled. "He tried to buy it from me at the Pawn Swan. Like a total stalker," I told Mauve.

"If he stole it, he wouldn't give it back," Mauve correctly pointed out.

"I wasn't stalking you," my captor added. "Mauve asked me to keep an eye out. And considering what happened at the witch house, you should be grateful I did." Then to Mauve he added, "she almost died the second she arrived."

"I was *attacked*." I wildly blushed. This somewhat softened Mauve.

"I was afraid of that." She watched me re-adjust the chain around my neck. "It looks nice. You wear it well."

"Thank you." I looked down at the chain, then back up. "It's one thing I still have of my Mom... although... who knows. After all of this, I'm beginning to think she was a nut."

Mauve didn't bother to refute the disparagement. "Your uncle was a powerful man."

"So I hear." I sighed.

"But he went a bit power hungry at the end. A little bit... *nuts*." She used my word.

"Power will do that to you," I guessed.

"Yes. But, power also gave him a lot of control. With that strength, your uncle took care of an item we call the Blood Stone." She checked my face for recognition, then went on. "It's a powerful totem which, if played right, would make all the witches in Plumpkin become witch bloods."

"I'm sorry, I don't—"

"Future vampires. Like Lark." She nodded at my driver, apparent protector, and sometimes stalker. I stared in horror at him.

"You're a *vampire*?" I choked the word out.

"Surprise," he flourished his hands in a wry joke. Mauve didn't bother to soften her blow.

"Focus, Persephone. Of course he is. You can always tell a vampire by the creases at the sides of their eyes. They replicate smile lines, but the tiny wrinkles come from the joy of drinking blood."

"Gross."

Lark grinned for us both, showing his off. "Does the body good."

My stomach gave a little flip. His was a dangerous smile. Too beckoning. I'd known that right from the start. Somehow learning what he was made sense to me. I felt newly drawn to him. Which was both twisted and messed up. I was attracted to a vampire? Of course I was. I blinked and turned away.

"We call the markings raven claws. Other than that small visual representation around their eyes, a vamp looks just like you or me, they fit right in. Until they don't. Most can't go out until night time, but some can. That's neither here nor there for your purposes. You have to beware. Your uncle kept the Blood Stone safe. If it's used, it would make all the witches here susceptible to the turn."

"And... we don't want that." It was a bit hard to follow along.

"Do you want a secret society of vampires running amok in the night? Of course not." Mauve looked at me like I had two heads. "Witches are bad enough. Look, the stories aren't true. Until now, becoming a vampire was a fairly rare thing. There's no cross contamination with humans, humans can't become a damn thing... but about twenty-five per cent of witches carry the witch blood gene mutation. It's automatic for anybody that does... if a vampire bites a witch with the mutation they will turn. Like creates like." Her words sunk in. "If a witch doesn't have the mutation and they're bitten they will lose their witch gifts." She swigged her coffee. "It's still hard to become a vampire because at the mere scent of blood, the creatures of the night have no self control. It's tough for them to stop drinking sweet witch nectar once they start, and both humans and witches can be killed. If a vampire drains all your blood, witch or not, you'll die. Simple enough. But with the Blood Stone..."

"My uncle guarded the rock so the town would be safe."

Lark scoffed.

"No," Mauve's answer was cold. "Child intended to use the stone. He wanted to become a witch blood. But he aspired to transform into a vampire when he was a powerful man... he didn't like the look of the never-ending twenty-something youth. No offense, Lark."

"None taken," Lark shrugged, rubbing his own chin. "For a hundred and fifty-six years old, I still look damn good."

"Your ego's large enough." Mauve slapped him down. Then refocused again. "Vamps can't procreate, they're dead. The only way to grow their numbers is to turn more witches and hunt for witch bloods in the coven. So some vampires want the Blood Stone—if every witch in Plumpkin makes the turn, their numbers will grow. Most think there's safety in a vampiric society. Some vampires don't."

"Men like *me,* think that more undead morons just means more problems," Lark chimed in.

"I'm inclined to agree with the latter group," Mauve said. "But that's not all. Some witches want the Blood Stone too. Because with a well-timed bite they can become immortal, invincible beasts... they'd like to turn. However, most witches would prefer not to be susceptible to the undead. It is, after all, a curse." Lark grunted. I stared at them.

"You two are a team?" They were the oddest couple I'd ever seen.

"We are aligned," Lark clarified.

"So you don't want to make anyone else into a vamp," I checked.

"More trouble for me," he shrugged.

"And more competition," I added.

"You catch on quick," Mauve said.

"And *you* want to keep the Blood Stone safe," I said to Mauve. "Well, good. I don't want more vampires either. If we can help it, let's do that."

"Good. All we need is the stone," the woman said.

"Great. Unhex the house and I'll give it to you," I shrugged. All this cloak and dagger drama seemed unnecessary to me.

"It's not there. I've searched his home top to bottom," Mauve said.

"We think it's in his office. At the school," Lark said.

"You must retrieve it," Mauve frowned.

"Me? You're a teacher there. Why don't you just go and get it?"

"I can't go near it. The coven elders have ordered me to lay low in the academy, and while I rarely listen to the idiots in charge, your arrival and Cornelius' will has offered us an alternate path to seek the result we desire."

Lark shifted on his stool, just a bit.

I could tell there was a bigger story there, but I didn't pry. It wasn't the time and Mauve definitely wasn't receptive to nosey inquiries. Not in the slightest.

"The witch world has floundered with Child gone… there's an embargo on his things while they're trying to sort it. However, I believe his grieving niece could enter the academy doors above reproach."

"They'll let me in?"

"Maybe." She stared me down. "Maybe not. Either way, I believe you'll be properly motivated to find a way to bring back the Blood Stone. I hear you are good on your feet."

I glanced at Lark. Had he seen me steal my way onto the bus?

Or did he know where the jewelry I pawned was originally found?

"What's in it for me?"

Mauve sat back. "Your illustrious inheritance. Child has several hundred thousand in savings in the bank and you'll receive the deed to his manor. All this will be yours when you complete this one tiny task."

I glanced down at the sandwich on the bench.

It was kind of Lark to buy it for me. I hadn't eaten earlier today because I didn't have the cash. The inheritance she spoke of would pay for a *lot* of taco Tuesdays…

It would be life changing…

"I don't know." I decided to hedge.

"Yes you do," Mauve cut right through the crap. "The paperwork of his death says you have to be under my tutelage for a witch education in order to inherit the lot. But, bad luck for you, the academy enrollment no longer exists as it once did. They are trying to get it up and running again." She flicked her hand in front of her face as if brushing away an annoying fly. "A new paranormal school is planned and growing, but it has yet to come to fruition. It may be years 'til it does. The current school is still in session, but you cannot join in. Good news is *education* is a vague term. You get the Stone, you'll learn a lot. Consider it a crash course in a supernatural school. You do this, Persephone, and I will call off the spell. When you deliver the Blood Stone to me I'll sign the paperwork and release all his belongings to you..."

"The house will be mine? Free and clear."

"And everything in it." Mauve agreed. "Yes. The payout is sizable. But only upon completion." She warned. I shook my head.

"I left my job, I need that money now."

"No."

"I can't do your evil bidding if I don't have somewhere to live and food to eat."

Mauve was about to snap at me again, but Lark cut in.

"My brother and I can give her an allowance."

"What?" I stared at him. "No. I won't owe you for anything. Forget it, vamp."

Lark half-smirked. "Consider it a gift."

"One that I never have to repay? And owe nothing for?"

He stiffly nodded.

"The vampires have plenty of money, just take it." Mauve waved a hand to dismiss all of that. "Lark will be your bodyguard 'til you're done. Won't you kid?" The vampire stiffened, but Mauve didn't care. "He'll keep you safe until the Stone is retrieved. Should be simple. You can do it tomorrow."

"Why the rush?"

"I told you, we're not the only ones who want to retrieve it." She said darkly. I checked with Lark, but his face offered little information. "Besides, I'm told when they reopen admissions to the school it'll be merit based, not fate decided. If you wait until then, you'll miss out on the magical education completely. You're not a witch, are you girl?"

She was taunting me with this, there wasn't really a right answer. Before arriving in town, being called a witch was an insult, nothing more. But now? The paranormal title held certain powers and privileges, neither of which I could currently claim.

"They finally gave up on Parabonds?" Lark sneered. Mauve shot him a look.

"What's parabonding?" I asked.

"This conversation is over." Mauve was done. "Do this one job and I'll waive the schooling, then you can live in the house and spend his cash free and clear. You can even enroll in the academy if you so desire."

Lark raised an eyebrow.

"I'm not going to some high school witch academy. I'm an *adult*."

"You seem real mature," Lark agreed.

"Sorry I'm not one hundred and ninety-seven like you." I snapped in return.

"One hundred and fifty-six." He corrected.

"Do we have a deal?" Mauve asked.

"Sure." I shook her hand. "But you should know, I'm not gonna live in some paranormal freak town like you seem to think I will. I plan to sell the witch house, take the money, and settle in some place not haunted by witches and vampires and magical monsters."

The two exchanged a last glance.

"What?" I snapped.

"Nothing," Mauve said. "I wish you well on your quest." She pushed out of the booth and stood to leave. But Lark was still grinning at me.

"Tell her the truth," he told Mauve. The woman shook her head and left.

"*What?*" I asked again. His jaw flexed.

"It's just... a town completely witch, vamp, and monster free? Persephone, you should know, no place like that exists."

8

PERSEPHONE

"Come on," Lark got up.

"I'm not going anywhere with you," I automatically replied. But that wasn't true. We stood in the empty diner in the midst of nowhere, miles out from town. With the promise of money and a new house deep on the horizon after I finished one job, he was my only option out of this roadside restaurant. That, or hitchhiking to... where? I weighed my options.

"If you want that allowance I offered, we'll need to visit a bank," he said.

"Right. Okay. Yes."

A ride back to town and a pile of free money.

Best offer I'd heard all day.

The vampire let me stew in my own juices for most of the car ride. I almost broke down to ask more about weird paranormal stuff, but I got the clear sense in the diner and from the shared looks between them, there were details I would not want to know.

Ignorance might be bliss and all that.

I waited on the curb while he pushed a card into the ATM on the road. Then the vampire handed me an envelope full of twenties. I didn't want to count the cash in front of him, I figured that would appear ungrateful or cheap, but I guessed it amounted to four or five hundred dollars. If he could afford to hand off that to a virtual stranger with no notice, he must be loaded.

"Thanks," I finally said. "I guess I'll see you tomorrow."

"No. All evening. I'm staying the night with you."

"You have got to be kidding." I turned on my heels and walked away.

"Mauve hired me to protect you. That's what I'll do," he said.

"The hell you will."

Money in hand, I no longer had use for this vampire. He grabbed my arm before I could blow by.

"Let me go, *right now*," I growled. I didn't give him the respect of looking his way.

"Or what?" He sneered. My head whipped around.

"Or I'll scream bloody murder and you'll have to compel the whole town or go to jail for the night like some rapist murderer."

"How 'bout I just compel *you*?" He stepped closer, upping the threat. His blue eyes pierced into my brain. But I'd developed a theory about that.

"Go ahead," I dared.

We locked into a staring contest, glaring in each other's pupils. His eyes were so blue. So cold. So wild. I could barely contain him. I felt the oxygen of each breath I took shake inside my lungs. My sympathetic nervous system ground to dust, sending up wild flares of panic and lust. But I held my ground. I didn't believe he could do it. The vampire couldn't persuade me. Not anymore.

It was because of my mother's necklace.

The one that he found, or that the other vamp stole.

The one he'd been so willing to pay to possess.

When the redheaded vampire at Child Manor tried to order me around, it didn't work. He couldn't compel me. And the first thing he did after he failed at compulsion was to stare at my chain. Plus, when Lark compelled me at Bug's house, my necklace was gone. He'd only begrudgingly given it back when the loss was discovered by Mauve. And now that the chain was hanging safely around my neck again, he didn't automatically try to bend my free will. There was something in the jewelry that warded off his powers.

Not just Lark's.

All vampires.

When wearing the necklace, I couldn't be compelled.

That was my guess. And I tested the hypothesis in real time.

Lark was so close.

So big.

So strong.

My whole arm grasped in just one of his hands.

But the compulsion didn't come.

"You can't, can you." I gritted my teeth out into a smile. I loved being right.

"You're impossible, Orphan Girl." He broke off the stare. Then let go of my arm.

"How 'bout you cool it with the nickname," I said. "I get it, my parents are dead."

"Join the club." He spit back.

My eyes grew wide. Lark flinched. That should have been obvious. If he was over one hundred and fifty years old, then of course they'd be gone. But it felt like a tiny piece of himself had just been revealed. Something he hadn't wanted to share. He hid it by turning away. The first sign of weakness I'd spotted since we'd met.

"They're not vampires too?" I asked, quieter.

"It doesn't work like that, *Persephone*." Lark used my real name like a jab. I half-smiled.

"Seph," I offered him the shorter form. An olive branch.

"Seph." He nodded at me. "I will stay with you tonight to protect you. It's no coincidence that a vampire found you at Child's house. They know you exist. They've been looking for you too. They understand you'll have access to all that he owned. And hid. And stole."

Lark was implying a lot of things.

Was the Blood Stone my uncle's rightful possession? Or stolen property?

Again, a detail I probably didn't want to know.

Part of me was pleased to stay by Lark's side, but another side of me was horrified. I wasn't about to spend the night curled up with the undead. No matter how well he filled out a pair of pants.

"Fine. I won't go back to Child's house tonight. I can't get in anyway. I'll stay in a hotel. There's got to be one around here somewhere." I whipped out my phone. Lark put his hand over the device and steered me back to his face.

"They'll hunt you down... they'll hunt your scent." Involuntarily, he breathed me in. It made me feel so exposed... and desired. His throat bobbed, but he hid any bigger physical response from my view. I ignored the clench of yearning that sparked between my own legs.

"Then what should I do?"

Lark moved in until we were only a whisper away. He dropped his voice, for fear of being heard, although we were alone on the empty evening street. I listened close. "You should know that a vampire can get to you inside a hotel. It's public space. You can only stop a vamp from entering a private residence that you or someone else owns. We have to ask permission to get in. Or be invited."

"Humans can say no?"

"To a vampire entering your private property, yes, you can say no as many times as you want. Only, once permission has been granted, the invitation lasts forever or until the ownership changes. So you have to be careful. It's the best protection you have. Especially at night."

The sun had already set.

Prime vampire timing.

"But I can't get into my new home until I finish Mauve's job."

"That's why I'll stay by your side. If Mauve knows you have value, other vampires know it too."

I hated to realize he was right.

"Like that first guy who tried to kill me."

"Malachai. Yes. He tried to *turn* you."

"Same difference."

"No." Lark touched a tendril of my hair. "One is much worse."

Involuntarily, I goose pimpled and shook. The words excited my skin. Or was it Lark's surprisingly gentle touch?

Being turned into a vampire was worse than death?

"You're cold." Lark took his coat and put it around me. "Here." I accepted the gesture, his arms wrapping about my shoulders, tucking me inside. For a brief moment the vampire almost looked kind. His coat was much bigger, cut to shield his wider shoulders and protect his longer legs. I felt like a kid cradled in a protective adult's arms. In this close, whispered proximity, his beauty was unmatched. I realized, although he was sterner and stronger and colder, he wasn't actually too much older than I was.

In human years, not vampire time.

"Why are you being nice to me all of a sudden?" I asked, looking up. Lark smiled down.

"I'm your vampire bodyguard for the night. It's my job to save your life."

"And can I ever repay you?"

"No..." he quietly dismissed the thought. "Unless you're really good in bed."

"Oh, come on." I dumped the coat off my shoulders. There was a puddle close by, but I didn't care. Instead, I marched off.

"I thought we were having a moment," he laughed.

"We were. You just ruined it."

"Don't take things so serious. That coat is expensive," he mused, picking it up.

"Buy yourself another one." I muttered. He retrieved it and easily fell into step.

"There's my girl. It's good that you're pissed. This is a working relationship, Orphan Girl. We're not friends. Or anything more." He added, turning me to him. I flushed red.

"Don't flatter yourself."

"I wouldn't dream of it... Seph."

The way he said my name made my breath catch. We stared at each other, locked in this twisted game. The heat from a moment ago was still there. Burning a new way. Heating hidden parts of my body. Drawing me to him. Not that I would ever tell him.

His words said no but his actions said yes.

He was pulling me in.

Stopped face-to-face.

The vampire stood so close.

Radiating intent.

I could practically feel the heightened breath in his chest.

Heaving, up and down.

Or was that my own breasts?

Lark was so near. I didn't let men like this into my world. Dangerous and brazen, and dead. Any moment we could kiss. We could give in, our lips pressing fast. And it wasn't just him turning my crank, I was here, too, still staring at him. Desiring and repelling this man. An impulse unlike any I had ever known or wanted before.

"This sucks." I broke us apart. "You suck."

"It's just part of who I am," he gave half a shrug. "Vampires suck." He showed off his fangs, but reeled them back again. "What you're doing is important," he tried to assure me.

"Yes. Less vampires in the world is a good thing. Obviously. I said I'd do it, but that doesn't give you the right to mess with my head."

"I can't," he agreed. "Not with this here." He lightly touched the necklace around my neck. With this intimacy, this graze, he lured me closer again. But this time, I fought back.

"I knew it." I stepped away from the vamp.

There *were* access rules.

The heirloom necklace prevented him from compelling my head. I had more control than I thought. I turned and marched away from Lark, further down the town block.

"Where are you going?" Lark asked. "It's not safe."

I pointed one shop over. The lights were still on.

"I'm going to the bookstore."

"Why? What do you need?"

"I don't *need,* I want. Books! If I've got to spend the night with you, I have to pass the time somehow. I used to work in a shop just like this. Are there any vampires inside?" I facetiously asked. But Lark took the query seriously. He cased the joint. Empty but for a few people browsing the stacks.

"No. But they might be coming," he warned.

"To *read?* Just wait outside." I marched through the shop door. Lark waltzed in right behind me, refusing my order. "You're impossible." I grumped.

"Right back 'atcha, Orphan Girl."

"Orphan Boy," I snapped in return.

Lark glanced at me for a moment. Then he actually laughed. A beautiful sound, deep from inside. It made me chuckle too. The vampire's face cracked open in genuine pleasure and I saw those raven claw lines at the sides of his eyes flourish. They were a beautiful sight.

He was such a handsome man.

He isn't a man at all, my gut reminded my heart.

But I'm not sure I cared.

I drank in the joy. Enjoying Lark enjoying me. For a moment we stared at each other, surprised and wide open and soft. Then behind me, I heard the shop girl walk up. She marched to the register to ring someone through. The vampire immediately tensed. Our goodwill collapsed. I turned to check out what spooked him. But nothing seemed weird in the store. Just a girl doing her job. When I glanced back to Lark, he'd disappeared in the stacks.

The customer rang out.

"We close in fifteen minutes." The shop girl gave me a nod.

"Thank you," I gestured back. "I'll be fast." I always hated when an indecisive customer arrived at the eleventh hour and made me stay past shift. I would grab a few books and get out. The familiar sound of the register and all the books made me miss the store from back home... but this was home now. "I don't suppose you guys are hiring?"

"No." She frowned.

I nodded.

Bad timing to ask. The girl clearly wanted to close.

"This is romance?" I pointed at the row marked plainly as such. She just stared, unimpressed. "Right. I got it." I nodded, stepping that way. The girl was cold as ice, but there was no way she was the owner of the store. I could come back tomorrow morning to meet him or her, *if*, after I retrieved the Blood Stone for Mauve and Lark, I decided to stay.

Would the vampire be happy if I stayed here in town?

I looked again for Lark. Where was my so-called bodyguard? When I turned the corner, a familiar voice rang out.

"Seph? Seph! Holy crap! It *is* you. How'd you find us?" Bug stood there. He beamed ear-to-ear, his bike helmet smushing his hair out on all sides. The girl behind the counter narrowed her eyes and frowned, but Bug acted like he'd just seen the oldest friend in all his life. "Come here, come here." He tugged my arm and brought me straight over to the shop girl. "Josie, this is the girl I was telling you about! The niece of Cornelius Child. Persephone Dawn meet Josie Jiu."

A welcome wagon with an ice brigade and a vampire hiding somewhere in the book stacks. What a weird night. I gave Josie the friendliest smile I could muster.

"Uh, hi. Nice to meet you, I'm Seph."

"If you take advantage of Bug, I'll string you up by your ears," Josie said.

9
PERSEPHONE

"Oh, *ha ha*, she's just joking," Bug laughed, but a look at her face said she was dead serious. Finally, Josie's mouth twitched upwards in a minuscule attempt at a smile. It immediately flattened again. "She's a jokester." Bug insisted.

"I'll keep that in mind."

Josie looked me up and down. She was probably the same age as Bug, but twice as mature. Twenty maybe? Twenty-one? With shiny black hair, almond-shaped black eyes, and pink cheeks on creamy tan skin making her appear far sweeter than her words and expression did. I could see why he loved her almost immediately; she was as tough as Bug was soft. As closed off as he was open. And as self-assured as he was meek. Also, she was not at all impressed to meet me. Joking or not.

"How did you find us?" Josie asked. Her skeptical look didn't budge.

"I didn't, I just came in for a few books."

"What are the chances?" Bug beamed.

"Are you here by yourself?" Josie stared me down.

"*Ah,* no—" I flinched. I didn't want to lie, certainly not at this point when I was already very much on the wrong foot with Bug's friend, but Lark's disappearing act implied he didn't want to be found, plus, the last time Bug had seen him, the vampire had forced a nap onto the whole Frankel crowd. Josie flagged my hesitation, but I was saved by the bell when the door entry chimed. A couple strolled into the store. We all looked up.

"Hey Jo, still open?" The guy asked although he could clearly see us here, standing around. "You got those bookie-books for Blue Moon? I'm double parked."

"Greggy, don't be rude!" The girl laughed. "She's clearly got company, hey you." She patted Bug's helmet.

Rat-tat-tat.

Both Josie and I stiffened at the sound.

"Hi, Marce," Bug gave half a wave.

"Hey to yourself." She told him. "Anything new in the bug world?"

"Nope, insects were first thought to have evolved almost 480 million years ago, so I doubt much has changed."

"Be right back." Josie grumped and left us to find their order in the back.

"You're so funny. And *that* is a disgusting fact," Marcy assured him. Bug beamed. Like her boyfriend, this girl was aggressive and loud, but also friendly and playful. No hint of malice. At least not so far. She turned to me, but realizing she didn't know me from town, she only offered a congenial smile. "Hello." She spun back to Greg. "While we're here we should get some kama sutra novels. I heard all about them." She wiggled her eyebrows.

"You can't learn crazy sex from books," her boyfriend groaned.

"*Uh,* how about the whole romance section of the store?" Marcy laughed. "You should hear some of the audiobooks." She spun to me for support. Her quick gaze caught sight of the title in my hand. "You know what I'm talking about, *yeah*?" Her eyes lit up. I couldn't help but grin back. The language in some of my favorite romance books on these shelves would turn her guy into a quivering mush, but I wasn't about to yuck on anyone's yum.

"Whatever works," I shrugged. Greg rolled his eyes. Marcy didn't give up.

"*Greggggg*. We could act a scene out," she whispered in his ear, pressing her breasts against his arm. Now her guy grinned like a mad man.

"Get five books. Right now. No, six!" He announced. "Six for sex!" He laughed at himself.

Eeee! Marcy squealed and picked a flurry of fantasy romance novels off the shelf just as Josie came back carrying a heavy box with a shipping label on the side. She thumped it on the counter.

"This is what we've got."

I read the address. *Lady Blue Moon. The High Council Witch Academy.*

Mauve was named Lady Mauve. At first I thought it was her first name, but now I could see it was a designation of sorts. A witch term. Like ladies and gentlemen... and the names finished with colors. Blue and Mauve? I newly stared at the friendly pair. Were they also witches? It seemed likely. *Was everyone a witch in this town?*

"Put these on the account too," Marcy grinned, dropping her collection of romantasy books on top of the box. I watched Greg squeeze her butt. She leaned herself into his hands. This couple was fun.

Josie started to number crunch. Bug practically put his head in his hands, staring at her and watching her work. She could do no wrong in his eyes. Maybe she wouldn't be such a helpful source of witchcraft knowledge as he first implied, but the academy... perhaps these two could get me inside.

"You go to the witch school?" I asked.

"Sure do," Marcy smiled.

"They're not supposed to talk about it," Josie reminded me and them at the same time.

"*Oops*," Marcy laughed. "Right. I think we're way beyond that." She rolled her eyes.

"Did ya hear about Beck?" Greg asked. Josie flinched. Bug's eyes widened.

"She doesn't want to know about that," Marcy chided her man.

"Sure she does. Ol' Beckety-Beck?" He *rat-tat-tatted*.

"He's her ex," Marcy supplied context for me, in case I planned to listen in on the conversation, which I absolutely did. I nodded, but to appear unobtrusive, I politely melted further back into the stacks.

"You wanna know? Jo? Hey, that rhymed." Greg said.

"He left with Mae." Josie managed to state and inquire at the same time, all while keeping a total straight face. Her tone confirmed that Marcy was right, she didn't really want to hear about her ex, but perhaps like a car crash, Josie couldn't look away.

"*Um hmm*. He and Mae-Mae moved to some ocean town with her Aunt. What was the name?" Greg asked.

"Aunt Abeline," Marcy confidently said.

"No, not the lady." He laughed. "The town!"

"She's sweet," Marcy added.

"We've met," Josie said.

"Killer Scrabble player." Marcy added.

"The town. The beach town. They just sent us that postcard..." Greg groaned.

"I don't know." Marcy laughed. "All geography's the same."

"I put it on the mini fridge."

"When they invite us to visit, *then* I'll care. I look real good on the beach."

"Yeah, you do." The boy goosed his girl. "You look good right here." He nipped her ear. She playfully yelped.

"I'd go to the beach," Bug agreed. "Doesn't that sound fun?" He asked Josie.

"No."

I was working up the courage to casually intercede and bring up the academy again, when Lark whispered in my ear.

"Miss me, Orphan Girl?" I almost jumped at the low growl. A warm hand wrapped around my waist, tugging me back in the stacks. My temperature rose. My whole body tensed. Fully on edge. Alive and alert to his touch.

"No. Miss yourself." I played it cool, pushing him back, trying to stay with the group. But Lark was so close, it was hard to concentrate on anything else. His lips were up near my ear.

"Wrap this up. We need to go. I told you, it's not safe in a public space."

"Then compel Bug to let me stay the night on his couch."

"*He* can sleep with you, but I can't?" Lark cocked an eyebrow.

"*He* will keep his hands to himself." I shot back.

"Don't flatter yourself." Lark echoed earlier me. But there was something deeper in his tone that told me I was right. That there was something here between us. Off-limits and hot to the touch. And the vampire felt it too. Whether he admitted it or not. Finally, his fingers released their possessive grip on my waist. We both felt the loss, I immediately missed the presence of him and I wanted it back. Like a fire that went out, but the coals were still hot. Our eyes met again. He stared at me too, surprised but fully in check. We swam in each other's gazes. Locked in a liquid fight, both getting wet.

What were we doing? Were we flirting?

Fighting?

Teasing?

Telling the truth? Were we lying?

Probably a little bit of all of the above.

I didn't trust Lark and I didn't trust myself. Not around this... *ache.* For now, ours was a working relationship. Nothing more. It was better to nip this chemistry in the bud. After I got the Blood Stone and acquired my house and Child's cash, if the vampire wanted to explore other options... we could...

I let that thought trail through my brain.

We could...

I considered it wholly.

But I didn't let the thought demonstrate on my body. I wouldn't voice all the things I might want from this undead man... that was seriously messed up.

"You sure he's what you want?" Lark asked. He seemed to be thinking all the same things. I swallowed, hard.

"Yes." That choice was smart. "You said I'd be safe in a residence. If the owner says no, a vampire can't enter. They're locked out. Right? You said so yourself. I'll feel safe there. In his house."

"Even with his gun-happy Pop guarding things on the first floor?"

"He was a terrible shot." I shrugged. Lark grinned back. "I'll be good. Bug's a sweet guy. I trust him."

"And me?"

Did I trust Lark?

Instinctually, yes. But that's not what he meant.

"You want me to wait all night in the woods outside the door, guarding the house just in case?"

"You do you." I maintained my tough stance. "*I'll* be fine."

"Fine." Lark sighed. "Then you can give me back your allowance." He unpeeled a hand and held it out.

"No way. You said that was a gift and I didn't need to repay it. The cash is mine."

Cha-ching.

We both looked forward at the sound of the till finishing the sale.

The couple's transaction was complete.

The academy students were headed out.

"Thanks babe." Greg waved to Josie. He smacked my pal's helmet again. "Bugaboo, see you around,"

"*Shoot.* You made me miss my chance." I frowned.

"Chance for what? A threesome with Marcy and Greg?" Lark's brain was obviously still on sex, just like mine.

"Bye," Bug pushed the protective headgear back out of his eyes.

"*No.*" I hissed at the vamp. "I wanted to ask about the school. The academy. Damn it." This was my fault. I hadn't been strong enough to pull away from the vampire's allure. I still wasn't strong enough now. Lark remained undeterred.

"There will be other chances," he murmured. As the couple left, a new boy strolled through the opened door. The passing trio exchanged nods. This guy was casual cool, in a light blue dress shirt with a tie strung open and hung 'round his neck. He probably just got off work. Bug looked down at his feet.

"Hey, Jo," the new guy came in like he owned the place. "Look what I found." He held up a small stone. Josie came out from behind the counter and snatched the jewel from his hands while he grinned.

"Where was it this time?" She frowned, checking the watch on her wrist.

"By Lumber Village. I'm telling you, you should get that thing fixed."

"I should just throw it out." She lied. Instead, she carefully returned the missing stone to its set spot on the watch.

"What a shock to see you here," the guy sneered at Bug.

"I could say the same," Bug whispered back.

"I work two doors down." He laughed too loud.

"Lucky us," Josie returned.

"Who's this?" The new guy stared me up and down, half in, half out of the stacks. Bug came around the corner.

"That is my new neighbor," Bug introduced me before I could reply.

"Persephone Dawn," Josie added. My name sounded cold as ice in her mouth.

"She doesn't like you," Lark whispered to me.

"I know," I shot back.

"Don't know why, you're delightful." Lark teased. I frowned.

"*Really*? New in town." The boy looked me up and down like a piece of meat, then his gaze floated behind me. "And him?" I turned.

Lark was still there? He wasn't hiding in the stacks this time?

No, the vampire stayed, appearing almost polite. Bug looked at me, surprised.

"Uh, this is Lark," I introduced. "You remember him, Bug?"

"No, I don't think we've met." Lark threw on a nice guy suave and leaned past me to shake Bug's hand. As he did, he shot me a look, like, *you don't call all the shots, girl*. "The name's Lark." Bug stared at the vampire with wide eyes, but shook his hand. When Lark turned next to Josie her body language shut him down.

"I know who you are," Josie said without an inch of a smile.

"Who is he?" Our new friend caught her vibe with a curious frown.

"He's *uh*, my boyfriend," I lied.

Lark's eyebrow hitched high. But my guess was right. The new boy instantly relaxed. Knowing the bigger, more handsome man was not a romantic rival for Josie dampened any growing tension he'd felt. I smirked at my bodyguard. A little *'see, I was right.'*

"Lark." The vampire shook his hand.

"Spade Polari. You guys going to tomorrow's Sundown

dance?" He asked us all, but the question was really for the girl by the till.

"I'd rather die." Josie shrugged.

"Just like last time at the High Council," Spade winked.

You were in the academy? I was about to ask.

"No. Last time I left." She shot back. "*You* stayed. And fought it out. And lost."

"There's nothing wrong with my magic." Spade darkened. "I didn't lose. Mae and I weren't a pair." Then his eyes flickered to life again. "Doesn't matter, the dress-up night is open to everyone, I hear it's an unofficial open house for the school." Spade shrugged. "Testing the waters to enlist a new class."

Bug's eyes shone. "Everyone's invited?"

"Even insect witches," Spade winked at him. "They say invitations and enrollment to the school will be based on merit instead of fate from now on. I think they want more numbers since Cornelius Child went a little bit–" he whistled and spun his finger by his head, the universal sign for cuckoo. Josie nodded at me.

"This is Child's niece."

I cocked my head, ready to watch the boy backtrack. Lark crossed his arms. But Spade wasn't embarrassed at all.

"Right on, Cracker Jack," he grinned, totally caught. But he couldn't care less. "Can't pick your family, can ya' girl."

"I only just found out he exists," I said.

"*Surprise,*" Spade whistled a bit.

"I was thinking I might like to check it out," Bug's voice squeaked. For a moment we'd all forgotten he was there. "The Sundown."

"Oh, Buggy, no." Josie frowned.

"I'll go," I offered. Josie shot me a look, but I held her gaze in a defiant stance. *Let the kid do what he wants.* Besides, it was already my plan the second Spade had offered it. I'd get in and get out of my uncle's office during the party. If Bug came along, that was a bonus. I could use a friendly face as a guide or a plant. The group looked to Lark.

"I'll go as well," he said through a clenched jaw.

"Well, maybe I'll see you there," Spade noted to me, and slightly less to the other two guys. "Lemme know if you change your mind," he told Josie, sauntering out. "You'd look fire in a dress and mask. It's a masquerade." Then he was gone.

"He likes you," I told her.

Bug immediately bristled, but Josie was like a beautiful stone statue, chiseled to perfect precision and cold as marble. Of course every man would want to claim her. The fact that she clearly wanted nothing to do with him or anyone else, including me, likely only heightened her pull on the opposite sex.

"He had his chance," Bug gruffed. Josie glared at him.

"Did you find your book?" She asked me casually, ignoring that last jab. She was not about to reveal any secrets. "We're closing. Now."

"Right, of course." I held up a swoony, romantic, steamy love story. One with impulsive mermaids and stoic mermen soldiers I'd already read a bazillion times. My favorite tale. "I'll take this one." Josie rang up the book.

"Isn't she great?" Bug whispered, coming closer.

"Tell *her*." I encouraged.

"Tell me what?" Josie snapped. But Bug shook his head.

"That Bug's going to the Sundown party tomorrow and he hopes you'll come too." I stood up for the guy.

"Is that right?"

"It would be cool to go around wearing a mask, don't you think?" Bug squeaked.

"No."

This girl wasn't going to tell me a damn thing about witchcraft, or vampires, or the history of the town. She handed me the romance book and glared.

"Is that all?"

But there were other information sources right here in the store.

"No." I said, holding her gaze. "I changed my mind. I wanna buy every book on witchcraft and Plumpkin and vampirism that you've got in this place. And he's paying." I motioned to my vampire bodyguard. Then I turned to the sweet kid. "And Bug, Lark's got something to ask you too. *That's* everything. Hope you won't have to stay late." I smiled sweetly at her. If Josie didn't want to be civil, then two could play at that game.

10

PERSEPHONE

It turned out the store had *a lot* of books about vampires and witches. Josie made sure to give me every title she could think of, just to shove them in my face. I took the lot and Lark ponied up his credit card. An exorbitant price tag–ghastly, really–but the vamp didn't flinch. My first big purchase in town was all on the undead's dime. And it took several trips to load Lark's car, but he never complained. When it was all packed, we offered to squeeze Bug in the back seat of the sporty coupe, but there was no room for his bike, so instead the vampire drove me back to the witch's house while Bug rode his five-speed. We were silent en route.

"Alright," Lark said, popping his trunk as we pulled up at the house. It made a loud sound. I glanced up at the farmhouse windows. Would Bug's father and his shotgun come blazing out? But no one stirred. They hadn't noticed or bothered with the car's arrival. It was only my wild scream that clued them in the last time.

Lark was an enemy then, now, he was Helpful-Harry by my side.

The vampire's trunk opened wide, with stacks and stacks of titles. "I'll help you take them inside."

"Absolutely not. You'll pile them right there," I pointed beside Bug's cellar door. "*I'll* take 'em inside. No one's inviting you in."

The vampire smiled. "You're catching on."

With the sound of puffing lungs, wheels crunching gravel, and a tinkling chain, Bug entered his lane. He swayed back and forth on the bike with each pump of his legs. The insect witch wheeled right past the spot where Lark earlier compelled him and he'd collapsed on the ground. The guy didn't notice it at all.

"Why didn't Bug know who you were at the store?"

"He does. In a general sense. But I blocked the memory of the confrontation this evening from his mind. And from his family's too." Lark shrugged. "I made it a part of the compulsion to forget, like it never happened at all. It's better for them to feel safe in their own home."

"'Cuz you can't get in."

Lark didn't nod. "He still knows who I am. What I am. The Korean girl knew too. I can't block out years of whispers in town. Only the last kid, Spade, had no clue. He's so obnoxious, he only thinks of himself."

"Kid, *huh?* He's not that much younger than you," I grinned.

"Before or after I died?" Lark asked.

The frank question gave me a chill I didn't expect.

There were parts of Lark I didn't want to focus on or to admit. He was not a kid. He wasn't even close to my age. He might have been young in vampire years but he was ancient in any human timeframe. I'd blocked out the darker details of what he was. The stuff I didn't like. When we were fighting, giving each other little jabs, I refused to acknowledge that he sucked blood. When my thighs heated and my skin buzzed in proximity to him, I didn't want to know who he really was. Who he'd hurt, or if he'd killed anyone. Because if Lark was a monster, then who was I to be reeled in by my lust? If I was drawn to a beast, an undead man, what sort of freak did that make me?

"Don't worry. He'll figure it out," Lark said.

I nodded. If I'd gathered anything from the trip to the bookstore and meeting the others, in a small town like this, news traveled fast. No secret was safe.

"Time to unload."

It took Lark and me a few trips to bring everything from the trunk into piles outside Bug's storm cellar doors, and then it required *many* trips for me and Bug to carry those same books inside the insect-lover's house. When we were finished, the bugboy was red in the face and huffing a lot. He flopped in a chair and kicked out his legs. I went back for the last book.

"Gimme a minute," I told Bug, going up the steps. He merely grunted, already resting.

Outside, Lark had gone back to leaning against his car, chest slightly concave, one leg bent up on the bumper, sleeves rolled up on both arms. Not a care in the world.

My eyes clocked his bare forearms and his expensive watch as he flipped through the last book. His familiar stance. I walked over to the vampire, glancing back at the house. When I arrived, he snapped the text shut and offered it to me. *Dancing Through Moonlight*, the title read. I watched his muscle flex as I took it from his hands.

"Good book?" I asked.

"Informative," he agreed.

"Right... well, this is it," I said. "Last one."

"I suppose you're here for the night," Lark agreed. Where I stopped, his feet framed either side of my hips, his knee bent into my world. The distance between us felt very close.

"I'll be fine without you," I agreed. I tucked the book to my chest.

"So you've said." He noticed the way the cover pressed against my breasts. His lips twitched. Then Lark looked up at my face. The attraction I felt caught up in my breath.

He was so beautiful, so stoic, so... *other*.

It was time to go.

But I didn't turn to depart. Not yet.

There was something about him.

Or something about me.

Every bone in my body kept me wanting. Standing right there.

Waiting. Hoping to see what might come next.

11

LARK

She didn't go in.

Child's niece stood so close between my legs, my whole body surged. Like a deer caught in headlights, Persephone didn't move. Was her fight or flight reflex broken? No.

She was waiting for me.

Waiting for this.

For what might come next.

I could easily pull her to me. I could take her and do anything that I liked. Grab her hips, bite her neck, crush her mouth.

My tongue grazed my fanged teeth underneath my closed lips.

I hadn't been bated like this, really intrigued, in a long, long time.

Persephone would taste good.

Her blood or her sex, I could barely care which. I inhaled her sweet scent.

I didn't dare to move or speak, lest my body betray my damn brain. Every skin cell was on fire for her.

What was wrong with this girl?

She should absolutely be afraid of me. Of what I could do. Why wasn't she scared?

Didn't she understand who I was?

"Thanks for all that. Buying the books." She gestured back towards town and the general direction of the store, biting her lip. I stifled a groan. I shifted slightly.

"It's not like I had much of a choice." My jaw flexed with a smile. We'd both liked it when she'd bossed my wallet around. I could throw money from the heavens and let her roll in it. But no.

For her good and mine, I maintained a brick wall.

I strong-armed my foundation to stay tough even with her red hair swaying on the evening breeze, caressing her skin.

Such a beautiful neck.

My eyes trailed from her clavicle down to her curves again.

I'd also like to suck on those breasts.

She grinned at the attention I paid. "You can handle it." She smirked.

Her boobs?

No, the bill. She was still talking about the cost at the store.

But this flirtation had a price too... and it was more than I was willing to pay.

Stay in control, you vampire fuck.

I reprimanded myself. 'Cuz I'd also been waiting for her.

For this.

I'd designed our final moment tonight. I held onto her last book. I beckoned her close. Like a damn ego check. When I learned Persephone wanted to spend the night with the kid, and not me, I dunno... I developed something like... a longing to see it through. I wanted her, or if I couldn't have that (and I couldn't), I wanted some small moment, some assurance that she would give in to me, where *I* was the one who got to say no.

Now here she was.

Still between my legs, breath caught in her chest, waiting to see my next move.

Did the girl have a death wish?

Who flirted hot and cold with a vamp? Nobody did.

The girl looked down my bare arms, then back up to my face, matching my scan of her skin. I could feel the ache of sex every place that she looked. This was a dangerous game we were playing. Someone was bound to get hurt.

And it wouldn't be me...

... even if this girl had caught my attention more than I wanted to admit.

We watched each other again.

The intensity of her expression made me want to reach out and touch her pink cheeks. Soft and smooth with a hint of blush that flared darker every time I got under her skin. Which happened a lot. A goddamn beautiful tick.

It was a cool, quiet night. But with Persephone here, I practically burned.

"I should go," I said.

"You'll be out here?" She asked. I nodded.

"Nearby. Yes."

"That's good."

Neither of us moved.

More silence and stillness.

I throbbed.

"You have a—" the movement stopped me. With her free hand, she reached out and picked a minuscule bit of lint from my shirt. I watched her fingers move, almost touch me, pinch the tiny fuzz, and pull it off. She pulled back, then opened her hand and blew on it to let the particle fall.

I raised both eyebrows and breathed out.

I'd touched the girl plenty, grabbed her, steered her, handled her, but this was her first time reaching my way. And I liked it.

A lot.

When she realized what she'd done, invading my space, she blushed.

Blood rushed to my dick.

I could douse myself in lint, I thought with a groan I didn't share.

"Sorry," she acquiesced.

"For what?"

"I don't know," Persephone admitted. And stayed. Right where she was. My legs had started to ache. She was so close, I could sense the blood pumping in her veins.

It *thump, thump, thumped* with expectation and longing.

It announced a raw sort of desire.

Feral and untamed.

I could normally control myself around anyone, but tonight... she had me. I had her.

What the hell was wrong with this girl?

I was a beautiful monster, sure. That was no excuse. She should not be here anymore. And I should definitely go too.

"I'll keep you safe," I finally said. I assured her in a soft, low voice.

I'd keep her safe from everyone.

Especially me.

"Thank you, Lark."

I shuddered at the sound on her lips.

How I could make her say that name.

Make her beg.

Energy hummed over my skin. I watched every flicker and flinch. It was clear she was conflicted too. Part of her wanted to scream and run, maybe beat me up with her book, but more of her seemed to want to hurl the text from her fingertips, climb on top of my waiting lap, push me back on the hood and...

Slow down, vampire. I controlled my breathing again.

Did she have the same craven thoughts?

Was that why she was still here?

I glanced down at her lips.

So tempting.

Deep purple-pink in the low light. The shadows suited her. Made her more like me. Was Child's niece actually a witch? And if I sunk my teeth in her neck, would this pretty girl turn into a vamp? Was there witch blood in her veins?

I could spend an immortal lifetime with her...

I laughed at myself.

You wanna fuck. Don't make it more than it is.

Just one night in her bed... *hell yes I would.*

Is that what you want, Orphan Girl? I wanted to ask. *One dangerous night with a vamp?*

But what if one night wasn't enough? What then?

Suddenly, Persephone frowned.

"Did you compel me?"

"What?"

She stepped back, a dawning look on her face. "To stay outside. With you. Are you controlling me?"

"No," I stifled a laugh.

"It's not funny. Is that why I haven't gone inside?" Persephone sputtered, shock on her face.

"No." I stared at her. "I wouldn't do that."

"'Cuz you're so noble, Lark? I can guess what vampires do. Make women their sex slaves."

"No one does that," I laughed again, but it was forced.

Lots of vampires did that, in fact. And she was dead serious.

"No? You just compelled a guy to let me stay at his house." She gestured towards the storm cellar. I narrowed my eyes.

"Because you asked me to."

"And I'm asking you now–"

"You're wearing Electrum," I pointed out. Her eyes registered the word. The proper name for the material of her necklace. She put together what it was. It made her even more angry.

"I don't know what that is!" She lied.

Or maybe that was true.

Perhaps she hadn't figured it out. Maybe she was totally in the dark. Either way, her reply to me came out far too loud. If she wasn't careful, she'd raise the ire of Bug's pop and bring him and his shotgun outside.

A future mess *I'd* have to clean up.

I lunged off the car and covered her mouth.

"Educate yourself." My voice hissed. Her eyes went wild with fear, then anger. "Quiet," I nodded back at the house and released.

"I am educating myself." She whisper-glowered. "That's why I bought all these books."

"*I* bought the books." My shadow towered over her. Her lusty angst wasn't my fault. Nor her ignorance. None of this was. She didn't need to lash out. I decided to shut this bad decision down. "You're broke. And weak. And a desperate, horny, human girl. *That's* why you're still out here in the dark. You're not compelled."

"At least *I'm* still alive." She shot right back.

"You can go to hell soon, Orphan Girl." I threatened, leaning in, showing my strength.

She should be afraid.

Afraid of me, afraid of this.

But Persephone refused to cower from me. She just glared.

I turned the screws again. "You're out here making goo goo eyes at me 'cuz you can't help yourself. I'm a hired gun, but you've been angling for me all night. Calling me your boyfriend and giving me fluttering eyes."

"My eyes don't flutter."

At this, I laughed. "The only reason we're not out here grinding in the back of my car, your tits in my mouth right now, is because *I* held back. I'd destroy you and your little smart mouth, but you're a freakin' job. And I do good work."

"Screw you."

"Not tonight." I taunted back.

"Go to hell." She whirled around and stalked into Bug's house.

"Already there, babe. This is my life."

12

PERSEPHONE

I roared down the basement steps and slammed the large sliding bar into place, making a terrible thunk. Bug looked up from where he was making up the sleeping linens on the couch.

"That went... well?"

"I don't want to talk about it." I fumed.

"You know he's a vampire, right?" Bug whispered.

"I *know*..." I looked up at Bug. He obviously knew too. "What's Electrum?"

"Metal that repels a vampire's dark talk. A mix of silver, bronze, gold. It's pink in color..."

"Like this?" I showed him my necklace.

"*Whoa*. Precisely like that. Is it authentic?"

"Yes. No. I'm not sure. It was a gift from my mother, but I think it might be."

"It's handsome. Your Mom was smart to give it to you."

"Thanks, Bug." The insect-witch always struck the right note. A guy who offered others kind compliments without any desire to get into their pants... unlike Lark.

The vampire wanted me one minute, the next he shoved me away.

It was clear, he couldn't control his urges or himself.

Or was that *my* problem?

I had a weird hard-on for the undead. Different than any romantic entanglement before. I'd known lots of guys, some I'd let have fun for a night here or there, but this vamp got under my skin, then tore me apart. Over and over. What did I expect? He was a verifiable monster. Beneath the crisp fabric of his shirt lay an old and broken heart.

Could vampires even feel?

Or was his soul permanently destroyed?

And why did I care?

His words tonight were like a slap to the face. Mostly because he spoke the truth. I would have jumped his bones. I was still thinking of him and the firm feel of his calloused hand when he covered my mouth. That dangerous look. Stern, right in my face. I liked how he felt. And *that* annoyed me most of all.

"I don't really have any pertinent details about that stuff," Bug shrugged, still on the jewelry conversation. "Josie could tell you better."

I snorted. "Bug, I don't know how to tell you this, but your dream girl hates my guts."

"No! She's a bit protective at first... she'll come around. You'll win her over, Seph, I'm sure of it." Bug's sweet belief in me melted my angst and made me feel guilty for getting Lark to manipulate me into his house. I could have just asked Bug to stay on his couch. He absolutely would have said yes. I was sorry about that. I refocused on the witch.

"I really appreciate you letting me stay," I told him, bagging a pillow for myself. It was so sweet of him to make up fresh linens, especially for a stranger he just met.

"No prob." Bug agreed. Then he hopped into the sofa's new, clean sheets.

"No, wait–" I yelped. But it was too late. The messy boy flopped down on the couch. All the linens were instantly marred. Bug laughed. My mouth dropped open.

"What's wrong? Oh, I think you misunderstood, Seph. I'm staying here," he said. "You're sleeping up on the bed."

"What?" I turned to see what he was gesturing to. His double mattress linens were bug-free tonight. He'd changed those too. He even swapped out the comforter for a new blanket without critters on it. "You didn't have to do that." The boy narrowed his eyes.

"*Mmmm*, I think I did." He flopped back on the pillow.

Did he know?

The words were more true than Bug intended.

Lark not only compelled Bug to invite me over tonight, I realized. He'd also ingrained the requirement that the boy sleep on the couch and give me his bed. If I wasn't so pissed at the vampire and feeling guilty myself, I'd have thanked him for that little bonus command.

"You've got a lot of reading to do," Bug noted, picking up one of the witchy texts. The books were stacked sky-high all around the room.

"I know. I know nothing about my uncle or the High Council world. What can you tell me about the coven?"

"They're a buncha witches."

"I know *that*."

"You said you knew nothing," he teased. "Okay, how about a demonstration. Check this out." Bug spun himself around on the couch and leaned over the side, balling his hand into a fist. Suddenly, one of the stacks of books across the room near the door picked itself up an inch or two off the ground. It hovered in the pile. Then it started to move. Coming over to me. There were six texts in the stack. When they arrived at the bed, I leaned down to the ground and picked them up. A colony of worker ants had formed underneath the books. A living, breathing conveyor belt. Bug released his palm and they dispersed.

"That's quite a trick," I said. "You must get covered with creepy crawlers while you sleep."

Bug shrugged. "*Nah*. They come and go. Plus, they listen to me. It's a harmonious, symbiotic relationship. I told you, I love bugs."

"Are all coven witches like you?"

Bug snorted. "No. I didn't even get in." He shrugged. "Marcy and Greg are there," he pointed out. I nodded recalling the handsy, boisterous pair. Who could forget?

"Do they also manipulate...?" I gestured at the insects.

"Oh no. For Marcy it's birds... I think Greg moves rocks? I forget. They're both harnesses. Josie's a chemist though."

"Like she does science?"

Bug shook no. "Well, kinda. You could think of it like that, I suppose. She makes potions and spells. She's super well-read."

"That explains her working at the bookstore."

"Precisely."

"And the other boy? Spade?"

"We're not *boys*, Seph. He's twenty," Bug clarified. "I'm almost twenty-one."

"If you still use *almost* before your age, you're not an adult yet, sorry man." I smirked.

"Yeah? How old are you?"

"Twenty-four." I bit back the reflex to say 'almost twenty-five.' "Lark's four hundred and seventy-seven." I outed the vamp.

"Really?"

"I don't know." I felt annoyed at myself for even bringing him up. I did know. He'd told me he was one hundred and fifty-six. The number was burned in my brain, but I was doing everything in my power to push the cocky vamp out of my mental real estate. "Back to Spade. Is he in the coven too?"

"He got kicked out."

This made me intrigued. "Really? What was his skill?"

"Lie-guard. It's like this: there are four basic talents." Bug held up one finger. "Casters see the future while they're sleeping." A second prong. "Chemists understand the scientific makeup of potions and stuff. Empaths," he pointed to himself, with finger three, "specialize in meteorological, elemental, mineral, and animal energies. And bugs. But nobody likes bugs. I dunno why. Insects can dig and fly and lift heavy stuff. The insecta class of animals within the phylum arthropoda are the base of almost every meal on the food chain. Insects are incredibly diverse with over a million described species. Everything in life relies on these organisms to survive through pollinating, assisting decomposi- tion, and being a food source. It's truly a splendid miracle. But people think insectual creatures are gross. Have you heard of bees? You think a butterfly is pretty? Hello! Those are bugs!" He railed against prejudice from an imaginary foe he'd faced all of his life.

"Casters, Chemists, and Empaths is three. You said four talents," I reeled him back.

"Oh, right." He raised his pinky finger. The fourth. "Lie-guards are last. Or first in the witch world," Bug grumped. "They put on a show. The big, magical stuff. Their power is built on illusions. The lie-guards make you see and feel things that aren't really there."

"Like a vampire compulsion?"

"No. For that, you need to protect yourself with Electrum."

I touched my necklace and nodded. "I've seen it in action."

"Compulsion is incredibly dangerous."

"Maybe," I agreed. "But you should know, it doesn't hurt. Lark did it to me once," I added, mostly to make myself feel better about the trick we were currently playing on Bug. "It didn't feel bad. I just had to do what he said."

"Right. But that's true even if the command is dangerous. When a vamp blocks your free will, they suggest a choice and you must accept it. It's a form of oppression. It's out of your hands."

"So how's that different from a witch?"

"Well, a lie-guard creates a fake experience right there." He pointed in front of his nose. His fingers tried to grasp the air. "They make it feel so real you undergo it as true, even though it's not." He opened his empty palm. It still wasn't clear.

"I guess I'll have to see it in action to better understand."

"That's just it. When a lie-guard does their magic well, you never know you were fooled. Their power warps the perceiver's mind."

"And Spade's a lie-guard." I could tell his rival had been blessed with a more significant magical gift. At least in Bug's eyes. He shrugged, yes.

"Every witch falls somewhere in those camps."

Every witch?

"And performing magic always takes its toll. I'm beat." Bug flopped back on his pillows blowing out a large breath. I pulled up the covers myself.

"Right, of course. Thanks again for letting me stay tonight."

"What are friends for?" Bug smiled. He reached an arm to flounder inside a bedside table drawer and pulled out wireless earbuds. "I like to sleep with noise cancelling headphones, it's a form of sensory deprivation. It blocks out the external features of the outside world," he noted. "You want a pair?"

"No, I'm good." Seconds before he put them in, I piped up again. "Do you think I have powers?" I asked. I had a powerful wizard for an uncle, a magical heirloom necklace, it seemed possible that magic was genetically passed down in my blood. Bug regarded me.

"I don't know. Do this." He balled up his fist.

I did.

"Concentrate, Seph."

"*I am*. How?"

"I dunno. Close your eyes. Try to pull something to you. Or make something appear. A ball. Imagine a ball. *Ooh*, set it on fire."

I felt silly but tried.

I squeezed and concentrated and thought about a flaming ball.

I willed it to happen.

Frustrated, I opened my eyes.

Nothing in his basement had changed.

"Feel anything?" Bug asked.

"No."

"Know how to make anything cool? Truth serum? Sleeping potions?"

"No.

"Maybe you're not a witch." He shrugged, turning over on the couch. "It's okay. I like you either way, Persephone Dawn." He put in his earbuds and laid his head down on the pillow. I laid down too.

Glad someone does.

I thought of Lark, out there, somewhere in the night.

Just waiting for bad things to happen.

Protecting me in the dark.

Like I was his job.

Because that's all I was.

Nothing more.

<h1 style="text-align:center">13</h1>

<h2 style="text-align:center">PERSEPHONE</h2>

It took hours for me to fall asleep in Bug's house. I could have seriously used the noise-cancelling earbuds. It turned out, the guy who loved creepy creatures had a penchant for snoring incredibly loudly, like a bear whose foot had been caught in a hunting trap, or a chainsaw eviscerating a thousand-year-old forest. The sawing sounds did not let up. I shoved a pillow over my face, but all the stuffing in the world couldn't drown out his guttural noise. In the end, I settled for reading more in-depth about the witch talents Bug had mentioned. I'd had no magic to show to my friend with a balled fist, but I was growing more and more suspicious that I might actually be a dreamcast.

The books said a lot of things about seeing the future.

Dreamcasts sometimes saw key details, or locations, or people while they slept. They might string several events together, or their brains would piece items into raw sequences. Some casters saw puzzles or riddles or games. But important things often repeated in visions. Especially when the witch was unsettled. Right up until the moment of the event.

It explained a lot of things I experienced, including why in new locations I often felt a sense of deja vu. Like I'd already been there.

Maybe I had, in my mind.

That night I decided to make note of and remember all the details of my dream.

It took forever, but I finally slipped off.

In my dream, I hurried down the thin winding halls. Clacking along marble floors, touching brocade decorative walls. Dress skirts swished around my high heels.

"Follow the blue moon," a voice seemed to instruct.

I looked to the sky, but I was inside.

And the edict both came from me and expected me to follow it.

I ran into a barren room. There was no one around.

Suddenly, a single white piece of paper shuddered and flew out from under a paperweight holding it down. It made a 'whip-clatter sound'. I stared in awe as the single sheet of paper kicked up on the unpredictable wind. It gusted forth, splattered against the left wall of the office, then fluttered, spreading wide against the surface. It quivered there for a breathless moment, then the wind disappeared and the paper dramatically died. It fell down to the floor.

I went to pick it up, but the ground had nothing to show.

More breezes wafted from the nearby window, pushing the curtains apart. Inviting me out to a magnificent forest.

I pushed open the old shutters and looked around. The grounds were silver and shone in the light from the large, wheat-colored moon.

It wasn't blue at all... was that normal?

My hair whirled in the heightened breeze. So did my skirts. I was up high. Fifth floor or sixth, maybe higher. I stepped out the window and stood on the ledge.

"No!" Somewhere, my new coven friends yelled.

I screamed too.

And someone fell.

I shot awake in bed. Sweat beaded the sheets where I'd lain. I pushed the damp hair from my face. If I was a dreamcast then that was my future?

Oh no.

I'd liked the idea at first.

Supernatural powers seemed like a cute quirk.

An advantage to use.

But, if the books and Bug were correct then a caster was someone who received visions of the future while they slept. And if my nightmare was true... someone was about to fall to their death.

14

PERSEPHONE

The Sundown dance didn't start until the time frame its name implied, so Bug and I spent the morning and early afternoon thumbing through more witch coven texts in his basement.

"How much of this is real?" I wondered.

"It's mostly supposition," Bug agreed. I glanced at him and his casual use of big words. Bug was clearly a smart guy. It was just socially he was a little bit stunted. And even then, was a love of creepy-crawly creatures really so strange? People had all sorts of pets. Why should Ugnacious be any different? "If people are knowledgeable about witchcraft, they're in the coven. They don't go around writing books for vanity presses."

"You're probably right." We both looked down at our texts, disgruntled with the process. The idea that these accessible authors were unknowledgeable blowhards took the wind right out of our reading sails.

"My parents won't discuss the High Council with me," Bug confessed. "They never have. They were so disappointed when I didn't get in during the intrinsic initiation that they suggested I move down here. To my own apartment, that's what they call it. I like it okay, it's my own space in this world. I know the spiders and centipedes creep them out and I think they've all but given up that I'll ever meet a nice girl. But it's cool. Mom still does my laundry, so that's nice. I like to think I'm totally self-sufficient. Meanwhile, they're holding out hope for Una, you know. Her powers have yet to emerge, but she's only a child."

"When do powers usually arrive?" I wondered.

"For everyone it's different. I was a late bloomer at ten. Maybe I'll bloom later for everything. Mom told me she'll always have a space in her home for her special little guy."

"You don't have to live here," I told him. He looked at me, genuinely perplexed.

"Where would I go?"

"I don't know, Bug. Anywhere. That's up to you."

"I like it here. I can go up to the main house and snag Pop-Tarts anytime I want. They always keep the shelves stocked with my snacks."

"That's nice," I genuinely smiled. I'd never had a parent looking out. I didn't know anything about that. He rifled in his closet, pulling out a dusty brown suit.

"These are my clothes." He held up a mask and looked through it. "What are you going to wear later tonight?"

"This." I looked down at my jeans and t-shirt. Bug giggled.

"You are not."

"What's wrong with what I'm wearing?" I frowned. Bug tested out his jacket. In the arms, the suit fell a little short.

"It's a Sundown, Seph."

"So, what? Like it's fancy?"

"Technically it's a masquerade ball."

"A ball? Like in Cinderella?" I stared at him, incredulous.

"Well, no. They didn't wear masks... did they? My fairytale lore is rudimentary at best." He was busy trying to do up the buttons on his dress shirt. They didn't quite align. He started all over again as I stared down at my own clothes.

"A ball. Why didn't you tell me?"

"I didn't realize you were unaware."

"I know nothing about anything around here!"

"Well, we'll fix you up. Don't stress. You can borrow my mom's dress."

My mouth gaped. I couldn't wear his mom's clothes. "Bug, I could have gone shopping!"

"I assumed you had an outfit stored in your bag."

I held up my limp backpack. "You thought I had a ballgown in here?"

"And heels," he squeaked.

"Oh my god."

"My Mom will be happy to loan you something." He nodded. "She's only like... two sizes bigger. Four at the most."

"*Bug*," I closed my eyes.

"What?"

"I can't."

"You promised, Seph. You said you'd be my wing woman," Bug said. "What if Josie is there?" I looked at that soft, squishy face. It held so much hope.

"Would you ask her to dance?"

"No." He wildly blushed. He'd stare across the room with love in his heart and have zero game. That's why he needed me in attendance! Plus, I had to go to my uncle's office for the task set by Lady Mauve. The Blood Stone was somewhere on the High Council grounds and tonight, those grounds were public and everyone was in costume. I had to get in there. It was my best, and possibly my only, option.

"Okay." I sighed. I'd wear his mother's tent, if that was the style.

"Plus you don't wanna disappoint your boyfriend, Lark."

"He's not my boyfriend," I groaned. "He's a vampire." I cringed afresh at the idea of the immortal man seeing me in some old lady's rags. Any sexual tension between us would be dead and gone. Immediately. "Go, see what she's got," I gestured above, giving in. Bug goofily grinned and ran upstairs. I sunk down on the bed.

Nothing in Plumpkin was going quite like I'd hoped.

Bug took longer than expected. Probably had to get all the cobwebs off his mom's fancy wardrobe. Who knows the last time she went to a masquerade. But finally, there was a stiff knock on the exterior storm cellar doors. I marched over.

"It's your house, you don't have to knock," I said to Bug, opening up. But it wasn't the insect-loving witch on the threshold.

"Hi." Lark stood in the doorway, the sun in his dark hair, making it shine.

"Hi." I blinked, surprised, then gathered my wits. "I'm not inviting you in."

"You couldn't, even if you wanted to. It's not your house." He looked ridiculously handsome in a fresh black button-up shirt and black slacks with a slight gray pinstripe. He held out a dress bag. He dangled it my way. "I thought you might need something to wear." He let his eyes drape down my casual clothes then back up and raised a single eyebrow. "Unless you're going in that."

"Bug's mom is giving me something." I admitted. He half-grinned at the idea, but waved the gift again. I didn't take it. I stood my ground.

"Suit yourself," he turned to go.

"Wait!" I broke. He came back, now fully smiling, his beautiful raven claw crinkles on full display at my expense. "I'll take it, please."

"Say please." He crooned.

"I *said* please." I complained. But the vampire wasn't done torturing me yet. He put his own masquerade mask up to his eyes and looked through it at me.

"Say '*thank you for saving me. You're my hero Lark.*'"

"Give it." I snatched it from his hands. "Thank you. Do you want me to get into my uncle's office or not?" He just smirked again and let me shut him out of the space. I shoved the wooden beam back across the doors, then took the dress bag over to Bug's bed and unzipped.

Holy crap.

I pulled out the gown and held it up just as Bug came back down stairs with two packages of Poparts and a brown paisley frock.

"*Whoa*." He dropped his mom's clothes in a heap on the stairs.

"It's from Lark." I admitted.

We both stared. I gently brought the gown out of the bag, all delicate and light. Pale blue gauzy layers of thin crinoline floated and danced, intercut with ribbons and petal curves, some with beautiful embroidered flowers, others with leaves. Several well-placed pink panels were sheer. The effect made a totally unique, one-of-a-kind, elegant lilac gown that layered and fluttered on the air. It looked different with every move, every reflection of light. The princess skirt tucked in tightly at the waist to a lace bodice that one could almost see through. There was padding and coverage over the breasts, and thin straps to hold it up, then a low, low back that looked sexy as hell. It was both tasteful and demure. Confident and bold. It even had pockets. The most beautiful dress I'd ever seen in my life.

"You should definitely wear that." Bug mooned. He looked in the almost-empty bag. "He even brought a mask and shoes." He pulled them out. They matched perfectly with the dress.

The man thought of everything, I realized, shaking my head. It was hard to stay mad at Lark and his infuriating, unpredictable behavior, but I'd do my best. Of course, wearing a dress like that to a dance required coiffed hair and a well made-up face, so I took my sweet time getting ready. I was going to a freakin' masquerade ball.

How cool was that?

The words made me feel like I was a part of a fairytale. Super fancy. It was surreal, which was actually a pretty authentic way to describe my whole experience in this town. Bug got himself into his old suit, which mostly fit. I helped him re-tie his tie the proper way, then together, we left his basement all done up.

Outside, Lark waited in the Frankel driveway, casually leaning against his car, just like he'd been doing the night before. And in my old town the night before that. He looked handsome and well-dressed in the dark suit that I'd previewed from Bug's door. The setting sun brought out the blue gleam in his eyes. Walking towards him, I had the opportunity to observe every part of the man. He had the same rolled sleeves, his arms casually crossed. The same smug look on his face. The same strong, muscled physique. The same pressed, wrinkle-free clothes. And those damn charming crinkle-claws, pointing to his sparkling blue eyes.

He watched me the whole time.

I hated Lark for spending the night in the woods or his car or wherever he'd been and still looking so good. But I appreciated the slight shift his body made as he saw me walk out of Bug's door and come near. The dress rustled as I walked, kissing my feet, swaying around my hips and other feminine curves. But Lark's eyes stayed on my face. My hair was twisted with a soft braid. I'd added a touch of blush to my cheeks, and swiped come-hither shine on my lips. My eyelashes were thick enough to look through and flutter at him. At least, that was my intent as I'd ruefully applied a mascara coat for the third time over Bug's sink. A few red curly wisps dangled down, lightly grazing my shoulder blades. My pink-gold necklace laid flat against my bare skin. The only touch of jewelry at my neck. It elevated my look. Lark drank it all in.

"You wore my dress," he said.

"I thought it was *my* dress."

"It is." He agreed. "You look…"

"Good enough to eat?" I sweetly asked.

"Don't tempt me, Orphan Girl." He swung off the front of the car towards my door and opened it for me. "Get in." I didn't move.

"I'm riding with Bug," I said.

"Oh," Bug leaned in. "I, uh, only have the bicycles, Seph. I don't have my license yet." Bug admitted, pulling on the neck of his itchy brown suit. "I failed the test seven times."

Lark raised an eyebrow at me. That threw a small wrench in my plan.

What will you do now? His infuriating brows asked. *In or out?*

"Fine," I gritted out, "bikes it is." I could be defiant to a fault.

Lark merely pursed his lips, hiding a smile.

"Are you sure? In those shoes?" The vampire casually asked. I looked down at the heels he'd also bought. I was wearing an awful lot of dress. But I wouldn't give him one inch, not after how poorly he'd acted last night. The things he'd said…

"I'm sure. Let's take the bikes," I said to Bug. My bunkmate warily eyed Lark, but agreed. He followed my lead to the front lawn. The vampire didn't flinch while we suited up and each took off on two wheels. I had to hitch half the dress fabric into my hand and hold onto one handlebar just to make it all work.

"I thought you said he was your boyfriend," Bug muttered from under his helmet as his legs pumped for the school. I left Una's mini helmet behind on the grass. I wouldn't have worn it even if it was the right size, for fear of ruining my hair. "Why aren't we riding with him?"

"Because *he* is a vampire we can't trust. I only said we were dating to deter Spade. The man is an egotistical beast." I grumped.

"Which one?"

"Both." I smirked. But the insect-witch remained wary.

"Please don't let the undead man hear you say that," Bug said. "I'd rather live to the end of the week."

"Why, what's on Saturday?" I laughed but Bug refused to play along with my joke. "It's okay, Bug. Lark knows how I feel."

He knows all too well.

"I think you've made it pretty clear," Bug agreed as we took off.

The vampire drove behind us in his car. The insect-witch purposefully took us through a shortcut path to get away from his wheels. Una's bike was small and low to the ground, but I didn't mind. It actually felt good to be free and riding around in the fancy, obtrusive dress. The wind in my hair and the elements on my skin would help me achieve that effortless slightly mussed look that I'd tried so hard to create in front of the bathroom mirror. I also liked the gentle look of surprise on Lark's face when I made my choice. He thought he'd had my number right from the start. But, I still had moves. I was a mysterious girl.

And last night he definitely compelled me somehow.

Whether he'd ever admit it or not, he manipulated something, I was sure. He wasn't *that* hot. Not hot enough to make me crazy like this. Crazy enough to wear a ballgown on a small bike just to prove a point? A sexy ballgown that he bought!

The whole thing was nuts!

And I was spending this whole bike ride thinking about him, I internally groaned. Why? Lark barely smiled. Except for that sexy half-grin he gave me whenever I made him surprised. Plus, I couldn't care less about his stunning blue eyes. The way he'd looked so cocky and smug all the time, like he knew he could take what he wanted. Like no matter what, at any moment I'd desire his juicy lips on my–

Whoa!

I swerved off the curb, bouncing hard at the last second and straightening myself out.

"You alright?" Bug followed behind. I shook out my brain.

No more thinking about Lark.

"Too slow. Come on!" I pumped my legs harder, racing ahead. Flying through the town.

The sooner I got Mauve the Blood Stone, the sooner I'd be free of this place.

Free of Lark.

With wads of cash.

I'd be fine.

Better than fine. I'd be damn fantastic!

And I wouldn't miss the vampire at all.

———

I wasn't sure what to expect at the Sundown Ball, but it did not disappoint. The evening was just like Cinderella or any other fairytale I'd seen. People wore luscious suits and beautiful gowns. Most women were in shades of purple, while the men wore crisp black. My dress fit right in yet somehow felt innovative and new in the crowd. Lark knew the dress code to a tee. While Bug... looked like Bug. But I was happy to arrive with him. Coming alone would have been hard.

Bug and I put on our masks and dropped our bikes on the far side of the lawn so they wouldn't be seen. When we walked across the grounds, my heels click-clacked on the pavement stones, and then sunk into the grass in the turf. I read an elaborate scripted sign in the entrance on my way in. The official title of the dance was the Amethyst Sundown Ball. That's why most women wore purple. Lark knew that too. The grounds of the High Council had been done up with twinkle lights as plentiful as the stars in the sky.

The academy was huge.

I'd never been to this kind of country estate before, unless you counted my inheritance home, which was stately, too, but nothing like this. All sprawling and private and expensive and old. Plus there were areas with stark new renovations. It looked part-traditional castle, part-modern, sleek hotel. The academy was over six stories tall with an impressive atrium entry made entirely of windows that stretched up, up in everyone's viewpoint. Wings spread out on either side of the building, with wraparound balconies and decadent pillars. A fountain in front of the academy's double door entrance was a focal piece of the party. It tossed water into the evening sky in a never ending cascade of opulence and splendor. Purple lights danced in those waves. The place was more spectacular than any school I'd ever attended. More rich in style and flavor than anything I'd seen. And the party outside...

...it was a real life *ball*.

No wonder everyone in town wanted their kids to get into this academy.

There were witches milling in the school's gardens. More swirled on the flat dance floor erected near a stage. Live music played. It wafted over the group. There were chairs and a dais. But for now, the podium was unmanned.

Would someone give speeches later tonight?

What about academy tours?

Along with the sea of purple dresses, a few attendees missed the point and stood out with hapless color, or basic wardrobe choices. They didn't fit in; I was thankful I hadn't been looped in with them, even if sweet Bug was. Instead, I had my eye on the other group.

The beautiful people.

Adults who clearly had their lives together.

They looked comfortable holding champagne flutes and gossiping in small clumps while also seamlessly interweaving their socializing together. They danced and chatted and looked elegant, and their laughter rang out in pearls. They wore white clothing of every shade: alabaster suits, vanilla dress shirts and parchment-colored dresses.

"Those are the Ladies and Fellows," Bug warned. "Graduates from the academy, teachers and professors."

"Good to know." I smiled demurely at anyone who deigned to look my way. I glanced around for someone who could let me into the school to let me get to my dead uncle's things. I clocked Lady Mauve chatting with other members of the coven near those front doors. It was clear she was part of the staff. Like Bug had said, the professors all wore white suits with a flash of a single, solid color in their shirts underneath. Black, gold, pale blue. The women wore white dresses but had single pops of color too, in their jewelry or their shoes. Mauve didn't wear a dress. My teacher wore white pants and a silk sleeveless blouse in her signature color. Her mauve fit in elegantly with the amethyst color code of the party. The cut of the fabric showed off her tattooed arms, which stayed firmly crossed as she spoke with the other professors at the school. Even in this beautiful sunset, her eye mask and her fancy dress clothes, she looked gritty and tough. She was arguing with another coven member in white pants whose dress shirt was onyx. I tried to catch her eye, but if Mauve saw me in the crowd, she didn't let on.

Low profile and all that.

That option was impossible for me, as Lark's exquisite dress choice made my clothing stick out from the crowd, garnering approving looks. Everyone seemed nice, but such a show-stopping wardrobe wasn't actually the best choice when I would be trying to sneak down the back halls of the academy soon enough. For now, I took it in stride and smiled a lot. Maybe I should have worn the old wrap dress to disappear.

"I'm gonna do a lap, see if anyone is here," Bug told me.

"Anyone?" I teased. He blushed. We both knew who that meant.

"She might have changed her mind."

"I hope she did," I said, then added, "good luck with that."

But I couldn't say much about his not-so-hidden secret agenda, because as soon as I was by myself, I did my own impromptu search, looking for my own very dangerous man, a vampire who I knew for a fact looked impossibly good in dress pants.

15
LARK

I watched her casually stroll the grounds, tucking errant hairs behind her ears every now and then. A few pieces had fallen looser in her bike ride to the school. She was red-cheeked and rosy from the effort. It suited her. So much so, that I couldn't resist.

"You're wasting your energy. I could have given you a lift," I said low in her ear, sliding a hand to her waist, letting her know I was there.

An inch behind those frothy skirts, my body was erect.

"I'll be in and out." Persephone didn't turn my way, but I heard a hint of a smile in her voice. She was glad to be found. We swayed with the music, masks on our faces.

"You shouldn't dismiss the danger so easily. There's a lot you don't understand about this world." I warned her. "You need to listen to me more."

"I said please and thank you for the dress. I don't owe more than that."

"You're enjoying another gift?"

"That's right."

"My charity case?"

"Screw you, Lark." She started to walk away but I caught her elbow and tugged.

"You're not in control, Orphan Girl."

She was surprised by my strength. And pissed.

"Are you in control, Lark?" She finally turned to glare. We locked eyes through the masks.

I loved her like this.

Fiery and sharp.

But I would not back down. My face was an inscrutable wall. It was a mistake for her to take me on, head-to-head. She acquiesced and turned back towards the dance floor.

"I asked you not to call me that." She added.

Orphan Girl, it suited her. Pity.

"You don't like me anymore?" I cheekily asked. Our bodies returned to swaying. Of course she didn't like me. She fucking loathed me. I'd been driving her away since the moment we met.

"I never liked you." Persephone lied. I half-smiled.

"All this animosity because I said we couldn't have sex?"

"It's not up to *you*." She flashed a look my way so I raised my eyebrow, intending to ask '*you sure?*'" Then caught myself.

"It's better this way." I quietly said.

"What *way*?"

I was about to say more when that cocky Spade strolled up, looking me up and down.

"You wanna enroll in the Academy. Aren't you a bit old?" He asked me. He regarded my Orphan Girl next. Persephone smiled. I stiffened at the way he checked out her curves.

"I'm just here for moral support," I said, keeping my eyes off Persephone's breasts. Spade made no such effort.

"Hey, new girl," the witch-boy flashed a smile and locked onto her tits. He'd cleaned up well in a grey vest with a purple pocket square. I had to admit, he looked suave. "Nice dress." His wandering eyes stayed far too long on her skin. I was about to grind him to dust, but Persephone wagged a finger leading him back up to her face.

"Up here. Seph," She reminded him of her name.

"Spade," he said back with rakish intent.

"I know," she sweetly smiled, rubbing it in my face. Spade's eyebrow kicked up.

"You *know*?" He flirted back.

"She met you last night," I cut in. "We both did. In the store." My hand threaded more obviously around Persephone's waist; I tugged her to me, clearly laying claim. "Or did you forget?"

She glanced down at the large hand spread above her hip. Holding her to me. Pressed against my legs. I had no right to touch her. Not like this. But she didn't twist from my strong hands. Her dress sparkled against me. I did my best to ignore the waves of heat in my fingertips, caressing her lace.

"Oh, I remember. I never forget a pretty face," Spade said, just to her. He grinned, still testing the waters. "Just think, Seph, if we enroll at the same time, we might all be in the same witch class for years."

"That would be nice, wouldn't it, Lark?" Persephone turned my way and raised both of her eyebrows over her mask in the same way I often teased her. I frowned at her, then frowned darker at Spade, about to answer when–

"–that's only if you get in," Josie interrupted our group.

Was she jabbing at Spade? Or Persephone? I involuntarily tightened my grip. The Orphan Girl melted further into my hand. I steadied my breath. *Easy, Lark.* These were just a buncha nosey witch-kids. Seph was barely mid-twenties herself.

Right around the age I'd been when I turned.

I shut that memory out.

I had a job to do tonight. I'd do it well.

"Look who I found," Bug squeaked, arriving last. He immediately realized that reconvening his two favorite ladies might have been a bad choice. As did everyone else. Josie stood still in a shimmery silver drape that slunk down her body and showed off her posture and sophisticated grace. While Persephone was all rhythm and swirls, Josie was streamlined and bare. Her black hair was perfectly straight with a comb picking up half her locks. Her black eyeliner was thick. A cat's eye.

"*Hot damn*, Jo," Spade turned to shine brightly at her. He puffed out a breath, a reaction she entirely deserved. "You came… and you brought Bug."

"Actually, Seph and I rode our bikes," the insect-witch clarified.

"You rode Una's bike in that?" Josie frowned at my girl.

"I'd like to see *you* ride something," Spade leered at Josie's dress.

"You can watch me slap your face, if you're not careful," the chemist warned back. "Anything else you'd like to say about my appearance?" She raised an eyebrow at him.

"I'm good." But Spade still undressed her with his eyes. I tugged Persephone's waist again, making her lean back. Her red braid and tendrils fell against my chest.

"We're supposed to be boyfriend and girlfriend, remember?" I complained in her ear. "Why are you flirting with *him*?"

"We broke up." She deadpanned, straightening, pushing my hand off of her hip. "Last night. I need a drink." Then she stalked out of my reach and walked through the crowd headed for the bar.

In getting away from me, she almost ran into Greg and Marcy, the boy piggy-backing his gal on his hips in her own frothy purple dress. The skirt was hitched up. Her bare thighs in his hands. Both laughed and had a great time. For a second I regretted all I'd said.

That's what Persephone needed. Sweet, casual love.

Not moody vampire lust.

I had no right to be pissed. She was right. She could flirt with whomever she'd like. I'd done everything in my power to drive her away. Now I wanted her back?

The music picked up and the party started humming.

Persephone took a champagne flute from the bar but she didn't slam it back.

Smart.

She wanted the appearance of a casual drink, but she intended to be fully aware when she went into her uncle's rooms.

"You're still here?" She frowned at me. I didn't reply, just stood at her heels. This was my job after all, to protect the girl. "The lost and found collection at this school must be insane," she muttered under her breath.

"Indeed."

"I could make a killing."

"You certainly could."

There were lots of handsome witches and wizards on the dance floor. Ball gowns swirled. Cufflinks clinked. Laughter rang out. I watched Persephone absorb the sights and sounds of the crowd, until her eye caught on a younger girl. She couldn't have been much more than thirteen years old. Her mom held a champagne flute of her own.

"Here," her mom aggressively licked her thumb and tried to clean some imperceptible smudge.

"*Ahh*, stop." The girl glanced around.

Persephone casually peered up at the sky, so they wouldn't think she was staring, but glanced back as soon as she knew they hadn't clocked her listening in. There was something about them she liked. I watched her eavesdrop.

"I just want you to look your best, darling. The academy rules are changing and we want you to get in."

"I know, Mom."

Her mother frowned. "I knew that bow was a mistake the

moment you put it on." They both looked around, trying to ascertain the audience who was judging her, when in fact, nobody cared except for Persephone. Not another soul but Cornelius Child's niece was listening in.

"Should I take it off?" The girl fretted, her hands going to the purple ribbon in her hair.

"No. God no, you made your choice, we live with it now," her Mom said. The girl's face cracked.

"What if I don't get in?"

"*Hey.*" Her mom lifted her daughter's chin. "We don't talk like that. You will. Because the High Council witches love talent and minushka, you got it. Your father and I are so proud of you. Are you proud of yourself?"

"Yes," she snuffled back tears.

"Are you proud of yourself?" the mother asked more insistently.

"I'm proud."

"Damn straight you are… and don't look now but someone is coming. Leave the bow, leave the bow!" She whispered rapid-fire to her daughter. Her face twisted in glee. "Poker face."

"Would you, uh, would you like to dance?" A boy around her age asked the girl in a stilted, formal tone. The girl glanced at her mom, who bobbed her head. Her face radiated familial pride.

"Okay," the girl agreed. He took her hand and they joined the other dancers with four left feet. Her mother watched her girl for a moment longer, downed the flute of alcohol, then turned away. She allowed her daughter the moment all to herself.

Persephone fingered the Electrum around her neck.

My parents were long… long… gone. And Wren, Finch and I were older than dirt so I barely thought of them anymore. But for the Orphan Girl, this town… this whole experience opened a new door… into a life and a possible family she probably thought that she'd never get to have. Her bloodline was right here. They had walked these same halls... in fact, she was tasked with getting into her own family member's office this evening. I hadn't considered she might feel conflicted or–

"What are you two stalling for?" Lady Mauve snapped.

She yanked us out of the stolen moment we'd separately shared.

"I–what?" Persephone stuttered.

"Give me that." Mauve grabbed the drink from her hand and shot me a glare. "You just let her stand here and gawk?"

I tightened at once.

"Go." She yelled at us both. We automatically moved, whether to get away from her, or to do our job. We hurried away. *"Get the Stone."*

"Excuse me. *Geez*. Sorry." Persephone tried to walk around the perimeter, but I picked up my pace and swooped her into my arms. The dance floor was between us and the Academy's front door.

"Come with me." Her body tucked into my gait, even with a sea of crashing skirts.

"What are you doing? No."

I didn't obey.

"The dance floor is the quickest way to the front door." One hand went around her waist the other slid into her palm. She was buttery soft.

"I can do this myself."

"Not happening, Seph." I picked up her fingers and put them up on my shoulder, warming my skin. Effortlessly, I started to move with the crowd, her feet falling into step. "You need to seem like you belong," I told her, "not just look the part." I moved her in an effortless whirl, making the girl look light as air under my control. The dress I'd provided swished and swirled as we moved in perfect sync.

Face to face.

I got lost in her grace.

The music swooned.

"Lark!" She objected when I passed the entrance and didn't release her. I kept hold of this beautiful girl, taking her round the dance floor a second time.

"You belong," I whispered in her ear.

She straightened in my hands.

Up and down our cadence moved.

In her mask, her green eyes drew back to me. I was already staring at her.

Like the other hundred witches at the gala didn't exist.

Like we weren't here for a damn job that we had to complete.

Like I hadn't rejected her again and again.

Last night.

Today.

Like she could get everything that she needed right here.

In my hands.

In my life.

In my bed.

My jaw twitched, but our gaze didn't break as I moved us close to two other swirling pairs of witches. So near we might crash. She trusted me to steer us through unscathed, my attention never leaving her perfect face.

"You look beautiful, by the way." I was unglued by that gaze.

"Thank you," she whispered back. "You look... I'm sure you know."

"I'm aware." I agreed. I played it off. Then changed my mind. I leaned in, my breath hot on her ear. "But a vampire still wants to hear compliments from the woman he'd like to bed."

I swayed back, our chests exhaling out, as if we'd been afraid to breathe with each other so close in our worlds. I watched her. This woman who made me feel desire and fear and rejection and attraction all at once.

Would she take the bait? Tell me what I wanted to hear?

Would she express how she felt?

I hung on every word.

"You look..."

The music slowed, the song at an end. And I fully stepped back, leaving her to discover that I'd swirled her to the exact place we needed to be at the end of the song. Steps from the front doors of the school.

"Saved by the bell," I smirked, taking her hand and turning us away from the dance. "All business again." She stiffened at that.

"Come on," was all she said. We walked to the front door.

Behind those ornate double doors was a huge atrium. Persephone marched right in, but I stopped.

"What are you doing?" She waved me on, but I couldn't budge. When a student of the academy passed by on his way out, I inquired to him.

"May we look around?"

"Uh, sure." The kid shrugged. "But the party's out here tonight. I think the professors are gonna make some introductions soon."

Nothing changed. Fuck.

She nodded at me, expecting me to walk inside, but I still didn't come. I couldn't.

She rolled her eyes, annoyed, and turned, deciding to explore for herself. That's when she saw a plump-figured woman with a sharp gray streak in her curly hair and a white dress coming right for us. Something about her direct manner told us both that she obviously needed to be avoided.

"Quit fooling around," Persephone hissed. But I looked down at the threshold of the school. Right before the frame of the dramatic double doors. The Academy wasn't a public space. This school was owned. And now that Child was gone, I didn't have permission.

"I can't come in."

"You can't enter?" She snapped.

"Please lower your voice."

"You can't–"

"That boy had no authority here," I shrugged. I held out a hand for her to come back. "Seph, come on."

"*No*," the Orphan Girl looked defiantly at me through her half-mask, and started to smile. "I don't need help, Lark. Vampire babysitter or not, I can do this alone."

<h1 style="text-align:center">16</h1>

<h2 style="text-align:center">PERSEPHONE</h2>

"No future students inside. We're not doing tours tonight." The woman in white gave an oppressively wide smile to me and Lark. Her gray curls bopped around. There was no choice but to retreat. "Off you go. Watch the show." She stood as the gatekeeper in the atrium. We were boxed out.

"That was your big play?" Lark immediately snarked.

"Shut up. There wasn't enough time." I glanced over my shoulder, but the professor was a bulldog, keeping guard. I felt like a mouse.

"You didn't ask for her help or explain who you were," Lark chuckled.

"And waste a request on the human embodiment of the word '*no*'? I'll ask someone else."

"A smart decision for once," he mused.

"Screw you."

"The moment you've all waited for has arrived," someone announced to the crowd via a microphone from the stage. The music cut to a fairly collective groan. Lark and I had no choice but to rejoin the party outdoors. So while the speeches were set up, I made my way back to Bug. He welcomed me to stand next to him in the crowd. Josie on his other side. We watched as a procession of professors went up to the podium, marching in line. They stood at attention and stared us all down. The party area quieted at once. An old man in a white pantsuit with a gold dress shirt ambled up to the microphone.

"That's Fellow Gold," Bug whispered to me and Lark.

"Hello and welcome, potential new recruits, old friends, students and Ladies and Fellows alike. Welcome to the Amethyst Sundown Ball." Fellow Gold spread his arms wide. The witches and their friends and families clapped. "The High Council is a wonderful coven of witches. Generations of fated parabonds and a magical education for the mystical elite. This is quite an occasion. We're opening the selection door wider for the first time in thirty years." He paused to let the crowd give a polite cheer. "Now, more than ever, being a witch is a dangerous business. Outside these walls, we are other. And the human race barely likes its own kind. Throughout history there have been flare-ups and slaughters. Witches have been hunted down, publicly drowned and burned at the stake. Out there, your powers put you at risk, but inside, these same powers make you rich! And strong! And powerful! And dare I say *beautiful* tonight?!" The audience genuinely liked this. Some cheered. I politely clapped my hands. The man in gold droned on and on.

He spoke about the history of the Amethyst party. How decades ago, four witches discovered they'd developed four very different ancestral gifts. They showed the town their perfect new powers at a remarkable sunset, when a hue of purple kissed the sky to say goodbye to daylight and welcome in the starry night and the moon.

I got the sense the old man liked to talk.

My uncle would have been up there on the stage with the

others, I knew. This was likely his speech. He'd been their boss. His replacement tonight was a pale substitute. Even the other professors on the stage looked bored while the pompous man droned on.

Behind my back, Lark stood close. His hand floating just above my hip. My bodyguard, doing his duty. I didn't want to admit I felt safer with him by my side. His quiet strength spread from his chest in ripples and tides, drawing me in, even as his hot and cold words made me angry with him.

What the hell did he mean on the dance floor?

I was a woman he wanted to bed? Could have fooled me.

"This is a new witch era, we're not content to hide in the sidelines anymore. It's not enough to know who your parents are, or your parabonds–"

"What are those?" I whisper-asked Bug. It wasn't the first time I'd heard the term.

"Fated mates."

"See, I told you they're opening up the Academy to all kinds of legacy members," Spade chimed in to Josie under his breath.

"That's good for the niece of Cornelius Child," Josie said a bit too loudly, staring my way.

Others turned.

More stirred at the first group's attention, like an echo in the crowd.

Soon they'd all know exactly who I was. I closed my eyes. I did not want our relationship broadcast tonight. Not until I'd retrieved the damn Blood Stone. Was that too much to ask?

"How 'bout you keep other's business to yourself," Lark growled at her.

"She can say what she wants." Spade stood up to the vampire, straightening up. He balled his fist as if readying to fight.

"Spade," Josie put a hand on Spade's arm, shutting him down. "I can speak for myself. I apologize. I thought it was common knowledge why you were in town. Bug said you inherited the manor." The bug-witch quickly agreed.

"It was magically locked last night, so Seph stayed with me. I slept on the couch."

"Is that so?" Josie's cold shoulder let me know she had opinions about that as well, but I was saved from another scathing rebuke when Fellow Gold pounded on the wooden pulpit on stage. His bravado made us all look towards the front.

"*It is an evolutionary process we must guide and protect! For years to come! You and me!*"

The crowd cheered. Right on command.

It was a lot of fire and brimstone talk for a fancy dress-up night. But Josie wasn't done with her inquisition of me. Quieter, for my ears only, she questioned. "And your *boyfriend*? Did he stay in the Frankel house too?"

"No." I shook my head. "Bug didn't invite him in. I made sure." I matched her tone and her dark glare.

"Good."

"I don't plan on staying long. Maybe one or two nights. Then you'll never see me again."

"I couldn't care less what you do. But don't take advantage of him." Josie frowned. Bug was involuntarily nodding along with the propaganda Fellow Gold spewed.

"I could say the same to you," I countered right back. "You know he's in love." I raised an eyebrow at her. Josie sighed.

"I have been trying to dissuade him for years."

"There's no accounting for taste," I snarked.

"I could say the same thing," she looked over my shoulder at the vampire guarding my back. I might have found another retort, but Fellow Gold's abrupt coughing fit in the microphone at the front stopped us both cold.

"Blue Moon, get me some water, I've got something in my throat." Like most of the other party-goers who'd drifted into boredom during his extended talk, my head spun forward to watch the melodrama evolve. A woman stepped forward with a water glass and the old-timer drank. My eyes widened more, newly surprised.

Follow the blue moon.

The words I heard in my dream as I slept.

Blue Moon was a person, not a star in the night sky.

Fellow Gold kept right on talking, the frog still in his throat. But I stared at the woman who had tiptoed forward and poured him a drink.

I knew who she was.

I gaped in surprise at the paper master from the law office of Dunwoody and Barge. Bonnie Main and Lady Blue Moon were one and the same. Their initials even matched. The paper master, having finished her fetching task, stumbled her way back across the stage then slunk away from the crowd.

This was great news! Bonnie Main also knew who I was. If I needed a tour guide to Child's offices, she would be the perfect choice. I grinned.

Bring it on.

17
PERSEPHONE

When Blue Moon finished serving Fellow Gold, she didn't stay. I followed her progress off the stage and watched her movement through the crowd as she headed back to the school. Like a liquid eel she made her way, a total nonentity in the crowd, slipping in and out. That's how I should have dressed for tonight. I pressed forward and moved with her thirty feet out.

"What is it? Who is she?" Lark asked in my ear, right on my tail.

"Never mind. I told you, I've got it."

"*Seph.*" His voice grew tight. He reached out, but I swerved right, expecting his controlling hand on my arm. He missed.

Get a new move, blood boy.

I wouldn't give the vamp the chance to agree or to change my mind. There was no point. He couldn't come anyway, since I was going inside. And that meant any other vampires on campus would also be stopped. The protection of his presence may have ceased at the threshold but I'd be alright. I followed the paper master inside. Blue Moon, or Bonnie Main, or the paper master, or whatever you wanted to call her, took a side door. She still had twenty feet on me when she entered, but I could close that gap in the interior hall.

"Excuse me, Bonnie?" I called as soon as we were both inside. "Blue Moon?"

Annoyed as he was, Lark didn't come in. He couldn't.

I turned back to see him one last time. "I'll be alright." Then I called forward. "Blue Moon? Can I have a moment?"

The witch in front either didn't hear me or wasn't slowing. We each hurried down a hallway full of office doors. The doorframes came at regular intervals. Professor offices. I read out the placards. Fellow this, Lady that... but none said Child or had any indication of belonging to my uncle. His office was somewhere else. And the paper master didn't slow, so I followed. Lady Blue Moon slipped out of the professor's area and through an exit into the main atrium. As I entered the next space, my eyes floated high.

Up, up, up.

Holy crap, the school was large.

The atrium felt grand. I'd only had a tiny glimpse of the structure when the curly-haired Lady had hurried me outside. Now, I saw its full impact and height. The Academy was built out of beautiful slab marble floors, wood beams, exposed brick, and industrial rails. The ceiling soared high above us, covered in skylights and centered by an extravagant chandelier as big as a car. The mammoth light hung down from the sky like an immaculate illusion, reflecting a glittery array of light and sparkle all over the polished foyer. Little pods of furniture and throw pillows in playful colors broke up the elegant space to let arrivals know that the atrium was meant to be gorgeous, but not too precious for the students it housed. Although that was probably a lie, as I'd not seen one person actually sit on a curated couch.

Lady Blue Moon's shoes clacked across the stone floors. She clearly knew where she was going. Again, I hurried to catch up, but the paper master was too quick. She headed directly to the central structure in the space, an ancient service elevator built to hold large equipment or a flux of ten-plus people. Almost steampunk looking. Opposite of every modern and sleek contemporary choice. It was functional too. Blue Moon hopped aboard the lift, going up.

"Wait!" I called, my dress swishing as I ran. "Hold the doors."

I scurried like Cinderella at midnight, but it was too late. The elevator shut just as I arrived. The doors closed in front of my face. The paper master saw me at the last second, her mouth opening into a surprised little 'O.' Lady Blue Moon reached forward to press the door open button as I pressed the exterior call button, but with no luck. The light above the elevator lit up, and the arrow which signified how the box would travel from floor to floor started to revolve.

I watched the arrow go up.

A quick glance around the atrium again told me there was only one lift. Beside it, an architectural stairway that the majority of the student body likely used snaked around the elevator box. The ascending arrow was almost at level two.

Could I beat the elevator to the second floor if I hoofed up the flight?

I took the steps two-at-a-time in my high heels, trying to keep pace with the ascent of the lift, but it was a lost cause.

On the second floor, the elevator didn't stop.

I slammed my finger into the indicator button when I arrived, but it was too late to get on. The arrow kept rising. The paper master was going higher in the school. My feet ached in Lark's pretty, not practical shoes. so I scooted them off into my hands and started scaling the staircase bare foot.

"*Damn it.*" My skin slapped the tiles as I barreled upstairs.

I didn't bother with the call sign on the third floor. The elevator had already passed, the witch still inside. I'd try again on the fourth. Only, now I was gassed. I might have completely given up, but something told me this was right, that along with connecting with Blue Moon and asking for her help, I also needed to get myself up nice and high.

High like I was in my dream.

I wasn't fast enough to keep pace anymore.

The elevator passed floor four before I arrived, and when I got to floor five my legs were burning, my heels were raw, my lungs were gasping for air. I was way too late to see if Blue Moon had stepped off or walked around on the fifth floor. So I had to go off my instincts alone. I glanced up and down the long halls. These were residential dorms. The students' homes. The staircase still rose up. I decided to go up one more floor. The elevator indicator light had stopped there.

The sixth floor.

The last stop.

Blue Moon's exit point.

My thighs were like jelly, but I forced my body to climb the last flight, gripping the handrail as I rose.

I was way too slow to surprise her now.

Or possibly even to catch her.

I huffed and puffed.

"Paper master."

Gasp.

"Blue Moon."

Nobody answered my breathless calls as I arrived.

I looked at the double elevator door. It was closed.

I checked the indicator light above the box and shoved my finger into the call button hole. The door obediently slid open. No one was inside. I looked left and right down the hall. She was here.

Where did she go?

I swallowed the nervous energy in my thick, dehydrated

throat. I'd been too slow. Blue Moon had disappeared through one of the sixth floor's fancy closed doors. There was a marked difference here from the floors below. Yes, there were more offices for the school, but this time I knew the individual offices were for the people with power within the coven. Everything felt richer in this hall.

They were rooms with a view.

And the space to spread out.

The hallway was decked out in all the finest finishes. I felt confident my uncle's office was here. After all, from what I'd heard, he'd been the coven's boss.

"Bonnie Main?" I now called quietly, pacing forward, keeping my voice respectful and hushed. "Blue Moon?"

It only seemed right to honor the space.

The hall felt expensive. The carpet beneath me was plush. My toes were grateful for the reprieve. Rich and luxe. The walls were lined with navy blue paper, accented with pinstriped lines. Thin gold. Even the office placards were fancier than the ones on the floors below... Fellow Nightshade... Lady White... Fellow Gold, he'd been the blowhard on stage... I read off the names.

Suddenly, I saw a rustle out of the corner of my eye. I spun.

Was someone there?

But the hallway was empty.

"No, wait!" I resorted to chasing the ghost. But, as soon as I hurried around the next corner on the sixth floor, the person or the impression was gone. My adrenaline had my mind playing tricks on me. Had someone ever been there at all?

I blew out a breath. Then looked ahead. I cocked my head.

Maybe it was okay I'd lost the help.

The dream voice had said *follow the Blue Moon.*

It never said we would talk.

This seemed like the exact right place to be. There were more offices here, in this final wing. And the one near the end of the hall had been taped closed with yellow caution tape in a hurried criss-cross.

That had to be it.

I moved towards the warning sign and read the owner's placard.

Fellow Black.

This was his. It had to be his.

My uncle's office.

Cornelius Child was Fellow Black.

A badass color for the leader of a witch clan.

The caution tape was a ward. No one was meant to go inside. But, that didn't include his family, I thought. I had permission from Lady Mauve, or at least from the last testament and will that Bonnie read out. What was his was now mine. More or less.

Besides, no one was up here in the midst of the ball.

It couldn't hurt to peek inside. I pulled off my mask.

I tried the handle. Nothing clicked.

I jimmied it hard. Definitely locked.

Was it sealed by magic?

I tossed the shoe in my hand at the wood, expecting a jolt of a spell. It thumped against the door and fell with no zing or sparks. Child or another witch hadn't magically sealed this space. It was merely locked by bolt. That should have been good news, but it still didn't help me get inside. I was a petty thief of school lost and founds, not some master criminal. I couldn't pick locks and there was no one with a key waiting around.

At least now you know where it is, I told myself. But that wasn't enough. I touched the door again. Gave it a little thump. *The Blood Stone is in there. You just go down and find another coven member dressed in white, maybe someone else who stood up on that stage or even Fellow Gold himself. You get him to bring you back up. He'll let you in. No one will notice you've gone. The party must be in full swing by now.*

Or I could save myself some time.

Blue Moon had to be around here somewhere… I could just knock on every door in the hall and find her right now. She'd know what to do. To be thorough, I turned around and rapped on the last door in the row.

"Blue Moon?" I shook the handle. It didn't open. Nobody was home.

I went to the next office to try again, the one beside Cornelius Child's.

Fellow Nightshade, the placard said.

"Bonnie?" I knocked and twisted the handle. This one opened in my palm. To my surprise, I pushed the door wide. "Hello?" I called, but didn't really expect anyone to answer. The office was dark. Shut down for the night.

It was also mostly empty. Fellow Nightshade didn't use his personal workspace much. Either that or he had no use for knick-knacks. There was almost nothing on his desk. Sparse shelves stood behind his chair back. In fact, his whole office was practically blank with streamlined, darkened walls. Still, I looked around and cautiously stepped in like at any moment, Blue Moon might magically pop out. "Is anyone here?"

A familiar sense of deja vu came over me. The same sort of strange, uneasy feelings I'd experienced for most of my life. I usually brushed it off as an odd little occurrence.

But if you're a dreamcast witch, this stuff matters, I reminded myself.

Under a paperweight on his desk, the only object in the room, a single sheet of paper flickered on a faint wind. I walked towards it. It was a page of legalese, fine print instructions. I didn't read it down. I didn't care about the paperwork. That didn't draw me. It was the breeze…

I'd seen a shaking, fluttering paper somewhere before…

Somewhere in my mind.

I looked further around. The window to the outside world was slightly ajar. The two halves of a frame were worn and tall, part of the original castle architecture style, maybe antiques? Definitely old. They were latched with a single hook and eye. The look lent the room a quaint, warm charm, but the lock was a feeble mechanism. On the sixth floor of a verifiable castle, maybe they didn't care about the locking device. I undid the latch and opened the two frames to look out. The fresh air pushed the tendrils of my hair off my face. It rustled my skirts and goose pimpled my skin. I sucked back the breeze. As I suspected, the windows weren't double-paned. And there was no screen to hold a night gazer in. On the outside of the building there was a stone ledge, around a foot wide, and a six-story drop to the gardens below.

I stared down in the dark.

The distance to the earth was sort of mesmerizing. Beautiful and scary and far. I gazed out, orienting myself. These offices were on the backside of the school, the places with the best vantage point, the windows over-looked well-tended gardens full of roses, hydrangeas and curated, colorful flowers. The garden was surrounded by a decorative wrought iron fence, and further afield, the deep, untouched forest stretched out. The buildings of the town were far, far away. Overall, it was a spectacular sight.

Behind me, the single piece of paper suddenly shuddered and flew out from under the weight holding it down. It made a whip-clatter as it fluttered. I spun around at the sound. The single sheet kicked up on the air flow, curved, careened and churned like the tendrils around my hairstyle. The paper splattered against the left office wall, sputtered, and fell.

My body shivered.

Holy crap.

The details were just like my dream. I'd been here before.

Was destiny really recounting my path?

I tested the theory further, pushing the curtains like I had in my mind. It felt identical too, and then an idea developed. The vision brought me here. I was next door to my uncle's office. I could use the ledge on the outside of the building and walk the path to the next window... if Cornelius' office had the same simple latch on its window like this one, I could easily get inside.

Then I'd get the Blood Stone.

And Lady Mauve would sign off.

I could sell the house and take the money and run.

Maybe even spend a night or two having vampire fun. After that, I'd be gone.

All that stood between myself and my goal was one narrow ledge walk. I'd climbed lots of trees and entered plenty of windows before... although never from the sixth floor.

Was the idea totally nuts?

The breeze rustled my hair.

I stared out at the night.

I'm supposed to do this, I knew. Deep in my gut. The answer pulsed in my bones.

The dream had brought me here.

And later in the dream someone would fall to their death...

Someone. Not me.

I thought of the remaining images in my brain.

Bug, Josie and Spade screaming and yelling.

Someone hitting the earth with a terrible crash.

Maybe I could change it to an alternate ending, I tried to tell myself.

Maybe I couldn't... perhaps it was fate.

Was I willing to take the chance?

Absolutely not.

There was no way I was climbing out there, I decided. You would have to be mad. No one should mess with a forecast of life and of death. I turned away and headed back to the hall, about to exit Fellow Nightshade's office, when two men's voices made me pause.

"Did you see Child's niece?"

I froze behind the door. *Oh no.*

"She was there?"

"*Um hmm.* In the crowd. Had a vampire with her."

"She did not."

"Swear to god. Gold nearly peed his pants."

"Well, let him. Hopeless old fart."

"They were wearing masks, but no one was fooled."

"I hate these dumb balls."

I slid on my shoes. That wasn't so bad. I'd reveal myself. They already knew I was here. I could press these two for help. Claim the bloodline. Insist they let me into my uncle's office right now.

"How'd she know to come? I thought they were estranged."

"Someone tipped her off. Or maybe the girl's already a member of the Flood."

"I always knew Ambrosia wasn't dead."

"Let's not go that far." The other one returned. "All we know is that her daughter's alive and well."

"*Not for long.*"

The hair went up on the back of my neck.

"Think she knows the power she yields?"

"For all our sake, let's hope not... but if she snoops around too much or becomes a problem, I'm sure the elders–" the man trailed off. The other grunted.

"It's either kill or be killed."

I let out a long slow breath.

What the hell had I gotten myself into? Who were these elders? And what were my powers? Dreamcasting?! I thought that was fairly common. I needed answers. Real, verifiable answers. Not half-truths and gossip and vague details spoon-fed to me to keep me quiet and on the right track. There'd been enough of that in these past two days. It was time for me to learn more real information for myself.

And the knowledge was there. In the next office down the ledge.

One short risky walk.

I went back to the window and decided to cross.

18

PERSEPHONE

You'll be fine.

I stood in the window frame, trying to gather my nerve, again removing my shoes.

Goddamn heels.

What were they good for? Their only purpose was to make a woman look hot. No wonder Lark bought them for me. I wished I had boots. Heavy black boots, like his. To kick ass and take names, not trot around like a princess.

I stared out in the darkness, steeling my nerves.

Who was I kidding? I wasn't that tough.

Where was my vampire bodyguard now, when I needed him?

Was I really doing this?

It was like I'd invoked his name. Led him to where I stood, because suddenly, six floors away, I saw something move. Quickly. With purpose. The vampire was there. In the garden. Not bothering to shroud himself.

It was Lark.

I'd recognize that dark hair and wool coat anywhere. He was racing around the garden fence, coming my way. He looked so small from way up here. When he got close, Lark slowed, then stopped. He glanced around, more carefully this time, checking to see if anyone watched. Sniffing? Maybe?

Then he stared up.

His head raised directly to me in the sixth story window.

The move chilled my bones. Lark knew exactly where I was. His chin angled up until I could see his tensed jaw and those vibrant blue eyes. From six floors away, I still felt his gaze.

No, his lips said.

He gave a slight shake of his head.

My hair swirled on the wind, more tendrils coming out.

How could he possibly know what I was thinking from way down there? Telling me to stop? Shouldn't he want me to proceed? After all, the Blood Stone was next door. In my uncle's locked office. This was my task. My choice. The vampire had no say. He never had. I was wearing Electrum. He couldn't compel me anymore. Or do blood-sucking jiu-jitsu to my brain. I touched the necklace. Lark had given it back to me with very little prompting... knowing it would stunt his powers to control me. Why would he do that, if he intended to manipulate me all day everyday?

I shook my head. Enough about him.

I needed answers and I had decided to do this. Honestly, Lark's trying to dissuade me might have been the thing that pushed me onto the ledge. *I needed the Blood Stone.* Or at least, I wanted it. Badly.

The rock *and* the answers about who and what my family truly was.

The ledge wasn't so bad. I could creep across the footholds without looking down, I'd done it plenty of times before in foster homes. Never this high, of course, but it was no sweat. I could do this.

And I would get the damn answers for myself.

I doubled back to the hall and closed Fellow Nightshade's

office door tightly, then I took his office chair and slid it under the window. I stood up on the cushion. This put me higher, more in line with the window shelf. I looked out. It would only be a small step onto the ledge. I put my bare feet up on the stone and tested the surface. The battlement was firm.

It's wide enough, I lied to myself.

The wind cooled my cheeks.

Even at this distance, I could tell Lark was pissed. If he could have, he would have run up the six floors, grabbed me by my waist and pulled me back in. But the lack of permission from the academy owner kept his vampire feet stuck where they were. On the outside, looking in. Watching me climb the terrifying ledge.

Concentrate, I chided myself.

This isn't for him.

You're doing this for you. For the house. For the cash.

Not for some hot and cold vampire who likes to boss you around.

I took another step, no longer seeing Lark or the grass, focusing solely on the narrow bridge I walked across.

What were the boundaries of his skills?

Could a vampire stop me from dying if I fell?

You won't fall.

I took a step forward. Knees shaking.

Both my hands were on the rock wall.

Skirts swaying in the wind.

My toes inching across.

Like a sloth in a fancy party dress, I made my way.

What if I *did* fall?

If I was dying, could Lark turn me? Like they did in the movies? Could I become an undead girl? I gripped at the rocks.

If he bit me, that might be a pleasant experience.

I pictured the sudden slip, my footing gave way, the whole world swirling like a blur, then hitting the earth. A desperate thud. My life draining out. Lark swooping me up in his arms... and suddenly his mouth would be diving down on my neck. His fangs would sink into my delicate skin. Making me cry out. Vicious in desire. Ripe with lust.

He'd suck on me hard.

My body would writhe.

And I'd succumb.

In Lark's strong manly hands. Under his total control.

He'd go feral and wild.

His blue eyes would glow. The claw lines around his eyes would crinkle in delight.

He'd take me.

All of me.

Every drip of my blood.

He'd lap it all up.

Everything he ever wanted. I'd give it all to this man. I'd want him so badly...

This was nuts.

I shook out my head. I was currently in the dumbest place on earth to be hallucinating about such things... risking my life, out on a ledge, six floors up, my imagination running wild about a disapproving bully of a vampire sucking on my neck.

But it actually worked.

Thinking of Lark kept me calm. And focused. The fantasies kept me out of fear while my feet inched slowly. So I moved forward again. Giving into the thoughts.

This time, we weren't out on a terrible ledge. Lark and I were on the hood of his car. No, in his back seat like he'd promised and planned. All cramped and snug in that dumb sportster. Pressing into each other in a tiny space that barely fit one person sitting up. We'd have zero room for romance. But neither of us would care about that, getting right down to business, ripping into each other's clothes. Our limbs knotting and pressing together. Desperate to connect.

He'd feel so good.

So strong and so sure. His hands would control me.

Showing me just how to contort.

How to provide for all of his needs. Oh, how I'd give them to him.

But first, he'd make it my turn.

Lark's lips would clamp down on my breast, sucking me deep into his mouth. He'd swirl my nipple under his tongue. I'd feel alive in his touch.

Aching forward.

Groaning his name.

My head rolling.

His heat crashing over me again and again.

I'd embrace his hard strength.

Rocking beneath my hips.

I'd straddle him. Clamp my thighs around his strong waist.

Until again his fangs sunk into my neck, plunging in...

My big toe struck the window pane.

I gasped. Back to fully aware.

Holy crap.

In front of my face was the next office. I looked at it, almost surprised. I'd inched across the divide in a methodic, sex-hungry trance, thinking of Lark.

I gently shimmied the old pane and watched the latch shake loose, then I opened the window frame. I dropped inside and gasped for breath. My cheeks flushed in pleasure.

I did it!

Next time I was in danger, I could imagine what was under Lark's shirt... or roam around in his vampire pants, I giggled, surfing the adrenaline rush of success. I turned back to look down at the real man, far below. I waved hello, just to bait him. The vampire remained unimpressed.

Lark spread his hands apart as if to ask *'was it worth the risk, Orphan Girl?'* Then he crossed his arms and stared up. We both knew that my brazen act of fortitude would only be of value if I actually found the Blood Stone and then got out of the school unscathed. Any celebration before that was far too early. But I insisted on staying pleased and smug.

Let me have my damn moment, Lark.

Still, when I turned away from him and looked around the room, my smile faded. The task still wouldn't be easy, I guessed. He was right. Of course he was. Stupid vampire.

Unlike Fellow Nightshade's workroom, my uncle's office was a fully functioning workstation carefully curated for beauty and elegance and possibly intimidation too. He had his own desk and chair, plus two seats for guests, aimed and styled to make the hierarchy crystal clear. Behind those seats was a sleek couch lined with throw pillows in shades of purple and green. Jewel tones. It all looked rich.

I flipped on the light switch. My uncle's desk was huge and ornate. A heavy wood. Impossible to lift. It took up half the space in the room, set on an off-white rug below an enormous chandelier, the design of which was a mirror image of the huge palatial light in the atrium. It seemed oversized here. The entire wall behind his expensive desk chair was an irregular bookcase laid out with texts and knickknacks.

Magical artifacts?

Perhaps the stone would be among them.

For the first time I realized I didn't even know what a Blood Stone looked like. Would it be red? That seemed obvious. So I was looking for a red rock? Why had Lark never described it? Why had I never thought to ask for myself?

Behind the open shelves was beige wallpaper with huge golden tree branches and twisted vines and buds yet to open in the design. The effect made you feel like you were trapped in an opulent forest.I hurried into the space and scanned the shelves, then started opening drawers, looking through paperwork.

Where would a magical wizard hide a powerful rock?

I noted a laptop, so I turned it on and searched the hard drive for the key words.

Blood Stone.

Eight hundred results came up, all of which held very little worth. I clicked through a plethora of files, mostly documents talking about witch bloods and potential side effects.

There were notations about a coven blood bank. Gross.

Attendance records for meetings.

My eyes raced over the files, looking for anything image based so I could see a picture of exactly what I was looking for. There was nothing to help.

I was still searching blind.

I went back to the desk, with no luck. But my frenzied exploration did unearth something else. Most of the photos I found in the office were of the burly, red-headed man. My uncle always stood tall with a strapping chest, a hearty smile on his face, or sometimes a stern frown. He was always the center of any group. That was my uncle, the boss. But in one photo... A bent one, shoved deep in the desk drawer, loose, not held by any frame, caught my eye.

It was Child with a look-alike woman when they were young.

She was slender and lithe, the opposite of the man's burly strength, but there was cunning in her eyes. Her gaze was sharp.

I put my finger to her. She kind of looked like me. In a distant, one-off way.

Could this be my mom?

I'd never thought much about the woman who'd birthed me. If I was her discard, she was also mine. The woman was a fool if she didn't see value in her own child, because I was top notch. I had never had reason to care for or search her out, but now I wondered... was my mom still alive? Would she care who I was? Regret what she'd given up?

I pocketed the photo in my dress, alongside my mask.

Focus, Seph. Ask those questions another time.

There'd probably be worlds of information about my whole extended family relations in the house once I'd acquired the keys from Lady Mauve. Just find the Blood Stone.

I searched for an hour. Maybe two.

I stayed hunting far after the Amethyst Sundown Ball must have wrapped up and the witches went home. I worked by the twinkling light of the great chandelier.

But no rock appeared in my search.

This couldn't be it.

When I'd been through every cranny and nook and inch for the seventh time, I judged the room. It was odd. From the inside hall and the outside ledge, Child's office appeared much larger than this. The space between doors was too long. His workspace should have been almost double the size... something wasn't right.

I felt under the desk, my fingers tracing the edges. I stared again at the wall of knickknacks and books and decided to methodically pull each one off the shelf. I accomplished two rows before one book wouldn't come off. The text only shifted. I couldn't remove it. I tilted it down.

Ker-plunk.

Behind me, a shelf section unlatched.

I definitely heard it.

I spun around and touched every inch of the wall-papered shelves until I found one with give. When I pressed it, the whole bookcase swung, revealing a second room.

Yes!

My uncle's *real* office was here. A secret room. An alcove locked behind a hidden passage door. The second workspace was way more used. With none of the gloss or showiness of the first space I'd just explored. This cubby was like a pig sty. Books strewn everywhere, paperwork in precarious heaps. Artifacts scattered haphazardly about. And photos and post-its with scribbles on every surface. It looked like my uncle had been studying twenty different subjects at once. Maybe he was. His work was still laid out like he'd return any moment. And there were stones. *So many rocks.*

Black stones, pink jewels, purple geodes. Shiny irregular pebbles. Plain gray fragments too. Most had at least a little color running through them. Lots of red. I had no choice but to just grab 'em all and sort it out later with Lark. I ran back into the larger office space and snatched one of the throw pillows from the couch. I stripped the cushion out of its case and shoved all the stones I could manage inside the jewel-toned fabric bag. I pushed within an inch of tearing the seams, but there were still plenty more rocks in the workroom.

I went over to the window. Lark had settled himself by the woods, arms crossed, one knee bent, his favorite style of perch, this time against a tree. When I emerged as a shadow in the picturesque window, he immediately unfurled. He moved forward. I looked around, but there was nobody else on the grounds and no delicate way to deliver him the stones. At least the moonlight kept my visibility low. I hoisted the pillow through the window then flung it down the six floors to the garden so he could retrieve it.

It thumped to the ground.

Lark hurried forward. He knelt to look inside the bag at the rocks. Then stared up to where I was waiting. The vampire shook his head, no. Lark gestured with his two fingers. An inch, maybe smaller. The rock was a small stone.

I held up a hand and tapped my empty ring finger.

Was the Blood Stone a jewel in a ring? I'd seen no jewelry in either room.

Lark made a sign, a shrug. He didn't know. He made the inch size again. He put it up to his eye. The size of a pupil.

Crap.

I packed up all the other red rocks, just to be safe, now almost certain they weren't important at all, but it was better to be thorough than sorry. I flung the second pillowcase of stones down to the vampire. He dutifully knelt and looked inside just in case they were relevant to our mission. But again he shook, no.

I felt dejected. I'd been over every inch of this place. Multiple times. There was no pupil-sized stone. If it wasn't in one of those bags, I didn't know how to locate what I was searching for.

Lark put his two palms together and laid his cheek against them like they were a bed. He closed his eyes and rested his head. The universal sign for sleep. He was suggesting I dream.

Because I was a dreamcast witch!

The visions were the only reason I had come this far. I'd visualized details that had led me directly to this path. I'd followed them like crumbs. I could do that again.

I looked back towards the couch.

The office was still locked from the outside world. *I could sleep.*

I looked back towards him and nodded. But as I did, something deeper in the forest caught my gaze. It looked like eyes.

Gleaming eyes.

Four sets.

Looking out from the tree line.

Was I seeing things?

As quickly as they'd been there, the glittering eyes disappeared.

It was impossible to actually discern such things from up here in my roost, but Lark sensed the direction of my apprehension and followed it. Even from six floors away. He turned to check out the forest, paused a moment, then ventured in. His coat and boots were the last thing I saw as he slipped into the trees.

Was it possible some enemy vampires had arrived? I wanted Lark to be careful. After all, I'd be safe, locked inside. If Lark couldn't get in the building, neither could any other vampires... I could sleep. I could cast. But he was in the dangerous woods, alone, late at night.

He'll be alright, I assured myself. *After all, he's my bodyguard.*

A dream would show me right where to look. And Lark would be fine.

I turned off the overhead light, lay down on the couch, closed my eyes, and let my imagination run wild.

19
LARK

hat did you see, Orphan Girl?

From her window ledge viewpoint Persephone's face flashed with fear, more from instinct than insight, but I'd been undead for far too long to ignore someone's gut. Especially a woman like hers. The dreamcast could sense danger, even when she didn't understand what it was. It beckoned her, it called to her, it claimed her, it was those heightened powers that drew her to me, and why I had to repel her so much.

At least, I did so when I wasn't being a weak prick. I rolled my eyes at myself. What the hell was I doing dancing the girl around at the ball? Witches rarely turned my head, all cowering and sniveling human-like bores, but this one... Child's niece was something else. Something more.

Careful, Lark. Think with your upstairs head.

I moved into the dark forest, blind, senses on high alert willing to check it out. I moved like a ghost in the thicket from years of hunting, my footsteps barely touching the mossy ground. I sniffed the air, felt the breeze, listened hard.

Nothing.

The moonlight sparkled around.

But they'd be coming, I knew.

We might have gotten the jump. After all, there were too many witches around at the party tonight for the Brotherhood's liking... they'd hold out. Of course, that was hours ago. And Dreven might slaughter a whole coven just for his own pleasure if provoked.

For the stone?

He'd murder everyone in sight.

Could Persephone get in and get out unscathed? I hoped so.

I paused, sheltered by a thick pine.

Her gut wasn't off. Something *was* wrong. My blood pumped wild. My breath grew shallow. It was too still. Too silent. There should have been rustlings and wiggles in the night. Squirrels and bunnies doing what animals do. But the scavengers were gone. Disappeared. Out of sight. Someone was here.

Waiting.

In the dark.

And since the wildlife weren't willing to risk their necks, that someone was scary as hell.

I bent low to the ground, looking for a sign.A flicker, a sound.

None came.

Was it possible I was reading too much into these signs?

I glanced back at the school. Had the witch understood my hand signal to sleep? Was Persephone dreaming now?

I visualized the Orphan Girl laying down on a bed, her body curved, her red hair splayed, her eyes closed, her face soft. The witch looked so beautiful as an outline in Child's tower window, out of reach. Her curls swirled around her shoulders like a goddess in a tornado. She'd also looked like that on the Sundown dance floor.

A goddamn force of nature. My fangs grew sharper in my mouth.

So far, I'd found Persephone infuriating but strong, hearty and quick, not at all as dainty as she looked in that dress. Which, by the way, was a perfect fit. When I'd bought it, I worried it might be too much, it could swallow an unconfident girl, but she filled it out and pulled it off and looked... wow.

It draped her bodice in jewels.

Her perky breasts balanced by the exquisite curve of bare back. And while there were too many skirts to get too close, I'd have loved to explore underneath that crinoline later tonight...

Not happening, Lark.

I stretched my jaw, tilting my head. Left and right.

I'd find some other form of release after the job.

The pillowcases she'd tossed down to me were nothing but sedimentary rocks. Child was studying geology or who knows what when he was killed, but they were nothing like the Blood Stone, which was packed with unrelenting power and looked like a scarlet-black jewel.

Crack, crack.

There it was, what I'd been waiting for.

A branch broke to my right.

I spun to my feet ready to get the jump, but the vampire who'd made the mistake was already hulking far too close.

A huge man.

A gym rat with more muscles than brains.

He wolfishly grinned, leering down as if I was a small child.

"What have we here?" He licked his fanged teeth. Showing them off. The man was a fresh turn, not yet in control of his dark urges. The baby vamp had probably been undead for less than a week's time. He still had that crazed look, where the hunger for blood pulsed over everything, threatening to drive the beast mad.

I remembered that time.

That terrible state.

When you weren't in control of anything and you feared that you may never be again.

"I'm not your enemy." I said, slowly raising to my feet. No quick movements yet. He had three inches on me, even if I was over six feet. His neck was as thick as my waist. The Brotherhood of Thorns was picking larger and larger witches to turn. On purpose. That's what Dreven ordered. When the selfish vampire refused to join the Crimson Flood or become one of the clan, everyone assumed he'd build his own army. He'd clearly put thought into making his officers stronger and larger than our soldiers.

Bigger, but dumber.

There was already blood on the vamp's shirt, he'd consumed a fresh dinner. That's why the forest felt quiet. Some bunny was dead. Or drained and limping home to its poor warren. It did not sate the man. The blood was still in his fangs and his urges made this undead rampant for more.

"I don't want to hurt you," I told him carefully.

"You won't." The man sneered. We catalogued each other for only a moment longer, then he lunged. I swerved, snapped a tree branch, and stabbed it deep into his back.

The vampire howled in pain.

I missed.

Before the hulk could turn or raise, I retracted and plunged again, this time finding my mark, embedded deep in his mammoth heart. Dispatching him in the second it hit.

"The bigger they are, the harder they fall," I muttered, disappointed in myself.

A second strike? I was losing my touch. I yanked my impromptu knife from his wound.

The vampire crumpled to the earth.

I turned him over to check the second death was complete. It was.

The man had been discharged again. Returned to his original maker.

"Rest in peace."

I glanced back at the school. Something felt off.

That wasn't a foe. At best, it was a joke.

A decoy.

Fuck.

I leapt up to my feet, raced through the trees, headed back to the academy.

I was a fool.

Hunting rabbits in the woods, while the real foxes broke into the pen.

As I broke the clearing, I saw the back door in the garden was open. Three vampires entered the school, Gattas plus two others, flanked by Fellow Gold and a Lady as well, her white skirt swished. She was clearly compelled and leaning heavily on the men who escorted her around.

Damn it.

I flew over the field in an all out sprint, revealing my position. The blood of the dead vamp still wet on my hands.

Gattas turned slightly and gave me a wink.

They went in. The door swung.

I closed the gap.

My feet landed hard on the pavement and stones. I did not slow. But I was too far behind. The door shut in my face. An impenetrable seal. I slammed into the magic keeping me out. The supernatural forcefield. Gold and the compelled woman let them in. They would take the trio straight to Child's office. I slammed my fists on the forcefield again. Pain surged in both arms. Out in the cold.

The Orphan Girl was upstairs on her own.

I raced back to my watching place and stared up at the sixth floor. A light was back on in the office, but she wasn't there in the window. I lunged for a pillowcase on the ground and dug out a small stone. I hurled the pebble up at the school, through the upper floor window. I had to warn her. It bounced through the opening. Nothing happened.

Come on.

Damn it, witch! I silently begged her.

Orphan Girl, come to the window.

Or die in that office alone.

20

PERSEPHONE

In my dream, *I stared directly into the sun, I shaded my eyes, blinded by the all-encompassing magnificent light.* It woke me up.

I shook my head.

So much for casting the future. That was short. And useless.

It was dark inside the room but every time I blinked, it was like the dream sun still burned, shining bright. It took the shape of the chandelier in the room. I flipped on the switch. Had I been on my uncle's couch for mere minutes or hours? My eyes went to the black liquid outside, still pure night. A quick scan of the forest said Lark hadn't returned. The grounds were stained with moonlight. Everything seemed still. I felt a pit in my gut.

Had the vampire encountered trouble in the forest?

Or perhaps he just got tired of waiting under the window for a small glimpse of me? He was the one who'd suggested I try taking a nap. But all I dreamt of was the dumb sun. Like this overhead light, shining so brightly, it hurt my eyes. Whoever thought an office required such an extravagant chandelier? It was a pompous design. My uncle had hung it and chosen it. That's who...

I rolled my eyes at the plethora of bulbs. The crystals that danced and swayed. The sparkles refracted throughout the room in a hundred different ways. Why had he put such a monstrosity here? Such a dramatic piece made sense in the academy atrium to demonstrate the witch school's reach and worth to newcomers and arrivals. But here? It was oversized and obtrusively large. You couldn't look at it without squinting or shading your sight... *just like in my vision*, I thought.

I stared up at the chandelier's arms.

Maybe the thing in my mind wasn't the sun, maybe it was *this*. I grabbed a chair and dragged it underneath the bejeweled swags. Most were simple sparkly glass, but I looked closer now. Was one of these the Blood Stone? I maneuvered around the light, looking for signs. In the center of the design was a gold-etched pair of wings. They surrounded a single black jewel. I stretched to try to touch the piece. And it had a little coloring of red. Just a shade. I reached up to unscrew it but the jewel was out of my wing span. I clamored onto the desk chair, one foot on the back rest, and extended my reach. It raised me up. The makeshift ladder was precarious, listing slightly, but I leaned out anyhow. I reached into the chandelier to grab the central jewel. The two carved wings were beautiful. I slid the black ball to the left, twisting it out. It started to roll.

Was this the Blood Stone?

Thwack-thack.

Something ricocheted into the room and landed on the rug.

What was that?

A pebble. A small rock had bounced through the open window into the room. I tried to analyze it too, just as the chair under my feet gave way.

Instinctively, I grabbed onto the chandelier as my footing rolled and fell. The fixture groaned. Hundreds of chains tinkled and twisted above me, wrenched by the drastic, sudden weight of my grasp. I made one last twist on the black jewel, releasing the stone from its winged home. The bauble fell. It bounced off the desk chair, hit my shin, smacked the drawer, and disappeared into Child's off-white colored rug.

Above me, the chandelier wiring lurched.

I dropped from the fixture, landing half on the desk, half on the ground. The chandelier rocketed back in place. Rattling around. Dangling chains broke off and crystals rained. I covered my head until the clattering calmed. Scattered pieces landed all around me, but I only cared about one black little ball.

About the size of a pupil.

I crawled to the back wall and reached under the unit. Jack pot. I pinched the black ball and pulled it near, but upon closer inspection my expectations fell. I was fairly certain it wasn't a magical something. Just a bauble, nothing more. I closed my eyes. It was a dead end. No Blood Stone. My vision was as useless as I felt.

Thwack-thack.

Another small stone hit the floor. This one bounced and came to a stop on one of the guest chairs. A second stone through the window. Was it Lark? I ran to the window ledge.

"*Seph*," the vampire hissed my name, reeling back, ready to throw another pebble. "*Seph!*" I stuck my face out into the night.

"Lark?"

My vampire was scaling the wall. Hanging off the side of the second floor like a freakin' spider man. He looked relieved.

"You have to go, right now."

"I didn't get the stone."

"Damn it, I'm not playing. *Leave now.*"

"But what about—"

"*Persephone!*" His voice chilled my bones. But worse, I heard a scraping sound in the door.

I ignored Lark and spun around. The noise came from the hall.

This is what the vampire was trying to warn me about.

There was a key in the lock.

Someone was coming inside.

21

PERSEPHONE

The sounds of entry grew louder. I heard the scrape of the caution tape being ripped down. The key finished connecting in the latch. I lunged into the secret room. I yanked the bookshelf door closed, heart pounding in my chest, then froze. There was a small crack to look out. The lights in the office were still on. The window was wide. The place was a mess.

"Well, here we are," Fellow Gold intoned as the office door swung.

I stared out through the crack.

The man from the stage was acting as tour guide for two others, a woman and man. What was he doing? This place was supposed to be out of bounds. Another coven woman followed him in, dressed in a white skirt and blouse. She was draped over a final guy's shoulder, gaping around.

"Do you boys need anything else?" She asked. The clingy woman was in her early fifties and had started the evening with perfectly coiffed shoulder-length hair in hot roller waves that she'd styled with pride. Now, one of her shirt tails was untucked and that beautiful hairstyle was mussed. She sounded a little drunk. Totally compelled.

"We'll tell ya,' love," her compatriot noted, pushing her off. She merely received a look of disdain from the man in charge.

"Did your people ransack the place?" He asked Gold.

"No, no, not at all. I'm not sure what's gone on." Gold frowned. He seemed disappointed the others weren't more grateful for the entry and also frowned at his peer. "Perhaps that's just Child's way. Creative genius and all that. He was a difficult man."

"Silence," the first man shut him down, clearly the leader of this pack. Fellow Gold seemed to swallow his tongue. With all five people coming inside the office space the room was crammed. Two coven elders and three... I sucked back my breath... three vampires.

Oh crap.

One woman, two men.

The telltale raven claw crinkles were there.

But there were other signs of vampirism I was starting to recognize. They all seemed distinctly beautiful. Ancient and stoic, although their physicality projected beauty and youth. They felt dangerous. Their answers were brisk. In control. Their cruelty came off in waves. They had pure disdain for the witches they were working with... the people whom they'd no doubt had to trick to invite them into the school. Although Gold wasn't near as forgone as the woman. He still toddled around.

I clenched myself further back inside the secret room.

"Where is it?" The female vamp hissed.

"I don't know," the Lady giggled. "I've never known. Child didn't tell me a thing, he thought I was no good."

"Keep her quiet," the first vampire snapped.

"With pleasure." The third vampire smiled, fangs popping out of his mouth. He swooped at her. I gasped, but he just moved the witch to the couch and cooed to her like she was a drunk sorority pledge.

"You're still gonna make me immortal," Fellow Gold stuttered, rubbing his own hands, watching the fuss.

"Yes, old man. The deal was struck, just hand over the stone."

"Gattas, I think she's been here," the woman vamp interrupted. She was rifling through items. She picked up a knickknack on the rug and took a deep inhale. "I can smell her on everything."

"She'll be more trouble than we thought." The named man agreed. The vampire, Gattas, was strapping and tall. His hair was ice blonde. Short. His eyes took in the details of the room. He had large lips that he used to scowl. "Was she here?" He sniffed deeply too. I shuddered when the scent turned his head. He didn't know a secret room was here, but he looked in the exact right way. He could smell me too.

"Of course not," Gold dismissed the idea.

"No one has been allowed in," the woman in white agreed. "I have the only key." She held it up.

"And does everyone always do what you say?" Gattas growled.

The third vampire snatched the key from her fingers. He licked her hand.

"Oh, yes," she agreed with both of them.

"How interesting..." The third man told her. "*Yum.*" The compelled woman giggled.

"Stop playing with your food," the woman vamp snapped.

The third vampire pulled back the Lady's hair, revealing her neck. His eyes flashed and his teeth grew. They sunk deep into the helpless woman's skin. At first, the Lady's eyes grew wide. She flailed but almost immediately, she fell limp, enjoying the vampire suck. He took deep gulps, smacking his lips.

"Gross," the woman vamp frowned.

"Jealous, Eve? I'll share her with you." Blood dripped. He taunted his peer, slowly sopping up the gore with languid licks.

"I can't work with him." The woman glared at their boss.

"Don't go too far," Gattas warned his underling, gesturing to Gold, who sniveled in the midst of the room. Scared out of his mind. "This one's a fool."

"Is she, did you just–" Gold whimpered. "*Oh no, oh no.*"

We all knew that he had.

When the vampire licked the woman's first teeth marks, they sealed, but he went back for more, biting again, until her neck spouted with blood.

"The gold man doesn't know squat." Eve frowned at the Fellow in shock.

"We need him," Gattas shrugged. "Know your role." The woman vamp pouted.

"I'm using all the tools at our disposal. Don't be so uptight." The third vamp, still bloody, piled on.

Much as I wanted to block the sight, I couldn't take my eyes from the lady on the couch. The vampire bite wasn't two innocent pinpricks like I'd seen in the movies. This monster had torn her skin apart. Blood spurted out. The vampire's whole mouth dripped with blood and the woman's life force rolled down her neck, pooling on the edges of her crisp, white shirt, dripping down on her skirts.

"Close her up." Gattas ordered. "I don't want a mess."

Too late.

The vampire frowned but changed his style of attack. The woman groaned, this time pleased with how his nibbling felt. The vamps had compelled her so deeply, she might actually enjoy her death. But that wasn't how I wanted to go out.

My eyes travelled to the window.

Where was Lark?

Was he out there? Climbing to come save me?

"Where's the stone?" Gattas roared at Gold.

"I–I–don't–Lady White *show them. Tell them.*"

"My love?" The third vampire cooed at the witch. "Answer your boss."

Lady White tried to affix her gaze, coming back around.

"Have you tried the secret room?" She asked. I swallowed hard.

Crap.

"Where?" Gattas growled.

The woman weakly pointed her fingers at the bookcase. "Behind there. Child had the place redesigned a few decades ago. That's when he put in this grotesque chandelier."

They all looked up, then towards the wall.

No, no, no.

"See? We serve a purpose." Gold had the nerve to look proud.

The vampire named Eve shot him a death look. Gattas nodded a silent order to her and the other vamp. With blood still on his lips, the undead beast dropped Lady White and marched to the bookshelf to look.

They came straight at me.

Caught in the secret room.

There was no way to get out... except through.

The moment they opened the secret door, I would be found.

"How do we get in?" Gattas barked at the witches. Gold knelt to help Lady White.

"Answer him, girl."

"Oh, my head. I feel dizzy. There's a shelf, a book," she murmured.

No.

She would lead them right to it. I had to get out now. But how?

The exit to the hallway of the school was blocked by three vampires. They'd be on me before I crossed the threshold. That route was impossible now. But the path to the open window was free. And when the secret door opened, the hinge would swing the door out towards them, putting the vampires behind the shelf, not in front.

It wasn't much, but that's what I had.

I could lunge for the window and go.

That was my best and only route of escape.

Plus, Lark was out there. Coming to save me.

I hoped.

I prayed.

He must be on the fourth or fifth floor by now… if he really was a spider man.

They worked systematically. Pulling each book. Any moment they'd find the secret latch. I steadied my feet. Ready to go.

The vampire henchman continued until in the second row, one book clicked. Something unlatched. They looked up and at each other, pleased. I swallowed.

Time was now up.

This was it.

The vampire pulled the book down, opening the shelf.

The door swung out.

The second it did, I ran for my life.

22

PERSEPHONE

As the secret entrance opened, I shoved the door, hard. It smacked the first vampire in the face. Making him roar.

"It's her!" The woman vampire yelled.

"No one should be in here," Fellow Gold frowned.

I ran as fast as my legs would take me towards the window ledge. I dove past the desk chair and didn't bother with a step stool to get me outside.

"Lark!" I screamed as I shot my body through the opening and scrambled out.

"I'm here!" He shouted, still two floors below. The moment he saw me, he started climbing twice as fast. No longer careful as he ascended the balcony heights. "Move left!"

"Get her!" Gattas ordered.

In her compulsive state, Lady White obeyed his command.

"Come back here, child!" The coven professor grabbed at my heels. As I tore out of the school, her hand caught my ankle. I blindly kicked.

"Your other left!" Lark yelled, seeing the direction I was headed. I tried to turn. Fabric from my dress ripped on the bricks.

"Go too," Gattas ordered his soldiers. His two vampires looked out to watch. They moved onto the ledge.

"Lark, help!" I kicked the woman again. But she was stronger than I gave her credit for. I should have turned immediately for Fellow Nightshade's office, but instead, I'd gone up, facing the garden, towards a brick dormer. My only hope was to climb. A gargoyle sat on top of the window. An ancient decoration. I scrambled for that totem.

Below me, Lark found new handholds and scaled up faster.

I scurried around the window mount, clawing my hands.

The roof was so high. The wind blew me hard. It had turned into a stormy, terrible night. The weather felt dangerous at this height, but I didn't care.

"Where do you think you're going?" The Lady cackled. Fellow Gold came to the window to stare.

"Oh dear," he muttered, ringing his hands.

Gattas nodded for Eve to go up, while he sent the male vamp straight at Lark. They poured out of the window to meet their foes.

"Gattas!" Lark bellowed at the leader of the strike. But he'd have to deal with his bloody underling first. The High Council woman caught my foot.

"You don't have permission to be here." Lady White didn't care one bit about the blood streaming from her the wounds on her neck, or the wind, or the height.

"You're being controlled," I kicked and kicked, clasping onto the gargoyle. It groaned. I glanced up. Would the stone creature hold? The woman's blood dripped all over the shingle tiles and dolloped like rain far below.

"Pull her off the roof," the vamp woman commanded. She was

only steps behind where the professor and I faced off. A sick smile on her lips. Lady White pulled on me with all her weight.

"Lark!" I screamed again, but his hands were now full. He punched the other vamp, who'd thrown him down on a balcony.

I stomped my feet at her. But the witch grabbed my skirts. Like a lunatic, she didn't care about her own perch. She barely stayed on the stone ledge at all, forcing all of her weight onto my dress.

"Stop!" I screamed. She just grinned from my skirts.

"Drag her down," the woman vamp egged her on. "Use everything that you have."

The witch blindly obeyed, stepping off of the ledge, forgoing all safety for herself. She dangled off the building, hanging over a six-story drop. My gown stretched in the dark, inky air.

Argh.

It felt like it might rip in two with her mass.

"You're coming with me," Lady White told me cheerfully, her face a distorted mess. Her free will was completely lost to the vamps.

"No, I'm not." I dropped one hand to tug at my own skirts. Hard as I could. But I wasn't trying to shake the woman's hands off anymore. She had twisted herself with my crinoline, her fingers like talons in my petticoats. Instead, I ripped the seam.

One thread popped.

Then the next.

And suddenly a whole swath of fabric tore away. The dress jerked, the skirts came loose. They dropped away from my limbs, down like a broken parachute. The woman went too, pink ribbons and blue bows still in her hands.

"*Noooo!*" The Lady howled as she fell.

She soared past Lark and the other vampire on the fifth floor. Down to the gardens below. The witch splattered on the ground with a terrible thud. A red puddle blossomed under her broken back.

"*Oh my god,*" I scrambled on top of the dormer. I'd never seen a dead body so up close. Even six floors away. The river of blood continued to grow under her limbs.

"Oops, *bye.*" Eve laughed, a vicious smile on her lips, enjoying the terrible result.

Lark was pinned on the ledge. The vampire leered over him, ready to bite his neck.

"No!" I broke off the gargoyle statue and it hurled down towards them. "Lark!" I shouted. Eve dodged out of the way, but her buddy caught the statue straight in the back. It gave Lark the edge he needed to break the hold. "*Yes!*" I cheered. My vampire lurched to his feet, back on the attack.

"Seph, don't stop!" Lark demanded as he punched the other vampire in the face.

"Come here, girl," Eve was moving fast.

"No." I swatted away the tears on my face. Eve climbed quicker and more certain than the council witch ever had. I scrambled onto the next ledge, but she was on me. She shot a hand around my throat, picking me up.

"What do we have here?"

"No! Let me go."

Lark managed to subdue the vampire down below. He was climbing up to reach me. He seemed to fly up the building now. But it was too late. I struggled and choked, dangling in the air.

"Where's the stone? *Tell me.*" Eve snarled in my face. Her eyes were focused, not wild. She was staring into my soul, trying to force my will, but the compulsion didn't hold. I had my Electrum necklace on. "*Where*?!"

"I... don't... know," I struggled to say.

"You will give it to me." She ordered, shaking me like a doll.

"I don't have it. Please." I admitted. I half-cried. I half-begged.

"Give it to me!"

"She's wearing Electrum," Gattas said from Child's window ledge. "You can't compel her, Eve."

"What's in your pocket?" Eve demanded. Reaching for the only part of the skirts that hadn't been ripped away.

"A photo of my mother, a black bauble." I wasn't under compulsion, but I was still being so honest. I wept. Tears streamed down my face. I didn't have the stone that they wanted so badly. There was nothing in my possession to give.

"Leave her!" Lark ordered. He closed the gap.

"You want her?" Eve whirled, thrusting me higher in her hand.

"Let her go!" He demanded.

Almost to us.

I stifled a breath, doing everything I could for the woman vampire not to crush me mid-air.

"As you wish. Bye little witch!" The monster hurled me away from her hands. She flung me down. Launched me towards the earth. My remaining skirts and my hair spread wild as I fell. My clothes filled up with air.

"*No!*" I screamed.

Things moved in slow motion.

I watched Lark take aim.

His wingspan extended.

His hands reached for mine.

His fingers came towards me. I stretched my hand towards him too. Reeling into his grasp.

Our faces twisted in concentration. His eyes on me.

With every ounce of effort.

My vampire closed the gap.

"*Lark–*"

His name on my lips.

His fingertips in my hands.

He was going to catch me. Snatch me out of free fall. Save me.

"*I've got you.*" He told me.

I let out a scared yelp.

Our fingers combined.

I felt his warm callouses scratch against mine.

His grip closed. Sealing it fast.

My body snapped. He stole me out of the sky.

For a second, it held.

But then gravity kept dragging me down.

Lark lost the hold.

My bodyguard was there. Then he wasn't.

The vampire couldn't contain me.

The weight, the angle, the momentum was too much for one man.

Our fingers snapped apart.

I wrenched outside of his grasp.

"*No!*" We both screamed.

Lark's voice stirred something deep in my soul.

Fear.

A sadness at a life yet unlived.

A heart unloved.

A moment snuffed out.

It was all happening far too fast.

But there was nothing more he could do.

My vampire bodyguard failed.

And I fell.

23
PERSEPHONE

Someone screamed.

Thwa-thwa-thwa-thwa.

A swirl of creatures roared up from the ground. Spindly legs. Antennae. Tiny backs. The beasts came at me from every direction,, beating gossamer wings in my face.

The sky became full of small bodies and sound.

I screamed too.

Several bugs flew into my mouth.

I swatted at my own lips.

I choked and gagged on their legs.

My body became encased in the swarm.

Bees, butterflies, moths, dragonflies, mosquitos, June bugs. On and on the monstrosity of forms. They coalesced, catching me, slapping me with their wings, droning in my ears, buffering my fall. A living crash pad.

Even ants and worms piled up on the ground.

Everything layered between me and the earth.

Then just as quickly as they appeared, the insects dispersed.

I collapsed on the grass, gasping in shock.

The bugs saved my life.

Bug saved my life.

I huffed and puffed, looking around. The insect witch was beside me in a flash. Josie at his side.

"Are you alright?" He looked at me while she stared higher for Lark. The vampire was still scaling the building. Now coming down. I barely spoke, my body thudded with adrenaline. *Did that really happen?*

"Thank you." I managed.

"You're alright." He squawked, then he embraced me with an awkward hug and a pat.

"Get her out! *Go*! All of you, *now*!" Lark's angry yells shook me into action again. We dropped our arms. Above us, my vampire tackled an on-coming vamp, the one who'd bitten Lady White. Lark smashed him into the patio stones.

I'd defied gravity when I fell and lived, but the vampires weren't done.

"Come on," Josie said. Behind us, we heard the two male vampires thrash. None of us looked back. I prayed Lark could handle himself. Bug thrust his hands under my armpits and pulled me up. I discovered, miraculously, nothing had broken. I was only bruised and stunned.

"Go!" Lark roared again. Then he grunted in pain.

"Lark!" I cried out. But the others grabbed me. Turned me. They forced me to flee from the building, almost blind in the darkness, until I tripped over something on the grass.

Someone.

I landed in blood.

"*Oh my god.*"

Lady White's gruesome body on the lawn.

No insects had come to save her. Her body was twisted and bent, her mouth wedged open in final yelp. I stared at her terrified eyes, frozen and glossy. Lost in time.

Totally dead.

"It's not safe, come on," Josie warned. "We need to move, Seph."

I picked myself up and we ran on.

The three of us hit the tree line and didn't stop. We ran all the way through the High Council parcel of forest and out to the road. The rural highway was barren. A dead strip of pavement, in the middle of the night. But the road was a sign of normal human life. A reminder of civilization. Everyone stopped to catch their breath.

We were out.

We escaped.

"What now?" Bug wondered out loud. Josie looked in my direction. I shrugged. We'd fled the grounds without any sense or purpose.

"I have a car in the school parking lot," she admitted. Perhaps we should have ran there.

"Our bikes," Bug also frowned.

"We're not going back. Not tonight. Not ever." I voiced what we were all thinking.

"Then we walk. Towards town," Josie pointed.

A long, lonely road.

Bug and I nodded. What choice did we have?

We'd follow the highway back to Plumpkin. It would take all night to walk. But then we'd be home. Safe. The alternative...

We fell into step, three single file, Josie in front, then Bug, with me at the rear. Picking our way down the road. Wordlessly, we'd all decided to stay away from the tarmac and instead travelled on the mountain bike path that Bug and I rode earlier.. It had some tree cover. It felt safer with a nearby natural shield.

"You shouldn't travel with me," I warned them. "I'm dangerous."

"We don't have much choice, there's only one route." Josie frowned.

"We could go our separate ways." I offered to turn back, although that would require me to walk past the academy acreage.

"Don't be dumb," Josie said. It was the nicest thing she'd offered me yet. "Come on." We walked in silence, afraid of every tree branch crack we heard in the woods. Our bodies still on high alert.

"What were you still doing there? At the school?" I finally asked. "The party ended hours ago." Our steady footfalls kicked at small rocks.

"I was waiting for you at the bikes. I deduced you were still at the school because you didn't take sissy's bike home. I didn't want to leave you behind," Bug shrugged.

"He was scared for you," Josie added from the front.

"Trouble has been following you around."

"It still is," Josie and I both groaned at once. This actually earned me a small smile from the girl.

"When we saw your vampire boyfriend lurking near the forest, I said we should go, but Bug wouldn't budge," Josie said.

"You don't know the town," Bug shrugged. "I didn't want you to get lost."

"That's... wow. Thanks, Bug. That's incredibly sweet."

He grinned. "Plus, Una would never forgive me if I lost her bike."

"Your bugs saved my life."

"I didn't even know they could do that." Bug agreed. "I just sort of pointed and yelled. I asked them for help and they helped."

"It was more like a screech, a demand," Josie smirked.

"My voice is still raw." Bug agreed.

"Really?" A low voice drawled just up ahead. "Too bad. I was gonna ask you to do it again."

We all froze.

The vampire boss stepped out of the trees. Gattas darkly smiled. He looked relaxed. And cruel.

Where was Lark?

"Get behind me, now," I instinctively protected Bug and Josie, sliding them behind my back. It was my fault this monster followed us out in the dark. I'd protect them the best that I could.

"Do what again?" The insect witch asked Gattas, scared out of his mind.

Josie and I exchanged a small glance.

The vampire's intense stare bore into Bug.

Surging deep in his brain.

"I would like you to scream," the terrible vampire ordered.

"No," I tried to stop him.

But it was too late.

24

PERSEPHONE

Bug screamed and screamed.

Terror ripped apart his vocal chords.

"Stop it, stop!" I implored both him and the vamp. I shook Bug, but nothing released the compulsion spell. "*Stop.*" I ordered to no avail. The dark vampire laughed.

"He can't help himself."

"Here." I grabbed Bug's hand and shoved it against the necklace still hung around my neck. The moment he touched the pink-gold Electrum, Bug relaxed. He came right back to himself. Huffing and puffing, catching his breath.

"Thanks, Seph." He croaked.

"Oh my god, you're welcome. You're alright."

"Electrum necklace, huh." Gattas' delight turned to a frown. "Is that why you didn't give Eve the Blood Stone?"

"No," I stepped away from my friends, actually moving slightly towards the vampire. "I didn't find it. I swear." My voice sounded defensive and small.

Gattas tilted his head and regarded me head to toe. I was a total mess in a half-ripped gown and no shoes. I began inching back. Behind me, Bug and Josie shifted too. We slipped towards the road in small increments, backing out of the vampire's range.

"It's not that I don't trust you," the dark monster sneered. "But I think I'll check your pockets once we're done." He grinned.

"Done?" I wanted to stall.

The idea that Gattas would be *done* with any of us soon chilled my bones.

His fangs glinted as he bared his teeth. Toying with our nervousness. His face growing twisted and gross.

"Who will be first?"

"Me. Leave the others alone."

"You're tough, but stupid." He laughed in my face. "Silver's my favorite color," Gattas leered at Josie's dress. "How 'bout a taste?"

"No," I shot back.

He growled, his fangs growing in anger between his lips. "I wasn't talking to you!"

"Run!" I said. "Go." I begged the others. I prayed he couldn't kill all of us at once.

"You wanna taste of a chemist?" Josie pulled a white baggie of powder from her clutch purse and hurled it at the terrible man. "Eat this." It exploded on Gattas in a cloud of white dust. The sludge immediately hardened into glue. "Go!"

We grabbed hands with Bug and raced towards the road, just as a car sped over the hill headed right at us. A sports car flying so fast it would flatten all three of us in seconds.

The car was coming too fast.

The driver swerved.

Gattas struggled to pull himself free of the glue in the trees.

Bug froze. He screamed.

I hauled him to me.

The red car barreled down.

Its headlights filled up our whole world.

The last thing we will see, I surmised.

But at the final moment it swerved and jerked onto the dirt shoulder, tearing up the rocks and the path. The driver's side door flew open and Lark jumped out as the vehicle careened straight for Gattas in the trees.

The sticky vampire leapt.

Just in time.

The engine exploded as the car collided with an ancient trunk.

Fiberglass crunched.

A terrible sound.

The sports car was destroyed.

Glass exploded everywhere on the grass.

The impact rattled our ears.

Josie, Bug and I huddled together on the centerline of the rural highway road. Totally unsure. Lark hit the asphalt and rolled across the ground. Gattas managed to land in a heap on the torn up grass. For a moment, the car fire raged and everything else went still.

My heart *beat, beat, beat.*

But then my vampire bodyguard rose up.

His wool coat was torn to shreds.

His dress slacks and pressed shirt were tattered and spent.

The sleeves were ripped. Some fabric half-dangled down his arms, and the earlier battle at the school had exposed most of his chest. Lark's body was bruised. He had cuts and he bled. But he'd still come to help.

To save me and my friends.

The car's engine groaned and collapsed, leaving the night in an eerie quiet after the wild and dangerous crash.

Bug whimpered. Josie and I just stared at the terrible men.

Heaving chests.

Faces of death.

Gattas rose next.

"Get further up the road," Lark ordered to me over his shoulder. He didn't dare turn from the vampire he faced. "Towards the sun."

The color of pink morning was already rising.

Sunlight getting its first glimpse.

We scurried backwards, like Lark's command.

The monsters faced off.

"You're out of time," my vampire said.

"Think you've won this night, Lark? No more Eve? No more Kyle?" Gattas tut-tutted. "We've got Gold."

"Go home, Gattas. Don't come back." Lark said. The order was cold. "Tell Dreven there's no stone. There never was."

"That's a lie." The vampire snapped. "There's no stone *yet*. But we know where to look. Your girlfriend will find it. Then find us next." He darkly smiled. He hissed one last time, then disappeared into the dark forest behind him.

"Not if I can help it," Lark muttered to himself.

He stayed coiled like a cat for an eternity longer, but then morning fully broke. When the first rays of sunlight hit the trees, Lark finally relaxed.

"It's alright," he said to us. The three of us stared at the disheveled man. "He can't attack." Lark signaled to the daylight. As if *that* made it okay.

"You totaled your car," Bug said.

"Vampires can only come out at night?" I checked, currently staring at a vampire in the daylight.

"Most." Josie and Lark answered in tandem.

"It's complicated," she added.

"Thank you for saving us," I said.

"I didn't think I would get here in time," he admitted. He pulled a knife out of a wound in his leg with a scrunched face. I hadn't even noticed it was there. An actual knife, stabbed into his thigh. His slacks blossomed bright red, but he just wiped off his own blood and slid the blade into the beltline of his pants. Josie,

Bug and I stared. "It was smart you had spells," he complimented the chemist witch.

Josie nodded. "Always be prepared."

"Isn't that the Boy Scouts' motto?" Bug wondered.

"It worked, didn't it?" Josie frowned at him.

"Absolutely, yes." He agreed.

"Do you have a car I can borrow? Mine's a little out of sorts," Lark said.

We stared at the remains of the sports car crash.

'Out of sorts' was an understatement. His car was totaled. Completely destroyed.

Only his license plate might be salvaged from that wreck.

Even then, it was half-burned.

"I have my truck at the academy," Josie offered.

"May I use it this morning?" He asked. "I need to clean up. I'll return it, unharmed, when the task is complete. Perhaps bring it back to the store?"

I stared at him. A request, not a compulsion. Josie considered her options.

We still had miles to walk down this road until we hit town. The school was fairly close. If the vampires were truly gone it might make more sense to go back...

"Alright."

With no more discussion, we reversed our direction and trudged back to the academy, this time not bothering to hide off the side of the highway at all. Instead we strode on the side of the road directly facing on-coming traffic as a foursome. We would have to dodge out of the way of any oncoming car, though none arrived. The sun at our backs made long morning shadows. Exhaustion and adrenaline leaked from our bones.

Everyone's but the vamp's.

Though he was the most beaten and broken of our foursome, Lark maintained perfect posture as he strode. His guard had not yet lowered. I kept peeking at his wounds. The caked blood on his chest and legs. His stern look. I'd given him nothing but grief since we'd met a few days ago. And yet tonight, he'd practically died trying to help me.

Trying and succeeding at saving my life.

He totaled his car. He'd been stabbed. I'd been a brat.

Any apology would not be enough.

I wanted to cover him with thanks and assurances but he barely looked up.

"Are you okay?" I finally managed to ask.

"Did you get it?" His eyes turned on me.

"It wasn't in one of the bags?"

Lark shook his head, no.

My throat bobbed. All this chaos and danger for zero result.

"Child must have been doing some geology project around the time that he died," Lark muttered. "Working with rocks." I nodded, disappointed as well. "They're worthless junk."

"Sorry," I said. "Thank you for protecting me."

"I didn't. Since you stormed in the academy alone, you were lucky you knew how to climb rooftops and that your friends stayed." He shrugged. "Otherwise you'd be dead." His tone was so cold I didn't dare speak again.

At the school, we loaded Bug's bikes into the back of Josie's truck. Lark went to the rear of the school grounds. He came back carrying the rock bags in his hands. He tossed them in the truck bed too. Without a word, he returned for a second pass. Josie and Bug exchanged a nervous look, but I followed him.

"How can I help?" I caught up with Lark.

"You can't." He frowned. "The bodies are gone."

"*Bodies*?" I squirmed.

That's what Lark had meant about cleaning up?

He didn't meet my eye, but I understood. I'd seen the poor coven witch smashed on the earth, twisted beyond repair. Definitely dead. She was missing? And Lark used the plural of the word. Bodies. There had been more? The vampires. Eve and Kyle? The other two creatures had been... dispatched.

I decided not to further try to understand or break down what that meant.

Especially since Lark seemed to have expected he could round up their limbs and toss them into the back of Josie's truck. He picked up the last bag of rocks. Removing any proof I'd been inside the Academy walls.

"What do we do now?" I asked him.

"*We* don't do anything."

I started to ask what that meant when a car rumbled over the gravel parking lot. It squealed to a stop in front of us, parked in an adjacent stall, and Lady Mauve got out of the hatchback.

"Did you get the Stone?" She barked.

"No–"

"Then I won't lift the curse." She was so sharp and so cold, it felt like a slap.

"We almost *died* last night," I hit back.

"It's daylight now." She glared. "No one said it would be easy, girl." Then she turned on Lark. "I expected more." His eyes glowered but the vampire held his tongue. "Find the stone." Lady Mauve ordered over her shoulder. She marched into the school.

"How can I win against a bunch of freakin' vampires," I moaned. "This is my life!" I yelled after Mauve, but the professor was already inside.

"Forget it. Go home, Orphan Girl." Lark said. His blue eyes became flat.

"I can't." I sighed. "Mauve won't lift the spell."

"Not here. Go back to your old life. Your old world."

"There's nothing there. I have nothing left." My tone got louder. "Child Manor is supposed to be mine."

"Is your life worth a set of keys?" He growled.

"No. But if I just find the stone—"

"You don't think that I'm trying?! It's not all about you, *Seph*. The Blood Stone will endanger this whole coven of witches. Possibly the whole world! The Stone will mean a vampire uprising, the likes of which no one has ever known. In the wrong hands, it's a death knell. A weapon of mass destruction that will destroy everything and everyone. *That's* the Stone. That's what *I'm* trying to collect. You're just some selfish chick who wants a sweet house and some cash. This was a mistake. *You're* a mistake. You're not equipped. And I won't have some weak human's blood on my hands."

His dispatch hurt even worse than Mauve's.

"I'm not just a human. I'm a *witch*."

"You're out of your depth. And you will die."

"I have nowhere else to go!"

"Not my problem, *Seph*." He shrugged. "Get out of my town."

Without any bodies to contend with, Lark didn't need Josie's vehicle after all. He simply stalked off into the forest, like Gattas had done. And he didn't look back.

I stared at his departure, raw with shock.

"So that's it?" I questioned the air where he'd gone. "*What the fuck, Lark?!*" I yelled it high into the air. I wanted to scream. I wanted to punch. But the vampire was gone. There was nothing to do but stalk back to the truck. Neither Bug or Josie were dumb enough to try to engage me. My silence pervaded the school parking lot.

"Where to?" Josie asked Bug.

"You can stay with me for a bit," Bug said. He put his hand on my arm. I glared down at the touch, he quickly pulled his fingers off.

"Lark compelled you before. He forced you to invite me over and made you sleep on the couch while I took your bed."

"I know." Bug answered quietly. "But he didn't compel me to

go to the party with you, or into staying last night at the school. And he's not compelling me now. I'm offering respite of my own volition, Seph. I mean it. You can stay if you want."

I looked up at him, surprised. "Why?"

"I dunno... I guess... it would've been nice to have had a neighbor I liked."

25
LARK

"Call the Flood!" I roared as soon as I entered the castle.

"What? Why?" My brother's wife hopped to her feet. Wren merely rolled his eyes. I glared at them as if this was somehow their fault. The fires within me burned brighter than the flame in the hearth.

"Your Mauve has gone mad." I shoved a finger towards her.

"Watch your tone," Wren growled. Lila put a hand on her man's arm. I glared at the pair, pacing between them. I wanted to break something or someone. "You look terrible, Lark."

"Go to hell."

"What's she done now?" Lila put the tension back on Mauve.

"She wants this girl, this *witch* to find the Blood Stone. Cornelius Child's niece."

"Ambrosia's daughter?" Lila's eyes both went wide. Even Wren was surprised.

"Yes." I said. They exchanged a look. "She's not up to the task."

"Well, no," Lila agreed, once a fledgling witch herself. "She hasn't had any training. She doesn't know her family's history or–"

"Dreven's sent a whole army." I snarled. "Led by *Gattas*. We should be matching him force for force."

"We both know the town's not ready for that." Wren shut me down.

"Well, what do you suggest?" I glared at the man.

I hated when my older brother was right. I hated when he was cold and calculated and smart and I looked like a hot-headed punk. But he wasn't there earlier tonight. He didn't see the vampires enter the school on Fellow Gold's arm. His fucking prom dates.

Things were changing. Fast.

The old treaties wouldn't hold.

Not with Child dead and a power vacuum to fill.

The Brotherhood was coming in hot.

There was no way Persephone could take care of herself.

"We can't let them have it," Lila feared.

"Why don't you just get it yourself?" Wren asked.

"*I'm trying.*" I wanted to punch my brother in the face.

What did he think I'd been doing all this time?

"It's bound to Child's blood," Lila reminded her man.

"Not only that, Child hid it. And his home has been locked. *By her.*" I glared at Lila again.

"My sister's way past listening to my convictions." Wren's vampire wife sighed.

Wren put out a hand between us as if to further protect his woman. "So, act independent of the High Council," he told me.

"I am. I'm calling the Flood." I pulled out my phone.

"More mouths to feed." Wren warned. His eyebrow crooked up. Calling in the reigning group of vampires had its own risks and fallout and costs.

"And if Dreven succeeds?" I snapped. "He'll create an army! Every witch here will die."

"Let's say he got the stone and started turning coven Fellows. Who says they'll do what he asks?" Lila asked.

"He'll kill a few subordinates, the rest will fall in line," Wren admitted.

"We've seen it before," I darkly agreed. "Before your time."

Lila wasn't exactly new, she'd been a vampire in our house for over thirty years. But she hadn't been *there*. Not in the dark days. Days to which Wren and I didn't want to return.

"You know I'm right." I said to my brother, pressing a button and putting the phone to my ear. The dial tone rang. I called the Flood consigliere. The others watched, their mouths pressed into firm lines.

"What I know is that you're playing with fire," Wren said, as the phone rang. "I'm just not sure if you're gonna get burned."

26

PERSEPHONE

After Josie dropped us at his home, Bug and I each fell straight into our beds in his room, although this time we did swap locations and sheets for our slumber, putting me square on the couch and the lumpy spot I deserved. Bug would have likely still let me have the mattress, but this time I insisted. It was only fair. We each slept until late afternoon, ordered pizzas, then camped out in his house for the night, reading witch books, talking, discussing the craziness that had just happened at the witch school.

I replayed things with Lark in my head. How dismissive and cruel he'd been at the end. How much I'd grown to like having him around, this dark shadow cloaking me, how I'd grown accustomed to his grumpy safety net.

I hoped he'd be careful tonight, wherever he was.

Doing god knows what.

I had no doubt that he'd continue to look for the Blood Stone with or without Child's only living relative's help. What good had I been to him as his partner? Not much.

"What will you do next?" Bug asked when we were both clean and well-fed and sitting on his couch armed with books.

"I don't know. This is all..." I couldn't find an adjective worthy of the emotions I felt.

"Messed?" He offered. I grinned.

"Exactly. It seems like such a shame to leave behind all that money, my family, that *house*, on the merits that I can't find a dumb rock. But it's too dangerous..."

"Plus, there's the ethical dilemma of putting all the witches in town at risk of becoming witch bloods and vampires if the Blood Stone falls in the wrong hands. I'm sure you're worried about that too," Bug added.

"Right." I stiffly smiled. "And..." I wasn't sure if I was gonna admit this, but here we were. "I kinda wanna go to the witch school. Is that nuts?" I unfurled the photo I'd stolen from Child's office. "I think my mom was a witch. I know my uncle was. I'd like..." I swallowed. This desire had never been part of my life before, but after getting a taste, I was hooked. "I'd like to know more about them, Bug. Who I am and what I can do? Her name's Ambrosia... Maybe."

"Ambrosia, that's pretty," Bug said. "She looks like you."

"You think?"

"I do."

We looked at the old photo, a family moment between siblings, frozen in time. I had almost no facts, I'd never heard any details of my mother's life. But there were answers out there. If there were people who knew my uncle... they likely also knew my mom and dad. My parents were probably both witches. And I was a witch too.

A dreamcast.

I had powers.

I saw things while I slept.

I didn't doubt or question that now. The abilities hadn't been explored but they were real. In my mind. In my soul. I wasn't just a normal human anymore. Maybe that's why I'd never fit in. Not really. Not completely. I'd thought it was 'cuz my parents were dead and people with all their family intact rarely understood the gaping hole that that left. But, there were truths here I couldn't ignore, like, why could I be more honest and more forthcoming with Bug, a guy I'd known for two days, than I'd ever been with the people back home? Even some with whom I'd gone to school for years?

The insect witch understood me.

When I first came to town, I thought the promise of money and the Child Manor meant a chance at a new life, but now it was so much more than that. It was a chance at *my* life. *My real life.* To become the woman I was meant to be. I didn't want my old, ignorant existence anymore.

I wanted to know.

I rolled my finger over the photo of the woman.

"If I get the Blood Stone, Mauve said I could enroll. And that I could live in the house beside yours." I added to Bug. We really could be neighbors. His eyes lit up. "But you're right–" I floated the next word, testing the waters.

There was more.

Lark's words chimed in my mind.

You were lucky your friends were around.

Without Josie and Bug, I'd have died, even with a vampire standing guard outside. Now without him... I hadn't given up, but I couldn't get the Blood Stone all by myself. I needed more help.

I peeked at Bug.

"–it's important to stop the vampires. We can't let this stone fall into the wrong hands. The danger... it's, well, it could end the whole world." I said. "I want to, no, I need to finish this thing. I have to get the Blood Stone. But, to succeed," I turned to him. "I'd need to partner with someone more familiar with the witch world. Someone with powers. And courage. And a really big brain."

Bug nodded gamely. "Too bad Lark said no."

"I meant you."

"*Me*?!" He was shocked. The kid who'd never been picked for gym class in all his life, I was asking him to join my team?

"Of course. You saved me at the academy with your bugs."

"That was a fluke," he sputtered. "I don't even know how I did it. I just did it."

"Fine, then I could use a teammate with raw instincts like yours. I mean it. I could use some serious help..." But I wasn't done. I slyly reframed it for him. "Plus, I bet when you save all of witch-kind from the vamps Josie will be super impressed."

Her love and adoration was the best carrot I had.

"Forget impressed!" Bug beamed. "We could ask her to join the squad!"

"It's not a squad."

"Not yet, but it could be."

"It's too dangerous." I frowned.

"All the more reason to ask her for help. You saw her with the spell in the forest. She could arm us to the teeth with potions and stuff." Bug glowed at the thought. He and Josie working side by side, night after night.

For me, an arsenal was appealing.

Working with Josie was not.

"She won't say yes," I pushed back. "I know girls like her."

I *am* a girl like her, I didn't add.

"Yes, she will," Bug said with certainty. "Leave it to me. I know just what to say."

27
PERSEPHONE

"Josie? Seph has something to ask," Bug squeaked, meek as a mouse, the moment we walked into her store the next morning, sunlight streaming down in the street.

"Gee, great plan," I grumped. Bug blushed, but Josie wasn't around to hear his weak pitch. A man with small circle wireframe glasses sat behind the counter today.

"She's off, Bug." He barely looked up from his sci-fi book. "Bug's friend." He added to me. I nodded hello.

"I know right where to go." Undeterred, Bug turned on his heels.

"To her house?" I half-guessed, half-grumbled.

"Somewhere else." The insect witch shook his head and we pedaled across town. "Just think, if she joins, we'll have access to her car!" Bug added as we both huffed and puffed. That same thought had already crossed my mind. So there was one plus to working with the girl. That and her spells. That glue was effective, whatever it was. Bug pulled up at the local barber/mechanic shop, a weird two-business combination roughshod onto the side of somebody's residential house. The mechanic bay was wide open.

Only in a small town.

"Come on around back."

"This belong to her folks?" I mildly asked, dropping the bike by the stoop. Bug shook his head no as we walked into the bay.

"It's her ex-boyfriend Beck's. Well, technically, it's his Dad's. Mr. Templeton runs the barbershop and the mechanic's, but he lets Josie use his lift to work on her car. Always has. She and Beck broke up 'cuz he wasn't her parabond and he's off now with Mae. Mae Kingsley? She lived with her Aunt?" I shook no. "*She* was supposed to parabond with Spade, but when they went into the High Council limbo–"

"–*Bug!*" Josie's sharp rebuke cut him off. Her death look said *shut up*. Josie was tightening the torque on a bolt, glaring our way, listening to him spill all her secrets. The insect witch turned bright red. He couldn't help but squeak out.

"See? Told 'ya she'd be here."

"Working... *alone*." She wiped some of the grease off her hands with a frown. We were coming to ask for a favor. This was a bad start. "What do you want?"

He turned to me, his baby face pleading. I sighed.

"Bug and I are thinking of trying to find the Blood Stone by ourselves."

"Wanna join the squad?" He said too fast.

"It's not a squad," I assured her, shooting him a dampening look. "*Not helping*." Bug knew my tone well. He'd heard the vague annoyance of others plenty of times before. The insect witch bowed out, touring down the driveway, looking around. He held his hands behind his back and whistled. I sighed. "We could really use a third."

"Why?" Josie narrowed her eyes.

"Uh, 'cuz on my own, a vampire could seriously kick my ass?"

"No, why me?"

"Bug wants you," I admitted. Then went an honest step

further. "And I don't know anyone else." Josie and I had already been over *how much* Bug wanted her. She wasn't interested in him, so that wasn't a selling feature for her. If I truly wanted her on the team, I'd have to level with her. "I agreed 'cuz I know you're not dumb. I think you could help."

"If I joined, I'd prove you wrong." She sneered.

"You couldn't help?"

"No. Joining your *death squad. That* would be dumb as hell." She was so smug.

"Look, the vampires only come out at night, right? Everyone minus Lark," I said. She nodded. Mostly true. "He's got some special day-walking power, I don't know. He didn't explain it well. But, you saw it. When the sun came out, Gattas had to go. We'll be smart. If we work in the daytime, we'll be okay. Getting the stone back could save thousands of witches and stop them from becoming undead creatures of the night. But if you'd rather not, if you're not interested, just say so."

"That's why Bug's doing it," she agreed. "What are *you* getting out of it?" Josie crossed her arms. "I know you don't care about the welfare of anyone but yourself."

It seemed like a tough act, but she still hadn't said no. There was hope.

I swallowed, carefully weighing what truths to expose. I'd lose all credibility with the chemist the moment I was caught in a lie, but I had no interest in revealing myself. It was a fine line to walk.

"Seph has a whole deal with Lady Mauve. When she breaks the spell, Seph gets several items in the will, then she plans to join the High Council Academy's ranks. As will I." Bug piped up. I turned to stare at the boy, now back at our sides. I'd told him those details in confidence and he certainly hadn't told me *his* part of our plan. *He wanted to attend the witch school too?*

But I supposed it made sense.

Bug should also get something for his risk. He wouldn't get *her*.

"It's not so fun when he's blurting *your* secrets, is it?" Josie smirked. A knowing smile.

"I'll have to remember to keep my business to myself." We each gave him a withering look. Bug looked chagrined, but I half-smiled to let him off the hook.

"What are you getting from Mauve?" Josie remained undeterred. "What's the spell?"

"The witch house." Bug said. "It'll be hers."

"The Child estate," I agreed, although I was sure Josie knew exactly which manor he was talking about. "It's been magically sealed."

"Only Mauve can release the hex. It was written in the will. Mauve said she would open it, but only if Seph gets the Blood Stone for her," Bug spilled. I gritted my teeth. Insect-brain had two awfully loose lips for information that wasn't technically his to share. Luckily, I'd left out any mention of the hefty bank accounts.

"Are you gonna reveal *all* our secrets?" I asked him.

"I didn't say anything about your mom," he pouted in return.

"Who's her Mom?" Josie asked.

"–don't!" I caught Bug just in time. An exchange Josie thoroughly enjoyed. She tossed the rag on a shelf. Another good sign. "So you'll help?"

"I'm not gonna risk my life for you to make a down payment on your house." Josie shrugged.

"What about the good will towards men?" I snarked. She rolled her eyes. But I wanted her on board. I needed her. She was a bigger and better witch than Bug, no matter how much the jibber jabber-er might want to help.

There were other things I could offer...

"I plan to sell the manor as soon as we're done. When I do, I'll split the earnings with you."

"Fifty-fifty?" Josie asked.

Damn, she thought to iron the percentages out.

"Ninety-ten."

Josie went back to work, sticking her head under the hood right in front of us. Bug looked to me, he shook his head. The conversation was getting away from me.

"Fine. Seventy-thirty," I offered. She didn't straighten up.

"Fifty-fifty," she answered.

"Seventy-thirty." I didn't budge down to her percentage. Bug held his breath. Josie paused.

"Sixty-forty. And you'll do what I say." She casually turned a wrench.

"No, but Bug will."

The corner of the chemist's mouth turned up in a grin. Slowly, she straightened.

"Deal." She put the wrench down and shook my hand, grease smearing my palm. Bug beamed ear-to-ear, his favorite girl and his new neighbor officially becoming his elite squad. I picked up a towel and wiped off the muck, fully aware she'd purposefully dirtied me up. But, that wasn't her only play. Josie had more to add. "But we're gonna need a lie-guard too. I know just who to ask."

"No, *no*," Bug groaned. "Anyone but him."

28

PERSEPHONE

We took Josie's truck to the quarry. Bug piled into the tiny cab backseat like the willing pup that he was. He didn't even have to be asked. In her truck, Josie cranked the tunes so we avoided the dullards of awkward small talk as she drove us out of town to the abandoned waterfront.

"Are you sure this is the right spot?" Bug worried from the back row.

"Yup." Josie spun out her tires, roaring over the road.

It was beautiful countryside, the trees thickly growing from both sides over the roadway leading us to the spot. I could see a sleek car parked at the water's edge beside the manmade aquamarine pool.

"Swimming in a quarry is dangerous. People have drowned." Bug grumbled. "Swimming alone? That's just stupid."

"Nobody said he was smart," Josie shrugged.

Then I saw him, a single man cutting through the water, using elegant form. Josie slammed on the brakes to park beside the lone car in the barren lot, a spray of gravel stones kicking up when we stopped. She hopped out of the truck. I followed, releasing the back row for Bug to clamber out. We joined her just in time to watch Spade emerge from the water.

All muscle.

Rippled and tanned.

His torso dripping wet.

"You've got to be kidding me," Bug moaned.

Spade shook out his hair like a dog, pleased to spatter water every which way, including our clothes. He grinned widely at us, straightening up. I could tell immediately from his physique he must come here a lot. He'd developed a beautiful swimmer's body. Spade was tall and trim, his arms were strong. It felt illicit to stare, us fully dressed while he stood in short shorts, but Spade was showing off. He toweled his shoulders and head as Josie waited, crossing her arms, then he tossed the fabric aside. He didn't bother to cover his chest, stretching one hand behind his head to show his full body off. His well-defined obliques created two magnificent arrows the eye could follow straight into his casual navy swim trunks. To avoid looking at all the bare skin, I focused on the mini duck print.

Little golden chicks.

If only my vampire could see him now.

Spade looked at the pile of clothes that awaited him, but inclined his head, waiting for one of us to talk. No doubt when he was alone in the quarry he didn't cover up or hide to swap clothes, just stripped the shorts where he stood. Free to bare bones.

I turned away, trying not to add *that* mental picture to my brain.

The last thing I needed in this tenuous new friendship with Josie was to accidentally flirt with a guy sniffing at her heels.

"Thrice in one week, must be some kinda record." He leered at her and me and Bug as if we were the half-naked ones on display.

"Put on a shirt," Bug muttered, not loud enough for his rival to hear.

Josie merely shrugged. "You still want in the Academy?"

"Who's asking?" Spade stared at me. "Where's your man?"

"Lark's not her–" Bug started but I shot the insect witch a look.

"He's busy today," I said.

"You like what you see?" Spade's mouth twisted up in a grin, taunting me.

"You missed a spot shaving," Josie noted near his nipples. This took the attention off me.

"I don't shave, babe. I wax. Hurts like a beast."

"You didn't answer my question." Josie refocused. "You want in or not?"

"Maybe."

"You saw him at the ball," I said. "Men don't go to dances for fun. He was there. He wants in."

"So what if I do?" Spade snapped.

"We might have an entry point," Josie said. "To get you on the good side of Mauve."

"I'm listening." As if to prove his point, he actually donned his gray t-shirt over his head. Spade flicked his hair again, a watery tick, and checked each of us out more closely now, trying to size up the group. "What would I have to do?"

It didn't take long to get him signed on. And I was impressed that Josie incentivized him without spending any of our house cash. I'd have rolled my eyes at Bug for saying so, but now we really did have a squad. A ragtag group of four. I wanted to call Lark and tell him about our new plan. I wanted any excuse to call him at all, but that wasn't possible. The vampire never gave me his number. What was I supposed to do? Howl at the moon? No.. that was werewolves. I sincerely hoped there weren't any werewolves in this town, but at this point...

Maybe a communication ban between Lark and myself was smart. It was probably better if no one knew what we were up to. I didn't have a plan to divulge anyway. Josie and Spade came back with Bug and I to his basement clubhouse.

"What's our plan of attack?" Spade asked.

"I dunno." I admitted.

"Cornelius Child was an evil super genius," Josie said.

"No offense," Bug chimed in to me. But I shrugged. She could call my uncle evil. He probably was. And I was getting used to Josie's frank assessments. I kind of liked them. She was in fact growing on me. She cut right to the point. Josie went on.

"It's not like he's gonna make up a treasure map. *X marks the spot.*'"

"That's true," I admitted. "But... I did have a dream in Child's office. I snuck in, that's where I was last night." I caught the others up. Bug's eyes went wide. Spade looked impressed.

"You broke into the school and you had a *nap*?" Josie frowned. I nodded.

"That's what you were doing? All that time?" Bug asked.

"It was Lark's idea. I'm a dreamcast," I said.

"Smart," Spade nodded. But Josie shook her head.

"No, it wasn't. It kept you out after dark."

"We were already out after dark," I countered. "The whole party started at sundown."

"I don't like it," she said.

"What did you see?" Bug asked. I tried to remember exactly how I imagined it, how to describe what I saw and what I felt.

"It was like this bright light, like the sun was in my uncle's office. And when I opened my eyes, it was just like I was staring into the bulbs of his chandelier. But that light was off."

"Well, you shoulda turned it on. The stone might be there, you should go back." Spade man-splained. I shook my head.

"No, I checked it thoroughly..."

"And then three vampires attacked her," Josie added on.

"Wait, what?" Spade's jaw dropped open. Bug nodded.

"Seph almost died, but Lark, Josie and I saved her."

"He's a vampire too," Josie added.

"Wait, *what*?" Spade yelped. "Hold up. I'm out." He peeled back. "Your boyfriend's a vampire?!"

"No! He's not–" I immediately interrupted. But then I realized I was objecting to the far less reprehensible part. "–he's not my boyfriend. He *is* a vampire."

"Oh, no. Hell, no. Those things are *real?!*" Spade's voice shot up an octave. "Count me out."

"But..." my wheels were turning.

There was another lighting fixture at the academy that looked just like the one in Child's office. Another copy cat chandelier that was always on. That was large like the sun.

"The one in his office is a duplicate of the main chandelier, the one in the atrium of the school. I saw it."

"*No, no, no.* It's not happening."

"It's big." I said. "Like the sun." It all made sense. The dream steered me to *that*, not to the small fixture in his office. We had to look *there*.

"Are you nuts?!" Spade was beyond flustered.

"If you wanna get in with Mauve, this is the deal," Josie shrugged.

"I wanna get in with my *life*." He balked. "Not dead. Or *undead*."

"Fine, we don't need him." I cut him out. This was taking too much time.

"Yes, you do." Spade shot back. "You'd be dead without me."

"Guys, don't fight," Bug looked like he was caught on both sides. "*I* said yes," he offered. Spade laughed.

"Big deal. You say yes to everything."

"If we work together in daylight, everything will be fine," Josie told him.

"You're on *board?*" He scoffed. "*Why?!*"

"The Blood Stone is a real threat," Josie said. "If the vampires use it, all the witches in town will be susceptible to becoming witch bloods. Including Jim and Ping."

"Josie's mum and dad," Bug supplied to me. I'd already guessed.

"And Ma," Josie added.

"Spade's mum." Bug said.

"*She gets it, Bug,*" Spade snapped. He stared at me. "You were there yesterday, why didn't you check it then?"

"*Uh... 'cuz there was a trio of scary vamps and we were running for our lives?*" Bug actually shot back at him. The bug-witch's voice shook. I patted his arm. It was alright.

"It's huge. And way up in the ceiling," I added. "Three floors high. Maybe more."

"So we go in again, with a ladder, and climb up there and get it," Josie said, matter of factly.

"No way," Spade said. "The coven's locked down tight. The party was only one night."

"And even then they didn't let you in without some guide," I remembered the plump woman with wild gray curls stopping me in my tracks.

"Well, maybe Lady Mauve or Lark–" Bug started. But I shook my head.

"We have to keep them out of this. The whole reason the professor's forcing me to get the stone is so that she can lie low in the coven. Keep clean hands. And Lark said we shouldn't be involved anymore."

"But you wanna prove yourself?" Spade asked. I half-shrugged. Yes. Amongst other reasons, that's exactly what I wanted. Bug and Josie nodded.

"If we do this for her, Mauve said she'd help me get into the Academy. I can extend the offer to you and them," I lied, noting the others. I had no proof she'd also help them, but it seemed reasonable to think it was true.

"So we do it ourselves. We go in as students," Josie said.

"But, we're not students," Bug said.

"No, but we *know* them..." She looked at Spade. "People you can copy the mannerisms of, who you know attend the academy. Who no one would think twice about if they saw them on the grounds. We could pretend to be them."

"Greg and Marcy?" Spade's mouth turned up in a smile.

The couple who collected Blue Moon's books.

Josie nodded. "Plus two others."

"I don't understand. How do we–" I started.

"–Spade's a lie-guard." Josie said. She stared at him. "Think how impressed Mauve would be if you did that."

Spade considered it, pleased at the challenge. Or intrigued to flex his skills.

She'd known.

Or at least Josie had guessed we might need to do something like this.

Something that required Spade's special skills.

I'd never seen a lie-guard before. I wasn't sure how it would work. Bug's explanation still wasn't clear, but the others caught on right away.

"Who's gonna fall for that?" Bug laughed.

Josie and Spade exchanged a glance. A memory showed on their faces. A distant flash, then it was gone. Clearly, at some time in their past, someone had fallen for it. Hard.

"You'd be surprised," was all Josie said.

29
LARK

"*This is a mistake.*" Wren's words of warning still rang in my ear. But when I called, Franz said "Come on over, Bird Brain. We'll talk." So I did.

The Crimson Flood was a last resort, but I was in over my head. The risk of losing the Blood Stone was too great. Of course, my local connection to the organization of the undead was Franz Nichtenfalke. And he was... not my favorite vamp.

Nefarious.

With morals like you might expect from a creature with no soul, no past, and no future. Except, this vamp did have a past. That's how he ended up in his chair. A vampire could heal almost anything except being burned alive or a stake right through the heart, so the dire injury to his legs must have come while he was still a witch.

Did that wound build any shred of compassion or humanity in Franz's heart?

Not one bit.

But, I needed more help.

Even if it came from a brothel strip club.

The place smelled like stale beer. When I pushed through the doors of his bar, all eyes turned my way. Surprised. It was morning. On a weekday. The last time anyone should be visiting their place. But inside the club it could be any day, anytime; all the windows were blacked out. The red neon signs were set on high alert. Emitting a garish glow and a hum. The girls in the club sat around in black bralettes and short skirts. Dark hair. Dark eyes. Already strung out. Ready and waiting, just in case a client or customer waltzed in.

Franz certainly had a type.

The group of women wore heavy black eyeliner that was smudged, making their eyes look hollowed out and empty. Or perhaps that was a natural effect of living in a darkened hole, cut off from the outside world.

I didn't go up to the bar.

I wasn't there for a drink or a good time.

Instead, I stood in the door and waited for the owner to come.

Some industrious girl went back to alert their boss. He rolled out through a beaded curtain like he had all the time in the world.

"Lark," Franz grinned, spreading his arms, feigning delighted surprise as if I hadn't announced my visit with a phone call before I arrived. "I always knew you'd return. Welcome back to my Vampire Club."

He sat in an old fashioned wheelchair. A medical antique from over a century ago, but the looks were deceiving. It was outfitted with a modern engine. Fully motorized. He didn't need to use the motor to move, preferring the slow motion of his own arms. But the mechanics were fully installed for a quick get away, or a fast lunge. Franz just enjoyed the old-timey look. Even his clothes dated back in time.

Perhaps to a saloon? A nod to when the vampire was last alive.

"Subtle." I rolled my eyes at the goth decor and the glowing red lights. The words *Vampire Club* buzzed in two-foot neon red cursive above the back of the bar.

"Hide in plain sight," Franz winked. "Men love a trashy dump. Lets 'em slum without thinking too much."

All these girls. His workers. They weren't fools. While every eye in the place trained on the actions of their boss, not a single woman actually looked up. They all kept to themselves. Silent as mice. Frozen to the spot.

"You ever feel bad?" I mused over his girls.

"No," he laughed. "They're alive, aren't they?"

That was the level of humanity here? I frowned. The vamp was distasteful as fuck.

"I need a meeting with the Flood." I got right to the point.

"No, you don't," Franz chuckled. "Unless you wanna stake there." He pointed at my heart, which was straight on par with his face. He spun around on his chair and rolled away from me, leading me back through the bevy of girls. "It doesn't happen, Lark. No one goes looking for the Flood. No one beckons their aid."

"I know." I followed. "But, you don't understand."

"Oh, I understand." He wheeled around and leered. "You're in love with some girl." When he caught sight of my face he actually laughed. "Oh, shit. You are. It's always a girl with you good guy vamps!" He flung his hands up, as if his women were proof. Franz wagged a finger my way. "I've always wondered why your bed stayed empty so long, 'specially after Wren and that witch started–" He made a vulgar gesture with his hands. "Lila." He said her name, taunting, as if she was *his* girl. I bristled again. "There's no need to save the world, Lark. If you can't bed some chick on your own, you're always welcome here."

I ground my teeth.

I felt a special type of rage for the way he mentioned my sister-in-law's name. As if Lila was just some trophy on Wren's shelf and not a living, breathing entity herself. But showing any weakness to Franz would only entice the vamp to further poke.

He was watching me now. Far too smug.

"So who is she, Lark? And why has she got you storming out to the Flood?"

"It's not about some witch."

Franz pretended to pout, but he couldn't hold the silence for long. "I happen to love women! Especially witches." He wheeled between his workers. The girls in his club parted as we moved back to the VIP rooms. Franz suddenly stopped. He looked a worker up and down. "Take this one." She opened her stance to him, just a hair. An invitation. He licked his lips. "Women are the best part of being undead, aren't they love?" He traced a hand over a dancer's bare midriff, then snatched her hand. He tugged her into his lap. She obediently fell, and when he didn't immediately push her away, she writhed like a snake on the top of his pants. Her nearby friend came to slither into my hair. I held up a firm hand.

"I'm good."

She fell back, a bit hurt. We both watched as Franz went all in. He pulled the woman by the hair, aligning her in his lap to dry hump and kiss. As he did, I saw the prick wounds already on her neck. She'd been bitten and sucked. Probably lots of times, at his whim. I averted my gaze, but Franz still caught my disgust.

"It's part of the show," he defended himself, waving towards the sign. "*Vampires*." He chomped down on his own teeth. "And I pay for the privilege. Handsomely. Don't I girls?!"

They tittered in response.

Half-compelled. Half out of their heads with no sleep, booze and drugs.

"Loosen up," Franz ordered me. "Finch used to come here all the time."

Another name-dropped family member.

The name of my younger brother was employed like a weapon, I was sure. Franz casually grinned. But I didn't give the vamp the satisfaction of getting to me. Showed no weakness.

"Leave that idiot out of this."

Franz threw his head back and howled in delight. "He was a fool, wasn't he? *Ah, kids.* You three were so young when you turned."

"We didn't have a choice."

"Tell that to *Wren*," Franz leaned in, hitting my family history right where it counted. When I still didn't react, he grew bored. He shoved the girl he'd been kissing off of him. She didn't see it coming. Her skirt ripped at the hem as he tossed her to the floor. She hit the ground hard.

The way her body curled.

The moment of shock.

The torn skirt...

My mind flashed back to Persephone, crumpled outside of the school. Having just fallen six floors. She survived. But I'd been so angry with her. I blew her right off. Where was she now? I hoped she'd gone home. Did she have a home to go back to? I didn't know.

"You like it rough?" Franz caught my gaze and misread the signs.

"No." I'd had enough. "I don't." I glared at him. I folded my full stance at the waist and leaned heavily into his personal space. In doing so, I met him down at his chair. "*But I will make it rough,*" I warned.

"Alright, okay." Franz shoved me away and wheeled into the other room. "Come back, come on."

I followed two steps behind. But he was through playing games. Franz pushed the beaded curtain aside and rolled into the furthest back room. His private quarters. The place was still red, even in here. His office/bedroom glowed from smaller ironic, illuminated signs, little jokes. Lips with sharp teeth. The word love. That sort of thing.

Over the bed the light fixture looked like a glowing orb.

A reminder of the moon.

Two witches lay on his bed. Spread out like sticky jam.

As we entered, they didn't move.

More compelled slaves.

"I can't call the Crimson Flood. I don't have a death wish. But I can do something better for you, Lark. Girls!" Franz clapped his hands loudly, waking up the sleeping women. "Tell Lark his future." He ordered. They wore fabric strips as nightgowns, the supposed dresses covering nothing at all. They each seemed vapid and listless. But rose up like snakes on his command. "Sit." Franz bumped me with his chair. The move shoved me down to the bed. I sat, about to object again. This was not what I came for. But the wheelchair vamp's eyes narrowed. "You wanted help. Listen."

"Fine."

"Tell him, girls."

The first witch crawled into my lap, laid down on my dick and stared up. The other witch seemed to crawl over my back and hum in my ear. Both dripped with sex. This was a mistake–

I was about to throw them off and punch Franz right out of his chair when the first girl spoke.

"I see her. She runs. A fiery comet. Red sparkling through a sea of starlight. You *like* her."

I froze.

Red sparkling... a fiery comet... Persephone?

Through a sea of starlight. At night time.

"Where?" I asked.

"*Ah, ah,*" Franz warned. He put a finger to his lips. "*Listen.*" He beckoned my lap girl to come over to him. She crawled off of me and cooed into his chair. "Go on." He told her. She stared at me across the divide. Vacant and empty.

"I see the lights on in the darkness. A city of them. All in one box."

"What does that mean? *Where?*" I ignored Franz's direction. Barking this time.

A city of lights in a box? That didn't help.

But there was no point in my asking for clarification. The witches barely registered I was there, they were so far gone. Franz canoodled with the first dreamcast, happy to have her company. He sucked on her skin. The girl over my shoulder rolled down to the bed, staring up at me with big liquid eyes. Locked in a trance.

"A man drinks her blood." This new witch warned me. The other nodded. "The beast's a wild one." The woman bared her teeth as if she had fangs, though her mouth was human and normal. "Only you can save her, *Lark.*"

My skin shivered at the sound of my name.

Was the girl just repeating Franz? Or did she actually know who I was? Had she seen me? In her dream? Saving Persephone? *How?*

This place was messing with my brain.

"Lark," the woman on the bed said it again, calling to me. It was some dangerous chemistry. Her eyes held such need. "Bird Brain, *Lark.*"

My name.

My need.

It was a whispered refrain.

She bore a hole deep inside.

My breath slowed right down. I didn't want to give in but the word struck a chord in me. My name. My goddamn lonely life.

"*Lark.*" She said it again.

Was it possible this witch could really see me? Know me?

I'd been solo for so long. So strong.

But that took constant energy.

My body ached to be free. To be loose. With a different sort of danger and violent tendency. Weaker men always partook. The dreamcast witch was right here. Laid out on the canopy. Breasts on display. Legs practically splayed. Her eyes were liquid pools. Wanting and waiting for me to give in. She was practically begging.

I could take a taste.

I could take everything that she offered me.

Tits. Neck. Legs.

A perfect little vampire treat on this bed.

I was suddenly very hungry and there was only one thing I ate.

Blood.

The undead weren't built to say no to any of our desires. We were designed to give in to our basest needs.

Our hunger.

Our thirst.

Our bloodlust.

The longing inside me was so powerful. I looked at Franz. He was already all over his girl. And she happily let him. If not happy, at least she didn't complain. Fully compelled. The witch played with him. My fangs started to throb with their own ancient desires.

Hold it together, I fought my own urgency and wanting. *You don't want that, Lark.*

But the dreamcast still had more to say.

"The kids are all dead. She was helping you! *This is how you repay her?*" She cried. Pressing and insistent. Her body convulsed.

"*Pay her back!*" The girl on the chair yelped.

Franz dove down on his own dreamcast's neck, stabbing and fierce with his fangs. He ravaged her. Sucking her blood. She flailed at first, but there was no holding him off. Her body arched at the depth of the stab wounds but she gave in to the lunge. He hungrily drank her blood, silencing her with his attack. His need. He took what he wanted and left her bereft.

"She was helping me!" I yelled. "They both were!" His cruelty brought me back to my head. I leapt up to my feet. Aghast and irate. "She could have dreamed again!"

"Relax," Franz laughed, blood spattering from his teeth. "I'll get a new girl. There's always more witches, Lark. That's my point. The coast is full of covens and dreamcasts." He didn't even bother to seal her up. Blood squirted out of the witch's skin. The wounds were sloppy and jagged. Franz stuck a finger in the puddle and licked it clean. He frowned. "Don't give me that look."

"You could bite me," the other witch offered me. She pushed her dark hair off her shoulder blades, showing me the smooth nape of her neck, laid out on the bed.

Waiting.

Wanting.

Projecting.

"Put me out of my misery," she said.

"Is that what this is?" I asked, looking from one to the other. "Misery?"

Franz merely leered. His witch's blood dripped from his fangs. The nasty vampire tongued his own teeth, licking their points, waiting to see what I'd do next.

"Save me, Lark." The witch on the bed genuinely wanted my bite. This was so messed. She was innocent. So beautiful. Practically begging someone to make her tenure here at the Vampire Club come to an end. In whatever way I desired. The witch didn't care. She wanted me to take her powers away. Because if she wasn't a dreamcast, she wouldn't have to stay in this place. Or remain with this man. I could bite her and free her from his chains.

It had been so long since I'd had a bloody taste.

The urge called.

Take her, Lark.

I could nibble.

Just a snack–

She'd be so delicious.

No!

That might make her a vamp.

A beast.

Like me.

And Franz.

I shook my head.

These thoughts were screwed up. I was fucked.

I had to get out of there. Right this instant.

I'd clearly gathered all I could get from the Vampire Club.

A girl, a fiery shooting comet? A box full of a city's worth of lights. Her friends were all dead. A wild and blood-sucking beast?

Seph was fucked too, I decided. It was wrong to push Persephone away. Clearly, her fate in this world was too tied to her family to ignore. I had to find her. Before it was too late...

But first–

I grabbed the bedside witch's hand. As I pulled her up to her feet, her dressing gown covered even less. *Damn.*

"Here." I took off my coat and put it around her empty skin. I tilted her face up to my gaze and stared deep in her eyes. "You are alright. You survived. You will leave this house right now and you will forget all your time with Franz and the Vampire Club. You will go home. You will find peace. You will have a good life." I compelled each word with as much strength as I could muster.

Her eyes flickered, breaking through the days, weeks, or months of counter-compelling from her wheelchair-bound master.

He did not interrupt.

She stared at me surprised.

"You're safe." I re-emphasized again. "There's money in your pocket. Go back to your old life." She dug her slim fingers into my oversized pockets. There was several hundred dollars in cash. She stared at it, then me, then at the door.

Suddenly, she found her legs. Without a word she ran. Escaping from Franz.

"Well," he muttered. "Now I need two replacements."

"Will you kill her?" I asked darkly, glancing at the messy woman he'd attacked. Blood spilled down her chest and dribbled between her round breasts.

"Of course not," Franz groaned. "I'm not a murderer, Lark." He hadn't liked me removing his plaything from his club, but he wasn't dumb enough to cross me in such close quarters. "It was just a small snack. You know how it is."

"Seal her up."

Franz did as I asked. He slurped over her breasts just to be gross, but languished at her neck with the final lick. The healing properties of his saliva closed up her wounds. Though he did his best to make it clear he enjoyed every drop.

"I didn't come here for this," I muttered.

"Got your answers though, didn't you kid?" Franz laughed.

"If she turns into a vamp, kill her." I ordered. That dreamcast may have actually been a witch blood, already infected by the undead. "Put her out of her misery. Swear that you will. If she becomes human–"

"–She can work in my club," Franz smiled. "I pay well."

I glared at him, then I stalked back through the house.

"You're no better than us!" Franz yelled from the back room, still scared to come out. "It's who we are, Lark. Me, you, your brothers. Birdie?! The urge drives you mad. I don't care how tightly you tie your soul knot every morning! *You want to give in!* The need. The ache comes for everyone. *It'll come for you too!*"

30
PERSEPHONE

We waited until morning the next day. Then hatched the new plan. We decided to park off a road nearby and walk into the academy on foot. None of us knew how well the school parking lot would be protected, or if the witches had some way of knowing who was or wasn't in their driveway and we didn't want Josie's empty truck to reveal our location or plan. Plus, the three of us had already crossed through the forest surrounding the grounds the other evening. It seemed like the wisest solution. And the trees were far less scary to traverse in the daylight without a maniacal vampire hunting our steps.

Although if we had to make a fast getaway...

I frowned at the thought. Then ignored it.

"You'll have to work quickly," Spade told our group. "I'm incredibly talented, but holding one identity is hard enough, maintaining four?" He flexed his hand into a fist, looking at it as if wondering how much strength he actually held deep inside. I guessed we'd soon find out.

"You'll do fine." Josie said. "Persephone and I will go up."

I nodded. We'd acquired a two-sided ladder. We could each climb on one side, and if my last interaction with the chandelier was any indication, having a second set of hands to retrieve the Blood Stone could definitely help.

"Hell, no." Spade immediately balked. "You're not going. *I'm* going up."

"We need your concentration on the floor," Josie told him.

"So you can have all the glory?" Spade sputtered.

"We're a squad," Bug countered. "It's everyone's glory."

"Don't call it a squad," Josie groaned.

"He's not strong enough to hold the ladder alone, we need your muscles." I didn't know why anyone was talking about glory. Instead, I appealed to the lie-guard's vanity.

Spade's expression turned.

My implication that we needed a big strong savior to hold the ladder made the dumb witch puff out his chest. Josie hid a grin. It was clear I understood how Spade ticked, and to his credit, Bug wasn't insulted at all.

"We go in, we set up the ladder directly below the chandelier, Josie and I go up, the stone should be right there in the center. In the middle of two carved golden wings. We grab the Blood Stone and get the hell out," I said. The other three heads nodded.

"These are your spell packets." Josie handed out the equipment.

We looked at the mixtures. Each spell was a combination of chemicals in separate baggies that could easily burst if you applied any pressure. "I gave you guys stuff I thought might stop a chase. Glue, glue release, snap ribbons–"

"What are they?" I asked, looking the package over.

"Only the Francou Butterfly's favorite snack," Bug beamed.

"Plants. Like climbing vines mixed with a Venus fly trap." Josie suggested. "They grow really fast."

"And they've got thorns and a vicious bite if you're not careful," Spade added.

"Got it." It should have given me comfort to see we were prepared, but this little plant lesson confirmed just how uninformed I was. Just like Lark had said.

Where was the vampire this morning?

We'd purposefully made use of the daylight hours for our heist, the added danger of running into students was far outweighed by the fear of more vamps.

But I still wondered what my bodyguard was doing?

How was he trying to find the Stone? And did he miss me?

Of course he didn't.

Don't be silly, Seph.

According to Lark, I was a detriment and a liability. A fragile girl.

Well, I'd love to see his damn face when I showed back up to Lady Mauve with the stone. I'd love to see a lot of things...

"*Earth to Seph,*" Spade interrupted my internal bravado.

"I'm listening," I lied, but now I refocused.

"I gave us each a sleeping spell as well," Josie told me. "If something happens below, like the boys are stuck, we can sprinkle it down. Just be careful, we need the guys conscious to steady the ladder when we're at the top, or while we're working."

"Yeah, wouldn't wantcha to get caught in the rafters," Bug chortled.

"I got it. In and out, won't be a problem," I said. My tone stayed casual cool, belying the tension I felt. "I think we're ready."

"As we'll ever be," Josie agreed.

"We can do it, Squad," Bug cheered us on.

"We're not a squad," the three of us unanimously told him.

"Fine, alright. We're just individual friends doing like-minded things in close proximity and in tandem." Bug frowned. He was so dejected it made me softly grin.

"That's a much longer cheer. I like it." I bolstered his spirits. "We can do it, individual friends doing like-minded things in close proximity and in tandem!" Bug giggled with me.

Then it was time.

We all stared up at the school. Then looked at Spade.

"Ready?" Josie asked.

"Here goes nothing." Spade balled up his hand.

His brown eyes flickered, growing darker, more vivid, and I felt a shimmering intensity release from him. Then the other three members around me physically changed.

I blinked. It was impossible to explain, hard to even describe, but we transformed. Our bodies realigned in the space. Spade became the guy from the store, the one I knew was Greg. And Josie was replaced with Marcy, his pretty, buxom mate. Bug morphed into a short Indian boy with thick black eyebrows and shaggy hair. My own locks became long, pin straight and blonde. Almost pure white hair. I glanced down at my own hands. Even my fingernails had been swapped. I looked like someone else. We all did.

"Go," Josie/Marcy instructed. She and Spade/Greg picked up the ladder and ran. Bug and I hurried to keep up.

"I'm Tej Mithaali, you're Sloane Lolant," he filled me in. "They were seniors and parabonds in the same year that Josie and Spade didn't get into the High Council. But they successfully entered. She's a dreamcast like you... I think."

"Tej wouldn't be telling Sloane who she is or how to act, *Tej*." Spade/Greg nitpicked. We weren't even inside yet.

"Think ethereal," Bug/Tej whispered, defying the lie-guard again.

I nodded. Bohemian and chill. Got it.

But we needn't have worried. The lobby was open and barren. Class was in session so the atrium was empty. There was no one for whom we needed to pretend.

"Too bad," Spade/Greg groaned. "I'm doing my life's best work and there's no one here to see it." Josie and I went straight to the ladder and started to climb. "I bet Greg would have felt his girlfriend's ass once or twice." He leered at Josie/Marcy's butt as she went. Spade had the other boy's personality down pat. Or he pretended to, in order to let his own desires be realized.

"*Babe*," Josie tossed her hair, pitched her tone and joyfully laughed, the perfect Marcy performance. "Stop looking at my bum." Then her voice fell down an octave to a Josie snarl. "Don't make me poke out your eyes."

"Up you go, hon." Spade shrugged, undeterred. "I'll watch from here," he winked. The perfect vantage point.

"I won't look," Bug told me.

"Would Tej?" I asked.

"I don't think so, no" he agreed.

I grinned. "Then that's the right choice."

Eight rungs up, Josie and I were close enough on the opposite legs of the ladder to put on the two-sided harness she'd designed. One half for each girl, connected via rope. With every rung we climbed higher, I felt the ladder weight shift. The boys held onto the legs. Even with the telescopic extensions, the ladder wasn't quite tall enough to reach all the way into the air. We'd have to climb up into the lower ceiling beams and cross a few joists to reach the chandelier.

"I hate heights." Josie muttered. "Don't fall."

"I won't."

"I'm tied to you."

"I know." I understood how the safety net worked. We'd stay on either side of any apparatus, the rope dangling between us so that if one of us fell, it would catch the other before we plunged to our death. "Besides, Bug will catch us in a cloud of flies." I tried to lighten the mood.

"That was a fluke," Josie admitted. "And even if that is his new skill, Bug can't save us both," she finally cracked a small smile. "And we both know who he loves." She fluttered her eyelids in Marcy-like fashion.

Talking about our likely deaths gave a weird, light-hearted irony to our climb.

"Sure, *now* you accept the guy's affections," I groaned.

"Better than compelling him the moment I got into town," she shot back.

"That was Lark's idea." I blamed my guard. Not entirely the truth, but close. I thought of the vampire. I briefly wished he was here, by my side. Climbing these rungs.

"And you should know, I slept on the couch last night," I added, grunting with the effort. Scaling even higher, as if that decision alone might prove my motives were pure as the driven snow.

"You want a medal?" Josie muttered.

"A little recognition would be nice," I smiled. She stuck out her tongue.

"Not happening, new girl."

We reached the top of the ladder and confirmed that we'd have to stand on the very top rung in order to reach the cross-joist.

On tippy toes.

After that, we could grasp hold of the beam and swing on. Getting down from the ceiling strut would be an even harder matter. But first things first.

One problem at a time, I supposed.

"We're out of view here." Josie muttered. "Spade should release our ruse and maintain his power. We might require it later."

"For what?" I wondered.

"For something on the way out. Something only a lie-guard can provide." She gestured vaguely. So for anything.

Anything at all.

"Hey," she tried to call down. Josie hissed. But neither boy's head turned upwards. "*Hey.*" She grew louder. The boys finally started to look, but their heads ratcheted back to earth when the clacking sound of professor shoes clattered on the marble floor. Someone was coming. There wasn't time to stall further. We needed off this ladder.

"I'm gonna go," I pressed forward.

This was my thing. My job. My one task. And my sixty per cent of the profits too. I'd go first and show how it was done. I stepped onto the top shelf of the ladder and firmly held the beam. I bear-hugged the wood and pushed off with my feet. Josie and the ladder swayed precariously, but I was too busy scrambling onto the joist to worry much about her. I sat up with the beam between my legs, like I was saddled on a horse.

"Oh, *wow.*" I groaned. "Don't look down."

The boys were small as ants. The ground seemed to rush beneath my feet. I pinched my eyes shut until the spinning room straightened.

"I can just do it alone," I offered. Josie shook her head.

"That's not how the safety net works." She jutted her chin at our rope.

Would it even work? I didn't ask. But I wondered.

"Besides, fate requires action," she muttered, climbing after. "I'll be good." Josie copied my moves, until she was death-gripping the beam between her own thighs. She looked both tough, and terrified. But the moment she accomplished the task, she wanted to keep going. "One more riser." She noted. The chemist did not slow down.

"Let's go."

We shimmied across the joist. There was actually quite a bit of structural woodwork in the rafters at this elevation. It was all painted to disappear into the skylight panes. We climbed across the largest beam, the one that cut across the full length of the floor. Sloane's long blonde strands blew in the open air. I tucked them away like I would with my own hair. It was just a short crawl into the middle of the room.

"We should stand here," I warned at the last crossbeam before the chandelier began. It would be much harder to get to our feet right under the light than it was here, safer on the sidelines.

"You stand," Josie said. "I'll crawl and anchor in case–"

We both looked down.

I didn't like the sound of that.

In case I fell to my doom?

With legs like jelly, I raised up to my feet and took a deep breath. While I didn't one hundred per cent recognize the body I was currently manipulating, I clung to my own inner strength. It might have looked like Sloane, but inside it was me. Persephone Dawn, and I always came through for myself in a pinch. I could do this too.

The chandelier was maybe ten feet away.

Ten feet across and a million stories up from the cold atrium floor where Spade and Bug were waiting. Fifteen steps, with nothing to hold onto but air.

You're fine, you're fine, you're fine, I repeated to myself.

"We can call it off," Josie/Marcy warned. She cocked her head, both sympathetic and curious at my choice. I shook her off and took my first step.

The building seemed to sway.

I crushed my eyes closed.

Adrenaline coursed through my veins.

Don't think about the fall. Just think about Lark.

It worked when I was climbing outside on the ledge.

Think about the vampire who'd claimed I wasn't up to this task.

I imagined the man without a shirt. Bare-chested for my gaze. Both arms over his head in a Chippendale's pose. I pictured him as dumb and as sexualized as I could, completely out of spite.

On the balance beam of death, I took another step.

I could make the imaginary vampire dance inside my mind. I compelled him with my thoughts. Made him come under my gaze and do whatever I wanted. Imaginary Chippendale Lark ground his body against an empty chair on a stage, rolling his abs, showing off his six-pack in a spotlight show. I smiled to myself and kept moving forward, as cool and calm as I could.

The real Lark had an incredibly symmetrical face. A sleek pointed nose. His jawline chiseled into his face like cut stone. His lower face was all strong chin and pink-purple lips. The top portion smoldered with dark lashes, raven claw crinkles and expressive brows. He controlled every element with steely blue eyes that saw everything. His black hair was wavy and curled.

The hair was thick, like I could really sink my hands into it.

I ignored the raunchy dance solo and imagined that now.

How it might feel. To really touch Lark.

To comb my fingers into his dark hair. To watch his eyes.

Step, step, step.

It was those raven claws that gave him character and style. He'd seen life as a twenty-five-year-old for over a hundred years. Nothing shocked him anymore, but I'd surprised him. That confident nonchalance made the butterflies in my stomach churn.

As I crossed the balance beam to the chandelier, I tried to go back to picturing the vampire shirtless, all rippled muscles and tanned torso, but whenever I tried to imagine lower than his throat, I became distracted by what was real. He was so beautiful.

Lark's neck was long and soft. His Adam's apple bobbed when he swallowed or paused. In great detail, I considered the cut of his jacket under his elegant jaw. I pictured the starched collar and lapels of his clothing, and his impeccable posture.

Step, step, step.

I was getting closer now.

One more time.

I pictured the vampire bodyguard fully clothed as my partner. *His shirt fell flat against his hard chest, his firm stomach, his strong core. Leading my path. His shirt sleeves always rolled up, like he was about to do serious work or get into trouble. By my side, invariably he did both. On his wrist, Lark clasped an expensive-looking watch that probably cost more money than everything that I owned. The car he'd leaned on and wrecked certainly did.*

With money like that the vampire didn't have a care in the world.

But of course, that was false.

Lark cared. And Lark tried to act. His primary desire right now was to obtain the Blood Stone. To stop it from falling into the wrong hands and changing the witches into fodder for the vampires. The man was altruistic to the core... unless... he had his own reasons for obtaining the binding rock. Reasons I didn't know.

That thought gave me pause.

I actually didn't know Lark that well. Was it wrong to believe him so good after such a short time? *I* wasn't that good. But he'd saved my life. *Twice.*

Still, those efforts could have been in support of an awful plan.

I shook off the fear and held onto the lust that I felt.

Stay with the heat, I instructed myself.

I wasn't sure I could handle anything else.

Not when I was so close.

Another two feet to cross.

More important than the timepiece Lark wore were his two limber hands. Calloused and strong, they were also tapered and well-cared for. All his fingernails were cut short. Veins appeared in the rippled skin anytime that Lark tensed. I wondered how those large hands would feel, entwined with my own. His strength on my soft skin. Holding me.

Keeping me warm. We could learn to trust. Learn where to touch. Learn how we each wanted to be desired and loved.

Step, step—

Suddenly, I grabbed a hold of the dangling chandelier. I'd made it across.

Nice work, Orphan Girl, imaginary Lark approved in my mind.

I blushed.

The insult he'd made of my past had turned into a term of endearment I liked.

And I really liked Lark.

I'll disrobe you on the walk back, I promised both the imaginary version of him and myself.

"You did it." Josie/Marcy said. It wasn't exactly praise. Merely a stated fact. But it seemed lighter coming from the mouth of Marcy, instead of Josie's actual tight frown. Still, her mind whirred two steps ahead. "The wings are there." She pointed to the central hub in the arms in the chandelier. The fixture's apex. It sat at an angle she could better see from her vantage nice and low on the beam. I nodded and took up a nearby spoke of the light.

"I can get it." I pulled the chandelier closer to where I stood. The crystals tinkled as the heavy weight moved. It was surprisingly large. Probably ten-times the size of the one in Child's office upstairs. I had to tug hard. The whole thing jangled like giant wind chimes. The crystal strands shifted like hourglass sands. Though I hadn't been rough, a few pieces jostled and broke. They snapped off and fell the long distance below. A glittering cloud of crystal jewels raining down.

"Careful," Josie/Marcy warned.

"I'm trying. Relax." I wondered if seeing Sloane's ethereal face instead of mine made Josie like the partner she was yoked to a little more, or a little less.

"Try *harder*," was all she said.

I pulled on the fixture again, swinging it up on its side to reach the central winged design. I grabbed the middle pole in my hands. It looked just like the one in my uncle's office.

"No." I hissed and sighed.

It was *exactly* like the one in my uncle's office. The waiting bauble was a simple black stone. I screwed it off, just to be sure, but looking up close only confirmed what I already knew.

The central piece in the structure was a sparkly bobble.

A glass marble.

A nothing.

I was washed with the embarrassment of failure. I'd interpreted the dream wrong. *Again.* I'd risked it all and put my friends in real danger, with nothing to show for it.

There was nothing to retrieve.

Nothing more to be done.

The Blood Stone wasn't there. And we weren't out of danger yet. That was the worst bit. Now a pair of limp fools, Josie and I would have to make our way back down the ladder and figure out another plan. With no hope and no point for all this danger and trouble. We couldn't retrieve the Blood Stone today. Perhaps we never could. My whole body felt spent.

"We were wrong," Josie said. She was gracious enough to include herself in the failing report.

"I'm sorry, I–" I shoved the shiny black ball into my pocket and let go of the fixture. The massive display shuddered and swung. The chandelier rotated too fast when it dropped from my hand and hit an opposite post. I should have been more careful, but I didn't much care. What was the point?

A fresh slew of crystals dropped.

Tinkling like piano keys on the floor.

The boys stared upwards and frowned.

But the final falling jewels were drowned out by an incoming sound.

A bell.

A murmur began. It rose down the halls. Footsteps flooded the foyer. Josie and I looked far below. The sounds grew, then erupted into the atrium where Spade, Bug and our ladder stood. Students poured out from every door. They zig-zagged across the floor.

"It's class change," Josie realized as the mass of students and teachers grew immeasurably. I stood and stared atop the post.

A silhouette of Sloane standing watch in the sky.

Josie/Marcy grabbed the safety rope between us and tugged it hard.

"Seph, get down!"

I clamped my hands around the joist just as Josie had done, two tiny bumps on the log. We were too far from the ladder to escape or climb down it. Our only choice was to wait the chaos out.

"Don't move," Josie warned.

I nodded and held on.

The pressure convulsed. Little ants streaming in lines. Hurrying to fulfill their next task. The hubbub moved students from class to class. Plenty of witches looked up. The ladder was like an arrow to the skies. But as long as no one saw us, they grew bored. We gripped the beam and made our bodies appear as small and as flat as we could. I stared at the fingernails of my hands. Sloane's hands. They were soft pink with fresh manicured tips, far more feminine than mine. I found a small peace staring at them. Until the vision sputtered and stopped.

What?

I looked up at Josie.

The visage of Marcy also flashed and broke.

I felt my hair. No longer platinum and long, it was back to my natural wild and red.

"You're you." I said.

Josie gritted her teeth. "Spade must be running out."

"Of what?"

"Of magic."

31
PERSEPHONE

"*Y*ou *can run out of magic?*" I asked.

"Of course. It's a source of energy. Like any power in this world. It runs weaker the longer you use it. Until you deplete it, then it all but disappears. He talks a good game." Josie shook her head.

"And then it's just *gone*?" I was horrified.

"Worse. It catches fire on the inside... and in the air... basically everywhere that you are. Your fingers will burn. It's a violent safeguard. The extirpation warns a witch that the end of the magic is coming. The field's used up. He hasn't practiced enough to maintain a ruse for this length," Josie realized. "We should have saved his strength."

We looked down at our boys. Indeed the tops of their hair styles were starting to stutter and show as well. Spade/Greg still gripped the side of the ladder. But now he appeared pained. Bug was definitely scared. They each remained as sentries at their posts.

Just hold on, I thought. *We'll come down and get you.*

Only...

"Look." I pointed at the stairwell that wrapped around the steampunk elevator. Clomping down the steps in a small group were the real Greg and Marcy. Tardy truants, unperturbed at the idea of running late to class. The group chattered loudly.

"Lady White is still missing, can you even imagine?" The thin willowy girl asked. From her blonde hair I guessed that's who I had been: Sloane Lolant.

Bug was right, she did look ethereal and calm.

Her hair seemed to float down her back as she walked.

"And now her parabond is missing too." The Indian boy said. Bug had been Tej.

"Fellow Egg," Greg guffawed. "Imagine having all the colors of the world available for your badass witch name and you chose the name *Egg*," Greg sniggered. "What a tool."

"You shouldn't speak ill of the dead," Sloane warned.

"You think?" Marcy gasped. Sloane merely shrugged.

"If history has anything to say about it," Tej darkly agreed. The teens considered the odds.

"Remember Lettie?" Marcy whispered to her man. I glanced at Josie. Did she know who they were talking about? Her expression didn't change. Marcy went on. "Oh, Greg. I wanna spend all my last moments with you."

"You got it, babe." They nuzzled each other.

"Get a room," Tej complained.

Instead of backing off their romance, this gave the couple an idea.

"We could skip Poly-Mag," Greg offered his girl.

Yes, go back up.

Marcy stopped on the stairs and looked back up the route they'd just come. "Tempting."

Yes, go back the way you came. Right now. Right now.

"No way," Tej shoved the goofy boy in the chest. "You're presenting with me on the underwater trade effects of the Stone

War on the mermaid coast in Political Magic," he complained. "You can't ditch, man. You swore. I need this grade." But Greg was fully ready to drop his friend for a romp with his mate.

"After school." Marcy winked. Greg hungrily grinned.

"They're on a collision course with Spade," Josie murmured.

"You mean second Greg and second Tej." I noted the boys still in their lie-guard wares.

"This is bad."

But what could we do?

Spade and Bug turned their backs and tried to shield their fake faces from the crowd.

"You boys, move that ladder," a nearby professor snapped. She marched right up. I recognized her, trying to facilitate traffic flow in the space. The Lady with the gray streak in her hair. The one who shooed me away the night of the Sundown. "What are you boys doing? Is someone up there?" She glared into the ceiling. Josie and I froze on the joist, out of sight, but the chandelier still ebbed and swayed, risking giving our location away. The witch shielded her eyes to better stare into the overhead light.

"No, ma'am," Bug/Tej said.

"Can't a guy just see how high he can climb?" Spade added way too much bravado, a total Greg answer. "You hold the legs." He made a show of offering her the position of spotter.

"Not on my watch." The teacher snatched him back down.

"But, but..." Spade/Greg pretended to protest. Each word bringing the real foursome of students closer at hand. Guaranteeing they'd be found out.

"Not too much," I warned from far away.

"Nevermind, the idea was silly," Bug agreed, glancing at the real group. Spade continued to ham it up.

"*Move on,* Spade," Josie willed our friends. "Get out, now."

I noted she was pulling a sleeping spell packet from the pocket in her pants and gently holding it. Ready to act. A magical recourse if things now went bad. I did the same.

"You will not climb to the heavens on my watch." The teacher snatched him back down again.

The real Greg and his crew reached the bottom of the stairs.

Get out of there, Spade.

"When I become a Fellow they're gonna call me Fellow Sex Knight," the real Greg declared. "That'll be my professor name."

"How's that a color?" Sloane wondered.

"Or one word?" Tej laughed.

"I like it," Marcy agreed.

"I knew you would."

Spade clocked the figures mere steps away.

"We'll put it back. Sorry, Lady Gray," he bowed out of the game. I was surprised he knew her name, but she frowned and nodded. Spade and Bug took down the ladder and scurried out the front door just as the real Greg, Marcy, Tej and Sloane passed under our perch.

That was too close.

As our boys stepped off the threshold of the atrium I saw them flash back to their real selves. Spade shook out his hand. His magic had started to burn.

"There goes our way out," I murmured, torn between relief for the guys and fear for myself. We'd been abandoned in the rafters. With no hope to get down.

"They'll come back. When the time is right," Josie said.

I didn't have the nerve to ask when that might be the case. I merely held on.

"Every Lady and Fellow is a *color*, Greg," Tej's conversation continued to float our way.

"Princess Gwendolyn doesn't worry about rainbow rules," Greg laughed, goosing his girl. "And nor does her man, Fellow Sex Knight!"

"Oooh, we'll be the most perfectest couple," she agreed, threading her arms around his waist.

"Those are the dumbest lady and professor names I've ever heard," Tej muttered.

"Everyone's free to chart their own course," Sloane lightly smiled. "Even love birds."

"*Greg*!" Lady Gray barked. She'd recrossed the atrium floor, and now marched straight at him. The couple pulled apart, surprised. "Where's that ladder?"

"What ladder?" He frowned.

"I just told you to put away a ladder." She glared at him. "Where is it?"

"When?"

"*Now*."

"*Now*, now?"

"Is there any other definition that might be clearer?" Her tone darkened. The boy changed his tactics as well.

"No, I got it. Do you see a ladder?" Greg finally asked. The others looked around.

"No," Lady Gray frowned.

"Then it must be away." Greg grinned. "I think we're square."

Lady Gray pointedly looked at her watch. "Well, get to class!"

"Coven teachers can be so weird," Greg shook his head as the foursome hurried out.

Josie and I exchanged a glance. The academy attendance thinned down to a trickle, as the changeover timing expired between periods. I closed my eyes. Good.

"The boys are safe," Josie said.

"What about us?" I asked.

Namely, how would we get down?

We waited, hoping an answer would appear. Instead, we were revisited by Lady Gray.

"He had the ladder right here." The professor's voice echoed in the empty hall. Lady Gray marched back in leading Fellow Gold. Today, the leader of the coven was dressed in a white tracksuit and gold shirt. He walked stiffly with a third man.

Not in white, I noted.

The new man was in his thirties, buff, and casual. He wore dark jeans and a t-shirt rolled at both sleeves. His head was smooth and bald, his chin styled with short-trimmed scruff. His teeth were sparkling white compared to his dark beard and tanned skin. They were his best asset. He knew it too. You had to earn a smile from him.

The Lady pointed at the air and also showed them the debris scuttled across the floor. Multiple chandelier crystals and threads. Evidence of where we now hid. Details the professor had come to suspect. The new threesome picked up the discarded jewels, piecing together their origin story from the hanging chandelier. Josie watched all the strangers with equal trepidation, but my gaze remained solely on the last man.

His posture and presence were reminiscent of Lark. Upright and firm. He seemed to observe everything at once. His chiseled face quickly became cut into a frown. He had dark eyes. Raven claws crinkled his gaze.

Vampire.

And not just any vampire. A daywalker, like Lark. The sun was still high in the sky.

The man's intense scrutiny rose up from the floor and looked to the overhead light.

"Could it possibly be here?" The vampire asked.

I didn't recognize him from the other night, this was someone new. *Someone even more scary?* My gut warned. Someone smarter than the minions he'd sent to Child's office and home on the other days of their hunt.

"Child wouldn't be fool enough–"

The vamp cut Gold off. "You said the girl was obsessed with this light?"

"The chandelier, yes, the one upstairs. But who knows what these kids do. It might have been a prank, the ladder here too."

"She's not one of your wayward students. She's a *Child*." The vampire said my uncle's proper name. "And she's partnered with Lark." He emphasized the letter k with disdain.

Hearing my vampire's name in this enemy's mouth gave me chills.

"They've been two steps ahead this whole time. But we're catching up," the vampire murmured.

More than he realized, I feared.

It was only a matter of time before he found Josie and I stranded in the joists.

"Who is that?" Josie whispered.

"I have no clue," I confessed. "But we've got to get out of here... *now*."

32
PERSEPHONE

Our obvious need to escape the rafters was easy to say but impossible to do. After all, we didn't have a ladder to climb down and there was nowhere to go on the beams. All we could do was to hide and lay still.

Or use Josie's magic.

She thought of it first.

"We need for them to come closer," she said, palming her baggie of sleeping spell. "Group them together." The three were spread over the scene, taking in more details.

I focused on him. The vampire.

Who was that man? He seemed powerful. Dangerous.

Sunlight streamed in from the overhead skylight. It was mid-afternoon. So much for our assumption that acting in daylight would keep us safe from their fangs. Other vampires could daywalk too. Just like Lark. Could he even swoop in to help? Lark hadn't been able to enter the academy before. But *this* vampire had Fellow Gold do his commands. The leader of the High Council coughed a little and sat slumped on a couch.

The sleeping powder was our best and only viable choice.

"I can drop this," I offered, showing Josie the black jewel I'd taken from the center of the chandelier. "If it bounces here..."

"Do it," Josie agreed. We prepped the two magic sleeping potion bags without making a sound.

"What do you think happened?" Lady Gray asked the man in charge.

"We'll find out soon enough," he growled. "Get a ladder."

"I don't know where the boys took the one I removed," the professor admitted.

Good. Spade and Bug took the ladder with them back into the forest when they left.

"Then get another one, *fool*." The vampire snarled. Lady Gray looked to Fellow Gold, unsure, but he was no help, a sniveling, worrying version of himself. "I am your leader now." The vampire growled. He stared intensely into Lady Gray's eyes. She balked, then softened under his gaze.

"Yes, sir." She answered. The teacher was compelled.

"Get me a ladder, now." He let his tone soften. No further need to boss her around. She ran from the room. "Oh, what a bore." He looked skyward. "Where'd you put it, Child?"

"If you can't get them all, just get that guy," I told Josie, pointing him out. She'd had the same idea, I was sure. "Ready?"

"Do it, Seph."

I dropped the little black ball. It soared to the floor three stories down and hit the marble stone with a ringing bounce. The ball rebounded once, twice, then rolled, making an exaggerated whirring sound.

The only motion in the whole world.

Gold stared.

The vampire perked up.

He walked a few steps forward. Then stared up to the rafters.

"*Closer*, you night of the living dead." Josie waited for him to walk under her crosshairs.

"That's good enough," I squirmed. She shook her head.

The vampire stopped. Still out of range.

"*I. See. You.*" He called up to the rafters. His voice a dangerous song. Josie and I gulped. "Little girls, trapped like mice overhead. Did you get the stone? My stone? Is it now in your hands?" He practically purred.

I put my head against the wood and concentrated on my own heart. It now beat out of my chest. A tingle filled my mind, but I fought the enticement off, keeping control of my own brain. Josie clenched her eyes closed trying to fight the compulsion as well.

"*Answer me, girl!*" The vampire roared. His anger filled up the space.

"No," Josie whimpered.

"Josie," I hissed. "Stop."

"*What?*" He barked.

"No!" She called out, louder now.

"*No?!*" He laughed. "You don't have it?"

"We don't have it."

"So all this was for not?"

"Yes," Josie answered.

"Josie, stop," I whimpered. Her eyes were big, glassy balls. Completely compelled. I grabbed the two baggies of spells from her hands and shoved them into my pockets to make sure she didn't use them or lose them somehow under the vampire's command. The monster controlled her, just as he manipulated Lady Gray, who'd come back into the hall with a ladder. Neither of them were under free will. The vampire had no qualms invading everyone's brains.

Everyone's but mine.

Because I still had a chain of Electrum around my throat.

"Who are you working for, girl?" The vampire asked.

Josie's face screwed up. She tried to fight the questions. She looked pained.

"Little witch?" He asked the beams.

I put my finger to my lips, trying to keep her shushed, but Josie spit out the words.

"I'm working for myself!"

True. I was the one working for Mauve, not Josie. But he didn't like the answer.

"*Who are you working for?!*" The vampire's anger rattled the walls.

"Me! Myself!" Josie yelled back down, growing more agitated as well. Mood for mood.

"Easy, Jo." I warned her.

"Sit up." The vampire said.

"No, don't."

Josie raised.

"There you are. Are you alone?" The vampire asked.

My look pleaded with her.

But Josie said. "No."

"Answer me, second little witch." The vampire said.

I stared at her.

He didn't know I had Electrum on and could not be compelled. Perhaps I could use that to my advantage.

"I'm here." I sat up. He grinned ear to ear.

"So you are. Who do *you* work for?" He asked. I tried to mirror Josie's dead affect.

"Myself." I held my breath.

"Dangle your feet over the ledge, girls," the vampire ordered. Josie robotically did what she was told. I followed suit.

"We are tied together," I whispered to Josie. "If he tells you to jump you cannot listen."

"I won't," Josie agreed. But the power of the vampire's mind-control would be too much for her, I knew.

"Now..." he relished the moment. "Fall."

Josie immediately moved, about to push off the joist.

"No!" I screamed and tackled her to the beam. She struggled to get free from me, eager to leap to her own death and mine. "Josie, *stop*," I wrestled with her.

"I'm *wai-ting*," the vampire called from below.

The black-haired girl shoved me hard.

"No." I clung on for dear life. "We'll both die."

We grappled on the balance beam.

"Here." I endeavored to take her hand. I shoved her fingers onto the pink-gold chain on my neck. "Hold on, hold on." I pressed her fingers onto the metal. As soon as she held the Electrum, her black eyes cleared.

"*JUMP!*" The vampire roared.

"*What, are you out of your mind?*" Josie shouted right back.

"Get them," the vampire said, low and calm. Lady Gray had come back with several other witch instructors. All carried ladders they'd set up under our spot. Now they stared up at the joists. "*I said move!*" He roared. The compelled professors climbed on command.

"We have to both hold this," I said, undoing the necklace and offering half to her, careful the special metal also didn't leave contact with my skin. "It's the only way to resist."

Josie took her half. "What do we do now?"

Four Ladies and Fellows were coming to get us while the vampire leader waited on the floor. Fellow Gold merely fretted on the couch.

"I can't watch this," he complained, but instead of helping, the leader of the coven up and left.

He left!

Psssssst.

We heard a strange sound. Like air letting out of a tire. It came from my right. I turned and noticed something moving, high on the wall. Perpendicular to where we gripped onto the joist, a grate came off its screws in the wall and opened like a door. It was an air shaft.

Someone crouched in the dark tunnel.

Spade? Bug?

But it wasn't the boys.

Lark?! No.

Lady Blue Moon, the paper master, was there, careful to stay in the shadows, silently waving a hand, gesturing for us to worm our way to her. We could exit that way. Over a dangerous, two-by-four rafter escape route. A risk no normal person would take. Still, nothing felt normal today.

We shimmied forward.

"One way or another, *we'll get you down*," the vampire taunted. His witches climbed. To get out, we would need to move faster. The moment the vamp realized where we were headed, he could send more compelled minions to catch us in the halls, or lock the doors of the school. He would trap us again. Blue Moon knew it too.

"You have to run," she hissed.

"It's too dangerous." Josie said.

"No, it's not. I cast a safety spell, you can't fall," Blue Moon said. Josie and I looked at each other. The climbing Ladies and Fellows had almost reached the first beam.

"Just a bit more," the vampire laughed.

There was no other choice.

"We can do it," I told her. "Come on." I stood first, Josie right behind me, the thin gold necklace shared between our hands, a second tether like the one around our waists. We scurried across the narrow balance beam.

"Where are you going, ladies?" The vampire wondered.

At first he must've thought we were squirreling away from his foursome of witches, but when he saw the small, open grate in the far wall, his whole demeanor changed. "No. *No!*"

We raced across the two-by-four. It was so narrow, half of my sneaker didn't land with each step.

"Josie, we can do this."

"You're gonna make it, you're so close," Blue Moon encouraged.

"Fall!" The vampire roared. That's when Josie slipped.

Ahhhh! The chemist screamed, her hand pulled away from my chain.

Josie dropped. The heavy tug of our tether yanked on my waist. I flew out of control. I hit the wood two-by-four hard, but fell on the other side of the board. Each of us dangled from the safety rope tethered between our two waists. Amazingly, the harnesses held.

Three cheers for safety equipment.

We spun, amazed and dazed in the air.

"Get them!" The vamp laughed. "Cut them down out of the sky."

The teachers who'd almost arrived at the joists climbed back down and raced their ladders to where we wildly swung. We were rag dolls, saved, but also trapped by our safety chain on either side of the beam.

There was no way to climb up.

Or maneuver down.

We were stuck.

Above us, the two-by-four beam groaned under our heft. Round and round I twisted and spun. The ground seemed to lurch up beneath my dangling shoes. I looked at the Electrum necklace, solely in my hands, none of its power transferred to Josie anymore.

"*Climb,*" Blue Moon warned. "You have to keep moving, girls."

"I can't," I said. I had little upper body strength. But Josie moved. She changed her body posture and started to climb up her side of the rope. Knees, feet and arms, leaving me carrying all the gravity and weight between the two.

"There was never a safety spell," I realized.

Blue Moon looked guilty as hell. "I'm sorry, no, it doesn't exist. I just thought it would help you to get here if you believed that you could."

"You miscalculated," Josie grimly said. She struggled to get back on the two-by-four and dropped. Struggled again. I hung helpless underneath. She managed one hand, then a leg. The girl strong-armed herself back onto the joist through sheer will.

What a bad-ass witch.

"Just hold on," Josie warned. She began to use her own weight as a leverage to pull me up too, leaning far back on the other side of the wood. It worked. Sort of.

"Stop," the vampire ordered her.

Josie immediately paused. I dropped, as the four witches came with ladders again.

"Josie, don't listen. You have to fight him off," I told her, holding the Electrum out. She couldn't reach it above me, kneeling on the two-by-four.

"She can't fight." The vampire smiled. He strolled towards our helpless location, a delighted smile on his face. His raven claws dug deep lines around his eyes. While they made Lark appear beautiful, this vampire's passion made him cruel. He was excited to cause me more pain. "Don't you understand Little Child? She's entranced by my voice. Aren't you, love? They all are. Blow me a kiss," the vampire ordered. Everyone in the room except Blue Moon and I raised their fingers to their lips and air-kissed his way. The vampire pretended to catch all the sentiments in his own hands.

"*Mwah, mwah.*" He air-kissed them back. Then his eyes darkened. "See?" In another light, he may have looked handsome, but today all that was left on his expression was cruelty. "She may not like it, but she's going to obey me when I say this next thing. You're not gonna like it, either," he taunted. His voice grew cold. "*Saw through the damn rope.*"

Josie stood up, leaned back and used the pressure of my weight to drag the safety harness against the rough edge of wood. Over and over. The tension rubbed on the rope. It stripped down the strands. The braiding groaned and frayed.

"Josie, *no.*" I begged.

"Josie, yes!" The vampire clapped in glee. Happy to watch me squirm. He stepped closer to have the best view. Josie rip-pulled our harness again. I glanced down at him in fear, then up to her.

"Here. Take my charm," I told her.

We had to get her out of his spell.

Break the compulsion with my Electrum. That was our best chance.

"Ready? It's coming."

Argh! I threw the necklace up to her. Josie tried to catch it but missed. My throw was bad. The jewelry arched up in the air, then fell down to the floor directly under me. As soon as the moment passed, Josie bared down with all her weight. She'd snap the cord bristle-by-bristle, if that's what it took. I was totally helpless. And now susceptible to compulsion myself. Plus, if I tried to fight back or pull free of the harness now, I'd probably yank her down too. Then we'd both plunge to our deaths. I stared at my chain on the floor, totally dismayed. I reached for it, as if it was possible to grab my mistake from three floors away.

"What do we have here?" The vampire cooed. He trotted under where I was trapped and picked up my necklace with his hands. He tut-tutted, showing me his fangs. "Bad move giving this up."

"Actually, it worked just as I planned." I dug into my pocket, grabbed one of the sleeping potion baggies and dumped it over the vampire's head.

"*Stop*! Foolish girl–," was all he managed before the chemicals took hold and the monster collapsed on the floor's stone slab. All around him the compelled witches froze, holding true to his last command.

Stop. He said to stop.

But Josie kept working the rope.

"Josie, he's gone. He's asleep." I said, but she didn't falter. "You don't have to do this." Desperation crept into my voice.

"Yes, I do." Josie strained against herself to no avail. She gritted her teeth and pulled and pulled. "The compulsion's still there. I have to cut the rope. I'm sorry, Seph."

"I don't understand."

"I don't think she sees herself as foolish, so the vampire's final command had no effect over her. She's trapped in his earlier instruction," Blue Moon worried.

"The one that will make me plunge to my doom?"

"Precisely, yes."

Snap, snap.

The ropes splintered again. Almost through.

"What do we do?" I asked Blue Moon.

"I have a ring..." Blue Moon said. But she doubtfully looked down at the same impossible route we'd tried to pass.

"Get it out to her," I begged. Blue Moon tried to step towards us, but froze. She shook her head. "You need to fight it." I ordered Josie. "Break the compulsion."

"I can't." Josie grunted. "*I can't!*" She raged against her own hands. But no matter what she tried, she could not reel them in.

"Don't fight it directly. Do whatever you can," Lady Blue Moon tried to coach from the grate. She tried to reach as far as she could from the sideline. "Apply his instruction in another way that would benefit us. Think about–." But Josie continued to split the strands.

"–I'm sorry. I don't know how."

Snap.

A big thread of tension broke, the whole safety rig groaned. It shuddered. My body swung. The harness would give out any second. There was no way I'd survive a multi-story drop. And Bug wasn't here to rush in with insects this time.

"Fight it, *please*. Jo. With whatever you have."

"Take the ring, here!" Blue Moon leaned and leaned.

Tears streamed down my partner's face.

"I'm trying," she said. "I can't!" But no matter the effort, she couldn't get control of her hands or break the compulsion in her brain. We were down to the very last cord.

"I'm sorry, Persephone. I was starting to like you." Josie made the last thrust.

Snap.

The tension broke.

I screamed as the rope cut clean through.

And Josie completed her task.

33
PERSEPHONE

"Hold on!" Lady Blue Moon dove out of the air shaft she was hiding in. She grabbed my broken half of the rope. The whole thing tugged horribly on my waist. The witch slammed her body against the two-by-four, desperately holding on. But she wasn't strong. Or brave. Her life had been devoted to the pushing of paper, not lifting weights. And my heft proved too much. She barely saved her own stance from tumbling down from the ceiling. "I've got you," she hoped.

It was a lie.

I gasped at the brief reprieve and the fresh danger it brought.

The rope dragged in the paper master's fingers.

She couldn't hold on.

"Don't–" my plea was cut off. "*Oh, god.*" I swung precariously, dropping further. "Don't let go!"

"*I'm trying!*"

The words jarred Josie out of her shock.

Now that the rope was severed, she'd completed her vampiric task. Any need to follow his commands dispersed on the wind. The chemist was free to act. Josie grabbed my dangling rope beside Blue Moon and each pulled with both hands. They strained. It took the women both of their full, collective weights to pull me back up. But they did it.

Inch by inch.

"We've got you," Josie said as they finally grabbed onto my limbs.

"Thank you," I panted. They yanked me onto the two-by-four, shoulders first. My fingers glommed onto the beam, gaining splinters in my palms. I didn't care. I held on for dear life.

Wood had never felt so good or so safe.

But there was no time to rest.

Blue Moon looked at the other Ladies in the room, blinking dumbly, waiting for their compulsions to release.

"Come on." She crawled back across the beam and into the air shaft vent. It wasn't elegant or quick but it got the job done. We followed at her safe, careful pace. "I knew, as soon as I saw Gray trying to round up the others, that something was happening. *And Gold was here?* Thank goodness for this," she showed us her Electrum ring, a thin twist of pink-gold that she'd tried to lend Josie on the rig. "It's a family heirloom."

We shimmied along the air duct until we came out in a janitor's closet on the third floor of the school. When we dropped into the small space, the paper master's white track suit was dirty brown at the elbows and knees and covered with grime. She stripped off her sweatshirt, and threw the dirty sweater over my shoulders, straightening my hair under the lit lightbulb overhead.

"This looks terrible," she worried. "No one would believe. Oh well. Here." She also handed Josie an overcoat and me a hat that was hanging on the back of the door. Some man's work clothes. "They'll know I helped you." She frowned. "They're probably already aware. And, oh gosh, oh no." While she'd been forced into action in the heat of the moment, the paper master unravelled now. Her hands shook, the adrenaline too much for her.

"It's alright." Josie said, she put the wardrobe on, I donned the hat. "Thank you for your help." They were pathetic disguises of who we actually were, but it didn't matter much now. The dramatic chandelier heist or whatever it was would be gossip all over the school by the end-of-day bell.

Josie opened the door and checked the hall.

"It's clear." She waved us both out. Lady Blue Moon immediately followed. There was no one around. "We need to keep moving." Josie ordered. She led us another way, down an internal staircase. We could slip right out the door, but I grabbed their arms.

"No, wait. My mother's necklace," I realized.

"There's no time," Josie said.

"*Yes*, there is." I frowned. "There has to be."

It wasn't sentimentality that made me pause. The chain was a valuable tool, the only defense we had against the powerful vamp's cruel will. I wouldn't leave it behind.

"Can I borrow your ring?" I asked. Blue Moon handed it over. Just in case. "I need to, Jo."

"Persephone, no." She objected, but I was already gone.

The women stopped in the doorway as I hurried across the hall.

The atrium was still frozen in the scene we'd observed from above. The vicious vampire slept in a collapsed pile on the floor, his witch cronies perched atop ladders, stuck in mid-air, following his last command to stay where they were. I wondered when, if ever, it would wear off.

I pulled the bill of my hat down, trying to protect my identity, or at least make it difficult to describe my appearance. Everyone seemed to know who I was.

The helpless witches watched from their roosts as I crouch-jogged across the floor to retrieve what was mine. Josie and Blue Moon hid just outside of the hall. On the way, I saw the fruitless black stone from the chandelier display. I snatched it up. Then I swooped down to retrieve my pink-gold chain near the vamp. It felt warm in my palm. I attached the clasp back around my neck and was about to run out, when suddenly, the vampire grabbed my ankle with his hand. His fingers were strong and hard.

"Stay," he hissed. Still half-drugged. He looked even more terrifying up close. All beauty and cruelty and ancient power. But his compulsion held no weight in my brain.

"You are not in control," I growled back, the Electrum safely around my neck.

This was only half-true.

The vampire couldn't take command of my mind, but he did have my limb.

His grasp was strong.

An immortal strength, holding me, stuck to the floor.

He knew it too. The bald vampire stared up with a lazy smile. Stalling until the rest of his body awoke from the chemist's sleeping spell.

"What's your rush?" He asked. I could see now, the intense shaved hairstyle was a manicured choice. All of it was. He was a calculated killer, with no need to rein his vile impulses in. I had to get out of there. *Now.*

I tried to kick the foot he held. I'd kick him right in the face if it helped. My attempt made him smile. A flexed foot he controlled. He stared up at me, trying to bore into my brain.

"I hear you've been running around with the birds... you think Lark's your friend? Maybe your mate?" He spit out the word, reading my face. I didn't flinch. I'd never thought that we could permanently pair, but I tried to keep my secrets buried inside.

I could stomp this guy with the other foot, I thought.

Kick in his pointy teeth, then he'd let me go.

"You're drawn to him, I understand." More awareness was

coming back to the vampire's frame. His body was waking up. "He's handsome and rogue. Almost as charming as me."

I'd get only one move.

This time, I had to make sure the kick made his fingers release.

Hit his stomach, perhaps?

In humans, attacking that soft, fleshy part made us buckle and gasp...

Or between his legs. If I could kick the vamp in the balls...

"*Listen to me.*" He flexed his strength, squeezing my ankle.

I winced at the sharp pain. My limb ached.

The vampire returned to his charm offensive.

"You should know, *Little Child*, he only wants the stone. He'll kill you in the end. They always do," the vampire warned. "In our world, good guys don't exist."

"So, what? You thought you'd save him a chore?" I sweetly asked.

"Something like that." He predatorily smiled. "I'll be your friend if you like."

"I think I'll pass." I raised my foot as if I were to strike, bringing his attention low. He prepared. "Sleep tight." Instead, I whipped out the second baggie of sleeping potion from my pocket and dumped it onto his head. The chemicals knocked him right out. He thudded hard to the floor and I wrenched his iron grasp from my calf.

The witches above all stared as I raced back to the two women waiting in the hall. Both Josie and Blue Moon were dumbstruck at what they saw.

I'd faced the terrible vampire close up and lived.

"I got my necklace," I said the obvious part. Handing back Blue Moon's ring. "And we need more sleeping spells."

"No shit," Josie agreed, still amazed.

We ran through the school, and out into the field to find Bug and Spade, and escape the witch school once and for all.

The Blood Stone still not in our grasp.

34
PERSEPHONE

The paper master's hands were shaking so badly when we tried to enter the old, converted farmhouse, I took the key from her to insert into the lock and open the door. Everyone followed in. Lady Blue Moon went straight into an office to work. The rest of us explored. Foyer, file room, bathroom, small kitchen, a dining room with a work table and conference chairs and a central stairway leading upstairs.

"What is this place?" I wondered.

"The Konya Thomas Collection," Blue Moon said, taking refuge and comfort behind a computer screen with piles of paperwork on every side. Here, she deftly thumbed through files and made computer drives whir, in her element again. "A specialized High Council document hub. There are three like it, on the outskirts of town." She pointed north and south.

Spade frowned. "It's now a hideout." He lowered the blinds on the windows and pulled drapes across. Blue Moon seemed to brush the statement off, in her own world.

"You'll be safe here for a while."

"Will we?" He sneered, peeking outside. Our official bodyguard since we'd reunited in the woods. The fellas had been hiding in the bushes next to the ladder, which they'd covered in bugs and leaves for a natural camouflage. Spade was favoring his right palm, holding it close. Although he hadn't admitted to anything, Josie was right in her earlier assumptions; Spade's power had been all but sapped in our attempted robbery at the school. He would need prolonged rest before he'd try to perform magic or create any new lie-guard.

Unfortunately, rest and safety were no longer real options for our group.

Guilt washed over me.

Our incognito mission had become very public.

That was nobody's fault, but it still wasn't good.

"There are cameras right there," she pointed to the lobby entry. Then her computer "But it's an in-house feed. I can delete it. No one will know you were here."

"Who owns this house?" I asked, checking the doorframe. Blue Moon looked up, surprised at the purpose in my voice.

"I just told you–"

"–vampires can only enter a private residence if the owner agrees." I told her.

"That's right," she replied. "I don't know. Your uncle did, I suppose... now, Fellow Gold? It's all the property of the Council, but like I told you, no one comes here. It's just me and the paper-work. We're happy left alone." She offered a sad smile. "We were."

"I'm sorry you had to help us," I told her.

"I'm not," she said, slightly prouder. "Changes are coming to the witch world." She darkly sighed.

"We can't stay." Josie said what we all knew in our hearts."Not overnight. If Gold's in charge? He's with them. And we're not going back to our own homes. They likely now know who we all are. I met Gray before, so did Spade, and when they put it together, they'll figure out you." She pointed at Bug. "You're always at the bookstore."

"Oh. Sorry about that."

They? I stared at the girl. *Who was they?* Did she mean the vampires? Or the angry coven who now knew we'd broken into their school?

"We didn't even get the Stone!" Bug complained.

"You just held a ladder," Spade snarked.

"So did you," he pouted.

"I also did magic."

"That was my job," Bug frowned.

"And you did it well," I cut into the fray before Spade could reply again. I glared at them both. There was no need to fight.

"What was the point?" Spade groused. I agreed, collapsing in a chair. We'd all been so busy, risking our lives. For what?

For some inheritance?

For an ancient spell?

All these witch and vampire problems weren't a part of my life before that damned letter arrived at my door. I wished for the millionth time that the paper master, the vampire, and the old witch had left me alone. I was doing just fine on my own. I hadn't cared or wanted to learn about the family who'd rejected me. I didn't long to know about the mother who'd cast me aside. She was nobody and nothing and I was content. I'd been good.

"Mauve shoulda just got the damn rock on her own," Spade muttered.

"Yeah, and left me out of it," I agreed.

"She can't." Blue Moon quietly said. We all turned. "A binding rock can only be yielded by the person it's tied to, or the remains of their bloodline." She nodded my way. Child's living relative. "Mauve could never have taken the Blood Stone without your help. You'd have to give it to her, or its magic protections would kill her. The vampires know that too. That's why Mauve and Lark want you to find it, or the vamps want to kill you and take it for themselves."

"Of course." I slumped.

This just kept getting worse.

"What? And you knew?!" Spade spun on me.

"I didn't!" I returned, but Spade was now on a roll.

"What if *I* had grabbed it, Persephone?! Or *Jo*?"

"*No!*" Bug's face went ashen in horror, his lips gaped. "*Oh my gosh*! Don't touch it, Josie."

"It's alright," Josie frowned at the men. "I'm fine. *I'm fine.*" She calmed them both down. "So are you. Nobody touched anything." Then she turned to the paper master. "What do the vampires want with it? If they can't behold it or yield its power?"

"They can." I realized. "They'll kill me to be sure, but they can try to take it themselves. The threat of death isn't really a threat if you're no longer alive."

Blue Moon nodded. "That's what Mauve thinks too. But it's a weapon, for sure. For a while now, the Crimson Flood and the High Council have sensed a new faction, an opposing vampire army, intent on growing their numbers. They were handling it in-house, building new weapons of their own, but with Child gone, there's a dangerous power imbalance in the coven that will need to be filled. New deals. Tentative bargains."

A whole magical underworld.

"Well, who are they?" Bug asked. "The other faction."

"Does it matter?" Spade snapped.

"Of course it matters. Classification and genus. Names give us order," Bug said. "There's the Flood and–"

"Blackrose," Blue Moon murmured. "He might be the vampire who runs it. Dreven Blackrose. Some people at the Council have taken to calling them the Brotherhood of Thorns. You met him today."

See, Bug's plaintive stare seemed to say.

Spade looked skyward, biting his tongue. "Super glad you rolled me into this, Jo," he muttered but she remained undeterred.

"Seph faced the leader of a vampire army and won?" She asked.

"I didn't win. We almost died. *Twice*. I only put him to sleep thanks to your spells. So if anyone deserves the credit, it's you."

"He wasn't looking for a fight, it was probably a routine meeting with Gold. We caught him unaware and alone," Blue Moon agreed. "Don't expect it to happen again."

"I won't." I agreed.

"Where can we learn more?" Josie asked.

"Come." Blue Moon left her office and took us upstairs into a bursting file room with wall-to-wall shelves on heavy rollers. Every bedroom on the second floor of the house had been repurposed for files. The space was crammed from floor to ceiling with organized folders and envelopes. The rolling shelves let the paper master cram in two more double-sided rows. I stared at the decades worth of documents.

Bug gulped. "That's a lotta—"

"Classification and genus," Spade echoed his terms.

"I was gonna say paperwork."

"The history of the coven is here," Blue Moon ignored his tone. She took us down the rabbit hole. "Look." The paper master rotated the crank, pushing a file system away and revealing another row. "We're digitizing now, but it will take time."

More of the same.

Hundreds of paper documents with labels and filenames. She slid into the stacks to retrieve the information she sought then quickly brought the folders back. On the table, she opened the file: paperwork, lists of names, medical documents and old photographs of handsome men in costume dress. They stood together in a group, all with dark stares. There were several women too. It was the females' extravagant hairstyles and petticoats that set the timeline for me, elaborate period dress, but the wardrobes weren't play acting. The photograph was legitimately old. The people pictured were likely dead and gone with age.

Or dead. But not gone.

The man who'd hunted us in the atrium that morning stood in the center of the group. Then with a trimmed black afro under a bowler hat. But it was him. Dreven Blackrose. Same facial hair. He looked just the same.

"These are some of the members of the Crimson Flood. The only group photo that I know of," Blue Moon explained. There were several printed copies and negatives in the file. All identical. "They're an organization of vampires who wish their undead presence and the influx of witch magic in the realm to remain undetected in the greater human world. Kind of like a paranormal police."

"Except they make their own rules," Spade muttered.

"Are they the good guys?" Bug asked.

I remembered back to Dreven's words.

There are no good guys.

"It's complicated." Blue Moon said, "the Flood want to hide their vampiric numbers. Like the witch hunts at the turn of the last century, the Flood believe bringing attention to magical powers, special beings, and paranormal undercurrents is too dangerous and troublesome to contain. They decided years ago they'd prefer to move in the shadows, hunt rather than be hunted, control over being controlled. They've maintained a sort of status quo in secret. Setting bargains and partnerships with witches and others."

"But that's him." I pointed back to the dangerous vamp. "He's in the Flood?"

"Blackrose was one of them... *then*. But he broke off. And this new group he's creating has no respect for their old laws. They want to increase in numbers. To overtake and overthrow. Instead of hiding, they're insistent on fighting. Showing off their true power. Blackrose tried it once before with smaller numbers, twenty-five years ago, but it didn't work. At least that's the wives' tale." Blue Moon would have been ten years old, maybe fifteen when that happened, so she didn't experience it much firsthand. "To do what they want to accomplish, the vampires need a dark army. If the Blood Stone causes every witch in Plumpkin to become a witch blood and then the Brotherhood sucks their blood, the vampire numbers will explode. They could control the whole town. Maybe more."

"That includes witches who aren't in the coven, like us," Josie murmured. "We'll be just as susceptible to their plan."

"That's not good," Bug said. "So the Flood's our hope."

"No, Persephone can save us," Josie said. She spoke of me like I was some goddamn super hero. "How do we meet with the Crimson Flood?" She asked. Blue Moon stared at her.

"You don't. They're a very private group."

"Lark?" I guessed.

"He might reach them, yes."

"He might also kill you," Josie quietly warned. I stared at her. "You heard her. There are no good vamps."

"Technically, she said that it's complicated, which isn't quite an affirmation or a negation," Bug pointed out.

"Well, I don't care. Let Lady Mauve deal with your murder boyfriend and the politics, Seph." Spade tossed the picture on the table. "We're done."

But I couldn't stand by and hope it worked out. "What other information do you have about the Stone?" I asked.

"There's not much. Nobody asks me to file the secret location of their magical artifacts," Blue Moon tried to joke. It fell flat. "There might be something here," she offered, moving on to the next room. The others followed. I was about to join them, but the photograph on the table stopped me. It kept me. I stared at it.

Dreven wasn't the only man pictured whom I recognized.

Another leaned against the wooden fence behind the lot. Real casual-like. He rested his butt back, one knee up on a horse trough, chest slightly concave, his arms crossed, sleeves rolled up showing forearms and strength. He looked at the camera with a bored stare. I'd know him anywhere.

Lark.

He was there.

The vampire stood in a photo from a hundred years ago.

Lark was there.

Lark was part of the Crimson Flood. Possibly a founding member.

My vampire told me to get out, I realized. To leave town. After our run-in on our first attempt to gain the binding rock. He knew. He'd said that the inheritance would cost me too much.

Get out of my town! He'd said.

He was right. I should have listened. I should probably listen now.

"I understand your point, but I want to help," I told the old blurry picture.

"Seph!" Josie barked from the other room, breaking into my reverie. Bug ran back to the doorway and hugged the frame, puffing.

"This isn't good. You should come."

I pocketed one of the copies of the old photo and followed the insect witch into the next room full of stacks.

"I don't understand–" Blue Moon was checking a new pile of paperwork. "*No, no, no.* This isn't happening." The paper master was freaking out, but nothing appeared to be wrong. I glanced at the other two.

"This was in the wrong spot. And that folder was bent." Josie filled me in.

It was a greenish-gray folder in question, similar to a thousand other files on a mountain of shelves. There were only a few papers inside. I barely noticed a wrinkle.

"*I put everything away.*" She vented. "*Always.* I'm meticulous. Look at this!" She gestured. I squinted at the small indent on a folder. The paper master was totally incensed.

"What are you saying? Someone was here?" I asked.

"*Yes!*"

"You said no one ever came here." I frowned.

"You said we'd be safe," Spade piled on.

"Someone was here. They came. Without me. And they put everything back in the wrong spot," Blue Moon wailed. She checked more and more files, looking for even more flaws.

"What did they touch?" I asked.

"*This.*" She shoved the paperwork on the table.

"Where did you find her?" Spade spun a finger beside his head, giving the universal gesture for someone who'd gone nuts. But I understood. This was terrible news. If whomever had come to the file room had only moved a few things, they were hunting for something. Something very specific. And the contents they'd touched should be examined for clues. It was a *big deal*.

"What does it say?" I asked. We opened the file. Blue Moon checked. She made quick work of the notations and paperwork.

"It's old receipts. From the architecture and blueprint days of the High Council Academy being remodelled. Lumber orders. Look, the skylights are here. This is tables and chairs for the dining hall area... the chandelier." We all straightened at that.

"Still think that she's nuts?" Josie snarked at Spade.

"Time will tell." He refused to concede.

But Blue Moon was off and running now. "When he rose to coven power, Child remodelled a lot of things. Policies and even the physical school." She pointed at a line of text half-blurred, half-faded with age. "Someone must've agreed with your dream, that Child hid the Blood Stone in the light fixture's wings."

"There was nothing there." I shook my head. "The dream was a lie. Or I interpreted it wrong. I've looked. *Twice.* In two different chandeliers. The Blood Stone isn't there. It's just a black jewel." I held them out. So far I'd collected two. The others looked them over, but there was nothing special about the stones.

"Why would they wanna look at an old receipt?" Spade frowned. "Waste of time."

"Because there are three." Blue Moon said. She looked up. She'd stopped reading at the very next line. "Three were built."

"What?"

"Look." She pointed out the quantity on the order. The document listed it plainly. One large chandelier and two small. Identical in makings. Three in total. "There's one more."

"The third one's the size of the one in the office," I realized.

"Maybe installed in a house?" Josie guessed.

"We have to climb into another ceiling?" Spade groaned.

"You stayed on the ground." Bug shut him down. "So did I."

"Where is it?" Josie asked.

"I don't know." Blue Moon shrugged.

"What's the shipping address?" I asked. "Child Manor?" That seemed like the obvious guess. Blue Moon scrolled down. She tried to make out the address, but the ink had worn out.

"That doesn't look like my street name," Bug said from the bits that were there.

"It looks like the word 'crypt,'" Josie squinted and read.

"Well, what do we do now?" Spade asked.

My eye scanned the top of the document. There was a company name on the purchase order line. Craylor Lighting.

"The manufacturer might still know where they went."

"It's the only lead that we have," Josie agreed. "We should go there."

"It's almost nighttime," Bug feared, peeking outside.

"I know, but waiting for daylight didn't work." I said. "There was a vampire compelling people at the school in mid-afternoon."

"Yes, but there will be *more* vampires at night." Spade rubbed his jaw. "And there's still a price on your head."

"Unfortunately, time's not on your side," Blue Moon said. "Whoever was rooting through these files got the information hours ago."

"We're already behind," I said.

"I still say we wait until daylight, like a reasonable person would do." Spade countered.

"And where would you sleep tonight?" Josie asked him. Her tone was clipped. "Here? At your house? Think you can sleep when the Brotherhood of Thorns and the High Council know who we are, and they know what we just did? What we tried? The only way to end this is to get the stone. To turn it over to Mauve."

"Or die," Spade said darkly.

"She'll know what to do," Blue Moon spoke over the dark thought. "My cover's likely blown, but I'll stay here and try to find whatever more that I can in these files."

"Can you warn their families?" I asked. I nodded at Josie, Spade and Bug. "Tell them not to invite anyone inside their homes. No matter how nice they appear at first glance."

"I will," Lady Blue Moon said.

"Alright. Look, I'm gonna go to Craylor Lighting. See what I can find, maybe learn the address of the third chandelier," I told my new friends. "You don't have to come. I definitely understand if—"

"—I'm in." Josie cut me off.

"I'm coming too." Bug raised a defiant chin. "We're a squad."

"Don't call us a squad," Josie, Spade and I all said at once. We all turned to Spade.

"Coming or going?" Josie asked the lie-guard witch. He eyed her up and down. Then Bug. Then me.

"Without a witch with real powers, you ladies would be toast."

Bug shifted his heels. "You forgot about me."

"No, I didn't." Spade shot him a cocky smirk. "Insects don't count."

"They saved my life," I stuck up for Bug. I threw an arm around the sweet guy. He stood taller under my protective hand.

"Thank you, Seph. If anyone is a hero around here, it's me." Bug took the bravado one step too far. Josie and I exchanged a glance. It was a lot of bluster from the two men who'd slinked out of the atrium at the first sign of trouble while Josie and I struggled not to fall several stories, be killed by a vampire, get the stone and/or be splattered to death.

"Hope both your egos can fit in my truck," Josie frowned.

"I guess we'll find out," Spade merely grinned.

As we left Blue Moon to work, she grabbed my arm. "Seph, wait." She pulled me back. "You're the one they'll gun for first, but they won't hesitate to kill the rest of the squad."

"I understand."

I didn't even quibble with the use of the term squad. This was too serious.

"Even the Flood," she warned. "Our goals might be aligned for now, but… you can't trust anyone." She echoed the words I'd heard before, in the mouth of my vamp.

Our goals are aligned.

He'd said that once. When I asked if he was a friend. Was Lark part of my squad? Yes. My ex-bodyguard was out there, fighting for me, for us. Fighting to stop the Blood Stone from falling into the wrong hands.

I knew it.

Even if I didn't see him.

Even when he kept me at arm's length.

But at some point, that might change. At some point…

"I'm serious, Persephone, I–"

"Bonnie." I put a hand on her hand. "I understand."

Since the first time that we'd met in that lawyer's office, I meant it. The dangers were clear, and I was irrevocably changed. I had no choice. I needed to finish this mission. I had to retrieve the Blood Stone. She nodded and sat down to work. I went out with the rest.

"You still wanna enroll in the witch school?" Bug asked me after he and I crammed in the back of Josie's truck. Since I planned to try to nap again and dreamcast, I'd let Spade have the front and Bug, bless his heart, always assumed he belonged in the back.

"I don't know," I admitted the truth.

"Me neither," Bug agreed. Because at this point, the boy next door and I were on the same page. We weren't worried about some future magical education in a mysterious small town where my uncle had lived and Bug had grown up. Our priorities were simple.

We wanted to find the Blood Stone.

And return it to Mauve.

And survive.

35
LARK

"It's gotta be inside the light." Birdie said. My sister-non-sister made a shove-over motion. Instead, Lila got out of her bench and slid around to my side. Birdie plopped in the booth of the diner not-so-secretly pleased to have scared Lila off. Hot coffees in everyone's hands. I tried not to hog all Lila's space on my side. The two women had to be family, but they did not have to like it. And they exercised that option. Wren lounged at the table head on a stool.

Birdie stuck out her tongue at me, then pulled out a photo-copied sheet. It was crumpled. A poor duplicate. An old receipt. She straightened the crumples to read. Half the input lines had gone missing with age.

"Three chandeliers were built." She tapped it. Proof. "Three."

"Where'd you get that?" I asked. She shrugged.

"While you ignored your brother's warning and went off chasing your tail, I stopped by a High Council records house to check. Cornelius Child gave me a key once, a long time ago. It was a private spot for certain activities, non-coven related." Her tongue toyed with her fangs and we all understood.

"You and Neil?" Wren groaned. "Gross."

"I get off on power." She shrugged. "We can't all fall in love with some young, pretty witch," Birdie looked Lila up and down.

I glanced at my hands. She wasn't talking about me, but my thoughts were consumed with a pretty, young witch of my own. Persephone was on my mind constantly now. It wasn't *love* that I felt for the Orphan Girl. It was...

Fear?

Respect?

The girl was brave. And dumb.

She made me laugh. She made me nuts.

And through no fault of her own, she'd been thrust into this world and asked to retrieve the dangerous Blood Stone. I didn't care at first, but now that we'd met, I didn't want her to needlessly die over inheriting some magical relic from a man she'd never known. Especially a prick like Child. And I also didn't want that artifact to fall in the wrong hands. But Birdie hadn't jabbed at me, she'd poked at Wren. He was the love-sick puppy she scathed.

"No offense." She chirped at Lila.

"I'm young." My sister-in-law compared herself to the ancient female. "We're in love. And you think I'm pretty." She dismissed the verbal attack. Birdie bit her own lip, dragging those fangs. The relationship between the two women had always been tense. For Birdie, my brother was the one who got away. She would have given up the title of *'honorary sister'* in our family in a heart-beat if Wren had invited her to his bed.

Since that had yet to become an option, she happily stayed in the familial ranks.

She'd already had me, I hated to admit it.

A one-night dalliance when I was newly a vamp.

And she'd had Finch, our other brother, I was pretty sure.

Plus half the town and most of the coven, I now guessed.

Oh well, get it girl. I knew for a fact she didn't compel a single male to that bed.

The raven-haired stunner was my sibling through and through. Not only did she look the part, with sharp black hair against her delicate cheeks and blue eyes that could cut a lesser man in half, but she'd acted it too, through decades of loyalty and trust. Birdie had our backs and fought hard, and I'd stand alongside her with my dying last breath. So would Wren. (And Finch would too, if he wasn't locked in a demon gate, but I digressed.) We were unequivocally family. She just hated Wren's mate.

"Anyway," Birdie ignored Lila and swung her attention to Wren, the smartest comeback she could play. She stabbed a finger onto the paper. "There's a third light. That's where it'll be. I'd bet my life on it."

"You're already dead," Wren noted.

"Har, har," she groaned.

"This is serious." I cut the bickering off. "Franz' dreamcasts said the orphan girl's in real trouble." I recounted the lines. "*She runs. A fiery comet. Red sparkling through a sea of starlight. Lights on in the darkness. A city of them. All in one box.*"

"That sounds like a chandelier, right?" Birdie shrugged.

"A warehouse full of chandeliers," Lila agreed.

"That's what I said," Birdie sniped.

"That's not all." I kept going."*A man drinks her blood. The beast's a wild one. Only you can save her, Lark. The kids are all dead. She was helping you! This is how you repay her? Pay her back!*"

"Sounds dramatic. I know how those club girls are. They'll do or say anything to get a rise. You didn't..." Birdie raised one finger like an elephant trunk. Or like the male junk.

"No," I said too fast.

"Alright by me if you did," she shrugged.

"That's not the point." I growled. My sex, or lack of sex, hadn't been Birdie's business in a long, long time.

"Dreven was at the school," Lila cut in. I stared agog. "That's what I heard." The strongest tie we had to the academy since the death of Fellow Black was now Lady Mauve. "He compelled four Ladies to climb ladders. I'm not sure what they found."

That was bad.

Publicly showing his face in daylight meant Blackrose was serious. He usually had his cronies do his dirty work at night, but Dreven had the power to go out in the day. Same as us.

"Child's niece was there," Lila added, watching my face.

"*Damn it.*" I crumpled the paper still in my hands.

"Hey, easy, that's a clue." Birdie grabbed the receipt before I accidentally tore it in half. I might have flipped the whole damn table if I wasn't penned in by my girls.

I smashed a fist on the formica. "I told her to leave town!"

"An uncompelled human ignored what you said, big shock," Birdie snarked.

"She's a witch," Lila corrected. "Not just human."

"We all were witches once," Birdie shot right back. "That's no prize."

"This one has Electrum," Wren added. Birdie cocked an eyebrow.

"The fight at the school was ugly, but she did alright," Lila said. "Apparently to escape she used a sleeping spell."

"Dreven had a nap, right in the Atrium." Wren grinned.

"Good for her," Birdie laughed.

The dreamcast used sleep as her protection, she was starting to get it, I smiled inside. But things could have gone much differently, incredibly fast.

"I told you we should've gone directly to the Flood," I growled.

"Hindsight," Birdie said. "I agree, *now.*"

"So do I," Wren admitted.

"It might be too late," Lila feared. I nodded at my closest family and friends.

"We have to try. His niece doesn't deserve any of this."

I pictured Persephone the first moment I'd met her in that pawnshop, bargaining with the stumpy business man. Working the angles. She was broke. She was alone. Her life might have sucked. But it was hers.

We'd taken everything away.

"None of them deserve this," Lila agreed. "Most witches and humans don't even know vampires exist."

"So we keep it that way." Wren agreed, darkly.

"I'm going after the girl, the club-witch was clear. *Only you can save her, Lark.*" I told them. The others exchanged a glance. I didn't like it. "What?"

"The niece? The girl? You can say her name," Lila told me gently.

"*Persephone.* Happy?" I snapped.

"Not particularly." She didn't back down. "But *I* didn't put her in this position and nor did you."

"I'm supposed to guard her. If they kill her, *it's my fault.*"

"That was a bullshit assignment," Wren groused.

"You've done all you can do," Birdie agreed.

"So far we've done *shit.*"

"That's not true. You saved her at the house. You introduced her to Mauve. You escorted her to the Sundown," Lila listed.

"And you fought Gattas off." Wren reminded me.

"I told her to run."

"Honestly, it's better she stayed. If they can't find the Blood Stone, they'll hunt her down in any new town. She would never be safe."

"Well, I guess we're all good, then. Too bad for Seph. I'll just bite her neck and see if she's a vamp." I snarled. I wasn't exactly sure what I was fighting against. Or who. I only knew I was pissed. This whole thing sucked.

"They'd still have to kill her to get the rock," Lila quietly said.

"She should just give it to them," I muttered. The whole table bristled.

"Watch what you say," Wren warned. I brushed a hand, giving up. I didn't mean it.

I wasn't like Finch. Or Dreven. Or Fellow Gold.

"I'm not sure Child's niece can be saved," Birdie warned. "You know that, right?" She stared me down. "If you can't save her *and* the stone, you pick the stone."

"I know."

"I'm just saying that 'cuz we—"

"I know." I agreed far too quickly. Another look exchanged between the clan. "*What?!*" I roared.

"They've never seen you act this way," Birdie murmured.

"I have," Wren countered, watching me closely. "Once before." I knew what he meant. I did not acknowledge the reference.

"I'm acting this way," I picked my words carefully. "Because someone's never threatened to destroy life as we know it—"

"*Uh*, yes, *they have*," Birdie laughed. "Remember the Mountain Pass?"

The others groaned.

Knowing.

Remembering.

I remembered too.

Who could forget the Mountain Pass? We'd been through a lot of terrible things together over the years. The Mountain Pass was *goddamn epic.*

This was my family.

We'd get through this too, no matter what happened to the Orphan Girl.

Birdie was right.

It was the stone that mattered.

I couldn't care about the fate of Persephone. Her well-being had to stay out of my mind.

"I'll get the Blood Stone." I agreed, once and for all.

"You do that," Birdie agreed. I took the receipt from her hands. We slid out of the booth. I tossed a generous tip on the table for the four coffees that nobody drank.

"Tomorrow, I'll go to the sea board. Jump over Mr. Gatekeeper, Franz. I'll be ready to let the Flood know what's going on, or ask for help if we need them." Wren stood beside Birdie.

"Need my help?" She asked. Lila frowned.

"I don't need to be babysat," Wren snarked. Birdie shrugged.

"Fine, then I have business in the Shadowscale Mountains," Birdie said. She'd be far out of town. We all nodded. "Handle it," she said with a frown.

"I will," I told her. Wren grimly nodded too.

"I'll meet with Mauve," Lila offered. We agreed with that, all departing, but after she slid out of the booth, Lila still blocked my route. "Be careful, Lark."

"I'll get the binding rock," I said. "No matter the cost."

"Don't talk like that," Lila said, stepping aside. "You'll save her too."

The words stirred something deep inside.

Hope.

But that kind of optimism was only a wish, not our real life.

We both knew if it came down to Persephone or the Blood Stone, there was only one choice.

36
PERSEPHONE

We made several stops. First, for supplies. Then for every magic spell Josie had in her arsenal, and dinner and snacks for the road. The drive to the lighting manufacturer was two towns over. The rural highway roads were open and long.

On the ride, I tried to make use of the only witch skill I had: taking a nap. But my adrenaline was too spiked, even after we drove out of the town limits and onto the empty country roads where it was all nature and farms.

"You have to sleep," Josie told me in the rearview mirror.

"I know." I grumped, making a face, stretching and bending, trying to find a more comfortable position in the narrow back row.

"Switch with Seph," Josie ordered Spade.

"No way, I'm not cramming in there."

"If you don't, she can't cast."

"Just give her some of your drugs. Sleeping potion, or whatever."

"I'm not taking that," I said from the back. "We don't know

what it'd do. Or if it would even work. I'll be fine. Just let me get comfortable."

"Bug could ride in the pick-up bed," Spade sweetly offered.

"Not funny." The insect witch frowned.

"Why not?" Spade grinned. "There are bugs. You'll feel right at home."

"Actually," I interrupted their spat.

"You're not gonna make me sit in the back of the truck, are you?" Bug looked pained.

"No, but maybe you should move forward and share the front with Spade. There's a middle seat belt."

"Absolutely not."

"No way!"

Josie pulled over. "Make the change. *Now.*"

The boys grumbled, but the two did what she said. There was further complaining about who should sit in the middle, and who could lean on the door. In the end, surprising no one, Bug drew the short stick. At least he got to ride closest to Josie. And in the back seat, I stretched out my legs.

"Tell me about the genus of moths," I requested from Bug.

"Really?!" The guy beamed. I didn't warn that I hoped the lesson would put me to bed. "Well, moths are insects that are closely related to butterflies. They both belong to the same insect order, called Lepidoptera. They each have two pairs of scale-covered wings and undergo a complete metamorphosis through egg, larva, pupa and adult stages, including the dissolution of an active chrysalis. They're also pollinators. And they have very pretty wings. Although moths are usually darker in color and hairier than the pretty butterflies you see. There are actually a lot of differences between them now that I think about it. One of the main variations is that moths are usually active at night."

"Like vampires," Spade muttered.

"Precisely. And butterflies are diurnal. Plus moths are

attracted to light. Which is why you see them fluttering around the porch lights on a farm. There are over one hundred thousand species of moths in the world. My favorite is probably the Atlas Moth, which has a wingspan of about ten inches that holds flat when they land. That's almost a foot."

"Gross," Josie groaned.

"It's not gross," Bug droned on. "But it is different than butterflies, who generally hold their wings upright when they are at rest–"

Before he could finish his next point, I was sound asleep in the back.

———

In my dream, *I walked through a field of rose plants that were nothing but thorns.*

Row upon row of twisted vines. Jagged enough to rip your skin clean in half. But amidst the nursery of mangled bushes bloomed one yellow rose.

I quickly moved towards it, smelling the air.

The flower housed no scent.

Suddenly, someone picked it. They held it out in a beautiful bouquet. But I didn't take it. I knew it was offered by Dreven.

No, Gattas. No, Fellow Black.

Or Lady White?

The identity kept changing.

I struck a match, and lit the rose bush on fire.

For a moment, I watched it burn.

Then I turned and fled.

I slammed out of a door. And fell right into a bed.

"Are you alright?" Lark leaned on the bed sheets. He stared down at me, I was still quivering and shaking in fright. But instead of his blue

pupils, there were two shining black stones in his eyeballs. He plucked them out and held them, one in each palm.

In the distance, a monster roared.

The sound was so cruel and so dissonant, I gasped and opened my eyes.

———

Go back to sleep, I told myself. *There were clues.*

A rose, a fire, a door, a bed. Two black stones. A monster? The black stones were like the ones I'd gathered from the other chandeliers.

There were other vampires there too.

And Lark.

They'd all been present in *some* form.

And that monster...

I kept my eyes closed, I willed my subconscious to return. To further explore. I had to figure out what it all meant. What could help? What might hurt? But the vision had vanished. I was back in the truck. Lying down. Listening to the motor and the wheels on the asphalt. Intercut only with the quiet murmurings of the others in the front seat of the cab.

"Can I ask you something?" Spade's gentle tone made my head twitch. It was so soft. Gone was that knowing, abrasive charm. The cocky grin. He sounded quiet and vulnerable. Not at all like him. I started to roll over to answer. Had he heard me rouse? Was the question for me? But Josie replied.

"You can ask..."

I started to stir more to join them but stopped at the lie-guard's next words.

"Why'd you invite me along?" His question felt exposed. "Why'd you include me in this, Jo? I mean, before you knew we were all gonna die?" He made light of the situation, just a hair. Josie paused.

In the front seat, I heard a guttural snore. A little snuffle between them. Bug must have also drifted off in the front of the cab, making Spade and Josie believe they were alone. I didn't roll over. I decided not to disturb them. Maybe Spade deserved an answer from her. She certainly wouldn't offer him insight if they weren't by themselves. I waited for more sounds. Outside it had grown dark. The only other noise was the *click-clack* of Josie's high beam headlights as she snapped them off and then back on for oncoming cars on the road.

"What makes you think you were my idea?" She finally asked.

"Please. Bug wouldn't share you with anyone and the new girl had no idea who I was."

"Can we ever really know each other?" Josie brushed him off.

"I'm serious, Jo."

"So am I." It came out hard.

They sat in silence, with me in the back row, Bug between them in front. The quiet stretched on for hours. Or minutes. Or seconds. Josie didn't turn her head from the road when she finally gave him another crumb.

"I asked you because I respect your witch powers," she offered. "We needed a lie-guard... why'd you come? Don't say that you wanted to help, I know you too well." She shot him a look. Spade shrugged.

"I want in the witch world."

"This might get you exiled for good," she countered.

"I know, *now*." Again, the silence crept in. "And I miss you." He floated the words.

I thought she might snarl or bite off his head, but the cold wall stayed lowered for now.

"Don't start." She muttered. "I'm not one of your girls."

"I know," he said. Then, "I know..." he offered it again. Truer.

Deeper. More honest. She wasn't like the other girls he'd known. *The other girls who'd come between them in the past,* I silently guessed. Josie and Spade definitely had a long past.

The quiet crept in again.

"I didn't like the way things ended between us." He finally shrugged.

"Which part?" The question was hard. She refused to give him an inch.

"We made a good team."

"Until you got bored."

"I was a kid."

"You're still a kid now."

"I was a jerk."

"You're still a jerk."

He finally got frustrated. "I made a bad choice. A lot of bad choices, Jo."

The way he said her name was a trigger.

"You broke my heart!" Josie snapped, far too loud.

They both shut up.

I winced and waited for the moment to pass.

I couldn't rouse now. Couldn't let them know I'd been listening. Not to that.

"Don't fight, Mom and Dad," Bug whimpered while he slept. He curled into Spade. The lie-guard patted his head.

"I'm trying to say I'm sorry." Spade said quietly. "I've been trying for a while," he added.

"I know." Josie at least gave him that much. The effort was there.

More silence.

"Do you miss him?"

She knew exactly which *him* he was speaking of.

"Do you miss *Mae*?" Josie immediately returned. Always volley for a volley.

"They weren't the same."

"I know." She said again.

"She didn't hurt me the way he–"

"–Beck would have stayed," she cut in. "He would have been my parabond. He would have forced it. He would have stayed. I let him go. It's better this way. But I don't, Spade. I don't accept your apology. It's too late. Fool me once..." she shook him off.

There would be no absolution today.

"Right. Well... I'm here if you need me." He sighed.

"I know," Josie answered again. The silence was growing. "And you won't die. Not if I can help it," she added. She looked over at him and slightly nodded her head. Then went back to the road.

Click-clack, click-clack went the lights while she drove.

———

The three of us jerked awake, sleepy and frayed at sudden pop music blasting through the cab. Our bodies groaned at the abrupt wake up call in the middle of the night, then our bones ached over the odd angles at which we'd slept. Josie turned the radio off.

"Oh good, you're awake." She deadpanned. The corner of her lip flirted with a smile.

"You did that on purpose," Spade said.

"Absolutely."

"Where are we?" Bug asked, rubbing his eyes.

"Craylor Lighting." I guessed.

37
PERSEPHONE

"It's... bright." Spade said.

We all sputtered agreement as Josie drove through the well-worn parking lot up to Craylor Lighting warehouse and showroom. The latter a beacon of flashy chandelier light in every inch of window display. The showroom entrance was ten feet tall, bejeweled in man-made light with more than twenty high-powered chandeliers. There might have been a whole city of blazing bulbs in that first window alone, but we could see the illumination went all the way back in the store. Nothing had been turned off for the night. Lamps hung high and low, multiple levels deep. Sconce lights lined the walls in rows. Under-mount lighting framed every dark shelf. The whole place glowed. Every fixture was ablaze even though the salesmen and craftspeople had long since gone home. The parking lot was empty. The business was shuttered for the night. Overhead, street lamps pooled in the parking lot and battled the would-be darkness, including at a workman's entry door.

"That's where we enter," Josie said. She parked under a pine tree, far from the spot. There hadn't been much discussion about whether or not to go into the store. We were on the same page. After hours was necessary since we doubted we'd gain actual permission from an unwitting person who worked here. But we only wanted to *look* at the files and not take any belongings, so no one had a qualm about sneaking in on our own terms. Plus, we'd be out before anyone realized that we'd been there.

And... since someone owned this business, we rationalized, it actually made more sense to enter after hours when things were closed. If the owner wasn't on site, they couldn't be compelled to invite a vampire inside.

It was win-win. Anyway, that was the plan.

Wordlessly, we got out of the car and regrouped by the cab of the truck.

"Here," Josie opened her backpack of spells. "Snap ribbon plants and quick sand," she gave to Bug. He nodded. "Six light bangs," she handed Spade the half dozen explosives. He took them gingerly. "This is the Udak," Josie warned me. She'd explained the short distance bomb in great detail to me early on the drive. An Udak was a short fuse explosive made by smashing chemicals together. We both hoped we wouldn't have to use it. "And more sleeping potion." My weapon of choice, and the only magic I had any experience with. I took it in hand. "I have the glue, the salve, and the truth serum," Josie told the group. With a lie-guard in our midst, we didn't need to take crowbars or lock picks. Instead we ran to the dark wall on the side of the building.

"The door's over here," Bug said, as we knelt by the brickwork.

"Doors have alarms, kid," Spade told him, balling his fist.

"We'll turn it off," Josie assured him, "once we're inside."

"Don't call me kid. We're the same age, in fact I'm half-a-year older than you," Bug forgot my lesson about keeping track of half-years.

"Fine, old man."

"Let's not bicker while we're completing felonies, everybody," Josie warned them. "Do it, Spade."

The lie-guard's eyes flickered shut. He balled his hand and the energy shifted beside us. The wall opened brick by brick, creating a hole until it looked like the builders had gone for lunch without patching the space. It was big enough to crawl through, and the metal shelves of the warehouse were visible behind.

"It's like it's really there," I mused.

"It is there," Josie agreed. She and Bug ducked their heads and scurried through. I reached out to touch the space, my fingers went right through open air. Where a solid wall had been, moments ago. I grazed the mortared edge of the square beside. It didn't seem real that these things could be here and then gone in a moment's notice.

"That's incredible," I murmured.

"I know," Spade wiggled his eyebrows at me.

"I don't understand it," I knelt. My fear stopped me from going through. I looked at the wall a little sideways. Spade grunted. The hole flickered. Then disappeared. The wall returned. Like it had always been there.

"You were supposed to go through," Spade frowned. "You have to believe. Doubt can mess with your perception." He flexed his hand. But the warehouse door cracked open, Josie popped her head out.

"We're in. Come on. Unless you'd rather stay outside with the vampires."

"Don't even joke." Spade grew a shade whiter at the thought.

I looked left and right just to check we weren't followed. A bad feeling washed over me. I half-expected to see Lark there in the darkness, leaning against his burgundy sports car, watching our task. But of course he wasn't. My vampire wasn't here and that car was gone. I'd seen him crash that vehicle myself. Still... I couldn't shake the feeling that something was out there. Waiting for us. The quicker we got in, found the old paperwork, and got out, the better.

"Bug took care of the alarm," Josie showed us.

"Technically, the termites did," he admitted. I looked over at the swarm of creepy creatures devouring the wires and walls.

"Gross," Spade shuddered.

"It's not gross, they're your peers."

Spade was about to say something more, but Josie shut him down.

"We can get the job done now, thanks to Bug's creepy friends."

Bug looked unsure whether he should accept the praise, or note the insult.

"Nice job," I piled my vote to the positive.

"They keep working even after I release my hand." The bug-lover grinned.

Spade merely grumbled. "This way."

I kept my eye out for the file room.

The warehouse was large. Unlike the showroom up front, which was all style, the chandeliers in the back shelves were packed away in boxes, and stacked up high on plain, functional shelves. The organizational structures rose far too high for us to grab the upper contents without climbing. A ladder or forklift would do. The greatest irony of the building was that the ware-house was not well lit. The fixtures here were a total afterthought. The space was illuminated by plain, dull fluorescent squares in the metal rafters. And they'd been dimmed to half-light since no one should've been there in the night.

We walked down the long hall, shelves on each side.

Half-way down, I turned and froze.

Something flipped in my stomach.

The others careened to a stop.

"What is it?" Josie asked. The stacks made no sound.

"I don't know…" I couldn't verbalize the moment, I only knew the bad feeling from outside had just gotten worse. While I didn't see or hear anything amiss, I could feel it. I knew it was coming in my bones. Then I saw the yellow rose.

I pointed at it.

The flower symbol was a stamp. Inked on a lamp box.

There was a whole shelf of them, but only one box was angled our way, with the rose clearly visible. The rest were turned in another fashion, or had been taped to the pallet. The twisted tape almost looked like vines. If I hadn't stopped, I might not have seen it at all.

My mind flashed to my dream.

In the vision, I scented that flower. I turned and walked into the aisle towards it.

"Something's here," I said. "From my dream. I think we should check this aisle."

"We can't just pick random rows." Spade frowned.

"You heard her, it's not random," Bug said.

"I think we should check out the office first," Josie agreed with Spade. "That could orient things. See if there's a direction where to go. We can always come back."

"No, this is it." I couldn't help but push. This was the section of the warehouse that we'd need. *I felt it.*

"We can split up," Spade offered. Then both guys at once said–
"I'll go with Josie."

"Gee, thanks for the vote of confidence, friends." I muttered.

"She's got the arsenal of spells," Spade countered. "And the experience."

Plus, you'd like to get in her pants.

Josie, to her credit, just looked at me with inquiry, *which one would I like?*

"I'll be fine on my own."

"Bug, you stay and help," Josie countered. "If anything goes wrong, we meet at the truck. The keys are under the mat," she added, in case we had to drive it without her.

"We'll be fine." I tried to play it off. "Won't we, Bug."

"Take a light bang," Spade gave me one of the six. "Be careful," he added. We nodded to the others. Then they split off. For a moment, we listened to their footsteps, then things went quiet.

"What's here?" Bug asked.

"I'm not sure. Read the labels, okay? Look for something amiss." We moved down the aisle. Staring at numbers. Labels. Packing slips.

I felt a flutter over my shoulder and turned to look.

There was nothing there.

"Seph!" Bug squealed, excited. I hurried to him and his outstretched, pointed finger. "Check the top shelf." There were packing boxes, plain brown with no manufacturing designs or imprints. Each simple box had a date markered in someone's messy handwriting. The numbers and months of each box went way into the past.

"You're a genius, Bug!" I slapped his back. The insect-guy beamed. I quickly called Blue Moon.

"Is everything alright?" She immediately asked.

"Everything's good. We found some old files. But they're listed chronologically. Does the receipt have a date?"

"*Ummm*, let me check. Yes. December sixteenth, nineteen-ninety-two."

"The nineties." I pointed for Bug. "Ninety-two." Of course the box with that date happened to be the highest on the shelf.

"What does it mean?" Blue Moon asked.

"Not sure yet."

"Good luck, Seph."

"Thanks. We'll call back."

I texted Josie as well. *Found something. December 16th, 1992.*

In the office now. She replied.

I slid the phone back into my pocket and stared up at the shelf. A new problem. How to get the box down from the upper echelon? Someone would have to go up, either climb, or ladder, or lift. I shuddered at the memory of my last ladder adventure. Maybe not that. I checked the nearby forklift to see if it would turn on, not that either of us knew how to drive it or make the retrieval prongs raise. But the machinery was also locked. That left one option. One of us would have to scale the shelf. Between Bug and I...

"I'll go up," I told him, starting to climb up the first box.

"Be careful, Seph." Bug didn't dare suggest that he take my place.

You can do it, I told myself. *Like a tree outside.* I'd maneuvered in and out of foster homes many times, climbing fences, scaling branches, but this metallic shelving was both taller and flimsier than any of that. The metal groaned when I placed my foot wrong. There was already so much weight on the shelves that adding one more body, especially a moving person, made the whole structure feel a bit dangerous.

"Hold, baby, hold," I whispered. But when I got as high as the third metal row, I could feel the shelf ebb and sway. If I fell, I'd take an apartment building's worth of chandeliers down with me.

"It's no good." I retraced down my steps.

"Should I try? I might be lighter, no offense." Bug was a waifish guy. Puberty had never quite hit. His final development was late. His muscles were light.

"There might be another way." I looked at his hand. "How's your magic tonight?"

"Good..." he frowned. "Why?"

"What about those moths... what did you say? The arctic ones?"

"Arctic... *oh*! Atlas moths! My favorite." He excitedly agreed.

"Right. Could they carry a box? They carried me."

"Actually, that wasn't moths. That was an assortment of bees and cicadas and other insecta genus. Whatever was nearby the school. Endemic to the grounds. I didn't call on a specific group. I don't know how moths would do that."

"Well, okay, just call on whoever's around here. This place is probably teeming with bugs."

"It is. Especially spiders. I also saw a nochticoladae and a blotted– you don't care." He gathered himself. I smiled and shook no. "They're cockroaches, by the way, the nochticoladae."

I squirmed. "Don't tell me that, Bug."

"And they're saving the day." Bug added. He balled up his hand, all heroic like. He was liking a new use for his powers, I could tell.

A flapping echoed.

A buzzing emerged.

I felt the unsettling stirring that came from tiny wings swooping too close by your ear.

A storm of creatures darted and wriggled, converging where we stood, feeding up, up over that metal shelf.

"I got it," Bug concentrated on the top line. The insects scuttled and buzzed like a cloud, rallying around the box, pushing it forward, then wriggling it off its high shelf. It shoved off. Fell, then the box smacked down on the concrete ground.

Splat.

It hit the warehouse floor. Hard. Cracking open like an egg. The contents spilled out. We were supposed to look but not touch, only now, the seams had split. Worse, we hadn't thought about how to get the box back on the shelf when we were done.

"Sorry," Bug frowned. He hadn't controlled it as well as he'd hoped. "Shoot." Bug released his palm and the circus of creatures dispersed.

"It's okay. You did great," I lied. He hadn't been able to hold it up or gently lower the box down, but oh well. The information was now in arm's reach. I rushed forward to see what we'd found, diving in. We picked through the errant scraps and opened the lid to pull out even more. As we did, an avalanche of paperwork fell out. No wonder the box was so heavy. There was a library's worth of information inside. We scrounged and read. Holding papers up to the light.

"It's got to be here," I told Bug, sounding way more confident than I felt.

It would take us all night to get through this lot, and that was if the address we needed to search for could be found in this box. I read and shoved aside, read and shoved aside. So did Bug, until we each had lengthy piles of discards.

When I reached for my fourth stack of papers, I yelped and pulled back.

Ow.

A feisty paper slid over my fingertip at the wrong angle and sliced through my skin. A dollop of blood fell onto the document. I thrust the small injury in my mouth and put the paper aside.

The tiny cut made a big impact. It hurt. And we still had too much to check.

Josie? Spade? I texted the pair. Where were they? They must have been done in the office by now. And we could definitely use two more sets of eyes.

Looks like the receipts are all there. Coming back, she replied.

"The others are coming," I relayed to Bug. A strange thrill brushed my skin, like a breeze in my hair and the sudden feeling of being watched.

I half-expected the other witches to return to our aisle. But no one was there.

It was just Bug and I and a mountain of receipts.

I looked down the aisle again, sucking on my small wound.

"Did you feel that?" I asked Bug.

"What?"

"Josie?" I asked the silent hall. "Spade?"

Had they returned?

The unsettling breeze blew on. It goose pimpled my skin. My head swiveled around. Looking for something, anything, coming.

"Hey," I put out my wounded hand to Bug, to silence his rattling papers. *Shhhh.*

"What?" He asked again. We paused.

My blood pounded, my heart thumped loudly.

"Nothing, I just thought–" I was scaring him. "It's nothing. I cut myself." I showed him. "But I'll live."

We both went back to the receipts. To the stack.

I didn't re-pick up the pile that had injured me, instead I chose a new bunch. I easily pushed the first three documents out of the way into my discard pile. Then I sucked back my breath. I read the words again.

Holy crap.

This was it!

Pay to the order of Craylor Lighting, courtesy of Cornelius Child, HCW Academy.

"Bug," I stared at the page.

The needle in the haystack. I'd found it.

"Bug–"

I read the contents down, absently reaching for his arm, totally excited. But before I could touch him, someone else's voice cut into my thoughts.

"What'd you find, child?"

38
PERSEPHONE

My head whipped around at the woman's voice, scared to have been found out. How would we explain how we got inside the warehouse? Or what we were doing now? But the woman who stood over us at the end of the aisle wasn't from the Craylor Lighting Company or its affiliated warehouse. She wore a white skirt and white dress shirt. Even white boots.

I recognized her from the school.

Bug did too.

A professor at the High Council Witch Academy.

When she said Child, she meant like Cornelius.

"You're the Lady who–*oh no.*" Bug whimpered. "That's not good."

"No, it's not." I agreed. I put out a hand to calm Bug, or at least to let him know he wasn't alone in the aisle. But this was the worst interloper we could have hoped for. Because the woman who stood blocking our way had last been seen crumpled and distorted and broken on the academy lawn.

And dead.

Definitely dead.

It was Lady White.

The witch who'd let the vampires into my uncle's office.

The High Council elder who'd been compelled, and had her blood sucked, and tried to pull me from the roof of the sixth floor. Who'd fallen. *Who died.* That very same woman stood before us now. Raven claw crinkles newly formed around her wild eyes.

"It's not possible." I said. Bug dumbly nodded, too. But we both knew, the paranormal dead could have a second life... if witch blood ran in her veins. "You're a–"

"Vampire, yes." Lady White smiled. She spread her lips, licking slowly over her teeth, showing them off. "You kicked me off the roof." She growled.

"You pulled off my skirt." I defended myself.

Hiss.

She bared her new fangs.

"I'm about to make your life a living hell."

"Run!" I leapt up to my feet. We were off like a shot. I pushed Bug ahead of me, helped him round the corner. As we raced, Spade and Josie were gunning towards us from the other direction.

"No!" I yelled. I threw up my hands trying to ward them off.

"What's wrong?"

They careened to a stop. Turned with us and we all tried to keep going, but Lady White was on me, too nimble for me to escape from her vampire form. She threw me down on the ground. She was now much stronger and faster than she'd been on the roof. Immortal.

I fell hard to the floor.

Immediately, I spun. I threw up my hands, my last line of defense.

A bead of my blood from my paper cut glinted on my fingertip.

The new vampire's eyes went wild with bloodlust. She dove at my hand.

"Stop!" I screamed. Josie grabbed a spell from her backpack. She hit the undead professor with a glue potion satchel.

Argh! Lady White convulsed, sticky and stuck.

I scrambled out from under her limbs.

"Wood. Does anyone see any wood–" I demanded, blindly looking around. The only way to kill a vampire was through daylight. Or fire. Or a stake to the heart. We needed wood.

Josie stared at the glue-monster she'd made. Spade seemed to have frozen in shock. They didn't answer quickly enough.

"*We need a stake,*" I screamed.

"Here!" Bug saw a wooden chair at the end of the aisle. We rushed for it.

"Break it apart!" I ordered. Bug tried to smash it on a diagonal leg. The kind of thing we'd seen action stars do in the movies. But the furniture construction was too strong. It sputtered and groaned, but didn't snap.

"Damn it." Josie and I went to help, twisting and bending the legs, pushing down with our weight, but the damn thing wouldn't bust. I kicked at the backrest while it was down. Terror strengthening my leg thrusts. Finally, the thinnest decorative pieces of the chair snapped off. We scurried to pick them up. Feeble shards to use against a woman who'd already shown terrible strength. Bug held up the rest of the chair like a lion-tamer, while Spade stared at the vampire professor. Totally stumped.

"She's getting out!" He warned.

Her vampire power seemed to grow, the angrier she got.

I looked at my measly stick. I handed it to Josie. "This won't be enough."

My dream had shown *fire*, not wood.

And I had a bomb.

"Stand back," I warned them.

"What are you gonna do?" Bug whimpered. I dug into my pocket and pulled out the witch potions that had been given to me. I showed them. Lady White was almost out of the sticky glue chains.

"I'm gonna blow this bitch up."

"Do it," Josie agreed. She hid.

"*Do it!*" Spade echoed. He grabbed Bug and pulled him back. I pushed the chemicals together to light the fuse, then hurled the Udak bomb at the vampire woman and dove out of the aisle.

Boom!

The short fuse bomb exploded, shattering boxes of chandeliers and exploding paperwork in every direction.

"Go!" Somebody screamed.

Maybe me.

We cried and ran. Back towards the wall where we'd come into the warehouse of lights. Back towards the safety of the truck. We slammed into the warehouse outer wall and sprinted for the termite-infested door. We couldn't get out of the building fast enough.

I looked over my shoulder but she wasn't coming.

I'd made a direct hit.

I saw Lady White's face a moment before the explosion went off. Her pupils dilated. Her raven claws spread for the last time. Her mouth bared the new fang teeth she couldn't quite control. And then the bomb blew up. There was no way she'd make it through that fire storm. Dead or alive. She was gone. Again. Dead a second time.

"Come on," Spade waved us through the open door.

Josie beckoned us outside.

"No, stop." I slowed. "We need that form. I saw it. Right before–"

"—Lady Murder tried to kill you and bite off your face?" Spade supplied.

"Exactly, yes."

"No." Josie said. "It's not worth it, Persephone. Your life for a house?"

"No... I know." I agreed. "But the stone."

"We gotta go," Spade insisted. "*Now.*"

Deeper inside the warehouse, a fire was burning. A fire we'd caused.

And the vampire was dead.

"We were only supposed to sneak in and out," I said. "Look at this place."

"What's done is done," Josie offered. I shook my head.

"Maybe so, but my blood is on some of the paperwork. I have to go back. She's gone."

"What if she wasn't... alone?" Bug whisper-asked. His words brought a chill to our skin.

"She was." I frowned. They couldn't talk me out of this. I had to. "I'll be arrested," I told the group. "With DNA, or... I don't know... we said we'd do no harm." We couldn't leave the fire going. The whole warehouse would burn. There were too many cardboard boxes. "I'll get the documents. Both the one with my blood and the receipt from Cornelius Child for the last light. You put out the fire."

Josie came around. "It's the right thing to do," she told Bug.

"Need I remind you, the right thing to do would have been not breaking and entering or doing anything illegal, but you were happy to cross that bridge when I punched a magic hole in the wall," Spade sighed.

"Can you magically stop the fire?" I asked.

He flexed his fist. How much magic did he have left?

"It's alright. You don't need to come back. We'll be fine." I didn't wait. I jogged away.

"Just wait here," Josie said, next in line.

"*Just wait here*," he mimicked her. "Oh no." Spade countered. "You know who dies in horror movies? The guys you leave behind. The guys who're just innocent, waiting for the wicked girls." He looked at Bug. "That and the sweet little guys. It breaks the audience's heart every time." Bug swallowed, hard. "We're not dying today, little buddy," he told him, following our path. "Come on, I think I saw a fire extinguisher on the wall." They joined our small chase. The bomb was still burning, but there was no body, no horrible smells. Nothing cooking or decomposing. Lady White was just gone.

"Is she alive?" Bug whispered.

"I don't know," Josie admitted. We exchanged a worried glance.

"Let's just hurry up," I ordered, like it hadn't been my plan that we double back. The others found fire extinguishers and sprayed out the foam. I grabbed my bloody fingerprint paperwork and the order form with the information stapled together for Child's final light.

"Umbrawick, like an umbrella," I read out the third chandelier shipping location to the others. They barely nodded. I balled the receipt up and shoved it into the empty pants pocket that had once held the bomb. We'd look at it closer when we were safely back in the truck. I didn't want to admit it, but I still had a bad feeling about things. "Did you get it?" Josie and Bug sprayed the fire remnants with safety foam. The row was a mess, but the fire was out.

"They're done." Out of frustration, Spade cracked the stupid wooden chair we'd been struggling with. He butchered it clean in half. He pretended to use a broken leg as a sword.

"You good?" I checked on the other two.

"Good." Bug agreed.

"Yes. Let's move." Josie said.

"I've still got a bad feeling about this," Bug admitted. So we were all experiencing the same dread. Spade lunged against an imaginary foe then stalled.

"Spade?" Josie called him. But he didn't answer or budge. We all looked at him. The fourth member of our group had lunged so far he was staring down the long back hall in the direction towards the office. The pretend dagger still frozen high in his palm.

"*Spade?*" I asked again.

The tenor of my voice brought his attention to me. But he didn't look our way. He put up his other hand, as if to silence us, as if asking us to give him a second.

"What do you see?" Josie quietly asked.

"Vampires... six more vampires," Spade hissed.

"A half-dozen?" Bug gasped. "That's not good."

"It's not ideal, that's for sure." Josie peeked too. "They're coming this way," she tugged Spade's arm, but the lie-guard couldn't stop staring down the aisle. Terror locked his limbs. "The White woman isn't with them."

"I knew we shouldn't have come back," Spade murmured. "This Stone is a death wish."

"What do we do?" Josie asked me for a plan at the same time my eyes questioned her. Our minds whirred. We were the only two in the group still maintaining our wits. It was clear I'd used the Udak explosive too soon.

"I wish Lark was here," Bug wailed.

"So do I," I sadly agreed.

I should have listened to Lark's warnings at every stage of this task.

But I didn't and now we were all here, paying the price.

Think, Sephy, think.

Time to develop a new, deadly rescue plan all on my own. Without my vampire bodyguard's help.

Fuck.

39
PERSEPHONE

"Up," I said.

The word shot out of my mouth.

The only advantage we had.

We were in the bombed aisle, they were walking the halls, checking row-by-row. They expected us to run and didn't know which lane we were hiding in. Yet.

They probably assumed we'd never go back to the place where the last vampire died. That we wouldn't be so dumb... but that's exactly where we were.

Your life for a house? Josie had asked.

We all knew, these vampires would come for me no matter what.

"*Up. Now.* We dump the sleeping spells on them like I did in the atrium." My plan spilled out. It was a good one. It had worked before. It could work again.

"Climb," Josie agreed and ordered. Sounding far more in control than I felt.

"Spread out," I told them. "The metal can't take too much weight in one spot."

"The wood ones aren't much better," Josie warned. We raced up the shelves. They groaned and ached with our boots and our hands, Bug's sneakers slipping as he scaled. We had to slow down. Move too fast and the whole thing might bend. The organizational frameworks had barely held my weight the first time. And now there were four of us climbing high...

...but that was wrong.

It was three.

There were three of us monkeying our way up the shelves.

The lie-guard was still rooted to the spot.

"Spade!" I hissed.

He hadn't budged from his peekaboo, staring at the undead group progressively making its way towards us. He watched them coming closer and closer.

"*Spade*," I gritted again. He still didn't look up.

"Spade, come on." Josie leapt down from the shelf and ran to the lie-guard.

"*Josie!*" Bug panicked as she went back towards the vampires. He wanted to jump after her, but I put out a hand.

"No. Bug, climb up."

She quickly reached Spade. "Hey." Josie grabbed the lie-guard's arm and when that didn't work, she manually twisted Spade's jaw to look her way. "We have to move," she told him gently. Years of understanding and empathy transferred between the two. Whatever hurt or insult and injury their relationship had sustained, it had nothing on the compassion coming from her. Their tangled dissidence washed away. "Spade, please. They know we're here, we have to go."

"Okay." Spade turned his head. He looked up, realized Bug and I were already halfway done climbing, and burst into action too. He shoved his broken piece of the chair into his belt, then he and Josie went up the opposite shelf, scaling the boxes of lights. Her first. Spade behind.

Bug and I made it to the top and stood on the highest row of boxes in the storeroom. The footing wasn't flat, uneven in the shapes of the collection of boxes, but it held. The metal shelves groaned.

"Don't do anything quickly," I warned. "This whole thing might go down."

"I won't." Bug agreed, watching Josie's assent.

I glanced behind me and immediately ducked. The six vampires were close in the hall. They walked in formation. Strutting. Assured and careful. Their eyes scanning the warehouse as they moved rows.

Hunting.

The word stopped me cold. This group of vampires didn't remind me of Lark. Did I expect them all to? Two were tall with dark hair like him, but one was short with brown curls. The other three were stark platinum blond. Most likely dyed. The tallest blonde–who strolled in the middle, clearly calling the shots–was a man I'd met before.

Gattas.

He moved as their commander, like he had all the time in the world.

He did, I realized, *or at least all night.*

Because there was no question of their dark hearts. Power thrummed from their skin. They burned with anger and confidence. They each had the same eye-framing raven claw wrinkles that I loved on Lark. But the lines twisted their faces, deeply dug. Like permanent scars.

The vampires squinted as they scanned down the rows.

The intensity of their gazes shuddered my skin.

To stay out of sight, I ducked lower.

"Bug, stay down."

He and I fumbled with our spells as Josie and Spade succeeded in their climb and rolled onto the opposite shelf on the other side of the aisle. The metal framework groaned but stood.

"I'm not sure it'll hold," Spade confessed. He was the biggest of our group, over six feet and around one hundred and eighty pounds. Mostly pure muscle. I'd seen that physique for myself back in the quarry days ago. I was astonished to realize the timeline. It felt like I'd been in this town fighting for my life for a long, long time.

Spade wasn't fool enough to try to stand, instead, he spread his mass out, lying flat. Those biceps and impressive abs wouldn't help him one bit if the wall of shelving collapsed. Josie prepared the sleeping potion spells in her hands. Spade gripped his stake. I wished I had a wooden dagger in hand for myself.

"Get ready," I warned from the best vantage spot.

The Brotherhood were enjoying themselves. Like it was a game.

Well, we can play too. I lay in wait. *Come into our web...*

My heart stilled.

They were so close.

Only a few more steps.

But the vampires didn't move into our trap.

"Witch boys and *girls*..." Gattas announced. He sang the last word, but then his voice turned to cold instruction. "Show yourselves." He stood at the end of the aisle, not dumb enough to walk down it. "It's not nice to hurt your new friends." He said. "We sent the professor in to retrieve her pesky students and you blew her to bits. *Oops.*"

A couple of the other vampires chuckled at the mess.

"Never send a newbie to do a real vamp's job," another said. More laughter at that.

They do have weaknesses, I reminded myself. *Fire, and Gattas was afraid of the light.*

So if we could hide or stall or do battle with him until morning, then we'd be safe... what time was it now? I turned my back, about to tell the others, expecting to find them hiding as I was, ducked and biding their time, but when I turned over my shoulder, all three were leaning out, showing their position to the vamps.

Exactly like he'd asked... like he'd compelled.

"What are you doing?" I groaned.

"Where's the fourth?" a blonde underling questioned.

"Child's niece is wearing Electrum," Gattas clicked through his teeth. "Where's the last girl?" He asked my three friends. All of them immediately pointed to me in my hidden spot.

"Sorry Seph," Bug said.

"*Damn it.*"

"Well, come down," the mouthy vampire said.

My three friends started to amble down when Gattas smacked his friend's chest.

"No. Stop." His order was far more fierce. An instruction to them and a warning to his man. Josie, Bug and Spade stopped. Their mouths were twisted in frustration.

What must be going through their heads? I feared, *forced to obey the enemy's commands?*

They had no choice. Their bodies just did what he said.

"Try to fight it," I whispered. "He's not in control."

"*Yes*, I am." Gattas growled my way.

The other vampires smirked. Gattas cocked his head.

"Witch kids, let's play King of the Castle. Throw each other down, off the shelving. Make your competitor fall. Hard as you can. Make them suffer... ready?"

I felt the insect witch stiffen beside me, coiling, ready for battle.

"Bug, no. Stop. I don't want to hurt you."

My sweet friend.

The guy who loved centipedes and moths.

"Then get off my shelf," he warned.

"It's a compulsion. You've been compelled." I said. Josie and Spade glared at each other too. "Please. We're on the same side. Don't listen to him."

"*Attack*." Gattas said the command like a puff of cold air.

Spade and Josie leapt. Their bodies clashed on top of the swaying metal shelves.

"Stop, careful. It's not safe." I tried to warn the other three. The shelves were precarious enough with small gentle moves, they'd never sustain an onslaught or attack. But Bug lunged for me too. I dove out of the way. He smacked hard on the boxes, slammed down his fists and roared, unlike I'd ever heard or seen from him before.

Josie and Spade sprawled across the boxes, intertwined, all fists and slaps. Him on top, their bodies smushed, backs twisted and bent on the uneven shelf. Spade grinned viciously in Josie's face, taunting the girl who'd been his support and his guidance only moments ago. Now he shoved her shoulders into cardboard hell.

"Don't hurt her, Spade!"

But being the lower person in their struggle brought advantages as well. Josie kicked back, rolling her body, shoving Spade towards the steep drop. He had to grab onto a random box for control. Packaged lights crashed to the floor. The box contents rattled with broken parts.

The sickening splatter on impact struck fear deep inside.

How would it sound when the first of us dropped?

Would we break bones?

Snap our necks?

Pulverize our lungs and our insides?

Bug was back on his feet, huffing at me like a bull. We paced back and forth.

"I won't fight," I told him, hands up in defense. "We're friends.

You don't want to do this." I had to get the Electrum to him, make it touch his skin. If he would just hold still–

"You're going over the side," he said. The darkness in his voice, in his eyes, told me someone else had taken over his mind. Even his body filled out. I'd never realized how much Bug recoiled his posture all the time, like he was hiding himself in plain sight, refusing to take up too much space for fear of rejection or hurt. He was far bigger than I gave him credit for. Unfortunately, he was wholly controlled.

Bug dove at me.

I ducked and squirmed.

I tried to push my necklace out towards him but the witch was too fast.

Bug caught my leg and yanked. I fell. I had to kick. At first, I booted his hands. Then I clenched my eyes shut and connected with more.

His face.

And his mouth.

I kicked Bug so hard I gave him a fat lip, but he still didn't let go of my leg.

He dragged me towards the edge.

I tried to hold onto a chandelier box, but my fingers ripped the cardboard I gripped. I had the damn sleeping potion clutched in one hand, the Electrum chain in the other, I wasn't equipped to hold on and there was nothing solid to grab.

Every box moved.

Cardboard caved in.

The shelving swayed.

If I didn't do something more, I'd be going over the side.

The vampires spread out in the aisle, curious to get a better vantage of the fight.

Spade pressed Josie's face into a lighting sconce. Attempting to crush her head.

"Spade, no!"

He maniacally laughed. Josie swung a hand and punched him right in the nuts.

"*Josie!*"

He collapsed and wheezed. But I couldn't shepherd their fight any better than I could control my own. Bug was trying to fling me off the shelf as best as he could.

"Get off my castle, Spade." Josie barked. He howled, scrunched in the fetal position, so she shoved him over the side. Straight at the vampires below.

Spade fell! But with one hand, the lie-guard caught himself on a box.

He hung by his arm. Mid-air.

Then with brute strength, he pulled himself back up.

Spade grabbed Josie's ankle, tugging her to the side.

The shelf let out a protest.

Screws started to pop.

There was too much weight on one angle.

"No, Spade. Please stop!" I watched Josie squirm. She huffed and puffed, trying to gather more strength for the next attack, while Bug dragged me down.

If I couldn't get him to touch the Electrum, I could use the sleeping spell on Bug, on all of them, I thought. But that would make my trio defenseless against the vampires. I couldn't leave them vulnerable to attack, even as I thrashed and hurt in Bug's hands. Instead, I let my body go limp.

Spade strong-armed Josie.

The shelf groaned as he yanked her down the side where he still hung in mid-air.

The thing leaned.

"Watch out!" I yelled.

Both teens fell.

The vampires cheered.

The witches hit boxes and lower shelves on their way down. They grabbed hand holds and clawed, each trying to regain status over the other at the top. They were desperate to win the King of the Castle over their bruises and cuts.

Bug picked me up.

Ahhhh! I screamed. *What the hell?*

I'd been too twisted up watching the other fight. The insect witch literally grabbed my limp body and clean jerked me up into his arms. Above his damn head.

Rawwwrrrr. He bellowed from deep inside.

"Bug, stop!"

But the insect witch had full control. I was like a rag-doll in his grip. The bug-lover hurled me in the direction of the other shelf, I flew, smashing me into the still warring Josie and Spade, like bowling pins.

I tried to catch and hold onto one of them, or both, but with all the stuff still in my hands, I had no grip, and the two shoved me off.

My body tumbled before I even had a chance to hold on.

I dropped the remaining half-distance and smacked to the ground.

Oh god.

My knees hurt.

My wrists throbbed.

Three vampires snatched me up by my arms and my hair while their buddies watched. They'd been itching for a plaything to come down. Six cold hands dug into my skin and tugged my hair. Their rough handling pulled me apart. Showing me off to Gattas.

Ahhhh.

My heart beat out of my chest at the terrible proximity of the closest vamps. Three dangerous men. While three other beasts watched. All scarier than I'd ever known. Hungry for my neck.

Practically salivating, fangs sticking out of their lips. I felt their hot breath in my ears, on my skin. But nobody bit down. Not yet.

They waited for Gattas to give the all clear.

I wanted to cry out, but held back.

"Looks like you're out." Their leader smirked from the other side of the aisle.

"She smells good," one of the blonde men crooned, breathing me in. "Fresh."

"She is," another one smiled.

"Look at this," the shorter, curly-haired man grabbed my fingers and spread them apart. He found the paper cut wound and stuck my finger in his mouth, sucking on me, letting out a gross groan. His head rolled back in joy.

"*No!*" I wrenched, but I was trapped. There were too many to pull away.

"I wanna lick," another complained. He too stuck my hand in his mouth like I was a lollipop.

"Stop. Leave me alone." I cried and writhed. Then suddenly, Josie and Spade smashed down to the floor. Each hit the concrete hard. Their battle equally lost.

"*I won!*" Bug roared from the top.

I stopped struggling and looked up. I realized in my skirmish, he'd actually jumped across the shelving divide and now stood in celebration at the top of the other's leaning shelf. His face twisted in evil, gloating, and proud.

"Be careful, Bug." Josie was back to herself. Raising, slowly. Since the game was over, she was no longer compelled.

"Are you alright?" Spade asked the girl he'd just kicked, punched, and fought. She nodded, sharp and tough. Then they stared at the vamps. Our mutual foes. The monsters were too close for any of us to properly breathe. Spade grabbed another piece of chair, he snapped it off. He'd lost his first stake some-where in the King of the Castle battle above. He held out the new, fresh wood like a weapon to protect Josie and himself, as best as he could from Gattas and his two men.

I tried in vain again to wrench away from the other three behind me, who were now sniffing my hair, humming with greed.

"What happened?" Bug asked. His voice was back to sweet and scared. The insect witch we all knew returned.

"You were compelled." I still struggled to no avail.

Josie smeared back her hair. Spade flexed his hand again.

"You won the game," one of the lesser vampires grinned up at him.

"So you did. And now for your prize," Gattas smiled. The gleam in his eye, the song in his voice chilled our skin. The vampires all smirked, knowing another terrible twist was coming. They practically beamed. "Insect witch," Gattas addressed only him. "*Kill your friends*. Use your powers. Make them squirm. Dispose of the witches, in whatever way that you can."

Bug's eyes darkened.

"No, *please–*" I started to beg. I didn't know how to make it stop.

"Ugnacious, don't." Josie tried his real name. "We're your friends. You love us."

We heard the swarm before we saw it coming.

"*Fuck*," Spade warned.

Then the creatures arrived. The buzz in the warehouse grew so loud that it roared. An army of wings, and stingers, and venomous creatures. Ants and mosquitos and gnats covered the room. Making it black.

A living cloud of bugs.

"Attack!" I screamed at the others. Creatures flew in my mouth, but this was our chance. Several flash bangs went off. I spit and stomped on the vampire's feet on my right. He groaned just enough. I wrenched free my hand. As it came momentarily loose, I hurled the sleeping potion from my pocket in an arc over my head, hitting all three vampires who'd been holding me. They hissed and screeched, but the spell did its job. They collapsed.

Spade raced at the next closest vamp, stabbing him with his stake.

Josie screamed and covered her head.

Spade missed the beast's heart and the monster threw him back. He splattered against boxes and heaved in a pile. The remaining vampires may have advanced, but the bugs grew too thick. We swatted and dashed, trying to get free. But Josie had it the worst. The creatures crawled into her black hair, biting her scalp. The other vampire and Gattas laughed, free and clear. Even the stabbed man was alright. He was starting to heal.

"*Jo!*" Spade yelled, but when he tried to talk, the bugs raced into his mouth.

She flailed and pointed up.

A hundred creatures bit me at once.

They flew down my pants.

Crawled under my shirt.

Burrowed into my skin.

But I understood Josie's command. There was no point in trying to hurt the vampires. We had to get to Bug. I started to climb back up the shelves.

"What are you doing?" Spade tried to ask. The bugs made him choke.

"He needs to touch Electrum!" I yelled, attacked by the mob. "Without it, we're as good as dead."

Ahhhh! When I tried to reach up to the top shelf, the weaker wooden one I was on snapped and broke. I dropped. But Spade was there. He caught my fall. He pushed up my butt. He helped me to climb.

"Do it, Seph." He ignored the bees stinging. He tried to protect me against the throng. It was no use. Spiders crawled onto my hands. They scurried down my arms. I fought the unending urge to swat at my skin. To scratch. To squirm. I battled not to go mad at their touch and to finish our plan.

"She's gonna stop the game," Spade's bloody vampire frowned.

"Where's the fun in that?" The third vamp stomped a foot, crushing bugs as he did.

"Let her try." Gattas enjoyed watching the spectacle play out.

On my next hand hold, a tarantula crawled on my fingertips. The furry body alternated legs. I screamed and turfed the whole box.

The vampires laughed.

"*Ah!*" Josie wept, getting stung. They crawled onto her. Bug must've called a whole army of arachnids as well as six-legged monsters, and they were now scaling the room.

Almost there, I told myself, pulling my body weight up. I ignored the metal's fresh groans. I climbed onto the top shelf, flinging off cockroaches and other bugs.

The whole framework lurched.

Ready to collapse.

Bug stood right on the edge, holding out his balled fist.

"Bug!" I yelled, I didn't dare stand. My cries didn't help. He was fixated on the death of our friends. On Gattas' command. His hand was bright red, fiery with the effort of churning out spells. Calling six-legged friends. Winged beasts. Demanding they feast. It was kill or be killed.

Josie screamed and screamed. She flailed. Overcome.

The first to fall.

Spade was covered in bugs who laid eggs and ate chunks of his skin. We were raw with insect bites, head to toe, trapped in ankle deep piles of writhing monsters, no matter how many we killed.

"*Bug, stop.*" I begged. I crawled across the top of the shelf. Totally spent. Narrowing the distance to him in any way I could.

Reaching my friend still seemed impossible, but I'd grown too close for the vamps. Gattas gave a small nod.

He wouldn't risk me actually stopping their fun. His sidekicks could jump in.

The non-bloody vampire burst into action, scaling the shelf.

"Where you going, girl?" He called, full of excitement. Fresh to the fight. I was beaten and exhausted and covered with bites. Going out of my mind. But I couldn't stop. Three more feet and I'd reach Bug. I'd share my necklace powers. Then he'd stop.

I tried to move faster. My body rebelled. Spade's first broken chair leg was there, stuck into a box. I yanked it out and used it like an ice pick, stabbing on cardboard, pulling my weight forward. Dragging myself.

"Bug, *please*. Look at Jo. You're hurting her. Your favorite girl. You're killing your *love*."

"And Spade," Bug agreed, his voice in a trance. "And you. I'll kill everyone."

I could see the extirpation had started to burn. He'd used so much magic, the natural world lit like a match. Embers of fire shot out of Bug's palm. Nicking the box pile below. Leaving charred spots. Any moment a bigger cinder might start a real blaze. And the insect witch was burning his own arm. His sleeve had singed.

"*Bug*—" I insisted. "Please." I crawled again.

"The witch doesn't care," Gattas laughed at me. His remaining crony clapped from the ground.

"Just wait," their third partner grinned, almost to the top. I looked back over my shoulder at him, stabbed the stake into another box and pulled.

Not if I get to Bug first.

Josie's screams were like blades in my ears.

I hauled my limbs across the divide.

I'd scaled this warehouse shelf once, fallen off, twice, and scaled again.

My legs roared in pain.

My muscles totally spent. But still, I moved.

This was our hope. Our only chance.

"Bug, *STOP!*" I held out the chain, I gripped it in my hand, and slapped it down on his leg.

The vampire leapt up onto the shelf.

He lunged at us with no plan, feeling it out, thinking we were dumb. But he underestimated my will to live. I still had the wood stake in my hand. I spun just in time and stabbed him right in the gut. It felt like meat, tearing apart. I didn't push hard enough. Afraid. It was too real.

This wasn't raw chicken in my hand. This was a *man*.

The monster made a slight face, and fell back on the shelf, bleeding into his shirt. But at least Josie's screaming had stopped. Bug had let go of his spell. He seemed in shock. His hand throbbed.

"*Not my hea-rt.*" The injured vampire had the gumption to actually sing-song mock.

My hand was covered. Slick with blood. His blood. And still, he thought it was a joke. I didn't realize it at first. Holding the stake, I tried to wipe the hair off my forehead, or brush off a remaining bug from my skin. The vampire's red sanguine slid across my cheek.

I winced in pain.

In horror at this monster's proof, bleeding on my face.

But the vampire only leered.

Ready to attack.

"She got him in the soul knot," his buddy laughed.

"Blaze doesn't have a soul knot," Gattas agreed.

"Josie?" Bug asked.

Neither she nor Spade had gotten back up.

"She barely hit me," Blaze called down to his pals. "Just a nick."

Bug fell apart at the seams. "What have I done?"

He released his harnessing hand. The insects disappeared.

Still, our friends did not move.

"*Josie*. Spade?" Bug wept.

I held him tight. "It's okay."

And then, a beautiful, suffering voice struggled to speak.

"Turn... them..." it said.

"*I'm coming for you*," Blaze taunted us.

"Turn... them..."

It was her.

"Turn... your bugs... on the vamps." Josie hissed out the words. Her voice barely a whimper. So weak. So pale. "If you have any power left, Bug. *Turn. It. On. Them.*"

Rawrrrrrr!

Bug's magical power roared back into his hands. He didn't care how badly it hurt. Or about the fire that burned. Or the sparks that flung out. The swarm buzzed right back. Even harder than before. They flew straight for the undead.

"Get away!" Blaze swatted at the micro beasts invading his space.

The vampires below did the same. Even the three sleeping monsters became covered in bites. But Bug's expression only grew more intense.

"Kill them!" Gattas ordered his man. Blaze shuttled our way.

"Leave him alone!" I swung at the vampire's chest. This time, I didn't hold back. I made a powerful thrust. Stabbing between his damn ribs. The stake sunk deep into Blaze's flesh. Hitting a bone. A terrible stab and gory mush. It pushed further and further in. Blood gushed over my fingers as insects swarmed down. It was hard to see the vampire's face in the melee of bugs. I didn't know where he ended and I began. But I felt it. *His ending.*

The vampire guttered on my hands. I shoved in the stake. Higher, harder.

Blaze's eyes went wide, and then dead.

Life force spewed from his lips, more blood gushed from his wound.

This time, I knew I'd connected with the monster's heart. And he was dead.

No longer standing by his own force, Blaze collapsed on me. Heavy as hell. I fell back under his heft, taking down Bug. The vampire's dead body landed hard on us and the three of us smashed onto the boxes on the top shelf.

The weight was too much.

The shelf bucked. The strain, the battle, the frame wasn't built for a war. The metal and wood shelving heaved under our weight. It groaned. Then–

Snap, snap.

Screws gave way. Two of them.

It was enough.

The mighty shelves lurched.

They sunk.

They collapsed.

Bug screamed. I cried out.

We tumbled down.

"Watch out!" One of the vampires yelled.

Spade and Josie both gasped.

The structures came down on all their heads.

They smashed in the aisle.

Bug reached out as we fell. Desperate to hold onto something. Anything. But there was no controlling this mess. The shelves collapsed in a thick cloud of insects, twisted metal, splintered wood, broken boxes, witch arms and legs, and vampire guts.

Bug's terrified scream echoed.

Then disappeared.

There was ringing in my ears.

Then silence.

40

PERSEPHONE

Ohhh.

I lay flat. Hard. Something heavy on top of me.

My head spun.

Silence pounded.

No, that was my blood.

My heart thumped out of my chest. But I was alright. Alive. Still high. Higher than most of the twisted wreck.

I turned my head slightly.

Ooooh.

Everything hurt. But it wasn't impossible. I could still move.

I began to put together the pieces of the broken scene. The wreckage of boxes and twisted shelves beneath my back and feet.

I'd landed on top of the forklift, the flat roof of the equipment's cab broke my fall. Probably saved my life. The rest of the shelves ended up in a terrible, violent pile somewhere below me, but I'd only tumbled five or ten feet, instead of twice as far.

My back groaned. My front was still covered with a heavy weight I recognized. Blaze's limp body. I shoved the dead vampire off my waist and legs. As he fell, I thought better of kicking the weapon away and at the last moment wrenched out the bloody, used stake. Gripping the weapon I sat up, ready to defend myself, trying to make sense of things. But there was stillness and quiet. No war in the warehouse.

"Jo–" I murmured. "Bug?" Getting a better view of the terrible collapse, I realized our shelf had brought down others in a chain effect. Things in the warehouse were smashed and garbled. Many aisles were wrecked. "Spade?"

No one answered my call.

I searched to find them but discovered Gattas' right-hand vampire impaled on a vertical stake, instead. A twisted piece of wooden shelf stuck out of his chest. He'd been gutted right through in the crash. One more dead.

I turned away in disgust.

His misfortune didn't lighten my mood, it only made me more fearful for my friends. I examined my legs, my arms, my neck. Everything worked. I slowly climbed down from the perch, testing each foothold as I went.

I clambered across more broken chandeliers. Several boxes had sprayed their contents into the heap or all over the ground. Most were indented and smashed. There was still no sign of my squad.

I lowered into the pile.

Where was Bug? He'd fallen like me.

Were Josie and Spade on the bottom of the mound?

Someone else started to rouse.

I started towards them, then stopped. Gattas groaned. A low, rumbling sound.

No, no, no.

I dug into the mess to find my group in a different spot.

We had to go, now.

"Where are you?" I threw more boxes aside, scared at what I might find. I lifted a garbled piece of metal shelf. I hurled it off. At the end of the aisle, other vampires also groaned. The three I'd knocked out with sleeping potion were coming around. They were bug-bitten, but untouched by the crash. And now the drugs were wearing off. They'd been far enough back from the collapse not to be crushed, but my friends...

"We have to go, *now*," I warned the others. Although, they might be hurt. They might have broken bones. No matter what, I would help. Someone coughed. Their voice rattled with blood. I spun.

It was Gattas. Gathering himself.

"Oh, you'll pay for that," he said.

Talking to me. Or himself. Or Bug. Or all of us.

We had to go. *Come on.*

"Where are you guys?" I whisper-cried.

"Come out, come out," Gattas called from where he lay down. He still hadn't stood. I hoped he was more injured than he let on.

"Leave us alone!" I yelled.

"I *can't*, now that I know that you're alive." He rose, picking dead bugs off of his clothes. I ignored the vampire and yanked more boxes back from the main pile. No longer precious or gentle with my exploration, my fingers went wild. Time had run out. I grabbed a third cardboard slice and cleared it off the wreckage by chucking it down the hall, then I gasped.

Bug, Josie and Spade were all there.

Ghost white.

Covered in blood.

Limp on the ground.

Eyes closed.

A huge metal bar had stabbed Josie in the chest. Bug's head was broken open, bits of his brain were spilled out on the floor. They were both gone.

"No." I burst into tears.

I thrust a finger to Bug's throat to see if there was any chance of a pulse. I felt nothing. Josie's black eyes were stone cold. I snuffled and thrust my hair out of my face to check on Spade. He had purple bruises blooming under both eyes. His hands balled in fists, like he intended to fight. I held my finger to his vein, but there was nothing there. No life.

"Spade, come on." I tried to lift him up, to pull him free. As I did, a bloom of blood soaked through the cardboard all around, leaking from his waist. His back.

They were all gone.

All three of my friends.

Their lives were snuffed out.

Oh my god.

I dropped Spade's limp body, still in shock. I let out a terrible cry, then snuffled.

What to do now?

They were dead.

This was my fault.

They came here because of me. They came back into the warehouse to retrieve my careless blood. I led them here and now they were gone. The agony melted my heart.

"*Uh, oh*. Are you alone?" Gattas asked. The cold, delighted delivery of his question brought me back to my head. I gasped. I still had to get out.

The other vampires were waking up too. The short curly-haired one sat up.

"What happened, Boss?"

I looked from him to Gattas, and leapt up as fast as I could stand. I didn't stop to think or to plan, I threw the one flash bang I still had in my pocket and ran. Raced as fast as my legs would go.

"Stop," one of the three sleepy vampires commanded.

"She's wearing Electrum," another one said. The compulsion was null and void. I did not slow down. The vamps came in pursuit. Hunted me as a group.

The door!

My only hope was the door.

If it was daylight outside, I could survive.

"Run for your life," Gattas seemed to whisper in my ear.

He taunted me. To him, this whole night had just been a joke.

First they'd sent in Lady White, to see how she'd handle things, a sick initiation of sorts. When she failed miserably, then the older, more experienced vampires toyed with our lives, pitting us against each other. Using Bug's powers for evil instead of his choice.

It was all so gross.

And even now the vampires let me run... as if I could ever get away from this group. I knew it was foolish to hope. My spells were all spent. I still had the bloody stake and the will to use it, but there was no way I'd catch a vamp unaware now. They were too strong and too fast. They knew right where I was. There was only one play.

Only one thing that had stopped Gattas before: daylight.

What time was it?

I ran. And I hoped.

Surely we'd been in this hellhole all night. That meant morning had to arrive. Either it was here, or it was coming on fast.

If I just got out of the warehouse doors and into the light, I stood a chance.

I ran.

I half-limped.

"You'll have to do better than that," Gattas laughed.

A cat toying with his mouse.

I gave it everything I had to get free.

My body ached with each step.

I couldn't slow down.

The door was right there.

Cold.

Painted gray.

The termite damage frayed the wires of the alarm.

I flung my body into the exit bar and shoved the latch with all my weight. The catch gave way. The exit swung open and I fell to the outside pavement in relief, surrounded by light.

I made it!

But the artificial glow wasn't the daylight I hoped. There was no sun. Just a street lamp. It shone down over the door. The incandescent illumination framed my battered body on the asphalt where I collapsed. I puddled in tears and gasped for breath. Because I had nothing more.

This was it.

The four remaining vampires exited the warehouse and gathered round their limp, exhausted snack. Disappointed that the game ended so poorly. In the end, I hadn't put up a worthy fight and that was no fun. I didn't care. I gave into my fate.

"Take her inside with the others," Gattas muttered.

"They're dead." The other blonde shook his head.

"What's the point?" The curly-haired vamp frowned.

"Fine," Gattas shrugged. "I'll end it here."

"We'll help." The other vampires toothily grinned.

I closed my eyes.

Too weakened to fight.

Too tired to even cry at this point.

Just get it over with...

"This won't hurt... at first." Gattas smiled. His men laughed. Their teeth glinted in the streetlamp light. Looming close overhead.

I had no doubt.

They'd each take a piece.

Suck out my blood.

End my life.

I said a final prayer. An apology for my friends. Sweet Bug.

Tough Josie. Wild card Spade. For Blue Moon, our ally still awaiting news at the file house. I said a curse for Lady Mauve. She knew the danger the search for the Blood Stone would yield, still, she sicked me on it. Made it into an offer I couldn't resist. Then she offered me a vampire bodyguard, but he deserted me next. Under the guise of keeping me safe. I couldn't hate him for that. He'd been correct. I was weak. I wasn't up to the task.

Bye, Lark, I said. *I hope you win out in the end. And good perseveres.*

The four vampires covered me.

Black as night.

Their danger and violence rolled over my skin.

The biggest, strongest vampire's presence sent a midnight shadow over my head and face and I knew it was time. My life had come to an end. But no fanged teeth sunk into my skin. No monster ripped me apart. Instead, I heard a terrible undead man say four words.

"Touch her and die."

It was Lark!

41
PERSEPHONE

Four on one was not a fair fight, but Lark whipped fresh wooden stakes out of a harness on his belt like they were knives and suddenly he was more armed and in control than the other four men.

Gattas nodded at a lesser soldier. The vampire rushed forward and Lark stabbed him with a targeted move, a direct hit to the vampire's heart, killing him instantly before any real fight could begin. Their first vampire fell with a thud beside where I lay on the ground.

"Where are the others?" Lark asked me.

"Dead, they're all dead," I told him. My vampire looked grim.

"Get to the truck," he ordered.

I didn't think I had an ounce of strength left in me, but at his command, I was on my feet, hobbling towards the old vehicle's cab. Not because I was compelled, but because I believed I had a chance. That Lark could save me.

The Brotherhood vampires believed that as well. They realized they'd never win in battles one-on-one against my bodyguard.

"What are you waiting for? Get him!" Gattas roared. He

moved with the remaining vamps. Now three on one. But Lark was quick, he grabbed a blonde man and threw him at the others. They bowled apart but didn't relent. I winced with every step. The sounds of meat punching meat and the grunting of men roared in my mind. I whimpered, moving faster.

Get to the truck.

Arghhhh! Lark cried out. Another vampire had landed some terrible impact.

I didn't look back.

I kept my sights on the vehicle and never stopped.

If I could just get to the cab, get in the truck I'd... I didn't know. *I'd lock the door? I'd feel safe?* 'Til these vampires smashed their way in. There still was no plan. But there was a goal, and an order given by my vampire bodyguard. And that was enough, so I moved best that I could.

Behind me, I heard boot connect to bone. Flesh scraped the pavement.

Almost there.

Go. Go. Go.

The refrain pounded my head and I reached for the door. I had just got my fingers around the handle when someone pulled back on my hair. His bony fingers were ice cold on my head. They dug into my red locks. They twisted and wrenched. My neck was exposed.

"No!" I cried.

It was the curly-haired vamp. The one who'd sucked on my hand.

"Where're *you* going?" He was done holding back. He hissed wildly and immediately went for my jugular, but before he made contact, Lark grabbed him by his own curls and yanked the vampire clean off the ground. The vampire's death grip didn't let up, pulling my whole head with him. We screamed and fell. I was dragged.

Lark swung at the monster's forearm with a wooden stake.

Bones crunched. Direct hit. The curly vamp screamed and released. His arm broke in half.

Oh my god.

My head dropped. I panted and clambered towards the truck again as Lark's elbow struck the vampire's nose and face. There was no time to rest. As the curly-haired vamp collapsed, Lark spun back to take on Gattas, who now lunged. He threw a right hook at my vampire's face. Lark used both arms to block, then jabbed down, throwing his weight on the Brotherhood leader's leg, attacking limbs rather than his core or his face.

I wrenched Josie's truck handle open and squirmed into the cab. I slammed the door, shoved down the lock, and hunkered back on the bench.

Sniveling.

Whimpering.

Lark turned and hurled a reverse elbow into Gattas' face, knocking his fangs through his lips. Blood squirted out.

"Watch out!" I screamed. The other blonde vampire snuck up. My warning was too late. He stabbed Lark's back with the bigger stake from the chair. The one *I'd* carried all the way outside the door, then left on the pavement without further thought. "*No!*"

Lark howled up to the moon, wrenching in agony, but the stake missed his heart.

The blonde tried to pull it back and stab again, but my black-haired vamp was too fast. Lark threw his own stake like a throwing star. It shucked the blonde vamp in the shoulder. Blood spurted, his arm dangled.

I cowered on the truck bench.

The men were more lethal and dangerous than anything I'd ever experienced in my whole life. Each attack made me gasp. Given a moment to rest, Lark became distracted by the wood stake still in his back. He tried to pull it out, but that gave his enemies a chance to regather. The blonde was coming from his right, and Gattas his left. They were each too fast.

Lark had to look up. He almost had the stake. *Why wasn't he looking up?!*

I smashed on the horn, blasting the sound.

The men jolted.

It gave Lark an edge.

He wrenched the stake from his own back, then took the same chair leg and landed a death blow to the blonde-haired man's chest. He yanked the weapon out and threatened Gattas next.

The leader balked. He took a shaky, slow breath.

Both men stood in attack mode, regarding the other, and shielded their wounds.

Lark's body blocked me from sight. He appeared as a shadow to Gattas, surrounded by the headlights I turned on in the truck. It blasted our enemy in artificial light.

Gattas held his stance, but no longer pressed. He tried to give me a glare in the truck, but I was no longer scared. Not while my vampire bodyguard was between us. Staring him down. Ready to pounce.

That's when I realized, it had grown lighter outside. The world was waking up.

The sun was coming out. Morning had arrived.

Lark raised his hands once more, as if encouraging Gattas into a final fight, winner takes all, ready to finish the fuss.

Gattas didn't bite. He snarled at us.

At me.

I glared right back.

My vampire stood as a fierce wall.

I was safe in the truck.

Finally, the Brotherhood vampire turned. He took off. I wanted to watch where he went. As if his path might reveal something that could help and we could keep winning this battle together. But as the enemy departed, Lark crumbled to the ground. Totally spent.

"Lark!" I scrambled out of the truck and caught him just as he fell to the pavement. "*Lark*," I said again, more insistent now, as if that might help. The beautiful man was almost passed out. "You're alright," I lied. I looked back at the truck.

What to do now?

42

PERSEPHONE

The keys were there, the engine was on, but the vehicle was a standard transmission and I didn't know how to drive that kind of truck. Instead, I turned it off and checked the lot for Lark's car. A new sports car was there, sleek and black. I leaned him against the truck license plate.

"We're getting out of here, now," I told him.

My vampire was bleeding everywhere.

His clothes were matted with blood. His and other vamps'.

I patted down his pockets looking for keys, then took them out. I ran over to his car and drove it up close. Then I scrambled to get Lark's arm over my shoulders and tried to force him to stand. I dragged him into the passenger seat, ignoring the other dead vampires strewn on the ground. I closed him into the passenger side and got in the driver's seat.

"Can I take you to the hospital? Where do we go?" I asked. Who could make a vampire well? He slumped back in the chair.

"Blood," he admitted. "I need blood."

"You want to bite me?" My eyes went wide.

His head lolled side-to-side. Lark was practically limp. He didn't say no... or yes...

"You said when a vamp bites a witch she'll either become a vampire or lose her magic abilities for good," I warned.

"You didn't even know you had abilities a week ago," he said.

"I know, but now I do. I don't want to lose... myself,"

He closed his eyes in agreement. "You said your friends were all dead, they still have blood." He struggled. "You could feed me... one of them."

I stared at him in shock. "What?"

He groaned.

The stab wound near his heart seemed to be gushing the most, his shirt heavy with blood, soaked and bright red, but the disgust on my face was enough.

"You want to–" I couldn't finish the words. He'd gone too far. "Oh, god."

Lark shook his head. His eyes were closed. "Forget it, Seph."

I nodded sadly.

It was too much.

But it was also very clear. Without ingesting blood he would die. Very soon.

What then?

Thunder clouds crack overhead. I look up as the first raindrops hit the earth. I drove us under the protection of the loading dock.

"What about the vampires' blood?" I asked. There were still three dead bodies out on the pavement, rain soaking their skin. Could he drink one of those? Lark shook his head.

"They've got too many coagulating properties in them. It doesn't ingest."

His lips were blue. A slight tremor shaking him.

"It's alright. Forget what I asked. I just thought if they were gone... it's too much. I understand..."

The rain pummeled harder now, hitting the pavement and

earth. Sounding like small smacks and pieces of hail. I felt like it was thumping onto my head, even sitting in his dry car. Stressing with Lark, while my vampire bled out from the wounds he earned saving my life.

Giving him the witches' blood could heal his chest?

Save his life?

Lark was right.

My friends were dead.

There was nothing left.

I could bring him their blood. They didn't need it anymore. And I didn't have to watch. But who should he drink? The question felt grotesque. Who would I feed to my vampire bodyguard? On which of my friends should he feast? I couldn't answer that. But I made up my mind to at least try to help.

"I'll be right back." Lark didn't budge. I wasn't sure if he even heard me anymore. The shock had set in. He moaned. His eyes flitted closed. "Hold on, Lark." I squeezed his hand. I ran out of the overhang, through the heavy rain to the adjacent door. I ducked back into the warehouse of hell. I ran back as fast as I could to the friends that I'd left, but every step made me feel sicker and sicker in the head.

Whose body would I give?

Whom should he drink?

The question had no answer.

The property backed onto a forest, could I hunt a wild animal for Lark?

I'd never been a hunter. I barely ate meat.

I might never eat meat again, I realized the new truth.

You have to do this, I steeled myself. Your friends are gone. Think of it like an organ donation. Or a life-saving blood transfusion. The witches you joined forces with would want to help him. *Everything about Bug screamed organ donor*, I reminded myself. Without his donation, Lark would die tonight.

I still wasn't convinced, but it was enough to keep me moving forwards.

I wasn't sure who I would pick. And I had no clue how I'd get them out to the car. But those questions proved moot the moment I got back to the broken aisle where the shelving had collapsed.

Because Josie, Spade and Bug's bodies were gone.

There was nobody there.

The vampires took all my dead friends.

I was left by myself.

43
PERSEPHONE

I fell to the concrete floor where the papers and light switches and twisted metal remained. There were bugs. So many dead insects, but the humans had been taken away.

I was the only one left.

Me and my dying vampire waiting out in the car.

What did they do with my friends?

Had Gattas come back? The rainclouds that rolled in were so dark, maybe he didn't need to hide in a storm? He only hid from the sun.

I needed Lark.

I *wanted* Lark.

He was the only good thing left in my life.

I had ruined and destroyed everything else. But Lark had come, had run in, just to help me. And now he was about to die. Unless...

I looked at the jagged pieces of shelf.

Unless I gave him the only blood I had. *My* blood.

Not a direct bite, but what if I made a cut? What if I poured some out? Like a transfusion that originated from my own vein. I dove towards the closest light box, digging through the chandelier parts looking for something, anything, that would work as a container of sorts. I found a votive shaped like a decorative bowl.

That could work.

I touched my arm. My smooth skin. Then went to the sharpest piece of glass I could find. I raked it over my vein, scratching down, ripping my arm. I hissed at the pain, opening up a new wound. It immediately ached. I gritted my teeth and held the injury over the container to catch my fresh blood. The red liquid seeped out. It dribbled into the cup. It was slow at this pace, but I was scared to widen the cut.

It wasn't much, but this would help, I rationalized my choice. When I had a small cup's worth, I wrapped up my arm with the papers scattered around, then ran back to Lark.

I pushed out of the warehouse door. The rain came down in full force. It was so thick, I could barely see in front of my face. I covered my head as I ran back to his car. I jumped in the front seat with my ruby red bowl of nectar for the vamp.

"Lark!" I slammed the door closed. He was a mess. An unconscious slump, low down in the seat. I'd already taken too long. "No, *Lark*," I turned to him, holding out the small bowl. I grabbed his face and turned his head. He flopped in my hands. "No, no, no."

I thrust the bowl under his nose so he could smell it, but his body didn't raise.

"I've got blood, I've got blood for you," I assured him. I tilted his head. I opened his lips, then inclined the bowl. I watched my crimson life roll across the votive and drip onto his tongue. "*Come on, Lark.*" I whispered. Madly. Softly.

More blood slid from the glass container into his mouth, and down his raw throat.

"*Come back to me, please.*"

I poured out everything. All that I had.

But it wasn't enough.

The bowl was too small.

I was too late.

Except...

...Lark's throat bobbed.

His body flexed.

His lips came together, smacking themselves.

He inhaled deeply.

Drinking in my smell and recovering. Something fluttered. Then he opened his eyes.

"*Lark*," I gladly whimpered. Happy to have my bodyguard back in the car. Until the vampire looked over my direction. His eyes were so dark. So vacant. All sign of the man I'd known was now gone. It was like he'd disappeared.

"What's happening?" I worried. "No."

I leaned back. Growing scared.

This wasn't Lark.

He snatched the glass bobble from my hand, lightning fast, and licked every drop from the vessel, snarling as he did. He seemed like a wild animal. Like all the other vampires he'd just killed. The man's eyes turned on me. Vicious and cold. Black as night. He sized me up, like I was a meal. Lark sniffed the air again. He realized the delicious smell came from me. He bared his teeth.

Horrible fangs. Razor sharp.

Glistening now.

My vampire bodyguard grabbed my wounded arm so hard, I gasped. He ripped off the pathetic paper wrapping I'd made. His eyes shone in delight.

"Lark, *no*. What are you doing? Please don't bite me. Stop." I begged. But Lark was gone. A cold, dark creature of the night replaced his spot in the car. "Please," I whimpered again. "You don't want to do this. *Lark!*"

I yanked my hand free and slapped his face, as hard as I could.

It left a stinging red handprint. For a moment, it seemed to reprieve my friend. My bodyguard. The man I'd been thinking of when I cut into myself, the one who fought hard and saved my life. For a brief second, I could see he was in there, somewhere in those eyes.

Surprised.

In shock.

That I could attack him.

That I would fight back.

But then that light version was gone, and the darkness returned.

"Orphan Girl," Lark said my nickname. He struggled with himself. A battle played out in real time. "Persephone."

"Lark?" I couldn't keep the terror from my voice.

He stared right at me.

"*Run!*"

44
PERSEPHONE

I jumped out of the car and slammed the door, half-expecting the vampire who I just saved to tackle me in the rain, dash my head on the ground, and suck all the blood from my veins. Instead, I ran like hell.

The storm blinded my eyes.

It made me feel dazed.

But I didn't stop.

I cried and I raced.

There was nowhere to go.

I had no one.

All my friends were gone.

Dead in a sick treasure hunt.

The only man that I trusted in this town had just turned.

He'd almost eaten me alive.

My world burned. My feet hit the hard earth. I headed for the wild forest behind the warehouse of death. Fast as I could go. My wound pounded, my legs hurt. I was exhausted and beaten and spent.

But still, I ran.

I raced 'til I could sprint no more.

The rain didn't wash away my tears. They compounded, like a flood. Like a river of pain. But it didn't matter. Nothing mattered now.

I thought he was good.

I thought *I* was good.

But my greed caused all of this.

My need to inherit my uncle's stuff. His house. His money. His life.

I could hide behind the good of all witch-kind, but my personal desires were the real impetus. This violence and destruction and death were all my fault.

My lungs ached.

My arms became loose. Same as my legs. Until the weight was too much for my flopping limbs. For my broken heart. I collapsed in a leafy pile of moss. I threw my head into my hands, falling over the round curve of a felled log. There I wept in gasping, ugly sobs, until my body held no more tears. Until my clothes were soaked and my hair was matted by the rain hitting me and the earth.

In agony, I pictured my murdered friends.

I couldn't outrun their twisted pain.

Sweet Bug.

My brain replayed the look of sad horror he experienced as he realized what his beloved insects had done to the woman he loved.

Fierce Josie.

Always thinking smart. Fighting back with every breath. With all the power that she possessed. Right 'til the end.

And bold and impulsive Spade. Cocky as hell. Along for the ride, completely unaware that the flighty decision he made to impress an ex-girlfriend would cause his demise.

I tried to hold on to their faces, but the twisted, mangled image of their deaths flooded over my brain. It overran my thoughts.

That should have been me, the voice inside me said. *I should be dead.*

I shook and wailed.

I stayed for hours in the rainfall until I heard the coming of heavy steps. Someone was searching the forest, looking for me.

Let them come. Take me, kill me. I no longer cared.

Being murdered by Gattas would be a relief.

Being butchered by Lark, a fitting end.

I didn't move.

I didn't hide.

Crunch, crunch, crunch.

The footsteps came straight my way, but I did not raise my head.

Just finish it.

The person kneeled.

"Persephone, you're hurt," Lark said. The voice was calculated and calm. Back in control. His presence too close. I didn't look up.

"Just kill me or leave me alone." I whispered to the tree. His body tensed. He paused.

"I deserve that. I'm sorry I scared you in the car. I wasn't in control." He admitted. "Can I sit down?"

I didn't answer, but he lowered himself beside me anyway.

The action made him groan. He was still as bruised and broken as I was from the fray.

"I'm sorry I told you to leave town," he offered.

"You were right," I didn't look up. "This is a death warrant."

"Yes," he agreed. "But I was wrong to make you fend for yourself, no one should have to do that," he mused. "Although you do have a pretty good slap," he said. He rubbed his jaw. "Is the imprint still there?"

I glanced up. Curious.

"No," I quietly said. He half-smiled. His mouth a straight line, the end slightly twitching up against his cheek. The monster was gone. He looked like Lark again.

My Lark.

Or at least like the version of Lark that I thought I'd known, until that terrifying moment in his car. This soaking wet Lark. With a stern but caring gaze.

It was a relief.

"When you fed me, you awakened something... primal. I haven't had the sanguine of a human or a witch in a long, long time. I thought I could control it, the need, the hunger, but I was wrong. Once I had a taste..." he trailed off. "I'm better now. I killed a rabbit in the forest, so I've had enough to calm my appetite. I'm back to normal, Seph."

"I'm not."

I didn't know what else to say. Even the thought of that evil creature feasting on an unsuspecting rabbit... it might have been better than dining on my veins, but... it didn't bring me any peace.

"Of course," he agreed. "You're in shock. You're still pretty hurt."

"I'm fine," I lied. Directly contradicting my previous words.

Lark went to put a hand on my shoulder but I jerked back, hissing at the tender spots. Every part of my body thrummed with an ache that would only grow more painful as the shock wore off.

"Vampire saliva has healing properties... I'd like to help." Lark said. He spit into his own hand. "May I?" This time, he asked for my arm.

I didn't move.

I didn't know if I could trust him or not. But it was either try with Lark or stay in the woods, in the rain, totally alone, broken and crushed. So there wasn't much choice. I let the vampire have my arm. Lark took the palm with his saliva and cupped it against my skin.

Fizz.

My eyes shot open wide as I felt the surge, like bubbles or carbonation tickling against my skin, covering the wound. Kissing my body. Helping it heal.

"How does that feel?" Lark quietly asked.

I let it wash over me.

A rush of peace. My body stitched up with his kiss.

"It feels good." I admitted, finally staring into his eyes, surprised. He held my gaze with care and patience. "Are you *good*? Lark?"

"Not all of the time," he admitted, removing his hand. Lark spit into his palm and applied the salve a second time. The movement was small and still, every other part of our bodies frozen, our gaze locked on each others' eyes. We were so close, it was like we breathed the same air. As if the rain didn't hit us at all.

Because that answer meant he was good at least some of the time.

Most of the time, I hoped.

I wanted to believe this vampire was trying to do right by me, by the witch world, maybe even by his fellow vamps, the ones who weren't out to tear nature and society apart. Lark tried and tried. There was a beast deep inside him. A monster he had to fight to control. An impulse that made this man fight wildly for me and protect my life, then also try to suck out my blood. Lark was both. I wanted to believe in the version right here, right now. To make that the truth. I wanted that desperately. After all, Lark was all that I had left in this world.

Please don't turn out to be a lie.

"Thank you, Persephone. You were willing to do an awful thing for me, getting me blood." Lark said, quietly. "I'm sorry I asked."

I thought of my friends, how they were taken. What did the vampires want with my dead? Same thing as Lark, I supposed. A hasty meal. An influx of fresh blood. The thought made me queasy again. But I didn't regret feeding Lark my blood to save his life.

"You saved me too," I admitted. "A lot. It was awful, but fair."

The abilities of the vampire saliva proved true. I looked down at the jagged cut I'd made on my forearm skin, it became sealed and light pink in color, only moments away from disappearing for good. It wouldn't even leave a scar. Not in the physical sense. Internally, though, it surely would.

"You have other cuts," Lark said. His discerning eyes examined my skin, nothing lost from his sight. He went to spit in his hand, to apply the touch again. But I wanted him closer than that. I wanted to wrap my body in his. To disappear into him.

"You don't have to use your hand," I said. "You could just... kiss. I mean, if you think you can control yourself."

"I can," Lark agreed.

We stared at each other a moment longer.

"I'd like to heal." I offered. The vampire's jaw flexed as he considered my ask, then he took my almost-recovered arm and gently brought it up to his lips.

He kissed the self-inflicted wound. His mouth pressed on my skin.

The injury surged with bubbles and fizz.

Twice as potent as the hand caress had been. So intense with medicinal healing powers, I shuddered in relief. My body released. Lark watched, locked onto me.

"How does that feel?"

"I'm not sure I can explain..." I murmured. "It feels a bit like fireworks exploding under my skin."

"And here?" Lark moved to my elbow and kissed another bruise he could see. I breathed deeply then sighed.

"The Fourth of July."

"And here?" He kissed my palm.

"New Year's Eve."

"Here?" Lark moved to the fingertip. The one the curly-haired vampire had sucked. I shuddered at the memory. He stopped, unsure.

"Do it," I said. "Please."

I wanted to reclaim my whole body from them. Replace it with a memory of Lark. My vampire's pink-purple lips caressed the top of my finger with gentle ease. He sucked on the paper cut slice. I tried not to groan in pleasure. I failed. Lark watched.

"How does this feel?" He whisper-asked. Taking my finger in his mouth again.

"I'm running out of celebratory occasions," I admitted.

"Should I stop kissing you?"

"Never, Lark."

The words popped out so quickly. I blushed. Of course he was teasing me. I'd fallen right into the sweet trap, proving everything he'd said before. I was like putty in his hands. But now that the physical threshold between us had passed, I didn't care. I wanted more.

"Don't you dare stop," I bossed, despite myself. "I have a thousand wounds." I offered my other arm as proof. Lark obeyed, finding any sprain, insect bite, or unclothed bruise and laying his lips on my skin. He leaned all over me.

The motion was full of care.

A slow, deliberate speed.

Here ventured a man who'd been so fast and violent with other terrible men, yet Lark could be liquid molasses with me. I had a large collection of other injuries under my shirt and my pants and I might have liked him to lick on them as well, kissing every inch, but the vampire didn't ask me to undress and I didn't push.

"That should be good," Lark murmured, pulling back.

"What about you?" I asked. Every visible inch of my skin had been buffered and cleaned by his vampire attention. But he was a mess.

"I'm healing alright," Lark said.

"I'll be the judge. Show me your wounds."

"Which one?"

"The worst one." I nodded at the caked blood on his shirt. He stirred a hair, raised an eyebrow then nodded down at his own chest, permission to look under the hood. I unbuttoned the mottled shirt as he watched.

The first fastener opened.

Then the next.

After a third and fourth button, I could see his tanned skin. His muscled pecs.

Lark wordlessly watched as I opened the cloth wider to have a view of his chest. The stab wound he sustained was jagged. His skin was gouged. Twisted. Blood red. But it was also true, Lark was already healing from his own internal gifts. Any blood was caked and old. Dried out. The wound no longer bled.

"It doesn't take long for a vampire to heal," he admitted. "Even from a stab in the back."

"Does it hurt?" I wondered out loud.

"Only when I laugh." Lark deadpanned. This made us both smirk. The morning had been so bleak, neither of us had cracked a genuine smile in hours. "*Ow*. See?" He pretended.

It probably did hurt, but he showed no real weakness. That wasn't Lark.

"Would you like me to kiss it?" I asked. My cheeks flushed red.

"Do you have healing powers in your saliva?" He cocked his head.

"No," I admitted, vulnerable and small. "But it still might feel good."

"It might." He considered the proposition.

I wanted his agreement so badly.

Take me away. Take me away.

Give me new memories, Lark.

Make me forget.

My vampire understood what I was suggesting. It was clear what would start between us if I kissed him like he'd done on my skin. Any pretense of practitioner's care or medical treatment would be gone. It would unleash a different sort of primal connection and need.

Lust.

Sex.

I wanted him so badly.

I felt certain he also wanted me.

But when the vampire didn't immediately agree, I realized how desperate and foolish the suggestion was. How sad and pathetic I must sound. A desperate girl. A human with no hope and no future and no friends.

A failure at Lady Mauve's simple task.

I couldn't do that.

I only wanted to open new complications to crowd out the pain of my past.

To make me feel whole once again.

To at least pretend.

For a while.

I pulled back, dropping his shirt. I wouldn't beg.

"I just think that might... complicate things," Lark finally said. He seemed chagrined. My cheeks burned. "I don't want you to get the wrong idea," he added, twisting the rejection. A knife in the wounds he'd just healed. I'd just been turned down by the man who'd spent the last twenty minutes kissing every bare inch of my skin. "Considering everything we still have to do," Lark added.

"You're still going after the Blood Stone?" I asked, surprised.

"If I can. Yes." He agreed. "You won't?" He seemed surprised by me too. At my opposite answer.

"I don't know." I admitted. "You said before, is a house really worth all this pain? I don't think that it is."

Could I possibly live in the home beside Bug's family, knowing the sweet boy died in effort to help me to live in his world? The thought made me gag. I spit on the grass. But if I didn't finish this task, then what was the point? What was the meaning behind my friends' deaths if the stone wasn't retrieved? There wasn't one. I was so overloaded with emotion over everything that had happened today I couldn't even fathom what might come next. But the High Council Witch Academy and Plumpkin weren't part of my plans anymore. Even if the vampires hunted me down to release the binding spell or even if I successfully passed the Blood Stone to Mauve. Gaining financial independence didn't seem right. Not anymore.

Lark nodded.

He understood. Or at least he pretended to.

Like I pretended with him.

"It's time we get you out of the rain," he finally said. At his suggestion, I didn't immediately stand. But he put out a hand so I let him help me to my feet.

I'd actually forgotten all about the weather that soaked us right to the skin. Sitting so close to Lark, so wrapped up in the fizzy blush of vampire kisses that the tactile feel of the wet weather had disappeared. Now his words brought me back to reality. My clothes were all ruined. Saggy and stretched. They were bloody and ripped. I was a dirty mess. I must have seemed like a drowned rat, not that I cared. But the disparity between us was apparent, even now. Lark still looked great. Tousled maybe, but handsome... only... more rugged and raw than before. It suited him.

"I don't have anywhere to go," I admitted. I'd been staying with Bug. But Bug was... I pushed the end of that thought out of my head. "And I don't own anything. The vampires can reach me wherever I land."

"Perhaps," Lark interrupted my dark thoughts, "you might like to see where I live?"

45
LARK

I shouldn't have kissed her skin, I beat myself up. *Or tried to suck her blood. I should've just used my hand to spread the saliva, or kept my fingers to myself. Goddamn it, Lark.*

That skin.

The way her whole body raised and writhed under my kiss.

She said it was fireworks.

I was a fire that burned.

I could blaze...

Christ, what was I thinking?

The girl almost died.

She just lost her friends. The only other people she knew in this town. And now I'm thinking of *sex? Of driving her back to my house?*

Why did I invite her home? Because I could no longer let her out of my sight.

The need in me had grown so great.

To protect her.

To keep her safe.

Even from herself.

I glanced across the front seat at Persephone, staring out the window, lost in her own thoughts.

This will blow up in your face, I chastised myself.

Seph looked so small in the seat. Like an adorable drowned rat. Her red hair hung down her back in a slick clump. I wanted to reach out and brush it with my fingers. I wanted to touch her. To take care of her. The vulnerability she displayed now belied the strength and resilience I'd seen back at that truck. Outside and inside the warehouse she fought for her life. And for mine. She would have carried each of her friends to safety on her back if she could have managed it. I admired her strong, healing body as well. Both softness and strength could be found in each curve. I snapped my eyes back to the road not to be discovered by her.

There was no way I'd let Dreven or Gattas take her.

Even if it did cause me trouble later on. I would protect Seph from the Brotherhood. I'd find a way. Then, once Persephone had the Blood Stone and we could finally, truly work together, then I'd see where we'd stand. Worst case, I could remove her Electrum necklace and compel her decisions. She'd do whatever I asked.

Fuck. When I said it like that, I was no better than the Brotherhood of Vampire idiots. That wouldn't happen, I assured myself. *We'll be on the same page.*

But there were no guarantees. Our relationship was already too messy. I was in too deep for us to be just bodyguard and charge, or something still innocent like that.

But you didn't let it get romantic, I reminded myself. *You stopped just in time.*

You controlled yourself, I lied. I said the words over and over again, even as I snuck another peek at the orphan girl. And a further glance right after that.

My body groaned with desire to touch her knee. To comfort her pain.

I cared so much.

I swallowed the feelings down and reminded myself of everything at stake.

Eyes on the road, you weak fuck.

I drove in silence the long way back to my house. She leaned against the window and waited for sleep to overtake her, but even in her exhausted state, true rest never arrived. I took as many peeks as I dared, but Persephone never looked up. Just stared dully ahead.

What was she thinking about?

"You sleeping?" I finally asked.

If she did dream, that could help. It was a good strategy. It would reveal more details or clues of where to look next. Though I knew she'd wished for it in the forest, the battle wasn't over for us. Until the Blood Stone was in our possession, there'd be another war to fight. It was simply a matter of time.

"I'm not sleeping," she said.

"Did you learn anything more about the possible location of the stone?" I gently asked. It had been a while since we strategized.

That was my fault.

I thought I could do this on my own, but she'd been one step ahead of me this whole time with those damn dreams. Or some other clue. I'd been lucky Birdie had stolen the files and we'd seen the warehouse name. It was time to team up with Child's niece full time.

Persephone glanced down at her wet pants.

We'd been driving for so long she was no longer soaked to the bone. The cargo material was merely clammy and damp at this point.

"I found a paper. A receipt," she said. "Before..." she swallowed the memories that came next. I saw her fight with herself, then regather. "It's proof that a third chandelier exists. That's what we went to the warehouse for. The paperwork had an address for each one. They weren't catalogued online, the purchases were made before mainstream internet."

"I remember the time," I agreed.

"Yes. But we found the hard copy. It was a different delivery point. The first two came to the school. The third–"

"Shipped directly to his house?" I supplied.

That seemed the next logical spot. A place I probably would have checked already if it hadn't been magically sealed from the world by the dead man. But, that wasn't the address she found.

"No." She glanced at me again, then stalled. "I don't know if I should give you this," she said.

"Probably not," I admitted. "I'm a vamp."

"It's not that," she kept looking. "I trust you, Lark. Completely," Persephone said.

I swallowed hard. *Had my lapse in the car not taught her anything? Trusting me was a terrible plan.*

She looked straight ahead, her voice drifted far away. "But everyone I've worked with is dead."

"I'm not alive," I gently reminded her.

"Nor are *they*."

The words squirted out with a fresh barrage of pain. Persephone quietly wept. I slammed on the brake and yanked at the wheel. My car squealed. The tires drifted and spun us around. The move was so intensely swift and vampiric that she should have screamed. Seph should have thrown up her hands and braced hard for certain doom. But the Orphan Girl didn't flinch. She didn't try to protect herself. And after a perfect donut on the highway, I stopped the car on the side bank, in sync with the road. I killed the engine. And stared at her.

"That's not your fault."

"Yes it is. They're all gone."

"You didn't ask for any of this, it was thrust upon you. You're innocent, Seph."

"And what, you all asked to become vamps?" She stared right back. "We're all dealt terrible stuff. This was *my* thing. *I* asked Bug for help. I asked you to compel him and you did. And he enlisted Jo and she asked Spade. *I* knew the danger, *you warned me* of the danger, and still I came, and *I made them go back–*"

"You did the right thing. The only thing you could." I shook my head. I hadn't heard all the details of what happened in the warehouse yet. I didn't need to know. That was the point. I'd seen who this witch was from the very first day we met. Sassy. Smart. Resilient. A damn capable woman. Strong enough to put me in my place. She'd done the best that she could, of that I was sure. And probably more. I grabbed the witch's beautiful face and steered her to look me in the eyes, but none of her spark remained. She shook her head.

"I could have stopped, Lark. I could have walked away. I should have. You said it yourself. Go. I knew the risks. I know I'm dead," she told me.

"What are you talking about?"

"Blue Moon explained about the binding on the Stone. It's mine, passed down by blood, controlled by magic that will hurt anyone who touches it but me. It's booby-trapped. But if I'm gone, there'll be no magical hex. If Gattas and his goons had just killed *me*, they could have let the other three live."

"Vamps don't work like that," I frowned.

"You do."

"They would have killed everyone in sight," I admitted.

"Then why am I still here?"

"I don't know," I sighed. *Why were any of us here?* "Maybe to stop a rogue legion of vampires from infecting the coven and making an unstoppable undead army. Maybe to put a chink in the plan to destroy this whole town? Maybe for me? To help me? To help me help you?"

She searched my face. Looking for answers. For connection. For a safe place.

I felt it too.

This girl, who'd almost been the death of me more than once. I was irrevocably entwined with her. I wanted more. I wanted all of her. She wasn't just my charge and I her bodyguard anymore. I cared. Way too much.

I'd move heaven and earth to keep her safe. But I couldn't explain how I felt.

I couldn't twist her up any more than we were enmeshed now.

It wasn't fair. Or smart.

My eyes accidentally drifted to her lips.

It took every ounce of strength I had not to lunge across the seats and kiss that mouth.

To let her know that she wasn't alone.

And that this wasn't her fault.

That I was here.

That I'd keep her safe.

"Please trust me, Seph." I whispered her name, like a kiss on my lips. The only part of her I could safely embrace. She finally nodded.

"I do. I trust you, Lark."

My dreamcast looked down. She reached into her pocket to retrieve something. As gently as she could, she pulled out the paperwork. The receipt.

"Here. It listed a place I didn't recognize. There was a family name… Umbrella-wick. Something like that." The old paper was damp. "No." She gave an exasperated gasp. The battle and rain and everything else had ruined the evidence she'd worked so hard to collect. It practically disintegrated in her hands. There was nothing left.

The exact location of the final chandelier was gone.

Totally destroyed.

All we had was a name.

A partial name.

It was a death knell to the mood in our car.

"What a waste," she muttered.

"We'll be alright," I said. Seph looked up.

"Tell that to my friends."

46

PERSEPHONE

I stared off into the distance, unfocused. Lark followed my lead, on autopilot, driving us back to his house. I took in nothing at all. Completely zoned out.

The vampire could have driven me anywhere.

I wouldn't have batted an eye.

Silence filled the car.

After who knew how long, Lark finally spoke. "Almost there."

The words made me jump, I'd gotten so used to the quiet I almost forgot where I was. Who I was with.

He turned his blinker on, I looked around at the road. I saw a flat, smooth stone laid down on its side. Then he swerved off the highway onto a winding dirt road with no sign. Not as tight of a corner as the donut-drift he'd done on the highway, but still an impressive maneuver. The road wound down through a thick forest. Lark took the turns in stride until the laneway twisted onto a large parcel of land. There were trees on all sides. The gravel crunched beneath his tires as I glimpsed the first vision of his home.

A castle. Made of stone.

Lark's vampire lair was ancient and large. Two hundred feet long or more. A fortress that spread out on several acres. The tallest turret pushed up into the clouds. All the glasswork and windows on the building were decades old. The architecture was ornate. The brickwork was curved.

Aged wood.

Medieval stone.

The structure had been built a long time ago.

Made to last through uncertain times. Uncertainty may have been all it had known.

The roof was cut into battlements. The parapets protected the inhabitants. There was a long, surrounding brick wall. The only thing missing was a moat.

We went through an impressive gate and drove up to a six-car garage.

"It was once a military college," Lark offered. "Welcome to the Bird Cage. Home, sweet, home."

We got out quickly. Lark came around to my car door to open it like a gentleman, but I was already stepping out. He held open the door into his house instead, so I went in. I immediately felt out of place as we journeyed into the first castle landing space. This wasn't the front door. He'd taken me in through a side entrance, directly into the heart of the home. Far too familiar. A kitchen, to my right. To my left, a long hall.

Lark ushered me further into his home. I wanted to feel warm and invited but he'd rejected me in the forest. Still, in the car on the side of the road, I could have sworn we'd had a connection again. Or was that me, merely projecting?

The mood in the house was at best professional, at worst downright cold. So I examined the details of the castle as we walked. It wasn't decorated by Lark. Nothing here seemed uniquely his, but maybe it was. Maybe I didn't know him at all. He definitely had money, and the castle was styled. The floors were wide planks, polished to a shine. Tapestries hung on the walls depicting nature and ancient languages I didn't know. Each of the alcoves had adornments from ancient times like suits of armor and coats of arms.

I hugged my hands to myself as we moved deeper. This wasn't my world.

Lark and I weren't a real team or a partnership. He'd made that clear several times. If it wasn't for my bloodline with Child, I wouldn't be here, in his house. I felt so exhausted and wrecked I just wanted to close my eyes and shut down. Push all these terrible thoughts and memories out of my head. But he expected me to help.

To find the damn Blood Stone.

Lark directed me to the castle's receiving room, a study where a giant fire blazed inside a massive hearth. The thing was huge. It took up half the wall. The flickering warmth drew me near, I hadn't been fully dry now for hours. The idea of heating by the fire was intoxicating. I might have walked right to it, laid down on the soft rug and slipped off into dreamland had it not been for the others in the room.

Three raised from their chairs.

I should have felt fear, but my emotions had run out several hours ago. I had no excitement left. No fear and no hope. This giant castle could have housed an entire army of vampires. I wouldn't be shocked. How many more lived in these dorms?

No matter the number, I didn't fear. This was Lark's home. His place in this world.

I was safe if he was close.

Still, the three people in the flickering orange light made me slow to a stop. It was obvious they had been waiting for Lark. Their eyes held questions.

He subtly shook his head. No.

"Persephone Dawn, meet Wren and Lila, his wife," Lark introduced us.

The couple were exquisitely beautiful, just like him. With delicate wrinkled lines around the sides of their eyes. Definitely vampires. The men shared similar hair and features, along with matching size and strength and style. Lark was possibly a year or two younger than Wren, but they each remained in that never-ending chasm of virility and handsomeness. They would stay there for the rest of their undead lives. The new man wore a pressed dress shirt, an expensive watch and smooth slacks, just like Lark's had been... before the rain and the fight had torn his wardrobe apart.

"You look terrible, brother," the vampire grinned.

Brother.

I guessed their relationship before Wren supplied it in words. Before he playfully smacked his sibling's shoulder in a familial way of offering both comfort and ridicule in the very same breath.

"Try to be nice. We have guests," Lila shook her head. Her blonde waves blossomed over each of her shoulders as she grinned at me. She was bohemian and relaxed in dark jeans, a dark tank top and a long flowy lace blouse tied in the front. "It's nice to meet you, Persephone." She genuinely squeezed my hand.

"Wren," Lark's brother labelled himself again and shook my hand.

"We've heard a lot about you. And I believe you know my twin sister," Lila swayed to the side, revealing the third party in the room, Lady Mauve.

Twin sister.

This I did *not* guess.

I stared between the two women. The disparity between their age and youth, between ethereal supernatural beauty and a mortal lifetime hard-lived, between long blonde locks and short gray hair, between smiles and kind words and judgy, death stares... *these two were twins?*

"How–" It was rude no matter how I tried to pose a follow up question, so I stopped.

"She's a vampire, I'm not." Lady Mauve snapped.

Both women frowned. Mauve at myself, Lila at her sibling's sharp tongue. For a brief moment I saw their similarities in the pose.

"Anna," Lila chastised.

"Close your mouth, girl, you look like a trout." Mauve told me. "Did you retrieve the stone?"

"No," I said.

"*Anna–*" Lark's brother tried to interrupt. Louder. But Mauve stared bullets at me.

"Why not?"

"There were complications, Dreven sent Gattas and five other stock," Lark cut in.

"There were seven vampires, actually. First, we blew up Lady White." I said.

"I never liked her," Mauve shrugged. "Weak-willed."

"Compelled," I corrected. "Then killed. We had no choice." But Lady Mauve didn't flinch at the death. Someone she'd known for years was gone and she didn't even blink.

"Gattas?" Wren was surprised. He and Lila exchanged frowns. "No wonder you look like you look."

"You should see the other guys," Lark muttered. His jaw flexed. I didn't enjoy their tone.

"Nine are dead," I said, coldly. "Including all my friends."

Lila sucked in her breath. Mauve was unmoved.

"I couldn't get inside," Lark agreed quietly. "Gattas' group did."

"Oh, honey," Lila started. Her sister cut her off.

"No one said she should enlist a ragtag group of witch kids.

That's her own fault." Mauve criticized my choices as if I wasn't even there.

It was all too much.

I burst into tears.

"Hey, no. Don't listen. You did your best. It's alright," Lila cooed. She held out her arms and I fell into this strange woman's embrace because she was nice, because I was spent, because Lark was full of mixed messages, and because I could no longer hold it together for their group. Lila asked for nothing in return. She let me collapse. She looked over my head at the others and glared.

"Look what you've done," she said to all or none of them. Lark, Mauve, and Wren merely watched. She seemed to realize their prying eyes wouldn't help me calm down. "Let's get you cleaned up." Lila steered me away from the crowd.

"Get that rock!" Mauve shouted over my soft sobs as I let the woman cradle me down the hall. The woman vampire was my age, at least she must have been when she turned, which was actually decades ago, judging by the appearance of Lady Mauve. If the women were twin sisters, Lila must have spent several seasons living here, in this house, looking the same every day, prim and proper in a castle with a beautiful, dangerous family of men. She'd likely seen her share. She was probably a monster as well. They all were, deep down. This new thought caused me to catch my ragged breath.

"So you're a dreamcast?" Lila asked.

"Maybe, I think. Yes. I have no training."

"Oh, you don't need that. I remember that feeling as well. I wasn't a member of the coven either, you know. Anna parabonded but I–"

"I don't know what that is." I interrupted.

"Nor does the High Council coven," Lila sniffed, but I wasn't in the mood for private jokes. She sensed it. "For your purposes, a parabond is a fate-bound partnership. A magical tie between you and one other. Witches used to prove their magical worth by finding the person they matched with. Not anymore."

"Like a soulmate?"

"No... much darker." Her eyes clouded momentarily, then she forced her cheery grin. She was as sweet as her twin sister was sour. "A story for another time," she assured me, patting my arm. "For now, some fresh clothes and a good night's sleep will help. You might even cast." Her eyes shone. They gave her away.

So that was it.

The reason he'd brought me here. It wasn't for my well-being at all.

Lark was hoping that in the comfort of his home, my visions might tell him where to look next. I was too tired to object.

Lila steered me to a guest bedroom on the first floor, away from the study and the giant staircase with rich blue carpet that led to the second landing where most of the bedrooms were. She swung open the door to another beautiful castle space with its own fireplace, cozy sitting area, rug, and couch. The room was painted in soft white, laid with the same plush carpet from the stairs. It was soft underfoot. Matching window treatments framed the windows to the world. The sight of four chandeliers dripping with glass and shining light in the space made me groan in despair.

"We'll keep those off," Lila flicked a switch and the lighting changed to wall sconces and the fireplace glow. The space was relaxed. Warm. "There's a closet here," Lila led me to a walk-in wardrobe with hanging things, and drawers of soft fabrics and underclothes. "Choose whatever you like. They're all for you." In the next room she turned on a light. It was an ensuite bath-room, almost as big as the bedroom itself, with marble floors and wallpapered shelves and faucets of bronze. She knelt and started a bath. The heavy sound of flowing water filled the space. "You can clean up first, then go to bed. No one will bother you here. Any questions?" She paused to feel the water to make sure the temperature was right. I hesitated. So Lila added. "You can ask me whatever you want, Persephone. I stayed here once, too, as a guest. I know what it's like." She was so gentle.

"How did you–" the words stalled. I wasn't quite sure of the verbiage to use not to insult my host. Turn? Die? "–how did you become..?" I trailed off. Her mouth twitched.

"Lark and Wren have another brother, Finch. He attacked me. When he tried to unleash something bad on the world, I fought back. He bit me during the fight just to spite Wren, to try to kill something he loved, but I was a witch blood, so here we are."

Lark... Wren... Finch.

My vampire had called this place the Bird Cage.

"So vampires can love?" I didn't mean to ask it out loud. Lila raised an eyebrow, but didn't ask why I cared.

"Yes, we can love. If we want to, it's possible. The boys love each other and I love Wren. I love Lark too, in a different sort of way. Just not Finch or Birdie."

"Who's that?"

"Birdie's... away. She'll be back soon." That wasn't an answer, but I didn't push.

"Is he–" I looked over my shoulder. "The brother. Finch. Does he–?"

"Finch isn't here. He's long gone. The boys made sure. But there are other vamps like him, ones who only think of them-selves." She must have noted the panic on my brow because she switched tracks. "There are good vampires and bad, Persephone. Just like anything. We try. Good vampires have something called the soul knot still intact. It ties us to the humanity we once knew." She put her hand to her chest. "It's located in the shadow of our hearts. Lark is a fierce protector. He'll do what is right. No matter the cost. If a vampire is cruel, it's likely that their tether is removed. Or destroyed. " I knew she meant to assure me, but a shiver ran through my bones at the thought.

"Look at me, prattling on. You're cold. The bath will help. Please rest and relax. I'll be right down that hall."

"Thank you," I said. Genuinely relieved. She smiled and reached out. She tucked an errant hair behind my ear. The gesture was so simple and caring, I almost broke apart at the seams. But Lila meant well.

"Any friend of Lark's is a friend of mine," she said. "You can count on that."

Then she turned and left.

I didn't have the nerve to explain we weren't really pals. I was just a means to his ends. She'd already departed anyhow. I touched the hot water for myself. It opened my aching fingertips. They sighed in a mix of relief and of pain. Before stripping down, I located fresh clothes and made myself a little pile. Lila had left a plump towel to dry myself on the edge of the tub. I checked the door latch twice to ensure it was locked before I undressed from my bloody rags and slipped into the bath.

It soothed me in a different way than Lark's kisses had done.

Now fully bare, I compared the injuries that had been in and out of the vampire's reach in the forest. The vampire-kissed cuts were markedly better off, almost healed to the touch. The lip service really was a medical marvel. Not romantic in the slightest, I now understood. There was so much I didn't know about this paranormal life. So much magic I didn't understand. Knowledge was power, but ignorance was bliss, and I knew in an instant which of the two I'd still have preferred.

I stayed in the bath 'til the water became tepid, verging on cool. Then I cuddled myself into the towel, a fresh tank top, clean underpants, and eventually the heavy blankets of the bed. Sleep came quickly, exhaustion finally winning the day. I started to dream the second I put down my head.

———

"*No!*" Someone screamed.

I shot up in bed, sweating and scared.

How long had I been out?

My throat hurt.

Lark smashed through the door. The vampire rushed to my side, ready to rumble, but the bedroom was still. The danger had only existed in my brain. He scanned the room.

"You're alright." He said. "You're in the Bird Cage and you're safe."

I'd been alone.

I stared at his beautiful, worried face, catching my breath.

It was me.

I'd screamed. I'd woken him and myself with my cries in the dark.

"I'm sorry I woke you," I said, covering up.

"I was awake." He must have been sitting right outside of my door to have crossed the distance to me at such a fast pace. Even with vampiric speed. "You need to rest," he said. Lark stepped back a respectful distance again.

"Tell that to my head," I sighed.

"Did you dream?"

I knew what he meant. *Did I have a vision that would help?*

"I don't think so," I shook no. "It was just that same bloody moment from today. When I picked up the cardboard piece and saw everything. All my friends. Josie's chest wound, then Bug. The way his brain was..."

I retched, clamping a hand over my lips. My body rejected the truth.

I tried to hold it in.

Gulp it down.

But the vomit surged.

I leapt from the bed, covering my lips, and raced into the bathroom to throw up. I fell in front of the toilet and puked. Then vomited again. Lark followed me there. Wordlessly, he scooped back my hair and held it away from my face as I clenched the porcelain bowl in my palms. He quietly rubbed my back until the agony relaxed. I sputtered and spat. He offered me a cold compress to wipe down my nostrils, neck and face. Then a glass of water. I leaned back against the tub, wholly spent, staring off into nothingness.

"Drink," he said. I obeyed. He poured a fresh glass and traded it out. "I'm sorry, Persephone. I should have been inside. I couldn't get in."

He didn't have permission to enter.

"How'd the other vampires get through?" I asked. I took another sip of water, hoping my stomach might calm. Lark considered this.

"They knew where you were going. At least, they must have guessed after you left each chandelier in the academy as a mess. Vampires can travel quite fast. Our reflexes mean we don't need to follow speed limits." I thought of Lark's penchant for fast cars. "They must have arrived before the warehouse closed. They either posed as buyers and hid or they compelled the owner to let them in before he locked up and went home," Lark said.

"We didn't find him dead," I said.

"Well that's something," Lark agreed. He also beat up himself. "I didn't think you'd go in. I didn't realize you were friends with a lie-guard to open a wall. Spade has powerful skills."

"Had." I said. "So did Bug. And Josie—" the past-tense of the words brought fresh agony to my throat. Spade *had* lie-guard powers. Josie *was* smart.

Not anymore.

"You need more rest," Lark finally said.

"So I can dreamcast you a vision, I know."

"So you can *rest*," Lark said. "Come on." He bent to pick me up.

"I can walk." I pushed back. Shoved him away. The vampire wouldn't allow me to kiss his chest in the forest, but he expected to carry me in my underwear off to my bed? These weren't even my clothes. I straightened to my feet, not bothering to hide the wincing pain in my bones. Every muscle still ached, but I padded under my own power the few steps, Lark one move behind the whole way, ready to swoop in. As soon as I reclaimed my spot under the covers, he brought the strewn blankets up to my chest, tucking me in.

"Good night," he said.

"Good night, Lark."

I expected him to go, but he didn't. His jaw twitched, a softness came into his voice. "I would like to stay, to sit in the chair and watch over you. I think it will help."

"Why?"

"If you know I'm right here, you won't have to be scared."

"You wanna stay in my room?"

"Yes."

"Still tryna' sleep with me?" I tried to make light like old times. But Lark took the playful tone out of the room.

"Near you. Yes. Would that be alright?"

"Okay," I became serious too. My voice broke with relief. "Thanks." He nodded once, then pulled over a wingback chair from the fireplace. He settled in close. My breath regulated as I finally relaxed. Letting the darkness wash over my soul. Embracing the night.

"I won't let anything happen to you," I thought I heard Lark say. But I couldn't be sure.

He sat silently in the dark in the chair.

I lay on my back and stared at the ceiling. We waited for my dreams to take me away with Lark standing guard. But time simply marched on. I couldn't sleep.

"Is it me?" He finally asked.

"Is what you?"

"The reason you can't sleep?"

"No." I sighed. "It's everything. I don't want to see them again," I admitted. "My friends." I started to tear up. "I'm sorry, I–" Trying to apologize or gather myself in front of Lark just made me more upset.

The vampire came over to the bed and sat on the edge. The mattress depressed under his thighs. He leaned over and brushed my hair away. Lark's fingers made the comforting movement again and again, calming me down.

"You have guilt." He told me softly. "I may not show it, but I understand. I lived once too. You've been through a lot, Orphan Girl."

I nodded, slightly choking on the once sharp nickname, said now with sweet care.

"Here," Lark pushed his bed sheets towards me, to use like a tissue. "Use this."

"I don't wanna mess up your bed," I snuffled. Wiping my face with my hands.

"Then here." He stood and ripped off the black t-shirt from his chest and handed it to me. I was so surprised, I took it. It was clean and dry and smelled like him. When I'd been bathing, he'd also changed, I noticed for the first time. Now he stood in light pajama pants and a bare chest, bed-side. He sat again.

"Now I'm messing up your shirt." I used it a bit to dry my eyes.

"I've got plenty more," he smiled. He reached out to stroke my hair once more and I let him. "And you're not messing up anything, Seph. I gave it to you... I've made my choice." Suddenly, the words felt heavy and we weren't discussing his clothing anymore. "I'm here," he said. Petting me.

Softly.

Gently.

Over and over.

The weight of his fingertips smoothed out my fears. Lark's eyes were so clear. So crystal blue. He watched me.

"I'm here too," I agreed. I stared at him through bleary, exhausted tears.

Were we talking about the same promise?

"Tell me about it," I asked.

"About what?"

"Your human life... or what it's like to be a vampire... tell me something, Lark."

"Will it help you sleep?"

"Yes," I lied.

He leaned in close to my ear. "I don't believe you."

I smiled. "Time will tell."

"Shift over," he acquiesced. I shimmied back. Lark laid down beside me on the bed, me under the covers, him on top. Very careful not to touch any of my limbs. I'd never seen him so close or so relaxed. I watched, taking in every detail I could manage of him.

The way his hair fell away from his face.

The warmth that radiated from his skin. Just being so near.

The sheer size of his arms and his chest.

He stared at the ceiling. "I was turned by my brother..." he started.

"No. Not that." I rolled onto my side, my hands tucked under my ear, fully facing him. "Not about how you turned. Or who you've killed, or what you've seen. I want to hear everything, every minute, I swear I do. But not tonight. Start with something good."

Lark rolled towards me too. His mouth twisted a bit, like I'd said something funny to him. His face inches from mine. "Something good?"

He looked younger and sweeter than I'd ever seen.

His smile lines gleamed in the low light of the room.

So close.

Face to face in the dark.

"*Um hmm.* Tell me something nice about vampire life. To help me sleep."

"I saved a witch once," he offered. "On a train."

"Yes, start there. Please."

47

LARK

My heart pounded in my chest.

Persephone could see right through me.

I stared at the beautiful girl in the guest room.

I'd brought her here, into my home, I'd put her here, in this bed. Then I'd climbed right in with her, touching her hair, comforting her. And now I was going to tell her about Gwen?

The story of the witch from my past had just eked out of my lips. Impulsively.

What are you doing, Lark?

I blasted myself. I'd marched right into a snake pit.

There was no denying the parallels here.

And now that the ball was rolling, I couldn't stop it if I wanted to. There were parts of my relationship with Gwen that were a nice story. That's how it started, anyway. With a meet-cute on a train. Would telling Persephone hurt me? Or help her?

She waited. I back-tracked.

"Forget it."

"No Lark, *please.*" She looked so happy for once. How could I deny her that?

"How well do you know your history?" I asked.

"Well enough," she shrugged. I gave her a look. "Okay, not great. But try me."

"There was a time in the past called the Great Depression."

"*Oh my god*, I went to school. I'm not dumb. It's in the textbooks."

"And I lived through it." I pushed back. "Would you like to hear about it or not?"

"Yes." She groaned, annoyed and enraptured at the idea. "Please continue."

"Like I said, I was there and–"

"What was it like?"

"Who's telling this story?" I frowned.

"Sorry. Go on. I'm listening. I swear."

"It was depressing," I said, "like the namesake. But for vampires, it was actually pretty good." I added that little detail before she could complain that this wasn't shaping into the happy story she'd requested. "People were transient. They moved around a lot, looking for work. The average citizen didn't have much, they started small gardens everywhere they could. Growing their own plants on any plot of land. Generating their own food. It's part of the reason why we have a greenhouse and a large garden here at the Bird Cage."

"I'd like to see it," Persephone told me.

"I'll show you," I promised her. Another day.

My eyes kept drifting to the witch's smooth skin. I'd seen almost all of her in the bathroom, wearing only panties and a tiny tank. It wasn't sexy then, her posture was so sad and anguished. I'd felt helpless as she'd clutched the toilet and puked, but now she was resting again, cuddled and soft in my bed. Her mind was calmer and free. She was imagining things with me, trying to picture another time. Another life.

The gash near her collar bone kept drawing my gaze. It was

maddening. The injured slit jogged from her neck down towards her right breast. When she shifted, it looked raw and red. It had been covered when I'd found her fully clothed out in the woods, but now in borrowed pajamas I had a view of a lot of fresh skin. Including the gash.

I could help her with that.

I could reach out and kiss it for her.

Lick her skin.

I could wrap my hands around Persephone's back.

Pull her in by the waist. Tuck her to me. Face to face.

I'd make it okay.

I'd help her forget all her pain.

Lick every inch.

Help her sleep, I reminded myself.

I kept the story on track.

"Anyway... it was common back then to ride the freight trains. It was mostly teens and young twenties youth that did that. People called them hobos, bos for short, the history books say it was men, but that's cuz women are often erased. At that time, it was really anyone not tied down with families or land. Men and women, common and plenty. We all shuttled around, looking for work. Wren, Finch and I did it too. It was safer if we didn't stick long in one place. Safer if no one knew who we were. So we followed the trend. People rode the rails. It was illegal, but that didn't stop many. Never does. And, from time to time we'd get caught up in hobo raids."

Persephone's eyes went wide. "Was it dangerous?"

"Yes."

"Tell me about the witch."

"Gwen." I said her real name. Persephone nodded.

"You saved her."

"We met during a raid. My brothers and I were sitting in a box car, minding our business, when a dumb girl jumped into the car and rammed the door closed. That was a stupid move, drawing attention to herself, as the bulls' always account for crashes and bangs. It's better just to hide in whatever's supplied in the car, blankets or boxes or stuff. Duck down and wait with a wide open door. But she didn't and we were stuck. We felt the brakes depress, and a bull opened the door."

"That's a train conductor?"

"A police officer. Yeah. Bulls. It's what we called them back then. He yelled *'unload.'* Well, Finch was pissed. We'd been perfectly hiding for hours, waiting for the train to roll and to get things going and in the last minute here comes this small, dumb girl making all kinds of noise. She gathered the copper's attention but *we* had to deal with the fallout. Only, not yet. It's dark in the car, so we're still hoping they don't notice us. *She* didn't. In those days, a ticket cost was basically anything the bulls could steal from migrant workers. They usually took half of whatever you carried. Have three dollars? Pay a dollar fifty. Have forty bucks? It's a twenty dollar fare from the man. Then the cops kept half of the loot for themselves. But Gwen stands up, and says *'no'*. And suddenly, the car is rammed with people. She has her fist balled. And looks between the crowd and says, '*I dunno Sarge. There's six bullets in that gun, and there's way more of us here. So you can kill six, sure, if you're a perfect aim, but then the rest might come and kill you. Whatdaya think? Like them odds?'* It was wild. She had this look on her face that said she was so desperate she might try cannibalism. All of them did." I was still impressed, all these years later.

"You cared for her," Persephone said. I lowered my gaze, but I was in too deep to mince words at this point.

"Not then, later," I agreed. "Yes."

"And she was a lie-guard?"

"A great one, yes."

"So what happened next?" The dreamcast watched me.

"The bull didn't realize that she was a witch. He was just a bully with a gun. He sneered right back at her and said he *'didn't have to use six bullets, just one,'* and cocked the gun in her face. Normally, I don't get involved. I had enough trouble with my brothers and I, but the girl was a supernatural too. And all alone. And he was twice as big. And goddamn ugly. And I just felt pissed. Wren, Finch and I stood up. I said *'she's with us.'* I bared my teeth and showed him what he was dealing with. The officer about peed his pants and jumped off the train."

"She must've been so grateful to you."

"No," I rubbed my chin at my favorite part of the memory. "She was mad. She said she'd been working that bull for hours, watching him, prepping. She wanted his gun and she'd planned to take it, that's why she drew him into her car. By standing up, I blew her whole cover. I saved her but the witch was pissed. All of us knew the bull would've rounded up the troops and met the train at the next stop with reinforcements and firepower of ten or twenty set on battling the vamps, so we hopped off in the fields somewhere mid-journey. I said she could go with us, at least for a little while, 'til she got back on her feet, to make up for her busted plan, but Gwen said *'she'd rather pluck out her eyes than spend time with three nefarious vampire brothers.'* And then, she took off in the field."

"What happened to her?" Persephone asked.

"I told you, we went separate ways."

"But she's not some random girl, you know her name. Gwen. You must've seen her again."

"I did."

"And?"

My smile fell off. "I thought you wanted me to stick to happy stories."

"Oh. Right." Persephone frowned. "You fell in love with that witch?"

"Yes."

"And she hurt you deeply?"

"Nothing hurts me," I lied. Persephone saw through it immediately.

"That can't be true."

Bringing up Gwen was clearly a dumb decision.

"I guess it wasn't the light-hearted story I hoped," I said.

"No, it's fine," she disagreed. "It took my mind off other things." Then she circled back. "Is that why you won't touch me? Because of her?"

"What?" I was surprised. "No."

"Because back in the forest, when you kissed me and healed me, I thought you liked things–"

"I did. Persephone. It's not a good idea."

"Are you afraid you'll get hurt?"

"No," I said, whisper-quiet. But I finally gave in. Locked in her gaze. Lying in her bed. I opened some truth. "I'm afraid that I'll destroy you, Orphan Girl."

Liquid fast, I spit into my hand and reached out for her. I put my healing palm against the cut on her chest. The wound had been calling to me all evening. Now I gave in. I touched her without warning. So fast that she gasped. The healing fizzed as the saliva hit her and she healed. She breathed deeply 'til the powers stopped invading her skin. I started to pull away but she stopped me there. Touching her upper chest.

"Lark, that feels good." It was an invitation to proceed.

"You can't handle me," I warned. She slid my hand further into her shirt.

"Feel my heart. It hasn't stopped beating. I'm alright. I can take it. Whatever you give."

I took the bait. I ignored her damn heartbeat. We stared at each other, as my pinky slid just a hair more beneath her shirt, I moved it slowly, grazing in circles, watching her experience. She didn't show much, watching me evenly. Instead, my fingers touched her curves, just like she'd hoped that I'd engage.

I wasn't strong enough to resist her again.

Not like this.

In her bed. Under her gaze. My hand by her tits.

She chewed on her lip. I watched the sensuous play of tongue and teeth.

My body dripped in heat. Ready to ravage this girl.

"This is a mistake," I said.

"Do I feel good?"

Yes, she felt good.

The need throbbed in my chest.

Take her, touch her, worship her skin.

"You should be sleeping," I managed. But my fingers again betrayed me. I found her nipple inside her shirt. I tweaked the pink hill. Persephone closed her eyes. She hummed a bit. I rolled it in my hand, eliciting a sweet groan. "I don't want to hurt you," I warned.

"I can take it, Lark" she said. "Just give it to me."

I pinched her more, just a hint. A penalty, or proof of the damage she was in for with me. Seph sucked back her breath. I went softer again.

"We should stop. I'm serious, Seph." I caressed her skin, embracing the feel. Longing to rip off her shirt and see the sweet breasts as they filled my hand. I was locked in a battle of what to do next. Let her loose, or shove my face into her tits. Persephone put a hand to my bare chest next. A lightning bolt shot through my skin.

I wasn't ready for her caress.

I thought I was driving this car. My dick went hard in my pants.

"I'm going to die like my friends, aren't I?" She asked, ignoring my suggestion to end our physical contact. She flicked my nipple with her nail. I grunted, exposed.

"Not if I can help it."

"Lark, tell me the truth." Her finger rolled around my sensitive point, drawing me in. I groaned. My fingers matched the pleasure and pace on her skin. We swirled in sync. Our faces impassive, like we weren't throbbing and longing or tempting our fate. "Am I going to die before you acquire the Stone?"

"You might," I decided to be honest with her. "I could go too. This won't be easy, Seph."

"I know."

She was all weakness and strength and sadness and sex lying here next to me. Caressing my chest, watching me touch her body too. The dichotomies of abandon and control were rolled into one gorgeous, perplexing package. A woman strong enough to feed a dying vampire her own blood. A woman so soft she needed someone to hold her touch while she slept.

"I want you here," she told me.

"This is a terrible idea," I answered.

"I know."

I'd never wanted anyone like I wanted Cornelius Child's niece. And if we crossed this physical barrier even once, I knew I'd never go back. I'd be forever changed.

"Well, okay." She stopped all motion and let me go.

I immediately felt the loss of her hand.

Then worse, Persephone rolled slightly, removing my fingers from her skin.

"Lark, it's your choice. I don't want you to do anything you don't want to do. But if we're going to die tomorrow... then right now, I'd like to live."

48

PERSEPHONE

I thought Lark might lunge for my lips, but he didn't.

"I can't." He admitted.

"Can't what?" I dared him to say it. To admit what he was thinking. Lark stared at my face, his gaze connected with mine and stayed. "What can't you do?"

He blew out a breath, long and slow.

"Lark–"

"Fuck it." Lark came right for me, slid between my red waves, cupped his hand around the back of my head. He held my gaze. He watched me a moment longer, taking all the confirmation he needed that I was here, *in this*, that this was exactly what I wanted, pausing even as desire and longing radiated off of his body. But he needn't have worried. I'd never wanted anyone like I longed for Lark. My vampire bodyguard was all I desired. "I want you."

My vampire kissed me.

It was like his healing kisses had been ratcheted up to one thousand. Because the chemistry and energy that swirled between us cut straight through my veins. His kiss flooded every part of me. I fed my hands around his waist. Clutching his bare skin. Scared he might take his perfection away. But instead, Lark slid his tongue between my teeth, tasting every inch.

His hands started to move.

I opened for him, his mouth, his body too, I turned his way. I curled my arms around his expanse. I groaned, wrapped up in his trance.

Lark kissed me again and again as we lay in his bed. I never wanted it to end, but finally, he pulled back. His fingers stayed in my hair, but his mouth released, lowering my face to his chest, kissing my forehead, embracing me, making me safe.

"You've been waiting for that since the day we met," Lark quipped. I swatted him. He laughed. It was beautiful and teasing and open. His lips raked apart in a sexy smile. Then he kissed me again. And another, and another until suddenly we were both moaning in the moment, all mouths and forward momentum. Searching each other out. Looking for answers. Excited and spent.

He tasted like heat.

Like hot peppermint candies, that stayed on your lips.

I licked up every inch.

His hands roamed, pulling me to him.

"You're incredible, Seph."

"I know," I giggled right back. "Lucky you."

He roared in delight.

"Get your ass up on top of me."

"Yes, sir." I rolled up and spread my thighs over his waist, straddling his hips. He felt thick under my thighs. Ready to fuck. "You've been waiting for this," I hotly whispered in his ear.

"I tried so hard to be good," he agreed.

"And now you're gonna be bad." I ground my center down on this length, for him and for me.

"You're killing me, Seph." Lark took up the motion of my hips, and aggressively rolled me on top of him.

Over and over.

Our friction built.

The fabric of his sleep pants was thin. My panties practically a non-existent barrier between my legs. As I moved, I felt every inch of the vamp. Hard and thick. Waiting to begin. We both were right there.

His fingers slid under my shirt and he fondled my breasts.

He grabbed my neck, pulled me to him. Kissing me harder than before.

The need growing.

The raw ache.

Lark's hands grabbed my hips and guided them down, pressing me. Grinding on him. I stared at my vamp, my clothed tits hanging down in his face, our two bodies lined up.

"*Oh my god*," I moaned, coming apart at the seams. Feeling every inch.

"Is this what you thought it would be?" He took full control, whispering in my ear. "Making out with a vamp?" He pushed me over his hips again and again. My body hummed. But I slid his hair out of his face

"I'm not in bed with a vamp," I told him. "it's you, it's Lark."

"*Holy fuck.*" Lark groaned in reply. I'd said the right thing. The exact words to light him up deep inside. He raised. The rapid move aligned me straight into his lap.

His pelvis throbbed below my ass. My legs spread apart.

"Take off your shirt." He didn't wait.

He grabbed the tiny sleep tank top from my waist and lifted it up over my head.

I let him strip me bare, releasing my curves, naked only inches from the vampire's hot skin. The move made me exposed. He appreciated everything he could feel.

"You look so good," he pressed my tits against his warm chest, rubbing my back, holding me near. "You feel, *oh god,* Seph."

I slid my tongue into his mouth, and he kissed me deeply again.

I slid my hands into his beautiful hair and wrapped my arms around his shoulders.

Lark nuzzled my jaw and my ear, he suckled my skin, knocking my head back, arching my body to him, revealing my neck.

Everything I had was on display. Like that was his plan.

"God, you are perfect in every way," he complimented my curves. But then his mouth became full, sucking on each of my breasts, taking the whole round nipples into his mouth, and tugging on them. "Baby, release."

He took a hold of my hips, and ground me down on his dick.

We were still clothed, but our bodies didn't care.

"Lark," I whispered his name.

There was rhythm and pattern with him.

Over and over, he rubbed us together.

Growing faster and stronger with each thrust.

"Lark!" I yelped and I begged.

Take the fabric away.

The build up.

The passion was too much.

It was more than I could bear.

"*Lark!*" I practically wept.

Then everything exploded.

I shattered on him.

Convulsing and pulsing in waves of desire and passion and exhaustion. He let me vibrate and shudder 'til I stilled. And when it was over, Lark released me and laid me down on the bed.

"No... I want more," I objected, tugging on him, suggesting he come over top of me. The vampire did, soft and slow. Lark pushed the hair out of my face. Kissing me here and there, both of us coming down from the throes.

I'd shuddered against his strength.

When it was over, we were both humming and happy, sweaty and consumed, lying prone on the bed. With wobbly legs.

"You alright?" Lark checked, still on top. I loved his weight, and the feel of his hips.

"I'm great." I contentedly sighed. Spent as I was, I tried to claw my nails into his back, grabbing hold to engage in a fresh ride. This one just for him. But the vampire shook his head.

"Not tonight." He took down my hands and kissed me once more on the lips. Lark pulled up the sheets, tucking me in, covering my curves. He settled on the bed covers, watching anew.

"You sure?" I turned, but his slight distance and sweet smile encouraged me to lie back.

"I'm sure, Orphan Girl. Tonight was all about you."

"Oh... alright. I have a question," I said.

"About what we just did?" Lark laughed.

"No, about something you said before." I glanced over at him. "In the Thirties." His expression tampered but refused to darken.

"Shoot."

"You said you used to travel with your brothers. Wren, but also with Finch?" I recounted.

"Yes."

"I thought he was bad."

Lark lay flat on his back, staring up at the ceiling. "In my experience, people, even vampires, aren't really bad, or good. It's about the circumstances they go through. They're just trying to survive. Responding to life. Anyone can make a poor choice."

"Does that include us?" I wondered.

I expected him to say no.

"What would you call having sex with a vampire?" He half-smirked. But a deeper sadness eked out.

So we were back to the honest truth.

That this was a bad idea. And we should not have given in.

I closed my eyes. I wanted to assure Lark with something sweet. A kind word. Proof that I saw who he truly was.

"I'd call it a pretty damn good night." I sleepily yawned.

My eyelids grew heavy. The night and morning finally catching up with my brain.

"I think so too," Lark might have whispered in reply.

But I couldn't be certain.

I was already asleep next to him in our bed.

———

My dream started off in the same way.

"No," dream-me frowned.

I hadn't drowned out the terrible vision with sex. I was back in the warehouse, beside the heap of cardboard and twisted metal and the marred limbs of my friends.

The same nightmare played out on a loop.

I frowned in uncertainty, knowing what had to be done next, who had to be revealed. I felt desperate for an alternative ending, a different option than exposing my murdered friends. But my unconscious mind would not relent.

Like a zombie, I picked up the cardboard sleeve and revealed the three of them looking just as I had feared. Josie, Bug and Spade, twisted and murdered. Ripped to pieces by the science of gravity, and the cruel vampire men. Emotion and horror welled up in my chest, but this time I stayed still. I unleashed no scream. I stared into the abyss of death, accepting my punishment. Their images burned into my brain.

I did this.

I chose.

I made the mistakes.

These murdered innocents were on my selfish hands.

I dissected each part over and over again until finally, Bug sat up from his wretched spot. He put together the pieces of his butchered brain and held the skin flap over the mess.

"Seph!" He grinned, pleased as punch. "Welcome back." The casual greeting caused tears to stream down my face.

"Oh, Bug." I started to weep.

"Hold on a sec." Bug took out the noise-cancelling earbuds he wore for sleep. "Can't hear anything with these. Where did you go?"

"I didn't go, Ugnacious… you did," I whispered his real name.

"You know I like Bug." He frowned and tilted his head. "It suits me best. Why are you crying?" He asked. No judgment, just curiosity in his gaze.

"'Cuz you're dead," I smeared a tear from my cheek, trying to clean up my face.

"No, I'm not. I'm right here."

"Your head's smashed in half."

"What, this?" He let the skin flap flop open, then picked it back up. "It's just a scratch. Spade says 'chicks dig scars,'"

"I should never have–" my tears came again.

"Hey, stop." Bug's kindness seeped out. He stood up, crossed the mangled wreckage and looped his arm in mine. He walked me from the warehouse into his basement bedroom, seamlessly leaping locations in a manner that only happened in dreams. We sat together on his couch. "You're okay."

"I wish you never met me, Bug."

"Don't say that, Seph. This has been the best time of my life. The scariest, for sure, but also the absolute bestest and that's not even a word." He winked, then leaned over, as if to share a dark secret with me. "Would you believe I've never had real friends before? And now Josie knows who I am. I think she was impressed with my bugs." He hopped up and went to his terrarium and stared inside. "I know I was."

"She's always known you, Bug." I stuttered a laugh between the tears that now fell, missing the real Bug and feeling his loss–even while a dream version of the boy engaged with his insects mere feet from

where I sat. He dug an earthworm out from the tank. He held it up to the light.

"True, but this is the first time Josie and I ever hung out. Me visiting her at work doesn't count. She's paid to be there. Plus, there's you."

"Me?"

"You burrowed into my heart," he showed off the creepy bug. "I've never had a friendly neighbor before." He put the worm back in the fresh earth.

"You still don't. I'm not getting that house," I shook my head. "I'm not finding the Stone."

"Why not?! We're so close."

"I killed you, Bug."

"Then I'm delicious worm food. Yum. It's okay to be dead, just ask Lark. The life cycle begins all over again."

49
LARK

It was a mistake.

I watched Persephone's breath rise and fall, in and out. So peaceful on our bed.

Fully spent.

I wanted the witch to release, to let go and feel safe. But I shouldn't have...

Made her come?

Sucked her breasts?

Introduced her to my dick.

I recounted the whole list of crimes. It went on and on.

Kissed her mouth?

Told her about Gwen?

I squeezed closed my eyes. I was weak. It didn't matter that I drew the line before we fucked. We'd done enough. Way more. I was hooked.

I'd already been hooked, I admitted to myself, *even before my first taste.*

And now?

Things would be much harder, I frowned.
And not the good kind of hard.

50
PERSEPHONE

My eyes fluttered open, wide awake.

"Lark?" I said his name. Even before I gathered myself, I felt his absence from the bed that we'd shared.

"Morning, Orphan Girl." The vampire was back in the chair where he'd sat down in the night. Fully dressed. "You dreamt." It wasn't a question. He knew it this time. I nodded. I tugged the sheets tighter around my naked breasts.

Why was he over there and not beside me, still in bed?

Lark seemed to feel my hesitation and came over. His thighs pressed weight on the mattress as he sat. "Tell me, Seph."

"I'm not sure what it means," I admitted, looking at him. Suddenly embarrassed to feel so raw and stripped. Lark was put back together and perfect while I was a total mess. He reached out and touched a wave of red hair.

"Why don't we start with breakfast," he offered.

I breathed out. "Yes."

He stood. "I'll let you get dressed." The offer was stiff and cold, back to total formality, as if he hadn't been the one to order me to strip off my top early this morning while grinding my hips. But maybe I just read too much into it.

"Okay, thanks."

He went out.

I wanted to bask in a late morning glow with my new man, but Lark was acting as if nothing had happened—or worse, something had, but it wasn't some earth-shattering matter. I guessed it wasn't to him.

So we made out?

Now it was business as usual for the vamp. Lark's plan was to focus solely on the next task. Apparently my consolation prize was that he was being a bit nicer to me.

I could understand his position.

After all, we had a lot to accomplish today. We needed the Stone. We were fighting a terrible Brotherhood with nefarious plans, and I'd clearly slept in. Plus, until the Blood Stone was actually in Lady Mauve's hands, with the binding spell transferred over to her, there was a magical price on my head. So yeah, I needed to get out of bed and get my brain in the game.

I glanced at the closed door.

Still, were we just going to pretend last night hadn't happened? Or would Lark use it as an excuse to make every interaction between us cold and distant, professional from here on out? Because I had news for him, he hadn't exactly been a warm, giving, ray of sunshine partner before I'd rubbed myself all over his pants.

I wrapped the sheet around me like a toga and took it into the wardrobe to look for some clothes to wear. It took a while to find a suitable outfit. My personal backpack was still at Bug's. These were all foreign things. Someone else's. It felt strange to borrow another woman's items without her say so, even with tacit permission to root around in the midst of old clothes. There were a lot of bohemian touches in the walk-in wardrobe so I was pretty sure the guest room clothing might have been Lila's at one time, long ago. The picks were reminiscent of the style from the nineties. Very out-dated. Although, I supposed it could have been worse, they might have been leftovers from the hundred years before. I settled on a white t-shirt with lace trim and wide cargo pants. Then I journeyed out of my room in search of my vampire friend.

Walking down the castle halls by myself was unnerving. But vague chatter from the main study told me which way I should go. So not just Lark was in attendance today. I steadied myself for a fresh confrontation from Lady Mauve. As I entered the heart of the home, the trio were looking over a textbook page. The talking all stopped. The group looked up. Thankfully, it was only my vampire, his brother, and Lila. No Mauve. Lark closed the book. They waited, like I was the star of the show.

"Good morning," I offered.

"Morning," Wren agreed. Lark nodded, having already said his greeting, Lila gave me a smile and gestured for me to come in. The three vampires waited for me to settle in front of a plate of crois-sants and several jams. Fresh fruit and eggs and bacon were piled on serving plates on the coffee table.

"Help yourself to breakfast, Persephone," Lila said. "I like that top."

"It's yours." I agreed.

"I have great taste." She grinned. "I should have looked through the closet down here years ago," she realized.

Lark stacked another book on top of the one he'd been read-ing, as if he didn't want me to see it. I read the spine's title anyway. *Moon Phases,* by Leroyticin Grant. Was Lark an astrology buff? That didn't suit him at all.

"Lie went a little crazy with the meal, didn't you, babe," Wren told her, pulling back my attention. She shot him a look. Lark half-grinned.

"I figured you might be hungry. Lark said–" She stopped, unsure if whatever Lark said should remain between just he and her... or should've been kept between just him and I, maybe. He stilled.

Did he tell them about my freak-out vomit session last night?

Or my orgasm? *Oh boy.*

The vampire woman didn't offer any more information, but I let Lila off the hook either way.

"I'm starving, thanks."

It wasn't a lie. In fact, my hunger was almost ravenous. I'd worked up quite an appetite from our fun and games, even if Lark wasn't hungry. I took a bun, some bacon and eggs, and shoveled down a few bites while watching my vampire before I realized none of the others were eating.

"You don't–"

"Sorry, no." Lila smiled.

"The vampire diet only consists of one thing," Lark reminded me.

"Oh. Right."

Blood.

I didn't care. I sunk my teeth into the next croissant and enjoyed the buttery flakes.

"I miss croissants," Lila sighed.

"Are you up for talking about it? What you saw?" Lark asked. "She dreamt." The others nodded expectantly.

"Uh, sure." I put the breakfast plate down. I didn't realize we'd have an audience as I spilled the details. But any friend of Lark's was a friend of mine, I supposed. And while Wren had mostly kept his distance, Lila was a real help. "It started with my murdered friends."

The vampires shared a look. Lark bristled.

"I had the vision over and over again. At first I couldn't take it. They were all dead at the warehouse, just like when I'd been there. I'd wake up screaming. I think I was blocked, too scared to let the cast continue until you helped me." I said to my vamp. The couple shot a look in his direction, but Lark gave me a small nod. So our late night stuff was a detail he hadn't shared. "The next time I dozed off, it came again but I stayed with the details. And Bug started to talk. He stood up, brain half-smashed, and he took me into his basement to show me his bugs. Worms." I specified. "It was worms. I know that sounds dumb, but he was really proud of his insect lines. And he was really insistent I see his terrarium again. I think it's a clue. I think there's something there. At his house. Not worms exactly, but maybe there is more information in one of the books that you bought?" I said to Lark. "Or maybe it really is worms. He said he's worm food now. I'm not sure. I'm not great at the dream interpretations yet." I dropped my gaze. "Whatever it is, I think we start there."

"I'll check it out." My vampire agreed. The others nodded.

The word '*I*' stuck out at me.

"Alone?" I asked.

It was hard to look at him today, stiff and tough, since we'd previously been so bare and soft. That vulnerable side was completely closed off again. He had perfect posture and not a hair out of place. In my borrowed clothes and top knot, I felt less than ideal. Still... we were supposed to be a team. This was *my* problem. *My* solution. *My dream.*

"Yes. Alone." Lark said. "You can rest."

"Uh, no, I can't." I looked from one vampire to another. "You need me. You haven't been invited into the Frankel house and a vampire can't just break in." I countered. Lark shrugged.

"His parents have proved... amenable in the past. I can be convincing."

Compulsion. He intended to persuade them into giving him eternal access to their sacred personal space without being granted real permission.

"*No.*" I said it tougher this time. "You're not doing that to them. I don't want you to do that to anybody. That's Bug's family. He may be gone, but I'll protect them. You're not going inside, Lark. None of you. It's not right. I'm coming," I insisted. "*I'll* look around. And you'll keep your vampire hands to yourself."

51
PERSEPHONE

"Y ou wanna talk about it?" He asked in the car.

"No." I lied. Then couldn't help myself. "Look, I'm sorry if I sounded harsh, but I don't see why you have to go around compelling people–" I fondled the pink-gold necklace hanging around my neck.

"I meant about last night," Lark said. "The physical stuff that happened between us."

It was the least romantic way a man had ever referenced his own groaning, half-naked presence in my bed.

"Do *you* wanna talk about it?" I countered, an edge in my voice.

"You needed a release to cast."

I snorted. "*Oh*, well thank god you were there. *Thank you, mighty vampire.*"

"That's not what I meant."

"Why *were* you there? Waiting for me while I slept? Just to help?"

He gritted his teeth. "I was protecting you."

"Well, thank god for that. *In my bed?* Telling me to strip? That was for my protection? Thank you, Lark." I made the condescension drip.

"It was a mistake," he agreed. The word slapped my face. "We should never have," he broke off. "I wanted you to heal, Persephone. That's why I–" he stopped again. My embarrassment stung. I practically blazed. "A witch and a vampire should never be together."

"Except you and Gwen." I threw her name out into the car.

The silence was epic.

"It's fine," I said. In truth, I understood. I think deep down, my brain already knew Lark wouldn't want to be with me long term. He wouldn't stay. Nobody did. After he got the stone that he wanted, he wouldn't continue this ruse.

I just hadn't expected his turn to happen so quickly.

Next morning reversal.

That was a new one.

"The make out sesh was good. You have a big dick. I'm glad you didn't put it in me." I shot the last bullet I had. At least we hadn't had sex. I would have, wholeheartedly. It was a small gift he'd given me. Or another thing he'd withheld. I wasn't sure which. I didn't care. As long as my apathy hurt him back. And it did.

The back-handed compliment stabbed at him like a spear. He nearly choked, jerking the wheel. "That's not–" He sputtered. "I shouldn't have–"

I enjoyed the small moment of twisting.

Suck it, Lark. I could be cold as ice too.

"We've got a job to do." I finished. Determined.

"I know. I just... I don't want to hurt you." He sounded so... foolish. Because he'd failed. Miserably. And he looked miserable too. I didn't answer, just let the silence grow louder between us.

After a few more turns, we were getting near to the farm

roads. We both concentrated on the difficulty we knew was coming. Get in, get the rock, never see each other again.

Fine by me.

"Have you considered what you'll say to the Frankel family?" Lark asked.

"I mean it," I snapped. "You are not going in." I couldn't protect Bug, but I could stop his parents from becoming a vampire's victims. To this vampire, at least.

"Fine. But you may not get close. There could be a police presence," Lark warned. My eyes bulged. I clenched them shut.

"Oh, *geez*." I'd been so concerned with the supernatural presence in their home, I hadn't thought about the regular old humans, the police, or the real effects my friends' deaths would have on their families. The entire sleepy village would be rocked to the core at the news.

The untimely murder of three teenagers in a chandelier warehouse would make the media. Everywhere. There was bound to be evidence of my being with them and I would be questioned. Maybe even be arrested.

"I'll be fine." I didn't even try to address the danger. We were past the point where he had to pretend to care about my welfare. "As long as *you* don't go inside."

"I understand, Orphan Girl."

"Don't call me that again."

The vampire drove quickly through the town. I noted the smooth way he commanded the car. It reminded me of the way Lark handled my body. Like he could anticipate the turns, like his car was one with the highway's folds. I didn't feel the speed, or the danger. In the car or in his arms. But, since Lark had decided to withhold any evidence of our connection this morning, I understood him more thoroughly. Maybe *he'd* needed the distraction. And now he'd had that rush of passion between us, *he'd* function better. I was just a tool in his arsenal. Used and discarded. Now he was ready to work.

As we arrived, Lark slowed down to normal traffic speeds. A few quick turns and we were at Bug's house. I half-expected to see a flood of rotating cherry lights and an army of cops on his lawn, but there was no one around. It was quiet. A simple farmhouse, bikes out front. Exactly like it had been when Bug and I left the other morning.

Lark pulled into the driveway.

"Let me talk, then I'll bring out the books. We can take them back to your house, read, and go from there," I said. Lark nodded. He kicked open his door at the same time as mine and got out. I shot him a look, but instead of following me to the front porch, he stopped at the front of his car and leaned on the hood. Resuming the familiar patient posture of waiting. I glared at him, climbed the steps of the porch, and rapped on the door. Inside, I heard a TV on that clicked off, followed by footsteps. Someone walked to the porch and swung the door wide.

"Yes?" It was Bug's mom. She looked tired and overworked. But she had no clue her life was about to get far, far worse. She clearly didn't know her son was dead. I swallowed, skirting the news.

"Hi. I, uh, we're friends of Bug's. I left my book in his room, I was wondering if–"

"Just go around back." She glanced up at Lark, unimpressed, then turned on her heel. The door clanked behind her butt.

"Right."

I glanced at the vampire too, but to his credit, Lark still hadn't moved. He was a patient man of his word. I hopped down off the porch and travelled around to the side storm cellar doors, the ones the insect witch had taken me through on the day we met. It would be sad and weird to enter his kingdom alone, but at least I had permission to be there. I pulled up on the creaking, oversized doors to the lower floor, and walked down the stairs. It felt foreign to be moving around amidst all the insect witch stuff without really knowing what I was looking at, but this was the only lead we had, so I focused on that.

I knew one thing, no matter what happened, I would honor the memory of my sweet friends and I would find a way to make the Brotherhood pay.

52

LARK

"I don't see anything," Persephone admitted. I followed her as far as the door, but true to my word, I stayed outside and watched her progress from there. She moved around the bug-witch's lair haphazardly at first, then concentrated on the terrarium by his bookcase. It seemed a smart bet. She shoved her hand into the dirt and rooted around. Looking for worms.

We weren't even sure if worms were a literal reference in her dream or a metaphor. A quick internet search of the creatures told us that worms weren't really bugs. Their skin was made up of collagen and they didn't have exoskeletons like other insects. But many of the creatures that one would call worms were actually insect larvae in early stages of development, and...

"We're wasting too much time," Seph complained. Already giving up. I wasn't sure what to say. Maybe she'd misread her vision. I couldn't see how earth's tiny creatures could help us solve this mess. But then again, I wasn't the witch.

"You can figure it out," I growled her way.

Persephone's eyes rounded with fear. Always fear before she dug into her strength. Like she had to be reminded of how amazing she was every time she tried something new. Why couldn't she see herself like I did? It frustrated me. But she was still in her twenties and her powers were new.

No one had taught the girl anything. She survived on instinct alone.

We'd just thrown her into this damn society, lied to her face, and then threatened her with death. And *still*, she faced down vampires and escaped. Again and again. Sure, I helped, her friends did too, but the girl was impressive. If she didn't know it, I did.

The spark in her eyes, I couldn't bear to see that fire extinguished… by me or by anyone else.

And the only way to completely free her from this mess was to acquire the damn rock.

I nodded my head, encouragingly.

Think, Orphan Girl. Think.

Her eyes flashed with sudden recognition.

She yanked out her hand from the earth and dusted off the grime.

"What do they eat?" She asked, but didn't expect me to answer her. It hit me too. The dream version of Bug, he hadn't said *worms*, he said *worm food.*

"The food," we both said at the same time.

She jostled around the tank looking for food. She picked up a small container.

"Dried flakes. Ucurbitaceae plant. It's these." She showed me. She sniffed and made a face, it smelled like decay, even here at the door.

"Give it to me," I suggested, but instead she glanced down. She stared at the stack of books that was under the worm-meal.

"It's your book," Persephone told me. I frowned, not knowing what she meant, but then I recognized the cover too: *Dancing Through Moonlight.* I'd flipped through it days earlier. How did she remember that detail?

"Let me see." I said. Reaching again, helpless to cross the threshold. This was stupid, I could just compel my way in, but a deal was a deal. Seph picked it up to carry it to me, but as she did, she checked the next book below it. It intrigued her too, but first, she gave me what I needed. I looked at the moonlight book.

"You think the answer's in there?" Seph asked, going back to the pile.

"Maybe." I made a big show of flipping the pages, but it was mostly a ruse. If this was the message, I already knew what direction fate was leading us, something I'd already suspected... the moon.

Specifically, the worm moon.

Tonight there was a worm moon eclipse at midnight. That's how I'd get into wherever the chandelier was located.

The eclipse was a gateway for a vampire to slip in. Uninvited. Wren, Lila and I had discovered it this morning. I still wasn't sure if I would share the loophole with Seph, so I kept my attention anywhere but that section of the text. The dreamcast didn't need to know how I'd acquire an entrance into the next house. Or how, with that knowledge, I intended to complete the mission by myself. It wasn't worth fighting over. She had no choice. I could slip in through a home's bones but she'd be locked out. Without a lie-guard or a key, Seph had no way to get through the walls.

The next book she held up was called *Veins of Darkness: Vampire Biology*. I snorted.

"There's no way a real vamp wrote that. The title has a pun? You have got to be kidding." I snarked.

"Well, I don't know." She frowned. She held it tightly anyway. I'd annoyed her. "Maybe we only need the first book."

"Yes."

The dreamcast didn't look convinced.

"What else?" I sighed. She looked further into the stack.

"There are five texts in the pile and there were five of us before…"

Before their deaths.

"You think that's a coincidence?" Persephone perused the remaining titles.

"Do *you* think it's a coincidence? The clue was worm food."

"It's a puzzle, there are pieces. We can put it together." She glanced at me, still stranded in Bug's doorway, then back at the books. She looked at my watch. Perhaps it wouldn't be such a smart idea to go all the way back to my home. "Let's read out in the barn."

"Fine." I reached for the other texts, but she kept them to herself. I was annoyed to be given the moonlight book alone. I wanted the answers I didn't have, *like which house would the moonlight let me slip through.* The location of the final chandelier was the missing piece. If we could figure out that, at midnight, I'd be set. We walked out to the barn, slid open the large tractor door and snuck inside. The sunlight filtered through the cracks. I pulled up bales of hay that we used as a table to read and we tucked in.

"The Eldrian Calendar," Persephone read the title aloud, then moved on to the next, arbitrarily handling them. Putting them down. I was smarter than to grab any title too fast. *"From Dust to Stone: Architectural Wonders in Plumpkin,"* she read. *"Altars of Time: Chronicles of Churches Lost to History."*

"You didn't stack these before?"

"No, but maybe Bug did?" She frowned.

"But you don't think so. You think it was fate?"

"Just read them, Lark."

Since Seph and Bug were the only two who'd stacked the books into his cubby hole room, it seemed like a pertinent detail we should suss out. Like a vampire compulsion, fate twisted everyone up from time to time. It could make you act surprisingly. That's why dreamcasts were such powerful witches. They unravelled bigger purpose from random details. Dreamcasts were a vital part of any mission or army or venture... *when they were kept in their homes, away from battle, safe in their beds.*

The idea of Seph back in my bed made my whole body yearn.

Focus, vampire stud.

I glanced over the witch's shoulder, trying to pick up more information as she read. Seph landed on a page subtitled: *Vampires and Eclipses.*

Fuck.

"Trade with me," I said, less casually than I'd hoped. I offered her the moonlight book.

"No," Persephone eyed me. "I thought you said this vampire stuff wasn't important, Lark." I'd tipped my hand. This only pushed her to examine it further. She read more thoroughly.

"I only said there was no way it was written by a vampire," I countered. I bit my lip. I'd practically switched on an alarm bell in her head. I paced again, waiting for her to stumble upon new information that would harm me or help me or both. This was taking too long. She flipped open the calendar book next.

"What do you see?" I asked, way too quickly.

"I'm looking up worm moon eclipses." She shot me a look, then flipped through the pages, still slightly uncertain. Until she found what she needed. She froze when she got to the right calendar date. Then she looked up. "There's one tonight. There's an eclipse." She said it to test me. I failed. She snatched the moonlight book from my hand and rifled it next. "But you already knew that."

"Yes."

"A vampire can slip through the bones of a house—"

"When the sun, the worm moon, and the planets align. Yes. With or without an invite."

"When were you planning to tell me?" She narrowed her eyes.

"I wasn't."

"*Lark.*" Her face screwed up in annoyance.

She was so smart. I wanted to hug her and kiss her forehead.

This was why she couldn't come on the mission.

Why we could never be together.

I wanted her too badly.

I enjoyed every question. Every frown. Every insight.

But, an evil vampire would latch onto any seed of weakness and use it to bring their enemies down. I couldn't take it. I couldn't have another person I loved snatched from my arms. Destroyed right before my eyes. I wouldn't put Seph in danger. Not like Gwen...

I shook the memory out of my head.

That was a long time ago.

"So we know the how, we just need the where." She switched books.

The fallout wasn't bad yet. She was annoyed, but she likely thought once I was in, I would open the door. It hadn't crossed her mind that I would leave her behind and go in alone. In Persephone's brain, we were a team. I didn't correct her. Instead, I strung her along as two heads were better than one. I picked up the old church book while Persephone searched through the architecture tome.

"Umbrawick." She looked up at me. "Remember the receipt?"

"The one the rain destroyed?"

Seph nodded. "The name was something like that, Umbrawick. At the time, I was thinking Umbrella and the rain, but this is it. They're right here, look."

"Who are they?"

"Who *were* they?" She clarified. "The Umbrawick family was like royalty here."

I leaned in towards her, catching the scent of her hair. I sucked back the sweet smell.

"According to this, they basically owned everything at one

time. And they had an ancient crypt that was built under the town church before the railroads were put in."

"What church?" I asked, already flipping pages fast.

"Maybe that's in your book?" Persephone said.

"Right. Give me a sec." I dug into my book. *Altars of Time* had to be the source.

"Look for Umbrawick, check the index." She hurried me.

"I got it," I grumbled. I was the immortal, I knew how to do things quickly. It was fine. "Oh. This is it." I abruptly stopped and stared.

"You found them?" Seph leaned over my arm. Her breasts pressed against my skin but I kept my head clear. There was a photograph of the remains of a church, a three piece dragon artwork. And a sketch of the house built overtop. An illustration demonstrating the present and past. It was a place we each immediately recognized.

"That's my witch house," she said.

"Your uncle's manor was built on–"

"The sacred grounds," she read out loud.

"It says that religious affiliations often tried to claim the title of sacred entities to get exemptions from taxes and the State. Therefore the house was built on the bones of an old church which housed the Umbrawick crypt." I read.

"Josie thought she read the word crypt on that old receipt," Seph muttered.

"Point is, that's where it is," I said.

"And you think the last chandelier is there, inside that crypt? You think it's buried beneath the house?"

"I do." It was a long shot, but I felt sure.

"I do too." The orphan girl was so close, the revelation alighting our skin. Energy surged between us. We breathed in sync. The connection growing stronger. "It's the perfect hiding place," Seph said. "If there's an ancient crypt under my uncle's house, no one's going near there. He wouldn't let anyone in." She meant he wouldn't let any vampires in.

But that wasn't true.

Child Manor had long been a fixture in town. It held many coven parties and clandestine meetings and like his father before him, Cornelius played ball with the Crimson Flood and my family too. There were several alliances and treaties. We'd all been inside his home many times before. Invited in. The doors only became locked when ownership transferred to her. Still, even in its heyday I'd never found myself traipsing into the basement or entering a burial crypt. In that way, he'd been hiding the Blood Stone in plain sight. I'd also never thought to examine his chandeliers.

"The entrance is likely hidden," I offered. "In the basement."

Seph put a hand on my arm, thinking about things. I looked down at the graze. She didn't even know she'd touched me, but I was buzzing, staying stiff, maintaining control.

"There might be more tricks and traps to get in." She agreed. She squeezed me a bit. I felt her energy growing. I breathed out heavily.

"I'll figure it out at midnight," I said.

"*I'll* figure it out before then." She countered with a fresh grin. "We just need to break the spell."

"You're not going in without me," I countered. "It's not safe."

"Yes, it is. It's daylight, Lark. And a vampire has to be invited in. I'm the rightful owner of that house. So any enemy vamp is trapped outside. It's the perfect place for me to search. Until the midnight eclipse, it'll be totally, totally safe."

"You're wrong. I could have forced my way into Bug's house fifty times by now."

"But you didn't," she said. Then she thought deeper about it. "You didn't. Why?" This time, she noticed her fingers on me. She drew back, uncertain. The absence of Seph sent fresh shivers over my skin.

"You asked me not to." I said quietly. "I complied with your wishes."

"You did." She agreed. We stared at each other, lost in a stalemate. Then she reached out and purposefully brushed my hair off my face, taking in more of my gaze. "Thanks, Orphan Boy," Persephone said.

The name was soft. A teasing jest. It tugged at my chest. An echo of the sweetness we'd discovered early this morning. One fucking amazing roll in the witch's bed.

An indiscretion that made everything harder going forward.

Oh well. You live and learn even when you're dead.

"Orphan Boy? So, I can call you by your nickname again?" I grunted and shifted a bit.

"In the right circumstance," she agreed.

"Keep reading, Orphan Girl." I tried to keep us on task. But Persephone's smile was so devious, I wanted more. I couldn't help but play. I gave right in. "You can call *me* Lark." I leaned in close to her ear. "*Especially in bed.*"

She sucked back her breath.

Oh shoot.

I clearly should have refrained. The low, growly words warmed both her and myself in ways I didn't expect. The flushed feeling spread to my abdomen. Hung out in my belly.

Playing with fire, again.

"Save my life and I'll say your name as many times as you want," Seph teased. She meant it so light, but that was the wrong thing to say. My eyes cleared of our sex. They became springs of sadness and longing and pain.

"You shouldn't need someone to save you, Seph."

"Sometimes I need you completely, Lark," she admitted. Totally raw.

My throat bobbed.

She was so vulnerable. The reality of our situation as witch and vampire bodyguard should have kept me at bay. I knew better. I'd promised to *do* better. But whatever time we spent together, I only wanted the dreamcast more and more, I couldn't push this away. I put a hand to the side of Persephone's face and stared deep in her eyes.

This beautiful girl. This woman, so broken and soft. And hard.

She made *me* hard.

"Say it again," I murmured. "Say my name."

Everything in my brain told me I should remove this witch from my world. But instead I moved into her orbit. Inexplicably pulled.

"Lark."

My whole body buzzed.

Seph stared up at me.

"Orphan Girl." I intoned.

She let out a held breath.

It was on. This was it. We were both raring for more.

"Lark." She bated me again. Or I bated myself, staring into those eyes.

Our bodies closed any gap. I leaned in.

"Say it again," I whisper-warned. My mouth only inches from hers.

She would like what I would do next. She would scream in fucking delight down in this hay.

I threaded my hand further into her hair, tugging, just a bit.

Her breath hitched with desire.

So close, so close, too close.

My face bowed.

Her lips raised.

Our mouths opened to each other.

"Lar–" she said my name.

I gave in.

Creeaaaak.

We both turned back towards Bug's farmhouse, surprised.

"What the hell?" I frowned. "Who was that?"

Immediately, we were back. A witch and a vampire body-guard, on high alert.

"It came from the Frankel storm cellar doors," Persephone said.

Someone was there.

We'd definitely heard it.

We looked at each other in fear and fresh worry, as someone went inside of Bug's family home.

53
PERSEPHONE

My body spun from the proximity of my vampire and my heart pounded in fear at the new sound. Who had just gone into Bug's storm cellar doors?

His parents, maybe? I doubted that. They'd seemed oblivious.

Someone else, looking for clues to the location of the Blood Stone? Why look here? Now? Were we followed? Lark and I leaned out of the barn door as a pair, the heated moment between us immediately dropped in favor of investigating the noise.

Could it be the police? I wondered.

But there were no sirens or cherry lights flashing on the lawn.

Lark stepped away from my side. I immediately missed the vampire's intensity. Being deprived felt like a freezing blast, but I didn't say more. How could I? I couldn't hold onto Lark's world. And there were more important things that we needed to focus on.

Like the Blood Stone.

Like breaking Mauve's spell.

"I'm gonna go in," I said.

"No," he immediately rejected the idea.

"Yes." I started to walk anyway.

"That's a bad idea," he frowned. Catching my arm.

Damn it, I should have swerved. *Or maybe I still wanted him to touch me again*, I admitted. *But it didn't feel as warm as I'd hoped.*

"Do you have a better plan?" I asked. Before he could answer, I wiggled free of his hand and crossed over the grass. It wasn't a vampire in the Frankel house. Like Lark, no monster was invited in. So I had nothing to fear. Not only that, I had permission to be there. Bug's Mom had said I could go around back, so if it was his parents lurking, they would expect me to be there. I shot Lark a final look, took a deep breath and stepped through the storm cellar doors, only to be faced with three ghosts of the past.

"You!" I gasped.

"Seph!" Lark barked. He raced for me, but slapped against the invisible barrier of the home. "Stop! Let me in!"

Josie, Spade and Bug all stood there, mouths open in shock.

Bug started to answer Lark, totally compelled.

"No!" I threw up my hand. "Take it back!" Lark realized who the new participants were.

"Released," he immediately said.

The witches fell out of the compulsion spell. My breath heaved in my chest.

"*Oh my god*," I yelped, still in shock. "You're alive. *Holy crap!* What are you doing here?!" I tried to gasp back tears but they fell too fast. Bug cried too.

"Seph!" He ran over to me. Arms wide. Even Josie's eyes became wet. Maybe Spade's? I was crying too hard to check. My three friends were here.

Alive.

And safe.

"We thought we'd never see you again!" Bug openly feared.

"Me too!" I told him, just as shocked. "Oh my god!" We squeezed each other. I let the realization sink in.

They were here.

They were alive!

We hugged in a heavy embrace. The other two joined our hug while Lark stayed trapped outside. I snuffled and then stepped back to see the whole group. Bug's fingers still in my hands. I suddenly started to hop, an involuntary reaction, actually jumping for joy. So happy to see they were here. They were alive. It was real.

Bug jumped too. Joined by Josie and Spade. Until we all jostled about in an excited group. Hopping up and down in a foolish, anxious glee that could not be contained. It wasn't until the excitement released that we actually unfurled. I continued to stare in amazement at the trio who'd only minutes ago been gone and destroyed in my mind.

How did this happen?

I stared and stared.

"Are you alright?" Josie asked. I must have looked dazed.

"She thought you were killed," Lark quietly said.

"Same with you," Spade told us. I kept touching Bug. I shuffled my hands through his hair, just to make sure a head wound wasn't hiding under the wild strands. The others were also healed.

"How–" I checked from one to the other.

"Spade made a lie-guard," Josie explained.

"What?" Tears of relief crowded my cheeks. I was still frantic, still greeting the witches, barely taking it in. Lark waited ten feet behind, watching us from outside.

"Come in, come in," Bug told me. They dragged me forward. Sat me down on the bed. The place where they'd been huddled when I had walked in. My bag was there, my belongings strewn on the comforter. I frowned a bit, *that was weird.* But I stayed focused on my resurrected friends.

"Tell me everything."

"We thought you were caught," Josie squeezed my hands.

"Or dead," Bug agreed, wiping tears from his eyes.

"Definitely dead." Spade agreed. "Damn vamps." He shot a look at Lark, but didn't feel guilty over slurring the supernatural group he belonged to in the vampire's presence.

"I thought *you* were dead," I shot back, still in shock. "All three of you. *How are you not dead?* A lie-guard? I don't understand."

"Spade used an illusion to make the vampires think we were hurt pretty bad," Josie explained.

"Like we were killed in the crash," Bug agreed. "Then we just stayed where we were."

"You played dead?" I checked for Josie's wound too. Nothing. "It was all pretend?"

"An illusion," Bug agreed. Spade looked guilty.

"Sorry I couldn't extend it to you, Seph."

"Why didn't you?" Lark asked Spade. His tone was sharp. Too pointed. I looked at my vampire. Then them.

Wait, why? What did Lark mean by that? Why was he pissed?

"By the time I got my bearings, the damn vamps had already seen her, heard you." He answered Lark and refocused my way. "Since they knew you survived, I had to make a quick choice. I covered Bug and Josie and myself with the lie-guard to save us."

"And left Persephone to fend for herself?" Lark growled in the doorway.

"*No,*" I spun back to the vampire to shake my head, then looked back at Spade. "He didn't." But my realization dawned from both parties... *yes, Seph, he did.*

Spade did exactly that.

He saved them and left me to fend all by myself.

"It's more complicated than that," Spade lied.

"How?" I asked.

Josie cut in. "When I realized what he'd done, how he'd left you out, I told him to knock it off. We got up. We tried to help. I swear it, Seph. We followed where you ran, even went outside, and–"

"I thought if there was sunlight–"

"I figured."

"It was a smart plan," Bug said.

"It didn't work." Lark shut that down.

I looked back at him, still uncertain. *Why was he acting so mad?*

Why was I growing angry too? These were my friends? What had they done?

New feelings bubbled up that I did not understand. I was so happy they were alright, but–

"When we got out there, you were already gone." Josie said. She gripped my hands. Pulling my attention back to her. "There were vampire bodies and blood on the pavement. So much blood. It led out to the truck, then disappeared. It was pouring with rain."

"We're sorry, Seph," Bug added.

"*Because of the rain?*" I frowned.

"We thought you must have fought hard, but–" she paused. The others exchanged looks. "When you weren't there and the main vampire was gone too... plus you didn't take my wheels. There was a lot of blood around the truck and..." Josie trailed off. "So much blood."

"We thought you were dead," Spade finished.

"Or taken," Josie said. Bug rushed back over to hug me again.

"I'm so glad we were wrong, Sephy!"

"Me too, Bug. Me too." I let him acquire a fresh embrace. But I suddenly felt dull. I barely hugged him back. Lark watched me internally collapse with these details. We had all been fighting together, when the cabinets tumbled and fell. Then my friends saved themselves and left me out in the cold.

They left me to face five angry vampires. All on my own.

Then, when they assumed that I'd died, they just went on with their lives. It was raining, so that was totally understandable, I guessed...?

"How'd you survive?" Spade wondered.

"I didn't." I said. "I would have died."

I only survived because I wasn't alone. I had a vampire bodyguard. Thank god.

"Lark saved me. He followed us there. Or figured it out?" I shook my head, uncertain. "He was waiting outside. If it wasn't for him... Lark saved my life."

Did they understand what I was saying?

"There was no way you could have stood up to the others or fought them off," Spade agreed. Josie nodded.

"The evil in their eyes..." Bug shuddered hard.

"But that was your choice," I said to Spade. A dark twinge entered my voice. "And you two went along."

This chilled the room.

"You knew I couldn't handle it, but you left me alone." I looked down at the bed. My backpack had been strewn open and my stuff was pulled out. "Then you went through my things?"

It was tit-for-tat, as the vamp and I had come to Bug's house... but I hadn't rifled through his drawers, or tried his underwear on. Plus, I thought they were *dead.*

"Were you divvying up my stuff?" I asked. The others looked aghast.

"Of course not, no. We were looking for help. For a clue, to try to figure out where you were, or how to contact you. To see if you were alright," Josie said.

"But in your mind, I was a goner." I narrowed my eyes. "*You wrote me off.*"

Spade bristled. "I did what I felt was right at the time."

Lark scoffed.

"Hey, it worked, it saved lives," Spade snapped.

"*And left one girl to die!*" Lark cut him off.

I stood up.

The vampire was on my side. The realization washed over me: *I thought the others were dead because of what I saw...* an illusion they let me see, and let me then act upon. That was on them. Then they thought *I* was dead, *because of what they did...* because *they left me alone.* To fend for myself against a very real enemy who was hunting me down.

When I needed them desperately, my squad hid.

"So you'd rather I did nothing?" Spade snarked right back at him.

"*I'd rather my Orphan Girl didn't get killed if I wasn't there, you stupid fuck.* You think she'd leave you to die? Any of you?" Lark roared. Anger seethed under my skin.

"I wouldn't. I would *never.*" I stared at their group.

But they'd abandoned me.

"It's not like that, Seph," Josie said. Bug started to cry anew.

"Yes, it is."

"Persephone would be dead and so would all of you if I hadn't been there. The vamps outside didn't *leave.* Your little trick didn't *work.* I killed them. I saved every one of your lives. But if I'd known what you did, I would have sent the Brotherhood back into that damn warehouse to finish the job. Such cowards. All of you. You disgust me. Come on, Seph." Lark glared at them and extended his hand. I grabbed my things and shoved them into my bag.

"I'm glad you're alright," I muttered. I headed out with my vamp.

"Don't go. We really tried–" Josie said.

"We're a squad, remember?" Bug whimpered.

"Guess I'm the biggest fool," Spade spat. "Shoulda let 'em kill me first."

"Damn right," Lark answered back.

"It's your fault we were there in the first place!" Spade told me, as we left.

"*No, no, no.*" Bug tried to intervene. But, I pushed him away.

"Just leave me alone."

"Let her go," Spade shrugged. "Let both of 'em go."

"She's our friend!" Bug said.

"She's not your friend," Spade told him. "She's been using you since the first moment you met. To get her house and her cash. We were just dumb enough to let her in. Like a vampire, we invited a monster into the house."

"That's not true. I really cared." I blurted. "When I thought you were killed I–"

"Spent the night in your sexy vampire's bed?" Spade sneered. "I can see it all over you, Seph."

My cheeks burned.

He was slut-shaming my relationship with Lark? *We didn't even have sex.*

"I thought you were dead!"

"Oh, Lark. *Hump me, vamp. My friends are murdered. Boo hoo, yeah.*"

"Stop it. *Stop it, Spade.*" Josie charged in. She turned against him."That's not how we feel."

But I was done.

Emotion clogged in my throat.

It was a simple betrayal.

"I was alone. So alone. *After your lie.* So when Lark offered a little compassion, I took it. Hell yeah. It was a goddamn life preserver and I was drowning in death. And I liked it, Spade. I goddamn loved it. *Lark made me feel good. For a second, things weren't so terrible here in my world.* But that didn't mean I wasn't wrecked by what I thought happened to my friends. *What you three made me believe!*" I glared at all of them. "I was wrecked."

"Seph," Bug tried again. So soft and sad.

"No. *This is over, Bug.* You made me think you were dead."

"I'm glad I did it," Spade said. Free of guilt.

"Fuck you, Spade."

"No thanks for saving your weaker friends' lives!" He shouted after me as I flew up the stairs. I was still holding it together out the door, but on the lawn I couldn't take another second. Every emotion breached my face. It all choked my throat. Lark reached for me and I fell into his arms, escaping the subterranean home. The storm cellar doors clanged shut behind us. But none of the others followed me out into the yard. They just let me go.

I huffed and puffed.

Raw emotion pouring out of my body.

Lark held me tight, he pulled me forward. He would never let me go.

"They left me alone," I whimpered.

"I know."

"But you didn't." I looked up at him, with fresh desire in my eyes. "You were there. You're always there."

"I'll protect you, Seph. With everything that I possess."

"You promise?"

"I swear."

"I know you will."

He was doing it right now. Sheltering me from the world.

"I'll protect you too," I agreed, sadly.

And I truly, deeply meant it.

Lark held me there.

Forever.

Just us.

Me and my amazing vampire bodyguard, the only thing I had

left in this whole world. I stared deep into his eyes, both lost and found.

"Well, isn't that nice. A little romance." The leader of the vampire Brotherhood said from his perch on the hood of Lark's car. His sudden voice tore us apart. I'd assumed we were alone. I was wrong. "Whaddaya know," Dreven said. "Just the two I was looking for."

54
PERSEPHONE

"Hello, folks," Dreven smirked. He leaned on Lark's sports car's hood like my vampire bodyguard had waited for me so many times before. The evil vampire had all the time in the world. A paranormal hood ornament.

But the Brotherhood goon wasn't here on his own.

As we approached, two other vampires opened huge black umbrellas to keep themselves out of the sunlight as they got out of the car. Awash in shadow. So that's how they got around in daytime, I realized. As long as the vamps themselves weren't exposed to the sun's rays, they all seemed to be good. The looming black covers had the effect of creating a wall of living night behind Dreven. His back-up support. Even under the heavy shade I recognized Gattas. The other large brute I didn't know. I didn't care to get acquainted with the new man today. They glowered in our direction.

I wiped any emotion from my face. Suddenly made of stone.

My heartbreak and agony and anger over my supposed friends and their betrayal immediately became hidden inside. Replaced by this larger threat. Beside me, Lark roiled in fury. Anger and aggression. While my stomach dropped in fear, my bodyguard readied for war. His mind reeled, probably deciphering the quickest way to kill the susceptible vampire soldiers with daylight, I guessed. His hands went to his belt, where thin wooden stake weapons sat waiting on his hips. He pulled two out. Lark had just promised to protect me forever, but neither of us thought he'd have to prove those words quite so soon. Still, here we were.

Dreven, for his part, was unarmed and unworried. He didn't stir from his casual roost.

"We thought we'd find you here, once we learned the identity of your friends at the academy heist. Naughty, girl. Very clever." He praised. "Although, technically you didn't steal anything when you broke into either location, did you girl?"

Just two worthless black jewels. I frowned to myself.

"We checked the Jius' and the Polaris' too. We're nothing if not thorough," Dreven gestured vaguely towards the Frankel home. He winked. My skin crawled. "But you were here. We saw your ride." He petted the car, goading Lark. "Parked out front of your little pal's house. You should be more careful, Mr. Vampire."

"They're not my friends," I said. Which was true, but also a ruse intended to draw the vampires away from the insect witch's home. His family were innocent. The Brotherhood monster smiled at the news.

"Good." Dreven raised himself up, but took a step to the side instead of towards us, pacing back and forth in front of his men, a calculated move to show he wouldn't attack. Not yet. "That's good to hear." Instead, he casually strolled, pretending to be lost in thought. Moving side to side. "Listen, I think we got off on the wrong foot... there's no reason *we* can't be friends, Persephone. Work alongside each other. I'm not sure what your vampire told you, but we have aligning goals. You want your uncle's house, I want the stone. This can be a win, win."

"She's not helping you start a vampire army," Lark growled.

"Why don't you let the lady speak for herself, boy," Dreven said.

Boy? Lark was almost two hundred years old. How ancient was Dreven?

"Lark's right." I stood as tall as I could, facing down the terrible leader of vamps. "I'm helping him and Mauve, not you."

"Mauve?" Dreven reared back at her name. He laughed and laughed. Gattas and the third vampire chuckled behind him, like I'd told some ridiculous joke. After taking a moment with his men, Dreven turned back to me. He looked like he pitied us both. "Lady Mauve? You must be pretty desperate to trust her."

"I never said that I trusted her," Lark scowled. This surprised me next.

I glanced at the vampire by my side. I'd always assumed he was on board with Mauve's plans. After all, she'd hired him to be my bodyguard and I'd seen her standing in his house just one night ago. But... he hadn't seemed particularly glad to see her, or interacted with her that evening. I'd assumed it was because we were both so broken and tired, but that might not have been it. Maybe he was only forced to entertain her whims because she was so closely related to his sister-in-law. I wanted to ask Lark about it, but now wasn't the time.

Still, it made me happy to hear the vampire had doubts. I didn't trust her either. And she hadn't proven very nice.

"Fine," I agreed with my man. "I'm doing this with Lark. Alone."

A united front.

"The whole Flood's on our side," Lark added. Giving us numbers. "You won't win."

Dreven rolled his eyes.

"Oh, come on. If the Flood were in, they'd be *here*." He gestured around. "They're clearly not. And I don't need to defeat the whole Flood tonight, Mr. Vampire, she said so herself... the girl's only ally is *you*. If I kill you, I'm as good as gold. And I can defeat you in my sleep. *Heh*, sleep." Dreven grinned a terrible smile at me. He knew I was a dreamcast too. Either that or he remembered the way I defeated him at the academy. "Do it."

He nodded at something behind us.

Someone on the Frankel porch.

We spun, far too late.

Fellow Gold stood there. He hurled a spell at us. Lark's eyes went wide. Everything happened so fast. Lark grabbed my hand, pulling me to him, I screamed. He spun, covering me with his back. The potion smashed onto his coat, puffing white powder everywhere. The outside became a cloud of dust. I coughed as a sleeping spell spread out on the lawn.

I'd seen them before, I'd even used the same spell against others. *Against Dreven.*

Just not in such a high dose.

"Run," Lark told me, as his body began to shut down.

The men under their black umbrellas couldn't chase me. There was a chance Dreven would let me go. I stuttered, coughing out potion. I tried to hold my breath but there was already enough inside to coat the roof of my mouth.

"No. I'm not leaving you."

Dreven and the other vampires strode towards us.

"Yes, you will. I'll be alright. Go," my vampire ordered. "Orphan Girl, *run.*"

"No," I cried out. But still, I turned my legs in order to escape. Lark pushed me forward. I started to move away from Fellow Gold and the other vampires and whatever danger came next.

But it was too late.

The spell entered my system.

It took over.

We both collapsed on the ground.

55

LARK

Fuck.

I awoke to pain. Everything ached. My arms and legs were stretched taut. Upright in chains. I'd clearly been worked over as I slept. My sides had been both kicked and punched. My whole body was dragged. Scratch marks and gouges healed on my skin. I'd been battered and mistreated out of hatred or carelessness or both. I shook out my head to clear out the cobwebs. The spell abated. I knew where we stood. We'd been blitz-attacked by Fellow Gold, who wasn't even trying to hide his allegiances anymore.

I was tied up to four hard points. Two on my wrists, two on my ankles, with long metal chains. I pulled on my hands, testing the ropes. My muscles groaned against the bindings. I couldn't move, stretched starburst ahead of the Witch House front door. I was trapped in the vestibule of Child Manor, in front of the large mahogany entrance and wood transom. Chained to the walls. A large black tent had been rudimentarily constructed next to the porch. It kept the sunlight out, although soon the extra darkness would be an unnecessary addendum to the grounds. Twilight had emerged. It would be followed soon by night.

"Come on," I willed the shackles to move.

They had no give.

The bindings were locked. There was probably some kind of extra magic on them too.

I flexed again, trying to rip out the hard contact points. But I stopped short of full strength. I was afraid to tear the brick columns down. I didn't want to destroy the whole entryway over my head. Not while I was tied to the bricks and Persephone slept on the concrete patio.

I stared down at the witch at my feet.

Seph laid on the ground, unbound. Her red hair was tossed around her shoulders and she slept. She looked small. So helpless. I'd tried to protect her from this world. This life. And I totally failed.

"She's cute," Gattas grinned at me, catching my eye. "She's got spunk. I see why you like her." In their man-made darkness he was free to preen and smirk. I yanked on my bindings, trying to throttle his neck.

"Temper, Mr. Vampire." Dreven stepped onto the porch. "It's not our fault you didn't protect your girl. She was all covered in Gold's sleeping potion, breathed it right in. She's been out for forever. So have you."

An hour at least, I mused. Probably more.

"Good," I snarled back. "She's a dreamcast. She'll figure out a way to stop you as she sleeps."

"I want her to dream," Dreven rolled his eyes. "Why do you think I doused the girl? Why do you think that we're here? You're not dead? The hex is still intact, the booby traps too, and I need her to figure out a way to get me inside the house and get the damn rock."

"Or we'll kill her," Gattas leered. "That's second choice."

A way in?

So Gattas and Dreven didn't know about the worm moon eclipse, I took in this news but didn't react. They also weren't confident about their chances of getting past future traps. A second point in our favor. Two against one million. I didn't love those odds.

But I'd take them.

Out of the corner of my eye, I saw Persephone stir.

"You don't have to kill her." I tried to stall. Clued her into their plan without directly speaking her way. Persephone heard me. She barely flinched. She was smart enough not to rise right away. Good girl. But Dreven also saw the beat that we shared.

"She's industrious. Aren't you girl?" He nudged her with his boot. I tried to yank my legs from the chains to stop him. But it just hurt my body more.

"Wakey, wakey," Gattas grabbed her by the ear and tugged. Persephone raked up to her feet, and he released. She stood in front of my frame, arms extended in a fighting stance, as if she could protect me with a karate chop. The men grinned.

"Leave us alone," she snarled with surprising vehemence. Dreven waved his vampire goon to step back.

"There you are." He patronized. "Did you dream?"

Yes. I could see it in her face. She had.

Persephone's eyes flashed between me, Dreven, and Gattas and searched out the other vampires behind, looming in the tent. She'd seen something. She was trying to figure it out.

"Let us go and I'll tell you how to get the rock." She bluffed.

"No, don't," I said. She glared my way. *Trust me*, the look said.

"No..." Dreven countered. "You'll get the Blood Stone for us, or Gatt'll kill this boy."

It was such a punk move for Dreven to act like a few decades between immortals meant anything, calling me boy. Gattas tapped a huge wooden stake in his palm. I had to admit, that looked like it would hurt. A lot.

"It happens at midnight," Persephone said. My eyes shuttled to her. She really was revealing the pertinent details.

Fuck.

Don't tell him that, I tried to say without words. She didn't listen.

"I saw what to do." Her voice was strong. "But I can't do it until then."

No, no, no.

"Fine. I'll just kill you both right now," Gattas purred.

"It's booby-trapped, but hey, your call." Seph stood against him, toe to toe. I'd never been so proud of a witch before, tough as nails—although if the Orphan Girl did have a plan, I couldn't figure it out. Dreven waved a hand to call him off again.

"Fine. Midnight," Dreven smiled. He stood waiting, as if he expected her to act.

"I have to go." Persephone said. "Prepare some stuff. I'll come back. At midnight," she lied. "And you're not following me either."

Yes. Get away. As far as you can.

She couldn't save me. She shouldn't want to anyway. I was a vampire. Hot and cold. Wild and dark. I'd caused her nothing but trouble since I'd met her, even as her damn bodyguard. This was her shot to escape. Persephone could save herself. Making them wait until midnight would give her enough time to run. She could get far, far from this town, far away from this life. If she stayed off the grid, the Brotherhood might never find her.

Do it, Orphan Girl. Run. Fast as your little feet will move.

"How do I know you'll return?" Dreven snarled.

"You don't. Guess you'll have to trust me." Persephone shrugged. "I'm trustworthy, right?"

"I don't trust, I verify." Dreven frowned. He didn't want to take the deal but he had to. The leader of the Brotherhood didn't know how to get into the house. He watched her for any sign of weakness. To her credit, she did not flinch. Finally, he decided on his own terms. "I'm going to incentivize this deal so I know you'll uphold your part," he said slowly. "This is a taste of what will happen to your precious vampire if you decide not to come back." He motioned to Gattas. My whole body tensed.

"No," Persephone said. Full of fear and regret. She hadn't meant to cause me any more pain. I readied for the blow.

"Do it." Dreven ordered. Gattas practically foamed at the mouth, his desire to do me harm was so great.

"I've been waiting for this." The monster smirked. Attacking a tied up man was pathetic and cheap, but Gattas didn't care. He kicked out my right leg, making my body drop. Gravity was a force that couldn't be swayed. As I fell, he impaled my gut on his stake. Deep in my stomach.

"No!" Seph raced forward as Gattas pulled out the wood, spattering my blood all over her. She fell to cover me, tumbling helpless to the patio stone, trying to hold me. To put me back together again. I huffed and puffed, but I deliberately held back my agonized face. I wouldn't give them the pleasure of seeing me struggle. I wouldn't give Seph anything more to fear or regret. Gattas raised to strike again.

"No!" Persephone clung to me, a human shield.

"Don't hurt her." My words croaked.

"*Stop, please!*" Persephone begged. She laid over my chest like a blanket.

"Enough," Dreven agreed. He sounded a bit bored.

Gattas frowned, but obeyed.

I closed my eyes, *thank god.* The pain was already too much to bear.

"Think the dreamcast gets the point?" Gattas smirked.

"Oh, Lark." Persephone whimpered with me, skin to skin. She

threw her arms around my neck. I buried myself in her goodness, wishing I could wrap her up in my arms.

"I'm alright, I'm alright." I repeatedly said.

It was true.

It was a lie.

Both were accurate and equal. The blow could heal. But it hurt like hell. And I was in no position to mend. We each swam deep in my blood.

"Vamps can regenerate," I reminded her. It wasn't a fatal blow. Only a stab through the heart would truly kill me, only the severing of my soul knot could destroy how I felt. Anything else was just a terrible flesh wound. Torture and pain. I was willing to endure it. I didn't care what happened to me, as long as Seph got out.

"It's all my fault," Persephone cried.

"No, it's not. *Shhh*, Orphan Girl. I'll be alright. You need to run." I whispered in her ear. "You go to Lila. Tell her to write you a check. Whatever amount. And then run. You don't look back. I'll be fine."

"No, Lark..." She struggled to hear me. Her whole body went into shock.

"Yes." I ordered. "Now, kiss me, goodbye."

Persephone let out a whimper, then dove onto my lips.

She smashed her body against mine, threw her hands around my head, into my hair. As if she could free me from my chains by the sheer force of her will. I closed my eyes, fully consumed by our final touch.

My body lit on fire.

I thrummed with the energy of life.

It was all that I was, all that I had.

Joy. Sorrow. Trust. I felt Persephone's soul in the depths of my heart. She'd wormed her way into my humanity, and the dark places long destroyed. It made me remember how everything mortal felt. All that I'd lost. And what I'd gained in my afterlife. Her kiss did all that.

And when she went running to Lila and told her what happened, my family would come. They'd arrive in a fucking blaze of glory, and I would be fine. And if they came too late, then I knew full well, Wren and Birdie would avenge my goddamn life. They wouldn't care how long it would take, they'd hunt every single member of the Brotherhood down. Either way I'd damn near enjoyed myself. We'd had a good run. I tried to convey to Seph everything that I felt. All the potential sex and longing and admiration and joy and pleasure and wanting and protection and...love, so much love between the Orphan Girl and myself—that would have been nice.

In another life.

In this realm, I gave her everything that I had to offer through my lips and my tongue. It wasn't much.

Feel me, drink me, my Orphan Girl. Say goodbye.

You're not stuck in this hell.

Be free.

Go live a long, happy life.

I tried to assure her, again and again. That's what I wanted. Persephone pulled back, her eyes searched my face.

"Lark," she whispered my name, about to say more, but Gattas yanked us apart. She cried out as she fell back to the stone porch. Covered in my blood.

"Time's a ticking, *Orphan Girl*," Gattas said.

I watched my girl's face drop as he used my pet name for her. She stared from him to me, then scrambled to her feet.

"Go," Dreven ordered.

I thought she might object again, but this time, Persephone let out a small cry, turned on her heels, and ran. I watched every step, knowing it was the last time I'd ever see that infuriating, adorable witch.

Goodbye, Seph.

56

PERSEPHONE

"Blue Moon?" I raced into the Konya Thomas Collection. "Are you here?" Tears streaked my face, I tried to shield the panic in my voice, but there was no hiding my body. Covered in Lark's blood.

"I'm here." She came running. "I'm here, what's–*oh, Persephone.*" She caught me in the lobby, eyes wide at the sight. I was dramatic. Fully unravelling. I collapsed in her hands, weeping, contorting.

"They took him. They have him. They said–and–I don't know–" It came out in a jumble. There were no proper words to share what I felt.

Gattas grabbing my vampire. The twist of pain on Lark's face as he was stabbed. My bodyguard a helpless victim in those cuffs. Tied across the entrance of the Witch House.

I was his only hope. And I was totally spent.

Blue Moon helped me to sit on the stairs.

"*Shhh*, slow down. What happened? Is this your blood." She checked.

"No." It came out as a wail. I wrenched away from her gentle touch, but I didn't answer a linear thought. I couldn't. My brain was whirring too fast. "The other vampires, we were leaving Bug's house. They have him."

"Who? The insect witch? Bug?"

"*Lark!*" I yelped.

"Is this *his* blood?"

"Yes." I snuffled out. "It's all my fault."

"*Shhh*, no it isn't. You're alright. But you've got to calm down." Blue Moon hugged me like a mother might do–at least that was my guess, being motherless myself. "Take a few deep breaths. You sound like me when I try to do much of anything," she joked. "My boyfriend in the Damocles coven says to do it like this." She inhaled and exhaled. Inhaled and exhaled. I struggled to follow until my breath finally slowed. "Good. Now start again. What happened?"

"Dreven got us. He was waiting. He threw out a sleeping spell. Lark blocked it with his body to protect me, but that only made things worse. He fell unconscious. I did too. I dreamt. *I saw a large blue moon in my mind, huge, looming over the whole town, it was so blue.* So I knew, I knew I should come here. But I'm not sure it will help. They grabbed him, and threatened me. Said if I don't get them the stone and hand it over to them, they'll kill Lark. Then they stabbed him in the gut. There was so much blood." Half the stained puddle of his life force was dried on my chest. "We know where it is, we figured it out. The Blood Stone is in a family crypt under the Child Manor. I think I even know how to get Lark in. But the house is still spelled. I can't get in my own home. And Bonnie, *I can't do this alone.*"

"You're not alone," she shushed me. "You're not, honey. You have me and the others. We'll figure it out, I swear. We will. Did you find your friends?"

"What others? What friends?" I murmured, broken.

"Josie. The boys."

My supposed squad?

The ones who left me to die?

I was about to rip off their heads or maybe cry all over again, but Blue Moon said more.

"They called me, panicked. Over and over, they were trying to figure out what to do. They spent all night trying to learn how to contact the vampires. The Flood. The good vampires. They said they needed to make sure you were alright. They feared you might have been taken. They were so scared and angry. And Spade, he just buried his head in his hands. He kept saying '*what have I done? This is all my fault.*' He looked so destroyed. They wouldn't tell me what happened, there wasn't time, but they sounded so worried. I was so sorry I couldn't help. They said they had to call someone. Anyone. I suggested Mauve or–"

"Wait, what." My face scrunched at this news processing. "They called you? My friends?"

"No. Well, yes, at first, but then they were here. In a group. They'd been everywhere, Seph. They were frantic all night. Said you'd been lost. Or taken. Or worse. And Spade was so sorry. They asked me for anything I could find to contact the Crimson Flood. But it's not like the vampires go around giving their number out to coven paper masters, you know? I didn't have the contact to offer. I'm not sure anyone but Child did, and he's gone. But I've been compiling leads all night." She gestured to a big pile of folders in her office. "No solid facts, exactly. I waited all morning to hear back, but no one called." Then she remembered something else. "Oh, and Mauve. I told her too. Last night–first thing–she said she'd handle things. When I didn't hear back, I kept looking for stuff but I'd figured it was probably done. I'd hoped you were all back together. I thought that she helped."

"She didn't help." I gritted it out.

I thought back to the professor's attitude last night. Mauve had called the friends I thought were dead a '*ragtag group of kids.*'

She'd been so careless and cruel. She must've known all along that the others were alive and looking for me. They were still trying to help! She knew how broken I was at their passing, how desperately they were trying to find me too, and *still*, she kept us apart. She let me believe...

"Mauve did not help." I repeated the news.

But what to do now?

The coven professor *was* involved in the solution. The older witch had been in my dream too, under the giant blue moon. *In the vision, Lady Mauve sat at a desk, staring into a mirror, regarding a reflection of herself. Slowly combing her hair.*

I didn't know what to make of it.

I couldn't go to her for help, she'd proven that.

"Mauve? You must be pretty desperate to trust her," the evil vampire had laughed.

"I never said that I trusted her," Lark replied.

More and more I understood that. I felt it too. The only side Mauve was on was her own.

"I'm sorry, Seph. I didn't know," Blue Moon patted my back.

"Nor did I," I admitted. But I could see things clearer now. "You'll really help?"

"However I can," Blue Moon agreed. "How can I help? I'm more of a behind-the-scenes support kinda witch," she added nervously. "But if you need me to fight, *oh gosh*," her voice wavered but she still looked determined.

"No, it's alright." Things started to form as a plan in my mind. "Behind the scenes is fine. Great, even. I'm not sure. It's a long-shot... but I think... I need someone to make up some spells. Can you do that for us?"

"Yes! *Us*?"

"Us." I looked at the clock on the wall, evening had arrived. We didn't have much time, only a few hours until midnight. I'd have to work fast. I nodded. "Old friends and new allies, I hope."

"Right. Okay." Blue Moon focused. "It's been a while since my academy days. I mostly push paper around, but I'll definitely try. What spells do you need?"

"I need like a bucket of sleeping potion," I generalized, "and the spell to reverse the hex on the Witch House."

"It's bound to Mauve." Blue Moon frowned. "I don't think, I mean, she refused to do it before. It's connected to her biological signal and..."

"I know."

I pictured the dream image of Mauve. *She sat in the chair looking in the mirror at herself. A second Mauve looking back.*

"I can get her biological stuff," I said.

"Oh."

My dream's bird's eye view circled the pair. Mauve stared at her reflection, combing her hair. Over and over. Long and blonde locks. But the real Mauve's hairstyle was short, gray and cropped.

The reflected woman looked young and soft.

The real Mauve was hard and worn.

Her reflected dream image was the witch she'd been years ago, the woman she was, not the Lady she was now... only, it wasn't Lady Mauve in the mirror at all, I realized, but someone else.

"Do you think she'll change her mind?" Blue Moon asked.

"No." I firmly set my jaw.

But there was somewhere Lark had told me to go. He thought I could get money from his home, but there was something in the Bird Cage that could help us much more.

Because the second woman in my vision wasn't Mauve.

It was Lila.

"I'm hoping Mauve's twin sister can help."

57
PERSEPHONE

I ran up the dirt road to the Bird Cage property.

The taxi driver thought I was nuts to want to be dropped off in the dark, beside a flat rock and a strange forest road in the middle of the country, with no neighbors and no signage—especially when I didn't have an address, just told him to 'drive' and then 'stop' when the trees bent in a way I recognized. It was foolish, maybe. But I had no other choice, I didn't have their proper address and had to find the property by sight. Plus, I purposefully kept the driver at a distance from the vampire house. I didn't want to bring any more innocent people into this paranormal world. Not if it wasn't necessary.

It was a courtesy I wished I had been shown.

Ever since I learned my dead uncle existed, everything had gone to hell in my life. Before the discovery, I'd always been alone, with no close friends and no family, but this was far worse. The worried look on Blue Moon's face, the fight with my friends, Lark being stabbed... I wasn't sure my heart could take much more.

My bodyguard had said to run, but there was nowhere to go.

Not without him.

I'd had a life. But I couldn't go back. My old job was gone, and my House Mum would've figured out that I'd ditched by now. She'd likely already rented the room. Everything of any value from my past I'd already sold, but the real truth was... I didn't want to run away and start again. This was my real life and my real home now. These were the only shards of history and family that I'd ever had. I would fix what was happening here or die trying.

I'd get my man.

I'd reunite with my friends... maybe... and if I was wrong, if Josie, Bug and Spade wouldn't accept my apology and agree to help, I'd do it all with Blue Moon... and Lila, I hoped. *Or, fuck it, I'd do it all by myself.*

I jogged down the lane, ecstatic to see my memory was correct about the forest road. After a few turns in the trees, the castle opened up in front of me, the gate propped wide open, waiting for its owners to come home. But for Lark to do that, he needed my help. I raced up to the front of the house. I rapped on the massive door knocker, feeling small and alone, but hopeful too. For a long breath, no one answered. I would have sat on the stoop of the castle. Camped and waited forever. But finally, Lila opened the door. Seeing me, her concerned expression changed to surprise. She looked behind me, beside me, likely checking for my vampire, but there was nobody else.

"Where's Lark?"

"He... sent me." I hedged. From the tone in my voice, she could tell something was wrong.

"Come in, Persephone." Lila frowned, stepping aside. We moved into the atrium. I hadn't been brought into their home through this formal entrance before. The welcome was grand and expensive. A beautiful water feature flowed in the foyer. I glanced at the sad statute of a water woman trapped in eternal bronze. The molded girl illustrated how I felt.

Cold. Alone. Frozen in time.

But there was something in the expression on her face. A kernel of hope.

Or maybe I was projecting, I didn't care.

Lila led me into the large study. We sat down in front of the hearth. From the book on the table I learned she'd been reading about renaissance architecture.

"Wren's out on business," she told me. "What's going on?"

I took a breath. I barely knew her, could I trust her?

But Lila was someone Lark had told me to run to when he knew I was in trouble. He'd said '*go to Lila.*' His sister-in-law. Even if she was the twin of Lady Mauve. I knew the witches would have still been identical looking women if the vampire gene mutation hadn't killed Lila several decades ago. But they weren't mirror images on the inside.

In all her time in the Bird Cage, had her allegiances shifted?

Would she go against her sister?

And could their near-identical bio-signals work on my spell?

There was only one way to know.

I took a deep breath. "Lark's been captured by Dreven and his men. The Brotherhood of Thorns."

"*Oh my gosh.*" Lila stood, like she was going to tell someone or immediately act.

"It's worse. They're at Child Manor. He's tied up. Dreven says he'll kill Lark if I don't hand the Blood Stone to the Brotherhood. I said I would."

"Persephone, *no.*" Lila twisted, sitting back down. "You can't."

"I know. Lark wants me to run. He swore to keep me safe, he said you'd give me money, but I don't want that, I want to help–I only have until midnight and then I have to return, so–"

"–why?" Lila cut me off. I looked at her surprised.

"Why what? Why at midnight? Well–"

"No. Persephone, stop. I understand. I'll tell Wren. He'll bring in the calvary for his brother. We'll rush in at midnight, I swear.

That's why Lark sent you to me. He'll be taken care of by far more powerful beings than you are. Or even I am. You've told me now, you can go. Free and clear. You don't have to return."

"Yes, I do." It immediately popped out of my lips. Her eyes flickered.

"Why?"

"I just told you, Lark's in trouble and I can—"

"—is it the home? The money that will release when you've completed the task?" She raised from her seat and moved towards a credenza at the back of the room. "I can write you a check."

Lark had said to go to Lila and take his money.

But that wasn't why I was here.

I shook my head, confused.

Did all vampires expect to pay their way out of trouble?

She held out the checkbook. "I can buy you a house. Persephone, I can buy you a development of houses."

"It's not about that. I don't care about my inheritance!"

"What's it about then?" She was so calm.

"I don't know..." I sputtered. "*Lark*! It's about what's right! *It's my life.*"

She swooped back to me, her money tossed to the wayside. "He cares about you."

"I'm not sure." I hesitated.

"No, he does. I've lived here with the brothers and sometimes their sister Birdie for... well, it must be decades now. Sometimes time flies. Sometimes it drags. You're the first girl he's ever brought home." She picked up my chin, to ensure her message was getting through. "He cares."

"What about Gwen?" I spoke the other witch's name. The woman from his past.

"He told you about her?" Lila looked surprised. I nodded. She faltered. "Gwen was before my time. He cared about her too." She admitted. The hurt couldn't be avoided.

"Were they together?"

Lila hesitated, but to her credit, she didn't lie to my face. "Yes. While she was alive. He loved her very much."

Oof. That hurt.

"What happened to her?"

"They were fighting and working together on a task, kind of like this. There's always danger and darkness in the witch/vampire world. Too much power will corrupt anyone. So our lives, well, they're not always easy, Seph. Immortal creatures tend to have trouble. Same with the paranormal. Humans fear what they do not know, and—"

"You sound like Gold."

"Well, he's a fool," she darkened. "But fools are not always wrong."

"So Lark and Gwen?"

"They fought together, but ultimately Lark could not save her."

"She died?"

Lila's face darkened. "Worse. Gwen became a vampire, only her soul knot untied. The woman she once was became lost. A monster evolved. A truly terrible creature. His brother's been lost to the darkness as well. So you can understand why Lark's a little messed up when it comes to... feelings of love."

I ingested that news. *A terrible end to a meet-cute on the train.*

And when I asked him to reach for a happy story, Lark stretched back for her... back to before she...

No wonder Lark always stopped us so cold.

"So when he tells you to go, he really means it," Lila said. This was her whole point. "He won't judge if you do. He'll be glad you got out. We all will be."

"He doesn't want my help?" I asked. Lila half-smiled.

"Probably not. No. When Lark said to run, he meant it. Wren's the same way. They think they can finish everything themselves.

They've lived a long time where that had to be true in their lives. But, things do change, and we've seen what can be taken in a blink of an eye. That's his hang up. Not yours. Persephone, the thing to understand is, even immortal, he might need your help. He may not be able to carry the burden alone. I'll do my best to save him, to help him, we all will, but Lark could be taken. There's consequences and risk in every decision. Is it better to run? Is he worth fighting for? Is this *really* worth risking your life? Only you can decide."

I thought of all the times Lark appeared out of nowhere to help me.

How his surprise arrival had saved my skin. Again and again.

How he made me laugh. How he listened and respected my wishes.

How we often disagreed, but I always knew he was trying to make the paranormal world a better and more fair place, even when he could use his powers for darker things and literally reign.

I relived all the beautiful, quiet moments. The sexy, undeniable pull. The snarky bits and bites where the man drove me nuts. I recounted the rare times when he let me see behind his curtain. And the surprising way I could be vulnerable and honest with him.

I'd never had that before... and I didn't want to let it go.

I didn't want to live another second without my vampire bodyguard.

Lark was definitely worth it.

My future and family were worth it.

I was willing to risk it all for this witch life.

I owed it to myself to explore it. I needed to at least try. I'd give it everything I had.

"He is. Lark's worth it," I said. "That's why I'm here. But Lila, I can't get in. There's a spell on the house. In his last will and testament, my uncle said I had to have a real magical education before the deed would be mine. The magic can only be broken by Mauve. And she won't remove it until the stone's in her hands... only, I can't get the rock until the spell is removed." It was a terrible catch-22. "I know where it is, in a crypt in the basement of Child Manor. We're certain it's there. And vampires can slip through the house bones at midnight."

"The eclipse," Lila knew.

"Right. So I have to get inside first. But the spell, if we don't break it..."

"They'll get in, get the stone, and kill Lark too," Lila agreed. "I'll call Wren, he's been waiting to hear. He can bring the Flood. We'll surround the house, we'll stop the Brotherhood." She darkened in a way I'd previously only seen from vampire men. But Lila had their power and violence too. I shuddered at the sheer force of her.

"There's more," I squeaked out. "From you."

"What do you need from me?" Lila asked.

"You're your sister's twin. Your biology might be the same. And I know it might be hard to cross her or go against her wishes, but I need you to break Mauve's bequeathment spell and let me in. If you can–"

Lila stared at me with a thick smile and fierce certainty.

"*Hell yeah, I will.*"

58

PERSEPHONE

"We're closed." Josie didn't look over her shoulder as the shop bell jostled above my head.

"Uh, hi," I said.

Josie, Bug and Spade all spun at my voice. Bug's jaw dropped open in surprise.

"Seph! What are you doing here?"

"Need a book?" Josie asked, her cool voice was clipped. Spade just stared.

"No." I looked between them. "I came to apologize." The others straightened slightly. "I was wrong. I took you all to task and I said some terrible things."

"Yes, you did," Josie said.

"Well, I shouldn't have– Blue Moon set me straight." I admitted. "She told me how you called and came for me, and looked, and even tried to contact the Flood. She explained how you never gave up. So, thanks."

"No need for thanks. We didn't succeed." Josie said.

"And we should never have split off from the squad," Bug

agreed. It would be counterproductive to point out that the 'squad' he just mentioned, after they'd left it, was only me. Solo.

"No, I'm glad you did," I told Bug. I included the others. "The vampires would have killed us all if Spade didn't create the perfect lie-guard to protect you." I admitted. "You saved them," I added to Spade. A clear olive branch. He swallowed. "And I know you would have saved me too if you could have."

He nodded quietly. "I felt really guilty, Seph."

"It's okay. Really. You did what you could do in a terrible circumstance, and I can appreciate the decision you made with only seconds to choose. For a moment, the shock of your returning and the thought that you'd all ditched me in the warehouse and didn't care what had happened, yeah, that hurt me. A lot. It sucked," I laughed at my own pain. "But it wasn't true, you were working behind the scenes, trying to get me right back."

"We really were." Bug assured me. "And we were really worried."

"We're so sorry, Seph," Josie said. "If I could do it again—"

"No, it's alright. You should know, the biggest reason I was hurt by the lie-guard wasn't my safety, it was the facts. It was thinking you were dead. Seeing you all so battered and beaten on the ground because you followed me in. It ripped me apart. You guys are my closest friends. I've grown to care about you a lot and I was just as fooled as the Brotherhood into thinking, into believing, you were gone. The loss devastated me... truly... I was destroyed. No matter *who* I let comfort me in my bed." I added. Spade had the good sense to seem embarrassed by the naughty accusations he'd made. "Especially since I knew you were only there in that warehouse in the first place because you came to help me."

"Well, what are friends for?" Bug said.

"So we're friends again?" I asked.

"Of course!" Bug beamed. The others agreed.

"If you'll have us," Josie said.

"I definitely will." I breathed out in relief.

"Even me?" Spade checked. My gaze fell on him.

"Uh huh. Thank you for saving my friends."

"Thank you for saving yourself, I couldn't have lived with myself if you hadn't, Seph."

"Me neither," I half-grinned, though the joke was clearly too soon.

"I can't believe we went back there because of a papercut," Bug mused. "Fate works in mysterious ways."

"Wait." Josie stopped. "That's not the only reason we were there," she stared at him, then me. "Don't forget my payout. When we finish, I still get half your house, remember?" Josie tried to hold the hard line, but couldn't. She smirked. This broke a smile open in me.

"Sixty-forty," I found myself shooting back. If that was the closest thing to a playful joke I'd get from the book-loving chemist I would absolutely take it. The levity was a relief. But Spade was still serious.

"I'm really glad you're alright," he said.

"You too," I said quietly. We each nodded, on equal footing.

"You *and* Lark," Bug agreed. Then frowned. He looked over my shoulder. "Wait. Where's our favorite vampire? He's not hiding in the stacks again, is he?" Bug looked between the bookshelves.

"No, he's not." I couldn't stop the darkness leaking into my voice. I looked down, then back up, finding the three staring, waiting. "They took him. The Brotherhood. They kidnapped us and then stabbed him in the chest." Bug gasped.

"Oh god," Spade moaned.

"Is he–" Josie watched my face.

"No," I answered quickly. "A vampire can heal from that kind of wound. But they still have him. He's in dire condition. I need… your help." I floated the words, watching their faces. The request was open, naked, asking for something I knew I didn't really deserve at this point.

Their help.

If they said no, I'd understand. We'd just made up, but I'd been short-sighted and assumed the worst. I'd attacked them when they'd been just as confused and lost as I was in an awful situation... and now I'd come back to see if they would jump in again. I wouldn't be surprised if I received three immediate *'hell nos.'* But, if I had any friends in this world, these were my people. And I didn't want to do things all alone anymore.

I couldn't. I wouldn't...

This was my life and I needed more.

I had to ask.

The answers were their choice.

"The reason I'm here is because the other vampires have agreed to come, at midnight. Lila's gathering the Crimson Flood to fight outside of the witch house, and they can shift through a house's bones at the moment of the eclipse, but I don't want to permanently let any vampire in–"

"What can we do?" Josie asked.

"Whatever you need," Spade said.

"We've got you, Seph. You and Lark!" Bug chimed in.

"Really?" A huge smile broke across my face, it released the heavy weight on my chest. "You might want to hear what it entails first..."

"No, we're good," Bug said at the same time that Josie agreed.

"Obviously, shoot," she said.

"The Blood Stone is in a crypt under the basement of Child Manor. We've got to break Mauve's spell, sneak inside, and set a trap so that when the vampires come, we beat them at their own game. It's going to be dangerous."

"Super dangerous." Spade agreed.

"I'm still in," Josie said.

"Me too," Bug added on.

"Me three. If you'll have me," Spade said. He understood the wound was still fresh. The forgiveness was there. But it would need more time to heal.

"We could really use a lie-guard, not to mention a chemist and a bug harness." I nodded. "Please, yes."

"*Oh my god,*" Bug beamed. "Does that mean... the squad's back together again?!" He squealed.

"Don't call it a squad." Josie, Spade and I all moaned at exactly the same time. But as we complained, we also grinned, because it was true. We were a squad. We were back together again, and we were committed to stopping the Brotherhood of Thorns, saving Lark, and getting the Blood Stone for ourselves, in any manner we could... as a team.

59

PERSEPHONE

"I let myself in, I hope you don't mind," Blue Moon admitted as we entered Bug's house.

"As long as it's you and no Brotherhood vampires," he agreed.

I checked the clock on his bedside table. Less than an hour 'til midnight. We were running out of time.

"Have you got the potion?" I asked the paper master.

"Right here."

"We need Lady Mauve's biometric signature," Josie said, helping.

"Lila spit in this vial," I handed it to them.

"Gross." Spade groaned. "Couldn't you do it more sterile?"

"These are ancient magical powers that were discovered when modern medicine wasn't even invented," Josie told him. "Magic's not sterile." Blue Moon nodded too.

The women carefully calculated a potion together. They poured it up, then shook the vial until the ingredients seemed to disappear like smoke. Blue Moon released the valve. I gripped a nearby chair. I expected a bright light or a spark or explosion, even a cloud of potion, but nothing happened. It fizzled and disappeared.

"*Magic*," Blue Moon whispered.

"The spell should be broken... if using Lila's twin biome was close enough to the real thing," Josie said.

"But there's nothing there," Bug worried.

"There is, you just can't see it."

"It's magic, Bug. Fate requires action, remember?" I echoed Josie's earlier sentiment. The chemist eyed me and nodded. I finally got it. "How will we know if it worked?"

"When you try to enter the house. If the spell doesn't smack you away from the door with a crazy shock of voltage, you'll know you're good," Josie said.

"Fun," Spade muttered.

"And if not, we stay trapped in the yard while the Brotherhood and Flood battle it out inside the witch house without us, so let's hope it does." Josie finished.

"Fun, again," Spade griped. "But seriously, what's the plan?"

The squad looked my way.

"When the eclipse starts, I think we should lure the group inside, ambush them, put the Brotherhood vampires to sleep, then drag them out of the house for the Flood to deal with. That way, nobody fights, nobody dies and no one was invited in," I said.

"And no one gets hurt," Bug added.

We all nodded at that.

"I'll be the bait," I told them, leaving the most dangerous job for myself. Dreven had already proven that he thought the threat of Lark's death was enough to keep me in line, so we should continue with that. "I'll lure them into the house and take them down a tunnel or hallway where Bug and Josie will be waiting on each side of the vamps to douse them with spells. As soon as they walk into the room." The two witches nodded. They could do that.

"What about Spade and Blue Moon?" Josie asked.

"Spade, you play clean up." I hoped. "Can you create some kind of lie-guard weapon that will take someone out if any of the vampires get by our initial defense? Like a stake gun, or, I don't know."

"How about this?" He balled up his hand and closed his eyes until a huge black crossbow with spiderweb-like strings for the bow and a body shaped like a crescent moon appeared. A six-shooter. He loaded it with thin wooden stakes instead of arrows. And instead of drawing the strings back by hand, mechanical gears would twist and shoot out the arrow-stakes with violent speed. He punched out a shot to demonstrate. The arrow-stake thumped into Bug's basement wall, leaving a gouge in his sheetrock. "I call it the Bloodletter."

Bug pulled out the stake and looked at the damage. "Mom's gonna be mad."

"I think that will work," Blue Moon agreed, very wide-eyed.

"Perfect. Don't drain your powers," I said. Spade released his palm and the weapon disappeared. "Blue Moon will stay here, she'll make more spells and watch who's coming and going."

"I'm more of a researcher than a fighter. I don't want to get in the way," the older witch said.

"But you're still a huge help." I argued. "Look at everything she's made." There were sleeping potions, quicksand spells, snap ribbon plants, glue, burn salve, the list went on.

"You've done so much," Josie agreed. She divvied up the spells.

"Plus, I have something else to ask, Bonnie." I said to the paper master. "If you're staying, and I think you should, do you think we could borrow your Electrum ring? I have my necklace, but the others have nothing. With compulsion, the Brotherhood can get us to turn on each other."

"As long as I get it back," Blue Moon agreed. She took it off and handed it to me.

"I promise you will."

"Who should wear it?" Bug asked. "Seph for sure, with your necklace, but the other one? Me?" We all remembered what he did with his bugs, if Bug could harness his own power for himself, he'd be a very formidable foe. We wouldn't want the vampires to get access to his abilities again. But I had another plan. A hint from my dream when dream-Bug couldn't hear me.

"Actually, I was thinking Spade," I admitted. "He's on our defense, whereas you two are the attack. And *you* could wear your noise-cancelling earbuds. Maybe play music in them? That way you can't hear what the vampires say. Josie, too. If you have another pair."

"I do! That's genius, Seph!" Bug cheered. He dug into a drawer to find his set and gave another pair to Josie.

"You gave me the idea in a dream, when I thought you were dead."

"Dream Bug is awesome," he beamed.

"Real Bug's awesome too." Josie complimented him as she took his extra pair. He grinned and grinned. Spade slid the Electrum ring on his pinky finger.

"I'll take good care of it for you, I swear it, Lady Blue Moon."

"I know you will."

"So we use the sister-spell release to get in the witch house, lure the vampires inside, bombard them with sleeping potion spell, save Lark, and while the Flood is dealing with the Brotherhood vampires, we'll go down into the crypt and Persephone will get the Blood Stone, because anyone else who tries to touch it might be magically destroyed?" Spade recounted the steps.

"That's the plan." I agreed to uneasy nods all around.

"What could go wrong?" Spade mused.

Everything, I admitted to myself.

But we were still going to do it.

Because it was the only life-saving, house-breaking-in, vampire-fighting, stone-acquiring strategy that we had. And our time was running out.

60

PERSEPHONE

Our foursome snuck through the property line and slunk onto the Child Manor grounds. We kept low to the grass and scurried along. But the vampire presence was concentrated on the front of the house. They were watching the gates, not scanning the trees on the sides of the lot. We snuck right up to the house and lined up against the warm yellow bricks. Directly beside the back door.

"Alright, here goes," I whispered to the squad. I took a deep breath. From my first experience at the house, I knew the spell would present like a magical shock. I tested it now, throwing one of the useless black balls that I'd taken from the earlier chandeliers against the house wall. It rapped against the door and fell into the grass; no bright light, no sharp buzz.

I scooped it back up.

"I think it worked."

The others nodded, hopeful as well. Of course, the real test would be my hand on the knob. I reached out, gathered my courage and grabbed the door. Nothing happened. The spell was gone!

I twisted the handle but it didn't open. The house was still locked.

I looked at the trees and the second floor window. "I'll be right back," I told the others. Then I scaled up a bough. It was a small risk, nothing like the rest of the evening we were planning. I scurried across a thick branch to the second story juliette balcony, jimmied the pane and the window opened.

"Go squad!" Bug quietly cheered. The others groaned and covered his mouth.

"Be right back," I whispered. I ducked into the house, ran over to the staircase, and hurried down to the door where they were waiting.

"You did it," Bug whisper-praised. The others peered inside.

"You gonna invite us in?" Spade asked. Josie simply crossed the threshold and went inside. Bug followed.

"It's only vampires who need an official homeowner's invite. Come on." I said. Just like that, the four of us made our way into my uncle's locked house. Everything was dark. No electricity was on. We didn't dare try a switch, for fear of being found out.

"Where to?" Bug still whispered like outside.

Spade turned on his cell phone flashlight.

"No phones, they might see," Josie grabbed some candlesticks. I found matches. We lit them. Like old fashioned explorers, we looked around over candlelight. None of us had been inside the Child house before and the manor was about ten times the size of its neighbor's home. We slipped through the hallways, speaking little, keeping our footsteps light as we could manage. It felt like we were sneaking through a museum after hours. Not like a home.

"Hey, over here, you can see Lark," Bug pointed through a crack in a drawn drape. We huddled to peek outside. My vampire was there, still tied up in his chains. His posture was slumped. They'd kept him tied up for hours with no rest and no break.

"Poor Lark." Even Spade frowned.

"We'll get him soon," I murmured.

The other vampires on the porch were busy looking for me to arrive from the road. Other than a small glimpse, we didn't have much viewpoint. We pushed away from the window.

"Let's find a good place to set the ambush," I told the group. "What time is it?"

"Ten to," Josie said.

"Forget waiting for midnight, let's grab the Blood Stone right now!" Spade realized. Josie's eyes widened. We hadn't considered that at Bug's house. There were ten minutes left. Could we snatch the stone out from under the vampires before they had a chance to arrive?

Without a word, we headed down the stairs, into the basement of the home. There were plenty of rooms, and a dumb waiter lift from the kitchen to the other floors. Each room in the basement had old heirlooms covered with sheets and a layer of dust.

"It could be anywhere," Spade groaned.

"No," I countered. "It's here." I stopped in front of three large wooden slats. Wall decor. Across the triptych was carved the head of a dragon, staring out at our group. Its face was as big as a door, on the other two panels were each of its hands. The palms were hollow. The art piece stretched out across the wall. "I've seen this carving before, in books. It's the seal of the Umbrawick crypt."

"How do we get in?" Josie asked.

The artwork slides looked almost like doors, they were large enough to walk through, but there was no obvious handle, or latch, or hinges to pull. We tried to push them around or make them move, to no avail. All four of us scoured the space, looking for the answer of how to get in. But in the candlelight, nothing came.

"There must be a hidden release," I suggested, thinking of Child's office bookshelf. We felt the shelves around the room and lifted detailed tchotchkes off the walls. I tried grabbing other random items in the basement. Nothing worked.

"There's nothing here," Spade frowned.

"That can't be right," Bug countered. "A house this old would have several hidden passageways, I should think." But he also had no luck. Josie looked down at her watch.

"We're out of time. Four minutes 'til 11:59 p.m. We have to go back." We'd used up all our wiggle room.

We went back up.

"Well, we know they'll have to go down," I suggested. "So this is a good spot." We aligned ourselves with the staircase entrance one floor up. Found resting places for our candles to illuminate the entry. Deciding the spot for our trap would be the atrium for the staircase. There was enough space on each side of the hall for the witches to hide out of sight, waiting.

"We can't hear, remember, so we'll each take a side and watch for your signal. Seph, when you cross the threshold, you should turn and raise both hands above your head, then we'll throw," Josie said and Bug was on board.

"I'll perch up here," Spade jogged up the next level of the staircase, two at a time. He rounded the corner, out of view. "I'll come round the bend the moment I hear the sleeping potions explode." He mimed the action he'd take with his lie-guard crossbow. "If anyone's still standing, the Bloodletter'll get 'em." He mimed shooting vampires like in a carnival shooting gallery. "I'll grab Lark and we'll escape your way," I agreed. "It goes without saying, but don't shoot my vamp. Do not shoot Lark."

"If it goes without saying, why'd you say it?" Spade frowned. An edge came into his voice.

"Two minutes 'til 11:59," Josie warned.

"I'm just making the communication crystal clear." I said, tension also brimming in me. We were pals again, we'd always been on the same side, but with our past miscommunication and missteps, this was not something I would leave to chance. Not with Spade. "Under no circumstances will you shoot Lark."

"Loud and clear," Spade muttered.

"One minute." Josie cut in. "You need to go, now."

I nodded. The other two put in their noise-cancelling headphones to block out all sound. Spade flexed his Electrum-wearing hand and rounded the staircase to his rendezvous point. I jogged down the hallway to the front door.

Thirty seconds.

I would open the door when it was exactly one minute to midnight, I counted the seconds on the inside, willing myself the strength to do what had to be done.

Twenty seconds.

Ten seconds.

"Ready?" I whispered, as if the others could hear me down the hall. They could not, but they were with me in spirit, I hoped. "Are we ready? Absolutely not," I answered the question myself.

Five seconds.

Four seconds.

Three seconds.

Two seconds.

It was now exactly one minute until midnight.

I took a deep breath.

Go.

61

LARK

The door behind me opened.

What the hell?

Persephone stood in the entrance, her shock of red hair illuminated by warm candlelight deeper inside the witch house. I glanced at the stars. It was almost exactly midnight. She'd come back just like she'd said.

"Hi," she said to the vampires still holding me on the porch. They were surprised. Dreven, Gattas, two other guards on his flank, five new burly soldiers, two of which kept me in my chains, and a new caped woman who looked thin as a rail all spun to Seph at her door.

Ten to one.

No, no, no.

I wrenched against the chains, useless tugs. My wrists and ankles ached from hours of strain. My girl was alone. She needed me now. More than ever. But I couldn't get to the witch. I couldn't do a cursed thing.

Damn it. Why'd she return? *The Orphan Girl never did what I told her.*

She didn't leave.

She didn't run.

Instead, she'd spent the last three hours figuring out how to get around Lady Mauve's spell and gotten herself into Child's house. Like that would save her.

Lila.

I hissed my sister-in-law's name.

Mauve's twin sister must have provided my dreamcast her bio-stuff. Spit or hair or blood, whatever the spell required, she'd given it freely. I'd sent Persephone back to her doorstep, but not for that. Never for that. I wanted to throttle Wren's woman. And rescue mine.

Why didn't she do what I told her?

Maybe it was too much to call Persephone my woman, but I didn't care. She was. And seeing the predatory look on Gattas' face looking at her was too much for me to handle. When he saw that the doorway into the witch house was now free and clear, I wanted to slice that smug expression clean off his dumb jaw.

The dreamcast witch was *mine*. Not *his*.

I'd claimed her.

Over and over again.

With kisses and romance, but more important, with trust and true partnership.

She was my girl. And I was her monster.

There was no stopping this.

We were way past witch and vampire bodyguard now.

The undead paranormal world couldn't have Seph, they couldn't kill her or compel her or bite down on her neck. I didn't care if I had to rip off my own damn legs to get out of these chains, I would stop that from happening.

To rescue the girl that I was supposed to protect.

To save the girl I cared for.

Seph was it.

All I wanted.

And I would not be denied.

Not today.

Not now.

Not ever.

After night fell, they'd taken down the tent, and I noticed Persephone's eyes opened wider when she saw the sheer number of vampires now waiting in the front of the house. In the hours since she'd gone, more than half of the Brotherhood had arrived. They waited on the front lawn, amped to join in a terrible war if one came.

And one was coming, I knew.

If Lila let Persephone in and helped my girl out, that meant she told Wren and the others where I was. And what was at stake. That the Brotherhood was about to get the Blood Stone. They would not let that happen. No matter the cost.

We were about to be washed away by a Crimson Flood.

"One minute early," Dreven grinned at her. "Prompt and beautiful."

I flexed a fist. But I knew he was only sexualizing her to wind me up. Still, it worked. I wanted to punch his goddamn face.

"What happens next?" Seph asked, staying safely inside the threshold of the house, watching his group.

Good girl. Don't take any more risks.

"I hope it's not too rude if I tell you I don't want you coming into my house," she said.

"You can say whatever you like," Dreven purred, delighted to toy with her a bit.

"I don't want you coming into my house," Persephone said flatly. "Ever."

"*Huh.* Well, I don't care. We're coming in. Like it or not." He clicked each word. The other men grinned.

Don't engage, I pleaded with her with my gaze. Seph locked eyes with me. It felt as though she could feel my fear and pain and she tried to take it away. Her eyes implored me.

'Lark, it'll all be okay. Trust in me.'

I knew she had some sort of plan. Either that or a death wish, and that wasn't like her. Seph was too smart and too courageous. Once she got over her initial fears, the witch was as tough as nails, so I knew to come back here, to face them, she had to have back-up or a twist or something in the works. That was good. But did she understand everything that the worm moon loophole entailed?

I glanced up at the sky, trying to communicate with her without words.

It was almost midnight. When the moon aligned with the planet below, no matter what she'd hoped, they'd be able to slip into her home.

All of them.

The whole Brotherhood army of vampires.

Right through the house bones.

"Is Lark alright?" Seph asked.

"I'm good," I spoke. It was far better she worry about herself, and what would be coming next, than my experience at the enemy's hands. I could handle their pain.

"In sixteen seconds you won't be," one of Gattas' goons laughed too loud, staring at his time piece. "When we storm your witch's home."

In the hours that passed, they'd figured out the secret eclipse entry too. As I knew they would. I thanked him silently, as I hadn't had an exact count down to the actual eclipse but now I knew.

"Get ready!" Dreven snarled out to the crowd.

Vampires of all shapes and sizes turned and headed towards the manor's brick walls.

"What are you doing?" Persephone asked. She spun to look at the legion over my shoulder. Fear broached her voice for the first time that night. I was right, she never considered he'd bring in a whole army.

"We're coming to visit," Gattas growled. "Hope there's enough food."

"Bite me," Seph said.

"You catch on quick," Gattas smiled. Dreven nodded and his henchmen took me down off the hard metal points on the porch and twisted my chains into their hands to walk me around with them.

"You'll have a front row seat," the vampire nearest to me grinned. "As I lick every ounce of blood from your girl."

"Slurp up those curves," the other nodded.

"I didn't even bother to learn your names," I told them each, coldly. "You are that insignificant." Then I roared and tried to shatter the chains to scare the crap out of them. The men faltered. Even Persephone fell back in fear. But their vampire buddies flocked to control my shackles, forcing me to my knees. Controlled by the men.

"Leave him alone," she ordered.

Damn it, Seph. You're in no position to make demands.

I couldn't protect her from every vamp in town.

Not when the eclipse aligned and the world went dark.

She seemed to sense it too and quickly changed tracks.

"You can't hurt me," Persephone warned. "I know where the entrance to the crypt is located and I've seen the booby-trapped door. Only I know the way in. So you have to keep me alive."

"That doesn't mean they can't have a taste," Dreven sneered.

Anger surged through my bones.

Rawrrrr! Another roar shook the home. It rattled the whole manor grounds. But it wasn't from my mouth. They were here!

The Crimson Flood had arrived.

They charged the house from all sides, appearing out of the neighboring forests, pouring in from the streets, grabbing Brotherhood members, taking them down, fighting. Killing any vampire who wasn't loyal to them. Waging battle, non-stop. The Flood washed over the witch house grounds.

Woo-hoo-hoo! I heard Wren's floating birdsong, like a battle cry, letting me know my family was here. Fighting alongside. I saw him in the distance, yielding two stakes like twin blades, carving his way through the far side of the lawn.

"*Damn it.* You get the stone, I'll take care of this," Dreven said to Gattas, as the worm moon and the planet and the sun all aligned. "*Attack!*" He ordered his minions.

The Brotherhood spun. They surged over the grass. Against the Flood, they fought back. The sounds of battle roared up as the world around us shadowed to black. Any starlight or sparkle was gone. Midnight steamrolled all over the town.

Every home in the vicinity came at risk, but it seemed all the vampires in existence were here on these grounds. Coming into this very house.

The only light in the property came from candles flickering deep inside the home.

Our group on the porch moved as one. Now nine foes against Seph and myself.

Someone jostled my chains. The vampires took me inside with Gattas' group. A grave miscalculation on their part. Because I wasn't free yet, but I soon would be, I knew.

I would protect my Orphan Girl with every breath and every beat of my heart.

And when I got free, one other thing would be true: *once I was out of my chains, not one of Gattas' vampire party would live through the night.*

62

PERSEPHONE

I stumbled back several steps as the men shoved their way into my home. There were a lot of them, eight in total, and a girl too. More than I anticipated, but they also brought Lark with them, so I was grateful. I didn't want him chained up outside in a black-out war. Even if Wren, Lila and the Flood were coming for him. There was no way me and my squad could have stopped a whole undead army of cruel vamps. Now all my witch friends and I only had to free Lark, stop nine vamps, secure the Blood Stone, and not get killed. The odds felt so stacked against us I almost chuckled.

Laugh or cry, I supposed.

I walked back down the hall, leading the vampires inside.

The candlelight flickered. An eerie gold shine.

I moved quickly, ten steps ahead. Could they hear my heart pounding out of my chest? It was only natural I'd be scared, but fear mixed with anticipation and adrenaline churned inside. Were Spade, Josie and Bug ready for this? The vamps were coming. I was bringing them now.

"Where's the crypt?" Gattas growled in the low fire glow.

"Down the stairs." I stayed out double his arm's-length, just in case. Lark watched every step. My beautiful vampire was so tired. The dark circles under his eyes seemed to have taken up his whole face.

We'll get you out soon, I promised.

I turned on my phone flash light, in ruse as if to guide my way. In truth, I wanted to signal Josie and Bug we were coming without using sound. They couldn't hear anything with the earbuds they wore and we'd created a signal, but I flashed the small light from right to left as a bonus as we walked, bouncing it around.

"Right this way," I maintained tour guide composure as best I could, but I must have seemed suspicious anyhow. Gattas sneered and stopped.

"Turn that off. *Now*."

I obeyed.

The extermination of the light inside the old mansion renewed the rosy, orange candlelight glow. The small flames danced in the main hall. We could see the outline of the stairs ahead. I hoped it appeared like an easy route, but Gattas was too smart for that.

"Wait." He told the others. He watched me carefully.

"Let's get this over with," I pushed.

"No. The witch wants us to follow her a little too much." He considered their position. "Let Lark go first." He ordered. His second-in-command grinned, showing his fangs, then stepped aside. The two vampire grunts holding onto Lark's shackles slid ahead, dragging my vampire along. Lark was wary, helpless in the middle. I played it cool watching the swap. I would have preferred Gattas go down first, but this still worked. We actually hadn't considered where Lark might be in the group, but if he fell uncon-scious with sleep that was definitely better than falling dead, so I considered it a win anyhow.

"Better?" I pushed Gattas, maybe too far.

"I'm gonna wipe that smirk from your lips," his guard threatened.

"You and everyone else. Come on. It's downstairs."

I stepped through the opening, holding my breath. I could feel my hidden witch friends on all sides of me tense. I didn't dare look at either one, but I could feel their coiled energy, ready to strike. Josie and Bug were ready and waiting, sleep bombs in their hands. I stared straight ahead, taking one step, maybe two, biding my time. We needed to hit them at the exact right time to spell as many of their group as we could before my reinforcements were found out.

Keep cool, keep cool.

One more step and the guards with Lark would be inside the atrium.

We had to strike first, before they could react. My witches couldn't hear a thing, they were relying on my signal. They were ready to go. *Hold... hold...* I waited.

"It's a beautiful home, isn't it?" I made boring small talk, over my shoulders. The men watched me move forward. Step by step they came into our trap...

One step farther...

"All this is now mine," I said. I spun around and threw my hands into the air. "Minus the vampires, of course."

Josie and Bug took the signal and launched sleep bombs at the group. Their timing was exceptional. The spells hit the men on either side of Lark as they entered the wider room. It smashed the two goons to the ground, drugged heavy, asleep. Lark whipped his chains out of their flaccid hands, like he'd been expecting some move.

Which of course he was, he knew I'd try something.

"Damn it, get the girl!" Someone roared and the remaining vampires poured in.

Josie and Bug smashed quicksand spells on the floor giving

themselves a protective shield and reached for more potions in their pouches.

Josie was the chemist, Bug had other powers. Harnessing would definitely help.

"Bug spell!" I yelled. We could use more attacking bugs. Josie saw me try to demonstrate balling up my hand, but not Bug. He couldn't hear my commands. Lark held out his arms.

"Here! Baby, come!"

He'd never called me that before, but still I ran to him. Tucked in beside my vampire bodyguard was the safest place in this whole damned world.

Spade spun 'round on the stairs in front of us with his magical crossbow.

Rat-a-tat-tat. Thwack.

All of us gaped. His lie-guard weapon, the Bloodletter, was now twice as automatic and double the size it had been when he'd practiced before. The lie-guard aimed it at the incoming vamps and started firing, but the stakes came out so fast and hard, he had trouble controlling the wild aim.

"Look out!" Someone yelled.

Another vampire went down.

He screamed in pain, hit with several wooden arrows lodged in his leg.

Ahhh! I caught friendly fire in the forearm while shielding my face. Running to my man. Lark caught me and pulled me to safety behind an overturned wood desk.

The enemy vampires took cover.

Josie and Bug did too.

We heard more feral thunk, thunk, thunks.

Spade was out of control with his device.

"This will hurt," Lark gruffed. He yanked the wooden weapon out of my arm. I gasped at the pain. Lark brandished it, like he'd stab anyone who came near us. On high alert. I sucked back the ache. I put a hand on my vamp's arm to bring his attention to me.

"It's not real, it's a lie-guard." I warned. The weapon could disintegrate, though the wound, the blood, and the pain were all definitely real.

"They don't know that," Lark agreed. Until Spade released the illusion, my vampire would grip it, ready like a weapon. Willing to strike. But for a moment, we had a tiny reprieve. Everyone hid. "Are you alright?" He looked concerned. Lark stripped off part of his already bloodied, ripped shirt, flashing bare skin. He hadn't caught a Spade-bullet, but his body was heavily cut and swollen and bruised from the beatings he'd endured all day.

"Oh god, you've been hurt," I stared so sadly at his wounds. What had they done to my vampire while I was away?

"I'm alright," he said darkly. "Are you? Wrap it up good." He nodded to my wound. "Don't show them the blood. They'll go crazy for it. Just a taste and they could double their strength. The sight will make them foam at the mouth. They'll be out of control, we don't want that Seph." He warned. I remembered how crazed Lark'd become when he drank me earlier. I covered the bloody wound with his shirt.

"I'm good."

Bees and hornets buzzed in our ears.

I looked up. I knew what that meant.

Josie must've got my message through to Bug via hand signals or something. He'd started harnessing too. The insect witch called on all sorts of tiny creatures to swamp into the room. In moments, the building was alive with his creepy-crawling things. The mini monsters attacked the Brotherhood of Thorns.

"Witches, stop!" From his hiding place, Gattas shouted a general compulsion for the room. Lark and I looked out from our hiding place. Two vampires were crashed asleep, one was a bloody dead mess, another had been trapped up to his neck in

Josie's swath of quicksand. She hit him with a fresh sleeping spell, rendering him unable to move.

Four were down, five to go.

The rest of Gattas' soldiers were hiding from Spade's wild weapon attack. He watched through the sight. Like us, he kept himself hidden between strikes. But Spade was definitely ready for more.

Josie snuck to the edge of the hallway opening and launched something new, a wild plant that landed under the hiding vampires' feet, spread out, and grew, attacking the undead with sharp thorns. Bug's legion of insects swarmed larger down the hall.

"They've got to retreat," I hoped.

"I wouldn't be so sure," Lark growled.

"Harness!" Gattas roared. "*Now.*"

"He can't hear you!" Spade laughed from his stairway perch, ready to shoot. But Gattas wasn't talking to Bug. Instead, from the swarm of creatures in the chaotic hall came the small woman in her cape.

"Who is that?" I asked. Lark shook his head.

Josie and Bug warily gave the woman a wide berth. She stepped into the center of the room, a strange breeze picking up the fabric around her feet. The caped-woman knocked back her shawl and balled up her hand. As her face became clear, I recognized her from the High Council Academy. She'd been in the atrium the day we climbed up to the chandelier. Just a student, nothing more. She balled up her hand, like a lie-guard or harness. She closed her eyes.

"Easy peasy," Spade looked down the barrel of his weapon, aiming at her.

"Spade, stop! She's a compelled witch!" I yelled. Too late.

Spade unleashed his weapon. But not as controlled as he hoped. Several shots blasted off everywhere. Stakes impacted into the manor's walls and ripped up the floors. Everyone ducked.

Not her.

The compelled witch glowered, staring ahead, completely controlled.

Winds grew stronger in the room.

"She's a harness!" Bug yelled, unable to hear his own voice.

"We've got to contain her," Josie also shouted. She launched a new glue potion and Bug sent his bugs straight at the girl. But the wind witch was a long-time student at the academy, and far more trained in the magic she possessed. As their weapons converged, her harness whipped a tornado into the room. The cyclone of power pummeled us and guarded the vamps. The wind harness blew Josie's glue spell back onto Spade, smothering his bow and his limbs with the sticky mess.

He released the illusion, his body trapped.

The stake disappeared from Lark's hands.

"No," I whispered, dismayed.

"It's alright. I've still got the chains." Lark changed posture with precision, moving the long metal strands from points of weakness into a weapon. He gathered them up, ready to unleash the length on an unsuspecting vamp.

All around us, items whipped around the room. Lamps flew. Small tables crashed. Drapes flapped and ripped from their rods. Any detritus not rooted down picked up and flew. Ready to take out an eye, or crack a skull, or smash on our heads.

Josie's spell collection was dashed all over the room, various pockets exploded this way and that. The flash bangs went off. The chemist gripped onto a couch to avoid being caught in the swirl. Bug's insects smashed on every surface, their guts popping like living bombs.

"No!" Bug wailed. Spade squirmed out of the glue.

The whole house became trashed.

The wind witch only grew stronger, taking control.

"We've got to–" I shook my head. I had no solution to stop her.

"I'm going in," Lark warned.

"No," I begged."

"It's alright." He looked deep into my eyes and I nodded. I knew he'd protect me. Not only was it his job, saving this stone gave meaning to the undead life that he lived.

"Watch your back." I conceded. His mouth crooked up in half a smile.

"Yes, ma'am." Lark dove out of our protective base. The chains unfurled from his hands as he weaved. They worked like extensions of his arms, cutting and sharp. He lunged at the girl, aimed directly for her hands. He flung a chain taut across his body and leveraged it back again. The wind harness redirected her gusts of nature, pushing furniture wildly at my man.

"Watch out!" I yelled. Lark dodged with only seconds to spare, but the maneuver put him too close to the opening hall where Gattas and his goons were biding their time. His second-in-command grabbed my vampire by the leg shackle, tripping him up.

Lark snapped his own chain like a brass knuckle to punch. The witch harness's wind picked up a lamp and smashed it into Lark's shoulder blade.

"Leave him alone!" I growled at her.

"Go in for the kill," Gattas murmured in the hall. "Anything sharp, anything heavy, throw it at them," he commanded the girl.

Josie and Bug stared in shock as candlesticks, the fireplace pokers, lamps and broken furniture rose up on the winds. Lark was too busy with the bodyguards who'd jumped into the fray to see what was coming his way.

"No," I hissed.

The compelled witch had to be stopped. There was only one

way. I broke into a run, dashing across the room as makeshift weapons whipped through the air.

"Seph, duck!" Spade yelled.

I didn't question his help, I just dropped to the floor as a fireplace poker hurled into the space. Lark struggled with Gattas' man, wrestling with him, but the same poker that missed me did not fall to the floor. It headed right for them. The two vampires were locked in a chokehold. The compelled harnessing witch darkened her gaze, aiming her wind and the weapon at the center of Lark's back.

"Lark!" I screamed from the floor. But my vampire didn't immediately move.

Was he frozen in fear?

Did the enemy vamp have control of his chains?

The poker hurtled straight at him.

It was metal, not wood. When it stabbed him, would it kill him?

"Lark! *Turn!*" I begged.

He waited one breath longer then spun, taking Gattas's bodyguard with him, and flung the unsuspecting Brotherhood vampire straight into the projectile's path. It stabbed through his back. The poker gutted the monster so deeply, the sharp point pushed through his stomach on the other side. Lark shoved the wounded beast to his left. The vampire tumbled into the quicksand on the floor. It swallowed his legs. But before Lark could take another step, another goon grabbed a different chain. The witch spun all new terrible things in my bodyguard's way.

"Oh, hell no." I picked myself up from where I lay and raced across the wooden floor. I shoved my Electrum necklace against the wind harness' skin. Pressing it to the girl. "Wake up. You're being controlled."

"*Oh my god.*" She gasped. Everything mid-air came crashing down. "The vampires," she shuddered. "Please, help."

"You're alright." I spun her around. I looked for safety for the girl. "Spade! Take her, go!" I showed him how to hold the Electrum between them both. We met halfway and Spade shoved his hand in hers to put Blue Moon's ring against the girl's skin. They took off down a side hall.

The vampires didn't care. They let them go.

The main event had always been myself and Lark.

I spun back to the scene. Josie and Bug were each hiding behind overturned chairs, disappeared from sight. Lark was again held hostage by two remaining Brotherhood vamps. They choked him with his own chains, locked in their arms. Gattas leered at me.

"Well, that was fun. Did your friends all depart?" He smoothly grinned.

"Yes," I lied.

The others couldn't hear us, but I didn't want them to take their earbuds out. I tried to signal them, laying both hands flat at my thighs, gesturing for calm and a signal to stay down. It worked, because neither Josie or Bug moved from the locations they held. "We're the only ones here."

"Seph, you should go too," Lark said. His voice was strained as one of the goons used his chains to choke my man.

"I'm not leaving you," I warned.

"That's right," Gattas grinned. "You're staying with us. We have unfinished business, me and you." He acted polite, but he couldn't quite pull off Dreven's chill. The storm clouds of anger still rolled into his eyes. "If you try something again, I will gut your precious vampire boyfriend right in front of your eyes. And before he dies, he will watch me drink from your neck," Gattas said. Voice ice cold. Then the genteel bravado returned. "So enough fun and games. Take us to the crypt."

63
LARK

I struggled against the massive bodies of the guards, but the four lengthy chains still dangling from my arms and legs proved too hard to control. I was trapped in the hands of two Brotherhood goons. Gattas' remaining men were a mismatched pair. But he didn't care. Dreven expected results from his top officer. It made him desperate, I hoped. I planned to exploit each of those weaknesses somehow. One of my captors was a lightweight man, the other was Gattas' closest battle friend. I could definitely take out the kid–a reverse chokehold, or something looped around his head–but Gattas' bodyguard could gut me before I got clear. Plus, with four dangling reins slowing me down, I didn't love my odds.

I would wait a little longer to strike back.

Persephone's face looked sad and pale. All her tricks had been played.

Her plan had shrunk their numbers, but it still failed. I wanted to tell her she had greatly improved our ratio with her magical trap, that there were three of them left to the two of us... it wasn't terrible math. Even with the damn chains dragging me down.

We'd likely also rolled through every scenario she'd seen in her dreams. She was flying blind now, like the rest of us. The weakest soul in a quartet of monsters. My once gray shirt around her arm had inked to a bloody red. So her injury continued to bleed. She needed medical help, or at the very least, the saliva of a vampire's kiss.

I would lick every inch of her when we were free.

I kept my eyes on Seph. Feeding her hope, keeping a stiff upper lip.

I will get you out.

Over and over, I promised my witch.

She trudged us down into the basement. We had to cross back across the length of the house on the lower floor, until she stopped in front of an art installation piece.

"This is it." She showed off the dragon carving on the wall.

"An entry fit for a crypt." Gattas clucked. He moved to the center piece that looked like a door, ready to open it. But there was nothing to grip, just an angry depicted dragon staring back at us. Seph lightly touched the triptych piece closest to herself. Traced the dragon's hand. "Where is the handle?" Gattas asked.

Persephone stayed back. She'd lost all her fight. "There isn't one."

Gattas flicked his fingers my way and his henchman tightened the reins, choking me, yanking me up to full height.

"Try again, witch," his second-in-command sneered.

She sighed and dug into her pockets. "You need these." She held up the black balls she'd retrieved from the two chandeliers at the academy. She'd kept them with her all this time. "Get your men to put them into the palms of the dragon. The door should open for you."

Gattas stared at my woman. "I don't believe you, witch."

"Suit yourself." She was beyond caring. Beyond being scared. "Guess you won't get your stone."

"My men will keep a firm hand on your boy. You and I will place the stones."

She gave one to him and took the other. They spread to each side of the installation, to feed the black jewels into the dragon's hands.

My captors forced me to stand directly in front of the beast's snout. I guess they thought if the dragon came alive, he could snack on me first. Or breathe out a stream of fire right in my ugly mug. I steeled myself either way.

"Raise," Gattas ordered her. Seph obeyed, lifting her jewel just like him, ready to put the stone into the dragon's hand.

I readied too.

I wasn't sure of my plan, but I knew the moment the doors opened, the two guards would be distracted, making it my best chance.

"Prepare," Gattas said. He and Seph turned the stones so they would slip inside the dragon's palms.

We all held our breath.

This was it. I'd unleash bloody hell. I'd give it all that I had. I'd take out the he-man first, then the small-fry next. And if I was lucky, I'd strangle Gattas before he even knew what happened to his men.

"*Wait*," Gattas also prepared himself.

His men shifted, nervous.

The second-in-command of the Brotherhood wasn't sure what to expect.

Seph looked unfazed, she waited for the order from him.

We locked eyes for a brief moment. She looked sad, but I shook my head.

We were alright.

We'd find a way.

It was my turn to lead.

Her mouth shifted into an almost indiscernible smile, but I saw her hope return.

Seph believed in me.

I would not let her down.

"Do it. Now!" Gattas barked. Both he and Seph shoved the black jewels into the dragon's hands. The wood carving let out a terrible roar, as if the dragon came alive in the hall.

I didn't wait. I lunged to my right, whipping my dangling chain like a snake, choking Gattas' right-hand man. The other vampire cried out. He'd been holding my chain so tight, my action flung him at the other Brotherhood guard.

Something below us clicked and churned.

I yanked back on my chain, as hard as I could. I took the bigger guard off his feet.

He bellowed. But suddenly, my footing disappeared too.

Not just my feet.

The whole damn floor.

And I was falling through the earth with my captors tied up at my wrists. The bodyguard's thick neck in my hands. Veins popping in his neck.

I couldn't see. I couldn't right myself up in the air.

Above me Persephone screamed.

Holy shit.

64

PERSEPHONE

I screamed as they dropped through the floor. Me next. Gattas flailed and hurled. Beneath us, Lark wrestled with two men. They all struggled mid-air. My vampire tried to free himself and use the surprise to his advantage. He choked the bigger soldier with his chain.

"*Lark!*" I helplessly cried. More fear than instruction or help. I landed with a thump and rolled towards the crypt's outer wall. Coming face to face with a human skull.

Ahhh! I recoiled.

This was the Umbrawick burial site. The whole back wall of the facility was made up of bones laid into the walls, designed by some sick anti-living architect.

Didn't anyone in this family believe in burial for the ones they loved?

I kicked back on my feet and hands. Ready to fight or run.

The men who landed together were now embattled. The hold the vampires had on Lark upstairs was totally gone, but any upperhand my vamp created when the Brotherhood were distracted by the opening dragon door had disappeared when they fell into the crypt. Lark struggled to keep a stranglehold on the larger man. Behind them, an unnatural body of water glowed neon blue. It creeped me out.

The liquid's sheen appeared strangely thick.

There were bubbles popping the surface from below with a menacing sound.

Every instinct in my soul said not to go near the liquid stuff.

"Watch the sides," I warned Lark.

"Kill him," Gattas hissed.

But Lark flipped his wrist chain around his own neck to make it taut and sharp, then hit the side of the Brotherhood's biggest guard, like he was swinging a baseball bat.

The evil vampire dodged.

He tried to grab hold of the chain to pull Lark, but missed. The momentum brought the awful vampire to a knee, which Lark swooped out with a swift kick. Gattas' smaller guard grabbed the ankle chain that Lark hadn't used. He ran away from my vamp, across the grave site to a metal fastener in the back of the crypt. He clanked the shackle in place. It snapped taut, pulling Lark back, but his other leg was still free. While the junior vamp dove for the second, dangling shackle, Lark swiftly kicked the bigger Brotherhood guard. The mighty brute fell to the ground. Gravity knocked him off-side. He toppled and reached out. For balance, he lurched into the water up to one knee.

Sizzzzzz.

We all heard the terrible sound.

Ahhh! The evil vampire roared.

He clawed wildly to stand, to get out of the muck, but his foot disappeared.

It was gone.

Whatever parts of the man had touched the neon blue stuff *melted away*.

They no longer existed.

Like a popsicle in a microwave.

Gattas' second-in-command couldn't rise up because all that was left of his foot was a nub, and his other limb fell in next. He howled in pain.

Sizzzzz.

This second sound was worse, because this time we all understood what it meant. The vampire couldn't right himself. He couldn't climb or scratch his way out of the neon bay.

Sizzzzz.

The sizzle mixed with the monster's terrible screams. Pure agony enveloped the room. We all stared at the ghastly slurp as the vampire's body submerged… then disappeared.

The liquid rippled and burped, swallowing the man. A small, tasty treat.

Clank, clank.

The smaller guard snapped another of Lark's chains to the wall. Lark roared and tugged, but too late. My vampire was trapped. *Again.* Two of Lark's cuffs were locked against the back wall of the crypt.

"Got 'im boss!" The smaller vampire beamed.

"Seph, come here," Lark ordered me. I ran to my vamp. He was locked, but safe, and also far from the moat. Plus he still had one free hand. "Stay behind."

"I'm here." I clung to his arms. Used his body as my shield. My vampire gripped the third chain in his fingers, like a weapon. His fists were balled, ready to fight. But the Brotherhood men were happy to leave us caged on the far side of the crypt.

"Good work, Matthias. Dreven will be proud." Gattas grinned toothily by the neon water. The kid beamed.

"Are you okay? You alright?" Lark quietly checked on me while we watched our foes.

I nodded, still feeling wild. I could see the primordial goo, or whatever the frothy neon moat was made of, had actually melted off the fourth of Lark's old chains. He'd been that close as the waters had killed a whole vampire–drowned, or cooked, or fried him–*right there* in front of our eyes. In seconds the man was destroyed. And Lark had been so close to the same fate that his bracelet had been singed.

A deadly moat, shackles to lock up people in chains, a wall full of skulls and raw bones... this crypt was seriously fucked up.

I flung my wounded arm around Lark's chest and felt his warmth.

His blood was pumping hard, adrenaline on high.

He was pressing hard on the edge of chaos.

I hoped my presence would calm him back down.

"I'm so glad you're okay," I said into his neck.

"Not yet," Lark gritted his teeth. We watched the two Brotherhood vamps.

Above the glowing, otherworldly waters hung the third, impressive winged chandelier. Identical to the two that hung in the witch school, this fixture was sized perfectly to illuminate the liquid floor of the crypt. In fact, it had been hung centered above the pond, so the deadly water was an intended booby-trap. And it was worth the effort to cross.

Because this time, the jewel at the apex of the wings wasn't some simple black rock.

It was a scarlet-onyx jewel.

Cut in a thousand dimensions to shine.

It sparkled clear across the room.

Lighting the room with its beauty and craftsmanship.

The Blood Stone.

It was real.

It was close.

"What do we do?" Lark asked me.

"I'm not sure. I didn't see any of this," I motioned around. I meant I hadn't pictured this scene in my dreams and to his credit

Lark understood. "I suppose they have to get across the moat and retrieve the stone from its perch."

"Without touching the water," he agreed.

"If you can call it water," I agreed. We both shuddered at that. Definitely not water.

We watched the Brotherhood men dismantle a coffin, shove a skeleton to the floor and to try to span the divide of molten magic with a wooden slat bridge.

"I don't have the strength to break a shackle," Lark admitted to me quietly. "I tried for hours upstairs."

I looked at my vamp. "It's alright."

"No, it's not."

I cupped his face with my hand. He was so beautiful and so worn. He'd given every inch that he had. He was afraid it wouldn't be enough, but I knew that it would be. It had to be. Or we would die in this crypt. And there was no point in either of us thinking that.

"Lark, we'll figure it out."

The Brotherhood guard laid down the plank. It floated on top of the acid. The soldier nudged the coffin side with his toes. The wood seemed like a viable path, but we all knew, once someone stood on top of the plank, the balance would change. It might not hold.

"I could take a run at 'em like a bowling ball, and knock 'em into the moat," I suggested.

"Don't even joke." Lark grabbed me to secure his point but he accidentally clamped down on my injured arm.

"*Ow!*" I hissed.

"Fuck, I'm sorry, Seph. I forgot."

It felt like the wound had gaped open again. The throbbing pain seared into my head. The arrow wound hurt way worse than I'd let on, and now he'd touched it again. It was probably bleeding heavily under Lark's cloth. Never stopped, I guessed. It was likely gushing. Dripping right down my arm. But, we couldn't let it show, as the other vamps would go mad.

Their raw hunger could drive them wild...

But even as I fought the urge to cry out, an idea came. It hit me. Hard.

"Lark."

My vampire knew my tone. He looked at me, eyes narrowed. The smaller vampire began to inch across the beam. Headed for the middle Stone. I squeezed my bodyguard's arm.

"You told me not to let the others see or get a taste of my blood because it might give them wild strength. Like we've never seen before," I said. Confirmation of facts. He nodded.

"So?"

"*You're a vampire too.*"

The words hung in the air.

The Brotherhood boy-soldier planted himself under the chandelier, the wooden plank held under his feet. He leaned out his clammy hands.

Lark could do the same thing.

Lark could see and consume my fresh blood.

Lark could unleash the terrible beast. The monster he kept locked deep inside. The darkest parts of my vampire would be strong enough to break the chains, to get us out. I knew that he would be. As long as he could control his violent urges to end my life...

"Seph, *no.*" Lark said it so sharply, it felt like I'd been cut again, sliced open by his vehemence. But I pressed forward anyway. "I'm not biting you. Ever. Absolutely not."

"I know." I assured him. "You wouldn't. That's not what I'm saying. What if I gave my blood to you, like I did in the car. It's already flowing down my arm."

His face revolted at the idea. "I won't risk turning you into a vamp. I won't take your witch skills when you're only beginning to know what you can do in your sleep."

"Lark, no. Don't *bite*, just lick my skin. Heal my wound. There's plenty of blood to lap up."

"I won't be able to control–"

"–yes, you will." I cut him off. "You did it in the car. The urge came on strong, but you stopped. You managed to warn me. You told me to get out, you let me escape, and you hunted something else. That's control."

"Maybe, but you can't escape from this room."

"*I don't have to.* I trust you, Lark. You won't hurt me. You just said you won't."

"*I would die before I would hurt you.*" He swore.

"I know. I believe you," I agreed again. Then sadder, softer, I added, already unrolling my sleeve, "and we don't have much other choice."

65
LARK

The smaller soldier reached out. Stretched his limbs as far as they would go. Not quite far enough. The chandelier hung just out of his reach.

"Get it," Gattas hissed. He practically compelled the younger vampire. So much desire dripped from his words. His soldier went on tippy-toes.

"You can stop them," Seph told me.

I knew what she was doing, but I refused to look down. She opened her wound to me. Revealed it completely. If I saw the red blood, if I even smelled the distinct tang of tin, it would all be too real.

She'd lose me.

I'd lose myself.

"Stop." Without looking, I wrenched my hand on her arm, stopping her full reveal.

Ahhh. She cried out again. It ached. I knew that was my fault. I'd pressed too hard, but I couldn't let go. Not when she was playing these games.

She thought I could control my urges. She was wrong.

Persephone didn't understand who I was.

She didn't know how dark it became inside a vampire's mind.

How hard I fought to keep the twisted madness contained.

She didn't know all the times I'd given in.

She didn't know the horrible mistakes I'd made.

And she wanted me to let it all out?

The Stone was right in the soldier's reach.

He grunted and stretched.

The Blood Stone was about to be claimed. It was about to unleash an army of helpless witches subsumed by vampiristic witch blood. Everyone in the coven would change. Creating an army that could never be stopped. All the Brotherhood had to do was obtain that small scarlet jewel.

We had to stop that from happening.

No matter the cost.

Seph was right.

"*Reach!*" Gattas ordered. The command echoed around the chamber. The soldier jumped up to grab the chandelier's arm. He jostled in the air, reaching high, snatching a shaky, spindly metal arm. The whole thing pitched, but the vampire hung on. His feet dragged away from the safety of his wooden walk. The soldier clung tight, but the chandelier swayed. His weight was too much.

The burning liquid waited for the soldier to drop.

Excited to lap him up.

Instead, the vampire tried valiantly to finish the task. He reached for the central jewel and tried to dislodge it using only one hand.

Persephone tried to force her arm into my face. But I watched.

The Brother soldier couldn't manage the light. The chandelier arm swayed and tilted, knocking him around. His reach faltered. He half-fell. The soldier dangled one-armed. He tried to right his direction, but there was nowhere to go. The soldier's fingers grasped at dead air. His feet reached for a wooden plank no longer under his feet. He held on by only one palm, over the gurgling, suckling neon mass.

When he faltered again, that was it.

I knew it. Gattas knew it too.

"*Reach!*" He barked. The soldier grasped one final time. It was too much. His fingertips spread. They opened. Inch by inch.

"*No!*" Persephone screamed for the life of the vampire who brought us here, trapped in chains. The undead who'd locked me up to this terrible wall. She still cared. She never wanted to see anyone die like that. Or burn alive in a pool of hell.

I braced.

The Brotherhood vampire fell hard.

One foot landed on his board, but he couldn't keep himself there. He pitched forward, both hands out. He landed in the acidic lake, fingers first. Full bodied. Subsumed at once.

"Oh my god, Lark." My orphan girl turned. She protected herself. She dug her face into my chest. I held her close. Cupped her head and breathed out. The Brotherhood soldier's screams echoed in our minds far after the sizzle faded from the crypt.

Then Gattas turned on me and my witch.

66

PERSEPHONE

"Your turn," Gattas grinned lasciviously and stalked forward.

I didn't know for certain if he meant me or my vampire, but I didn't care.

"No." I clung to my vampire's chest. "Lark, drink my blood."

"No." Lark had one arm free, and one chain to use as a weapon. It was clenched in his hand, perhaps that would be enough. I hoped and hoped.

"I can bite first," Gattas warned, licking his fangs.

Now we knew.

I was his next victim.

The Brotherhood officer was deciding how best to rip me away from my vampire with the least amount of wounds while Lark remained chained.

"Or second," he finished at the threat.

"The hell you will," Lark growled. He tugged at his chain.

"Why don't we let the girl choose?" Gattas picked up his own weapon. When they broke apart the coffin to use as a bridge, he and his dead soldier left some sharp shards on the floor. Wooden stakes. Gattas snatched up a long scrap of wood with a very sharp point.

"No," I said to the Brotherhood vampire. "Lick my skin," I begged my man.

"I'll hurt you."

"No, you won't." I wrenched my arm from his grip and ripped the clothing clean off. "I trust you, Lark. Do it. Save our lives. I know you can."

Gattas walked forward, a curious smile. Then his eyes went black as night, as a twisted desire reached the depths of his gaze. He too saw all my blood. His fangs grew out of his mouth.

Lark grabbed my arm with force.

To protect me.

To let his own demons out.

I wanted to cry at the pain. The handling was too hard. But my vampire was already fighting too many internal demons to add more complaints to his pile. Lark stared at Gattas, who'd gone slack and loose, dripping with death.

"Let's play, little bird," the Brotherhood leader taunted my man.

Lark sniffed my scent. His whole body rose with the dramatic inhale, his eyes rolled back in his head. *"Oh, Seph."* Then he licked, long and slow up my skin, slurping my fresh blood. His fangs dragged along, as his tongue deeply indulged.

It filled my brain with vampire fizz, healing my wounds, drinking the blood that had been spilled. But there was still more. So much more. The cut was too deep. Lark could easily push in.

Find my vein.

Drain my whole life.

His breathing heaved.

He went on and on.

Until my arm was clean.

Until the cut had coagulated with his saliva and no fresh sanguine seeped out.

Still, he wanted more.

"*Lark*," I whispered his name.

Gattas came near.

My vampire didn't care. He was consumed with my skin, watching for any fresh leak of life. Ready to sop it all up. Panting in heat. Sucking on me.

Gattas lunged!

Lark tossed him aside without so much as a grunt.

But his fascination filled me with fear.

Too much. It was too much.

"*Lark*," I tried again. "It's healed." I pulled back.

When I removed the limb, my bodyguard looked up.

His gaze connected with my eyes.

His own eyes raged to black.

"*Lark, no*. It's me, Seph." I tugged my arm in, protected the wound.

I stared at him, at this man I did not recognize.

He hissed. His fangs stretched out.

Lark was gone.

Replaced wholeheartedly by his vampire self.

It was like he couldn't see who I was.

With abandon, the monster dove for my neck.

67

PERSEPHONE

ot my neck.

Lark dove for my ear.

"Get back!" My vampire growled in a voice I did not recognize. Lark pushed me away. He was so strong, he yanked the locks clear out of the wall. I fell. I crawled back.

Oh my god.

Lark took off running at Gattas, full force.

The Brotherhood vampire gunned for Lark.

A stake and the chains in their hands. Makeshift weapons they found. Intent on death. Two massive vampires in a terrible crypt, under my family's home. I cowered as they clashed.

With the smell and sight of my blood, they'd become more beasts than men.

Lark jumped and smashed his chains of metal, missing Gattas by only an inch, but it knocked the stake from his hand. Gattas grabbed one of Lark's loose chains instead, whipping my vampire around his legs, then punching him right in the jaw. Lark's head snapped back. But he stayed on his feet. He cracked his wrist chain in the air. Gattas tried to jump over it, but failed. It tangled him and took the Brotherhood vampire off of his feet. But he landed a head blow on my man as it did. Lark buckled. They both fell.

Get up, I silently begged.

On the ground, the men muttered curse words and gathered themselves. They rose again.

This time, Gattas attacked first. He jumped onto my vampire's back as he rose, stretching his ankle tether to trip out Lark's stance, and used the metal as an impromptu garrote. Lark swung back, but his fist failed to hit. The Brotherhood leader pulled tighter and tighter on Lark's neck.

"I'm coming for you, next," he threw over his shoulder, my way. "Only, I bite." He said. "I'll fucking devour your skin."

Lark roared in disgust.

It wasn't a fair fight, Gattas cared for nothing and no one.

He hurt with abandon.

While Lark...

My protector was there. Fighting for me.

I decided to use it to my advantage.

"*Save me, Lark*!" I yelled. "Don't let him get me!" My vampire beast looked over. Gattas tugged even harder. The monster in Lark and I locked eyes. I nodded and willed. "Do it. Take him down."

Lark bent hard and then shot off of his feet in a jump that almost reached the roof of the crypt. He lunged backwards, body-slamming Gattas down with him, still clawing around my vampire's neck with a chain. They collapsed onto the earth, both men's full weight landing squarely on the Brotherhood vamp. He gasped and choked.

Lark rolled off.

Gattas limped.

My vampire regrouped. He went towards the fiery moat.

No, what are you doing?

I stared in shock.

But Lark actually pushed his second ankle shackle into the goo. Let it sizzle and burn, then released it from his leg. He did the same on his weaker wrist, too, so he had only one chain whip left—the one tied on his dominant hand.

By then, Gattas was up. Back on his feet. Growling at us. He snarled like a rabid dog.

Lark flipped his single chain expertly in his hands. A weapon and a tool.

The men raced at each other, Lark with the dangerous metal punch in his hands.

He hit once, twice, before Gattas clocked my vamp in his gut.

Lark let the chain out, sharp as a blade. He swung and sliced.

But Gattas dodged.

Lark reversed his footing, striking in a new way from the back.

Gattas roared. Blood spurted from his wounds.

I sat forward where I was.

Lark could go for the kill.

My vampire twisted the chain whip, he flung it hard. The metal rope whistled and hit.

Gattas howled, but grabbed the recoil. He locked the end of it onto his own arm, and jerked it around. Pulling Lark in a loop-de-loop, then, Gattas let go. Lark flew towards the neon pond.

"No!" I screamed.

My mouth ran dry.

Lark landed in a heap, mere inches from liquid death. Just as Gattas planned.

The Brotherhood vamp jumped on top of him, panting. He grinned ear-to-ear.

He used the chain to choke Lark. And he pushed my vampire towards the lake.

There wasn't room to breathe, or for Lark to get free.

It was either choke, or burn to death in the watery crypt.

Either way, Gattas would win.

My vampire struggled.

No.

This wasn't our end, a voice said inside my mind. *If Lark can't save you, you go save him.*

I got to my feet, my wits suddenly clear.

I ran across the flat earth of the crypt. The mens' struggling grunts filled my ears.

I grabbed the wooden stake from the ground.

"It's over, Lark." Gattas grinned. "I'll take good care of your girl." He said. Lark couldn't budge, but I could.

"*I can take care of myself!*" I stabbed the stake deep into Gattas' back. Pushing as hard as I could through his muscles and bones. Aimed straight at his heart. I yanked it out, let out a primal battle cry, and I stabbed him again.

The evil vampire roared and pitched. He swatted me off. It gave Lark just the moment he'd needed.

I saw my vampire rise.

I watched Gattas fall. Dying as he collapsed on the ground.

In slow motion, the battle was won.

We did it.

We'd survived.

But as he collapsed, Gattas latched onto my hurt arm.

His fingers dug cruelly into my wound, attacking my bone.

Ahhh! I screamed. The slice reopened where we stood. Blood spurted out.

Lark dove.

He reached for me.

But Gattas also pulled.

Gattas yanked me towards the neon waters below.

"If I go, so do you," Gattas' lips formed the cruel words.

"*Nooooo!*" Lark's twisted mouth screamed in return.

The Brotherhood vampire sneered, pulling me in.

Making us both fall.

"*Lark*," I said my vampire's name. I breathed out and took all of him in.

But it was too late.

Gattas won.

I plunged into the fiery lake of death. Head first.

68

LARK

Nooooooo!

I fell to the ground.

Seph was gone.

Gattas lay limp on the side of the pool, a sick smile on his mouth.

"*Oops.*" He tried to laugh but made no sound. Blood leaked out of the stab wound in his back, blooming ever larger on the ground. "Did I kill your girl?" The Brotherhood monster asked. He coughed and his eyes grew glassy with distant pain, with his inevitable end. "To be fair, she killed me first." He let out a bitter sigh. Then nothing more.

The crypt fell silent.

No Brotherhood and no Seph. I was alone.

I couldn't manage to raise my head. I couldn't rise. The pain I'd once felt with Gwen had hurt me to my very core, but this was worse. Far worse. *This was my girl.*

She was mine.

I'd known her one week. And she'd become my whole world.

Persephone was so strong. She came back for me, to rescue me, to get the stone, and I let her down.

The beautiful orphan girl gave me her damn life.

And for what?

I looked up at the rock, the fucking jewel in the chandelier, and I let out a terrible roar.

A bellow of horror.

Of pain.

Of loss.

Of anger.

Why had I dragged Persephone into this terrible realm?

Witches and vampires and all the others. She'd been alright on her own. She could have survived. She could have lived a long, long time.

The emotions all hitched in my throat.

I did this to her, I knew.

I drank from her wound, I kissed her mouth, I made her groan. I pulled her into this world, I gave her the job. I knew how dangerous it was. Yet still, I baited her in that pawn shop and waited on the hood of my car. I tempted her. Flirted with her. Made her feel desired, all so she'd be better controlled.

And it worked!

Too well.

Because she surprised me too.

Persephone Dawn could not be compelled. She could not be forced into any task but her own. The decisions she made for herself. She chose this life. Chose this mission. Chose me and my world.

She chose me because she thought I could... win.

Instead, I had failed.

And she was gone.

We'd only known each other a fraction of my immortal life,

but I was forever changed. The Orphan Girl reminded me of all that was good. What I was fighting for. The humanity, the ingenuity, the incredible verve of the innocent world. I would never take it for granted again. And I would never let myself weaken or be so foolish as to love...

Persephone!

I pictured her beautiful face.

That narrowed, tight gaze she wore when she was annoyed. Which was a lot of her time with me, if I was honest. And the sparkle in her eye when she accomplished something great, which happened frequently too.

It had all been destroyed.

For what?!

For a stone?!

"*Arghhhh.*" I beat the ground and wept into my hands.

Lark. I could almost hear her sweet voice.

In my ear.

In my heart.

The woman I might have loved.

I should just go ahead and kill myself.

There would never be another. Not like this, not for me. Not again. I would not allow it. I wouldn't be so weak as to enjoy it, as to imagine a perfect someone could stay in my world.

No, I was alone.

With a damn job to do.

Always alone.

I would ensure the Blood Stone would always be secured away from the Brotherhood. I would not let Persephone's death be in vain.

Lark.

Her voice haunted me so.

But then, the next sound of my name was followed by a splash and a kick. I was hallucinating all sorts of noises and things. Sounds. Next to me.

"*Lark.*"

The word was so real. It was real!

I looked up, amazed, as Seph pulled herself out of the liquid death. Neon water splashing the shore as she did. It wasn't possible. How?

"*Oh my god,*" I scooped up to my feet, ready to lunge at her myself. But when she saw my intent, she held a hand up.

"I'm alright. But don't."

I panted in shock. "What? Why?"

Seph.

My Seph.

I was frozen on a rope, staring at the redhead.

She looked a drowned rat. The most beautiful rodent in the whole world.

"I don't understand."

"It didn't hurt me. 'Cuz I'm bound to the stone, remember? This is my magical booby-trap, I guess. But you... you should stay clear." Her fingers said no. I wanted to swoop her into my world. But we obeyed. For now.

"You're sure you're alright?" I huffed, scared out of my wits.

Persephone squeezed the liquid from her hair, a remarkably normal, womanly thing to do. The dangerous fluid spattered on the ground. Some hit Gattas' side, it singed his paled skin.

"Yes, Lark. I'm really fine." She looked up at the chandelier.

"I thought I'd lost–" Emotion overcame me. "Don't ever do that again."

She broke into a grin. "*Yeah.* I'll do my best not to die." Our breath rose and fell in perfect sync. I smiled at her, she grinned at me. We may not have yet been able to touch, but she was right there with me, and I was with her.

A lifetime of connection in our gaze.

Finally one of us looked at the chandelier. The other spoke, although I couldn't say who, because in this finite moment, I was her and she was me.

"Before we go, there's one more thing."

69

PERSEPHONE

"Are you sure," Lark asked again as I took my first step on the plank.

"If it didn't kill me the first time, I think we're good."

He knew it too, so he didn't strongly object as I moved the next step, and several more after that. I walked the thin coffin floor out into the moat and stood directly under the chandelier. I took Lark's final chain from my hand. We'd carefully severed it from his wrist with the acidic moat, and strategically maintained its length to use as a rope. I threw the chain up and hooked it over one of the light fixture arms. I half-pulled the chandelier to me, half dragged the wooden floating bridge over to it, until the golden wings etched in the apex of the fixture hung directly above my outstretched hand.

I reached for the jewel, tentative at first, in case it was booby-trapped as well. But, my magic was bound to the jewel. It waited for me, mine to take. I unscrewed the scarlet stone into my hand.

I released the chandelier and watched it swing without its

central piece. Then inched my way to shore again. Lark gave me his hand as I crossed to dry ground.

"All this for that." I held it out. The jewel wasn't even the size of a quarter in my hand.

"All the power that's in there," Lark agreed, equally moved.

"It should be destroyed." The words slipped out of my mouth. Lark went stiff like a board. I stared up at my vampire. "Do you really trust Mauve?"

"Without it, she won't release your spell."

"I don't care."

Lark weighed the odds. "We've seen how easily it can be found, no matter how complicated the hiding spot." He was on board.

"Are we doing this? Are we going to destroy the Blood Stone?" I asked. Putting the jewel on the ground.

"It's your rock, it's your choice," Lark said. He smirked.

"Give me the chain." I put a large flat rock under the jewel, laid it on top, then balled the chain into my hand. I smashed the inter-locking whip as hard as I could onto the Blood Stone. It opened a first crack. "Here." I handed the weapon to Lark.

He did the same as I had.

Over and over.

We crashed the chain onto the rock, until even the whip and the stone underneath were pulverized into sand. The red dust still had an unworldly glow, but it mixed and mashed with iron shards and regular stone. We flung all the dust into the neon water source. Lark pushed Gattas' limp body in after that. We listened to the gurgle and sizzle as it consumed his bones.

"What are you gonna tell Mauve?" He asked.

"We tried our hardest," I told Lark. "We got as far as the cavern, but Gattas and the stone both fell in the middle of the poisonous neon pond."

"We watched him die."

"And the Blood Stone was forever consumed by its own spell."

"It hissed and popped in the booby-trap, breaking apart, then the minuscule pieces sunk to the bottom of the moat."

"There was nothing more to be done. The power was lost."

"The Blood Stone was destroyed," Lark agreed. He held my gaze and slowly smiled. I looked down at my palm. Any dangerous neon liquid that had previously been there had drip-dried or fell off. I offered Lark my hand. He interlaced his fingers in mine. A warmth flooded my whole body from that small connected spot.

Full of future and promise.

I nodded at Lark, each of us fully at peace since the first time fate had brought the vampire into my life. He looked at me with a calm knowing too. We were as one.

"Well, my big bad vampire bodyguard, what do you say we go tell Mauve the bad news, and move on with the rest of our lives," I asked Lark. He grinned. The pleasure creasing all the way into his deep raven claws.

"I'd like that very much, Orphan Girl. But one more thing..."

And then he grabbed me and pulled me to his chest and kissed me open-mouthed, so passionately it made my toes curl.

The best kiss of my life.

When it was over, he breathed into my lips. We both smiled.

"*Now* we can go."

70

PERSEPHONE

Two days later, the deed was mine.

All I had to do was sign on the dotted line.

Bug insisted that we have a party in my new backyard, and hang out where our vampire friends could join to celebrate the momentous occasion. My new home! It was my first ever permanent tie to a real community. Even if it was inside a dangerous paranormal world. The weather was beautiful and warm, so it was a great evening to stay outdoors, and it was also a practical choice. Most of the inside of the manor was trashed. The tornado the wind harness created during our battle destroyed more than half of the first floor. Plus, the basement still had a giant hole in the ground.

But, it was all mine.

All mine.

And it was sweet and thoughtful and totally Bug of him to gather the people that mattered together to celebrate my new transition.

My makeshift, found family.

My new life.

I'd come to town to try and meet my unknown relatives, of which I still seemed to have none, and find a fresh start on my own. No one here owed me a damn thing, but that didn't matter. People cared. People let me into their world. And for the first time, maybe ever, I wanted to invite those wonderful people right back. Maybe it was just the trauma-bonding talking but I had a feeling these witches and vampires would always remain part of my life.

So, Bug and I went to the store, bought patio string lights, snacks, soda and beers, ordered pizza and dragged random chairs out from the house so everyone could have a place to sit down. As the sun set, we lit up the small patch of grass near the back entrance. We had to do the party on a small budget, as I was totally broke. When Mauve heard our news about the shattered, buried Blood Stone, she refused to remove even one inch of the hex from Child's bequeathed bank accounts.

"You never finished your magical education," she frowned. "If this was a class, you failed."

"Well, how do I pass?" I had asked. Mauve's eyes darkened, bringing decades of anger and injustice down on me. She stared me down.

"Next time, *succeed.*"

It was meant to be a threat, and a disheartening dismissal, maybe even a slap. But I heard it for what it was. She'd said *next time...* there would be another shot. If I just bided my time. For now, Blue Moon ran the official documents over for me to sign. The building was transferred. The property was all mine. That part of my Uncle's will was granted, thanks to Lila's bio-spell. So money or no money, I owned Child Manor out right. I'd figure the rest out. I always did. I could take some old antiques to a pawn shop, for a start.

I looked up at the property. The Midnight Witch House.

Three vampires joined me as the moonlight shone down.

"You sure there's no lingering effect from the eclipse when

the vampires came into my home?" I asked Lark. He'd read extensively on the subject in the days since the event. Did that paranormal entry transfer into a permanent invitation to my home? Could those vampires return? Again and again? We didn't know. But since every undead person who'd been inside other than Lark had been killed, it seemed moot to worry too much.

"You're locked up tight. There isn't another eclipse like that for another three hundred and forty-seven years," he said.

Wren rapped a hearty slap on his brother's back. "A drop in the bucket of time."

I smiled at them. "Maybe for you." They both grinned as Lila joined. "Thank you for bringing the Flood and breaking the spell against your sister's wishes," I told his family members.

"Mauve said she'd kill me if I did it again," Lila admitted. "But I'm already dead."

"And we couldn't leave Larky to have all the fun," Wren teased. My vampire groaned.

"Is that what I was doing?" He groused.

"If you weren't, you were doing it wrong," Wren easily smiled. "Birdie and I had a blast." They'd told us epic battle stories of a fight that raged until morning light. Then everyone on both sides disappeared to avoid being burned by the sun.

Dreven got away.

Of course he did.

So the Brotherhood of Thorns would be back with a new plan at some point.

"Where is dear old sis?" Lark wondered about Birdie, whom I'd still never met.

"She had work to do further upstate," Lila said. The men shared a glance.

I didn't ask what that meant. I'd prefer not to have the details. I'd experienced more than enough vampire stuff this week to last me a long, long time. So when it came to new revelations, I was good.

The biggest result of the outside battle was that my house's gardens were also in shreds. That's why we'd put the party in the backyard. Still, I wanted to invite the witches and vampires over to see what was left of the manor, and welcome them in my space. Especially Josie. After all, this home was forty per cent her investment. She deserved to see how it fared.

"Oh wow," the chemist murmured, as we walked end to end inside taking in the details. The place was in ribbons, but luckily, the battle with the vampires and wind harness hadn't destroyed the manor's old bones. Although there were crossbow arrow holes in the walls, wind damage, quicksand on the floor, and dangerous snap ribbons plants growing everywhere. It could all be repaired.

There was something else I wanted to float in her direction as well.

"You know, this place is pretty beaten up."

She snorted. "I see that, Seph."

"It's big, but it won't fetch a great price in this state. I know I promised your share." I swallowed, coming to the big swing. Josie eyed me.

"What're you trying to say?"

"Well, maybe we should wait a bit to sell. Fix it up... we could live in it 'til then..." I watched her reaction. "Me and you?"

"You wanna be roomies?" Josie stared. "With me?"

"Is that dumb?" I blushed. "I've never had a place to myself."

"Actually, no. That sounds... good."

"Yeah?" I crooked an eyebrow at her tepid response.

"Yes." Josie finally broke into a slight grin. Her eyes shone.

"Good," I replied.

"*Good*??? It's great!" Bug beamed. "Now I'll have two neighbors I like!"

We heard a knock on the front door.

"Who's that?" Bug wondered.

"Come on," Josie dragged Bug away, leaving me to answer. "*Neighbor.*"

"Maybe you could get her a job at the bookstore too?" Bug said.

"Don't push it, Ugnacious."

"Yes, ma'am."

"I'll meet you guys outside," I said, then I opened the door. Spade stood on the stoop, illuminated by the overhead light. I swung the door open for him. He looked embarrassed to realize that I'd answered, although I wasn't sure what he expected. After all, this was *my* house. And *my* night.

"Hey. Come on in." I stepped aside.

"Uh, hey." He paused, uncertain. "I brought you a house-warming plant." He held up a small succulent. I laughed. I picked a receiving table up off the floor, righted its legs, then put the offering front and center in the chaotic foyer. One normal item in the total mess.

"Thanks. We're all around back."

Spade didn't stroll through the house. In fact, uncharacteristically, the lie-guard stalled.

"Are you sure you want me here after all that happened before? I mean, in the warehouse?" Spade checked. I moved behind him and walked to guide him down the hall until we joined with the rest of the group out the patio door. His eyes took in all the destruction as we went.

"Yes, I'm sure... you're off the hook for that. We made mistakes. Spade, we made the choices we made. And it all worked out in the end, so there's no point in beating ourselves up." He straightened. I watched his full smile return. "*But...*" I couldn't help but knock him down just a peg. "You also shot me with the Blood-letter," I complained as we stepped out into the patio lights. I showed him my healing arm. "*That* still hurts."

"With great power comes great responsibility," Josie cat-called.

"You think my powers are great?" Spade shot back.

"Hey, you weren't done apologizing to me." I pretended to give him the gears.

"Tell Lark to suck on it," Spade suggested.

"He will, he sucks on everything." I grinned. I wouldn't be shamed or deterred. "But I think you should feel hella guilty too."

"Yeah," Josie agreed. We crossed our arms, making up a fake, disapproving wall.

"I do. *I'm sorry!*" Spade groaned. We still didn't immediately relent. "If I'm in such trouble, then why am I here?"

"I dunno. Jo invited you to the party, not me... take it up with her," I lied. I winked and left the pair.

"Wait, did you invite me here as your date?" Spade smirked at the other girl. His trademark confidence roared back in.

"No." Josie groaned. "It's a friendly drink at a neighborhood barbecue. Don't get the wrong idea. We're friends."

"We're friends?" He asked, seriously.

"Yes," she said. "Friends."

"You've forgiven me?" He pushed. Spade searched her face.

"I forgive, I don't forget." Josie warned. But she couldn't hold up the tough exterior for long. Her mouth twigged with the start of a grin and Spade let out a huge whoop.

"You don't know how long I've been waiting for that!" He beamed.

"Just *friends.*"

"I know. Wait, with pity sex?" Spade immediately pressed. "Friends with benefits?"

"I rescind my offer," Josie groaned.

"Too late!" Spade scooped the chemist up over his shoulder and ran her around the grass. "We're friends!" He cheered. "I wore you down!"

Bug watched, a little pleased, a little sad, a little jealous.

"She'll never love him again. Not like that," I said.

The two witches joked around. Old friends, reunited at last.

"Maybe," Bug agreed, but he didn't seem sure.

Or maybe he realized she'd never love him like that either.

I didn't have a solution for that. So I did the next best thing and distracted him with praise. "You know, without you, none of this would be possible," I told the insect witch.

"Thanks. I just wish..." He watched and watched. Josie was a brick wall with everyone, but Spade knew how to slip under her defenses. Bring them down a bit. He made her laugh. Bug deserved his own happily ever after too.

"Life is long, there are plenty of fish in the sea..." I mussed his hair.

"And worms in the ground?" Bug asked.

"Uh... exactly, Bug. You really held your own out there. You should be proud. I mean it, You just stopped everyone in town from becoming an army of the undead. Even if they never know it, that's a pretty big deal."

"Vampires aren't all bad," Bug said. We looked at Lark, Wren and Lila chatting, beers that no one drank held in all their hands. They looked almost normal... almost. If not for those raven claw wrinkles around their eyes, and their unnatural, immortal youth and beauty. I smiled, staring at the world's most impossible man. My vampire bodyguard.

"Seriously, I owe you a lot." I told Bug. "Thanks for giving me a chance."

"Best neighbor I ever had," he agreed. We cheers-ed our soda cans.

"Really? 'Cuz I heard Cornelius Child gave out full-sized chocolate bars at Halloween," I teased. "That's pretty good." We both laughed.

"You've got a legacy to uphold," Bug agreed.

"I'll see what we can do in October," I said.

"Sorry I'm late!" Blue Moon blew into the backyard with a huge pile of paperwork in her stead. "Persephone, come over here," she called, laying the documents out, pushing her glasses up her nose. Josie and Spade came back to watch. The vampires converged

"Don't tell me I have to sign everything again," I groaned.

"You don't. You already signed, remember? On the first day we met at the law office?"

"That seems like a lifetime ago."

A wholly different life.

I looked up, Lark caught my eye. We both smiled.

"Well, I can give you the keys with one last signature." Blue Moon pointed to the final notation. She gave me a pen. I squiggled my signature as Lark, Josie, Spade, Bug, Blue Moon, Lila and Wren all politely watched. The group clapped. When the signing was done, I took a playful bow. Upon rising, Lark's mouth curved up in a sly smile.

I was officially a member of town.

Just then, light rain started to fall.

It hit the earth in plump dollops, the night sky threatening to build into a storm.

"Quick," Josie said. "Get everything inside."

The others grabbed paperwork and food and chairs.

"We're gonna run," Wren politely told me, with Lila by his side. "Congratulations on your purchase of the neighborhood dump," Lark's older brother joked of the torn up lot.

"I hope we'll see you soon," Lila added.

"I hope so too." The two jogged back to their car to avoid getting soaked. It started raining harder, but Lark didn't run away with his vampire friends.

"I like the rain," he offered, his shirt growing wet.

"Me too," I grinned. "You're getting damp."

The rain clung to his shirt and skin, showing the muscles in his chest, his broad shoulders, his strong arms. His dark hair flattened on his head.

"You're wet too," he noted.

The words heated me straight to my core.

And now it was just me and my vampire out in the rain.

Our other witch friends had gone inside to stay dry and warm. The weather drizzled on our heads, but neither of us moved out of the elements.

Lark stared at my wet breasts. My damp hair.

I gazed right back at him.

Drinking in his height, his muscles. His sex.

How I wanted Lark.

The vampire stepped closer.

My heart beat so wild in my chest.

"We've done a fair bit of kissing when you've been damp," he noted.

I thought back. In the forest, after I'd gotten out of the moat, how true. The memory of Lark's kiss in the basement made my whole body throb.

"I guess we have," I lightly agreed.

I wanted more like that.

More Lark.

More vampire heat.

He was the strongest, sexiest man I'd ever known and I was ready to fully give in.

Lark imposed himself with a fresh step. Our bodies met, he moved again and I couldn't help but slide back, letting him lead. Like a dance, he moved me across the wet grass, getting so close, but not touching.

Not yet.

He walked me backwards, until I felt the brick wall loom behind me, then he threaded his hand into my hair and gently pressed me up against the house. I was delighted and trapped.

His body curved, boxing me there, pushing my back against the stones.

He deeply inhaled. My heart beat wild under my skin.

"You're mine, Orphan Girl."

"*Lark*." I said his name just the way he liked it.

He bent down and kissed my lips.

My whole body moaned.

Eagerly, I fed my hands up into his hair as his tongue slipped into my mouth.

Lark's touch moved lower, under the tender slide of my arm, then swooped back up to fondle my neck and caress my back. He wrapped himself up in my hair.

I felt my body rise to greet him.

So ready for this.

But his kiss released. My face just inches from his.

He smiled at me, wrapped so deep in his embrace.

"This is nice."

"Yes, it is," I murmured right back.

Lark touched more, he grazed all my curves, and as an afterthought, he fondled the rose gold necklace around my neck, only inches from my piqued breasts.

"You know, if you took this off, I could make you do all sorts of things," Lark whispered in my hair. His thigh pressed deeper between my legs. As I spread open for him, Lark lightly groaned.

"You can make me do whatever you want, with Electrum or without," I offered my man. He breathed in my scent again, our bodies dripping with intent.

"I'll take you up on that."

"Now?"

"Soon. Very soon." He kissed me again. Soft and slow.

I felt him thicken, pressing in.

Maybe sooner than I'd think.

On the lawn.

In the rain.

I didn't care.

I just wanted more of my vamp.

But Lark released me.

"I should go." He huffed out his breath.

"You should stay," I countered. "I'm your girl."

"Hell yeah, you are. You're mine." He claimed me, his voice full of sex. "And I'm your vamp."

"Like there was ever any doubt." We panted and promised.

It was all I wanted from him.

All that I could offer.

I gave it. Freely. Repeatedly, to him.

"Lark," I said his name, spoke it right on his lips.

He groaned and suckled my neck. I let him pin me in sweet heat, but finally, I pulled his attention back to my face. There was something that still needed to be said.

This was Josie's home now too, but I knew she'd agree.

She'd have to.

This was something I *needed* to give.

One question I still had to ask.

An offer I needed to extend.

"Lark," I brushed his hair from his face. Bringing his full attention back to my words. When he gazed in my eyes, I took a deep breath. *"Lark, would you like to come in?"*

———

WANT a BONUS EPILOGUE with Lark, Persephone, Josie, Bug and Spade on Halloween? Click here.

https://juliecatherine.myflodesk.com/ midnightwitchhouseepilogue

———

AND if you enjoyed the fantasy romance between Lark and Persephone, plus you love reading fantasy quests, desperate battles, and lots of underwater magic, you'll love the *Broken Mermaids* series by Julie Catherine.

Sailor-girl told me she'd help me mate with a human. Any dream man... except *him*.

When a modern-day mermaid wrecks a human ship with her beauty, she discovers she can use a sailor-girl's help to land her dream man. In exchange, all sailor-girl wants is to learn the secrets of the sea. It's an easy deal. The woman has only one requirement... no one can mate with her off-limits, handsome brother.

Can the mermaid resist?

Can Sailor Girl's brother?

Cruel and Splendid Mermaids is a best friend's brother paranormal romance, where a desperate maid will try anything for love.

· · ·

Readers love the *Broken Mermaids* series!

★ "Mermaids and Mythology— YES PLEASE" - Amazon Reviewer

★ "I loved Julie's world building, it is phenomenal I could imagine everything clear as day." - Amazon Reviewer

★ "Intriguing, fun, imaginative... This book made me think of mermaids in a whole new way." - Amazon Reviewer

The completed Broken Mermaids series is best read in order:
Book #1 *Cruel and Splendid Mermaids*
Book #2 *Dark and Lovely Mermaids*
Book #3 *Fierce and Delicate Mermaids*
Book #4 *Wild and Elegant Mermaids*
Available now in kindle unlimited. Read all four.

———

WANT to learn more about the *High Council Witch Academy* and the origins of Lady Mauve, Cornelius Child, Josie, Spade and others? Join new girl in town, Mae Kingsley, as she arrives in the small town of Plumpkin, where not everything is as it seems.

· · ·

Magic. Mystery. Witch school. Students are dying to get in.

My whole world changed when I started at the new school. Everything about this small town feels a little... strange. I wish Mom was still here. Now it's just me and my aunt. And she's acting... weird.

Family secrets. Magic discovery. A legacy worth saving.

Then there's Spade. The cocky town boy knows *exactly* what's going on. He makes me feel *crazy*, but also *pulled*. Like maybe it's fate that we met? And not just him... also Josie, and Beck, her off-limits man.

Fated mates. Love triangles. Slow-burn romance.

My only hope of survival lies with the gays and town girls. The Peters and Kate know so much more than me. A paranormal bonding season? A secret witch school? An exclusive, deadly invite? With connections to my family?

It's no coincidence that I'm fresh meat at the season's first full moon. Enrollment is beginning— **but if I'm gonna get involved in some ancient, mystical witch world, I'm gonna do it *my* way.**

. . .

Paranormal Bonds **is the first captivating, addictive paranormal fantasy story in the six-book, completed High Council Witch Academy series.**

The High Council Witch Academy series is best enjoyed in order.
    Reading Order:
    Book #1: Paranormal Bonds
    Book #2: Predetermined Bonds
    Book #3: Poisoned Bonds
    Book #4: Planted Bonds
    Book #5: Paternal Bonds
    Book #6: Powerful Bonds

Available now in kindle unlimited. Read all six.

WHAT NOW?

Want to dig into sneak peeks, learn about the next releases and find all the other freebies and literary goodies? Join my newsletter at www.juliecatherineauthor.com.

Xo
  Julie

ACKNOWLEDGMENTS

Welcome back to Plumpkin! And a whole new layer on the High Council witch world. I hope you love Lark and Persephone and all the new vampires. It felt so good to make my way back to the witch world!

This is my first book with full on male POV chapters. I was really nervous to get inside Lark's head, but he was so nice to me! I had such a blast.

This book is a bit more... um... rough and swear-y. But that's just how Lark speaks. You'd be a little jaded after one hundred and fifty-six years too. And he can totally pull it off. At least, in my humble opinion he does.

Thank you as always to my beautiful editor, Allana. I hate each and every tiny criticism you give me (there are thousands of them, after all), but I also value your critique so, so much. My rule remains the same - I make (almost) every change and if it feels weird in the next pass I can always change it back, but by the time I get there in the re-read, it seems like a totally smart choice. Who knew! Oh, wait. You did. So thank you for that.

Thanks to Maria at Artscandare for this beautiful cover. I love it so much!

Thank you to all my fellow authors. I really value the indie-book writing community. Thanks to the Fractured Fairytale group for giving me the push I needed to start writing vamps!

Thanks to my darling hubby. Mr. Catherine, you're the best. And I'm sending so much love to my friends who ask things like -

how's the book coming, and let me prattle on about my fictitious men.

And thanks the most to my readers! I love you all so much. Whether it's replies to my newsletters, chatting on socials, or ratings and reviews that you leave - I'm so excited to interact. I truly love the characters and stories I write, I have such a great time crafting each book that it warms my heart to know even one other person loves them too.

Thank you, thank you so much!
Xo
Julie

ALSO BY JULIE CATHERINE

Midnight Witch House

Midnight Witch House

Dragon Witch House (coming soon)

Midnight Witch House prequel

Beauty and Fanged Teeth

The High Council Witch Academy

Paranormal Bonds

Predetermined Bonds

Poisoned Bonds

Planted Bonds

Paternal Bonds

Powerful Bonds

The High Council Witch Academy prequels

Enchanted Bonds (a prequel novella)

Broken Mermaids

Cruel & Splendid Mermaids

Dark & Lovely Mermaids

Fierce & Delicate Mermaids

Wild and Elegant Mermaids

The S.P.Y. Girl Academy

The Truth About the Spy

The Secrets in the Skies

The Motives of the Guy